Happy Holidays
Kidney Foundation of
New York

MISS *Lillian Russell*

Other Works by James Brough

MARGARET: THE TRAGIC PRINCESS
MOTHER R: ELEANOR ROOSEVELT'S UNTOLD STORY
(WITH ELLIOT ROOSEVELT)
THE PRINCE AND THE LILY
A RENDEZVOUS WITH DESTINY:
THE ROOSEVELTS OF WASHINGTON
AN UNTOLD STORY: THE ROOSEVELTS OF HYDE PARK
(WITH ELLIOT ROOSEVELT)
PRINCESS ALICE:
A BIOGRAPHY OF ALICE ROOSEVELT LONGWORTH

Miss
Lillian Russell

A NOVEL MEMOIR

by

James Brough

McGraw-Hill Book Company
NEW YORK ST. LOUIS SAN FRANCISCO
DÜSSELDORF MEXICO TORONTO

Book design by Mary Brown.

1 2 3 4 5 6 7 8 9 B P B P 7 8 3 2 1 0 9 8

Library of Congress Cataloging in Publication Data

Brough, James, 1918–
Miss Lillian Russell.
1. Russell, Lillian, 1861–1922—Fiction. I. Title.
PZ4.B87453Mi [PS3552.R68] 813′.5′4 78–6448
ISBN 0–07–008120–0

For Bruce Gould *in token of gratitude*

Prologue

A NICKEL bought a shoeshine, a barbershop shave, a ride on the El, or a seidel of beer and all the free lunch a man could eat belly against the bar, where ladies were rare and flies, in from the livery stables, thick. Godliness was popular, and the churches whose spires lanced the skyline were packed with seekers after a Sunday dose of fire and brimstone; but cleanliness was only just coming into fashion now that a few high-minded New Yorkers had rebelled against the reek of garbage and worse that overhung the teeming streets of the Empire City.

Public improvements spelled private graft. The bloated, be-whiskered sachems of Tammany Hall, where Mayor Oakey Hall fronted for Boss William Tweed, reaped a harvest of millions, hundreds of millions, when the new civic buildings began to sprout. Tweed was now in Ludlow Street prison, but Tammany's hold was as strong as before. How could it be otherwise when the Democratic ward heelers marshaled the living and the dead, registered citizens, and dumfounded immigrants to vote the straight ticket every election day?

From the huddle of huts the Hollanders had planted on the south end of the rocky island, New York had grown like Jack's beanstalk, squeezing out the woods and pastures, spreading so far north that the city limits had just been jumped across the Harlem River to take in thousands more acres of farmland in the Bronx.

To the caste-ridden refugees from the Old World, New York was America, a land that promised freedom and fortune. There was no Statue of Liberty to welcome them yet. First contact with the New World came in a converted theater, Castle Garden, where Jenny Lind had sung in the calm old days, which were hard to imagine in the present babble.

"Melting pot" was an inept, sentimental description of a city where aliens hunkered down in their own separate foxholes. In the ghetto around Hester Street, where the Jews clustered, Yiddish was the language and the caftan a not uncommon costume. Mulberry Street sliced through Little Italy, where fire escapes, festooned with quilts by day, became outdoor bedrooms at night. Cantonese, with pigtails dangling down their necks or coiled up under their felt caps, padded on thick-soled slippers through the triangle between the Bowery, Fell and Mott Streets. Chinatown surged every weekend when the laundrymen came in for a pipe of opium or a fantan game.

The immigrants' New York was an alfresco metropolis. Families who labored in airless workrooms wanted to spend their evenings and holidays outside the walls of a stifling tenement. Stoops, stairways and the street were the places to meet and chat and daydream, helped along by a song or a bottle, with the cries of passing pushcart peddlers as an accompaniment.

The city was a national as well as an international marvel. Visitors arrived by the trainload from as far off as the tracks had reached in their thrust across the thirty-seven states that made up the Union and the territories that still awaited admission. New York was the capital of the fearsome East, the power center run by bankers who didn't hesitate to ruin a man by foreclosing his mortgage or bring a President to heel if he got uppity.

New Yorkers boasted that they had raised $300,000,000 to beat Johnny Reb, but nobody had piled up such profits in the process as they had, and they'd best not brag about that after hundreds of them had been killed in five days of rioting over Mr. Lincoln's draft laws.

Strangers came to gape at the sights: the theaters lining Broadway; the new hotels that outdid each other in splendor and steam heat; the gingerbread mansions of the tycoons that went up ever farther northward away from the downtown clatter of iron-tired wheels rumbling over cobblestones; the department stores where, just imagine, you could buy genuine Paris gowns and Brussels carpets and pay as much as $2,000 for a shawl; the lacquered carriages of the rich with coachmen up front and foot-men in the rear done up in the monkey suits they called livery.

People here never seemed to go to bed at all. Day or night, there was always somebody about on even the meanest streets, and the sidewalks of the grand avenues like Broadway overflowed in the yellow glow of gaslight streaming from hotel lobbies, theater entrances, restaurants and oyster houses until early dawn. Most of the time, the busiest thoroughfares were jammed with a tangle of hansom cabs, wagons, carriages in all sizes, horse cars, and it took a body a good fifteen minutes to pick a way safely across, and you had to watch your step because of the droppings.

There was no other place in the world like it for extravagance, entertainment, spectacle, debauchery, and cash. It was the mag-net that, on this March morning in 1877, drew a girl christened Helen Louise Leonard who was to rename herself Lillian Russell.

MISS *Lillian Russell*

"GRAND CENTRAL TERMINAL, ma'am. End of the line."

The conductor paused, a black-serged bulk, in the aisle beside Mama and touched the peak of his cap. An odor of peppermint enveloped the three of us. He had been fretting over us for the past twenty miles while every other woman in the car, young or old, primped herself in anticipation of arrival.

Mama declined to let excitement infect her. She kept her nose where it had passed most of the night, in the pages of *Science and Health with Key to the Scriptures.* Christian Science was one of the newest of her fervors. My younger sister and I had no choice about our moods—hers dictated ours. If she remained in her seat, so must we. She had waved away the bobbing Negro who came to collect our luggage at the door. "I am not incapable of carrying my own possessions, thank you." We would have to do the same.

Metal clanged against metal as the train jolted to a stop, and the conductor braced himself against her upholstered chair. She snapped her book shut and turned pale, disapproving eyes upon him. "Here we are at last. Gather your things together, girls. Let us be on our way."

He tried last-minute appeasement by pulling out from a vest pocket a watch as big as his meaty fist. "Seven A.M. precisely, New York Central time. Right on the dot, ma'am." She ignored him. "Want help with your bags?" She ignored him again.

Suzanne rose, smoothed the creases from her lap and retied

the strings of her new bonnet. "Do I look as bad as I feel, Nellie, after sitting up all night?"

"I'd hate to feel as bad as you look. Thirty-six hours is thirty-five too many. Why couldn't we have ridden in the sleeping car, Mama?"

Her eyes took a turn at faulting me. "You ought to have learned by now that extravagance has no place in a thoughtful life. Fortunately, your father was in a position to supply passes for the ladies' car, and Vanderbilt railways have a reputation for comfort. We needed nothing more splendid."

I slipped the little dyed rabbit-fur cape that was a parting gift from him over my shoulders and picked up my valise. So far as I knew, the rest of our clothes would be forwarded once we had written to tell him where we had found a place to stay. The Negro in the white mess jacket extended a hand after he had smiled us down onto the platform. Mama left it empty. Tipping was contrary to her principles.

At least the "Atlantic Express" had brought us from Van Buren Street Station, Chicago, without the bother of changing trains, which was something coach passengers had to cope with when we had stopped for a meal in Buffalo. I'd had a notion to sample a little more of that ugly city than luncheon in the railroad restaurant allowed; Mama had been born in Buffalo nearly fifty years ago. But time was short, the wind blowing in off the lake was cold, and she could not be considered a sentimentalist.

She had forked the last sliver of hard-crusted apple pie from her plate before she spoke. "I first encountered your father when he worked here for the *Express*. I was twenty-four with soaring hopes for Mr. Leonard when we were married. I was disappointed; we all have learned what that entails. We have better things to do with life henceforth than continue to depend on a man's limited beneficence."

So my entry into New York City was made, sleepy-eyed and grimy, limping along an endless platform behind Mama, one hand raising tweed skirt, the other clutching the old valise that grew more burdensome with every step. Her lean nose twitched in the reek of hot axle grease and coal dust. Her lofty forehead wrinkled like a frost-bitten peach at the din of chattering crowds, rattle of luggage carts, hiss of steam from giant locomotives champing impatiently on their bright steel rails in the sulfurous glass-roofed train shed.

According to an ambition I automatically shared with Mama, my destiny was to sing in opera. She'd kept me in training for ten years now. Mother Superior at the Convent of the Sacred Heart fanned the fire when I was nine, contributing a little dance and a jingling tambourine as well as a song or two to commencement exercises. "She will one day be a grand prima donna."

Though Mama took some precepts of all religion with a grain of salt, this particular forecast had become an article of faith for her and, therefore, for me. Hadn't Jenny Lind earned $12,600 when Barnum brought her over for her first concert at Castle Garden? And then, to her eternal Swedish glory, didn't she proceed to donate every penny of it to New York charitable institutions?

I would feel happier if I knew where our heads might lie this Friday, March 3, 1877, and where we would spend the days thereafter until such time as Mama made her mark or my silvery soprano was accepted by the world.

We had not yet reached the gates when a candy butcher advanced down the platform toward the throng. In the past day or so I had grown accustomed to his kind, peddling their wares through the train, crying "*Life, Puck, Judge* and *Truth*; lemon drops; Ridley's peppermints." This shabby vendor, however, had something different to purvey: "Extry, extry! Hayes elected President! Crisis over. Four cents, and read all about it."

Mama stopped so short my valise bumped into her bustle. She set down her leather-strapped hamper and dipped into her reticule. She seized the newspaper and, while the crowd pressed by on each side of us, mumbled aloud the gist of the story. "House at 3:50 this morning voted not to count the vote of the elector from Wisconsin.... Ten votes of Wisconsin then counted for Hayes and Wheeler.... These gentlemen declared President and Vice President of the United States, having received a majority of all the Electoral votes.... Eighteen hours in continuous session...185 votes to 184—and not a woman's among them!"

The snort Mama emitted would have done justice to a yard

engine. Then she shook out her shawl in silence, and we resumed our procession among the last of those straggling out. The cream-hued stone walls of the vast concourse we entered rose to a vaulted ceiling that seemed to reach halfway to heaven. The tapping of our heels echoed on the marble floor. This palace of the Vanderbilts was now strangely deserted except for silent cleaning crews with brooms and buckets. I had no doubt that very soon the empty halls would be transformed into a sort of Valhalla, thronged with the inhabitants of the most fascinating, dangerous, delightful metropolis in the universe.

Mama interrupted her stride again and sniffed. "Rutherfraud B. Hayes. A colorless ninny with less right to be in the White House than I have."

"You know you couldn't have abided a Dem, Ma."

"True enough. Never, never forget, girls, that it was Republicans who freed the slaves and saved the Union. But the skullduggery and shillyshallying that's been going on among those politicians down in Washington, D.C., for the past four months while they made up their minds who won the election makes an intelligent woman want to—to expectorate." Suzanne winced.

I felt an increasing desire for us to find somewhere to unpack and freshen up before we saw much more of the city. "Mama, do you think we might find a lodging advertised in the newspaper?"

"Corruption." She was talking to herself again. "On every side there is corruption, and we are here in corruption's capital city. Graft in the post office. Fraud in the Customs House. That monster Tweed back from Spain and clapped into prison. And now His Fraudulency the Dishonorable Mr. Hayes—"

"Where do we go next, Ma?" I was growing nervous.

She accepted an interruption for once without rebuking me and descended to my level. "I thought I had told you. Everything has been arranged."

"Perhaps it slipped your mind, Mama. We left in such a hurry."

"We are to board for the present with a lady in Brooklyn. She was recommended by a workmate of your father's when Mr. Leonard mentioned the plans we had in mind for going to New York City. Mrs. Walker, a cultivated person of English extraction, I am told. A number of people connected with the press live in the house, I believe, so we should be able to count on some interesting company."

"Can we afford it?"

A brumal smile. "Your father can."

"Where is Brooklyn, anyway?"

A cold finger brushed my cheek. "Leave it to me, child. I have the directions. First, we must take a ferry across a river. We shall find our way there as in all things, never fear."

We emerged into a cool morning under a gray sky that daylight had not yet fully brightened and stood shivering for a moment while we took in the scene before us. Compared with Chicago, where almost everything downtown was fresh and clean, New York looked frowzy, a hodgepodge of buildings of all shapes and sizes in stone, brick, and wood. I could just picture how fast this city would burn if they had a fire like we did. If the street we were standing on was typical, they weren't any too fussy about where they threw their litter, either, but the air smelled crisp in the wind that was whipping across from one river to the other, not quite so cold as what we were used to but helpful in getting the grit of the train out of our eyes.

Twin flags flapping on either side of the Stars and Stripes on the three mansarded peaks of a barracks of a building across the broad thoroughfare proclaimed it to be the Grand Union Hotel. An ornate sign on our side of the street extolled its virtues: "Over 450 elegantly furnished rooms reduced to $1.00 and upward per day." Behind iron railings, railroad tracks climbed out of a deep cut that ran in front of the main entrance.

The streets were still but skimpily occupied by carriages of assorted sizes and a few early risers. I reminded myself that soon they would be awash with people, scurrying along at the pace expected by every visitor, not dawdling like most of these in sight now. Mama beckoned the solitary policeman who stood idly swinging his truncheon in a doorway of the terminal, dark blue tunic buttoned up to the throat under his bearded chin, cap pulled down on a headful of curls.

"We wish to go to Brooklyn, Officer. What is the least expensive means of getting there?"

His Irish eyes glinted. "Well, now, I might recommend swimming. Or you could walk there if they ever get to finishing the bridge they've been building for the last seven years. But today you couldn't do better in my opinion than take a ride to the ferry. This here's Fourth Avenue. The ferry's a fair stretch away. Shall I be getting a cab for you?"

She was not amused by anybody's blarneying, but she was tired to the marrow. "I should appreciate the courtesy."

He glanced at my sister and stared at me. I was becoming accustomed to such inspections. "Your daughters?"

"They are."

He raised his club to signal a weatherbeaten four-wheeler, its musty driver and a swaybacked horse. "You've got a real beauty in this one," said our policeman.

Mama's thin eyebrows flickered. "I think I have seen more handsome turnouts in my day."

His whiskers rippled with laughter. "I wasn't meaning the old growler but your daughter, ma'am. A fine-looking girl, all pink and gold, and a credit to you, I'm sure." I had heard such things said enough times before to have learned to restrain my blushes.

"She is a student of the opera. We entertain hopes for her so long as she works hard and—" her gaze erased his smile—"does not permit her head to be turned by flattery."

Riding in any kind of carriage except a horse car was something of a novelty. It was no particular pleasure to sit on scratchy horsehair in an odor of dust, stale perspiration and the whiff of cigars smoked by previous passengers, so I unfastened the worn leather strap to lower a window and hang my head out. The streets grew shabbier as we headed eastward, like the increasing numbers of pedestrians who hurried along the broken sidewalks. Gray-faced men bearing dinner pails and pale women with shopping baskets on their arms jostled each other as if they were involved in a foot race instead of being on their way to work or market. White-aproned shopkeepers were raising the shutters over store-front windows while sleepy-eyed boys swept the night's accumulation of garbage into already clogged gutters.

I could not recognize half the words exchanged by these denizens of a different world as we trundled past them. English was uncommon here, it seemed, yet most of the signs that covered shop windows, awnings, the lintels over doorways, and every available inch of brickwork were in that tongue. I wondered how many New Yorkers could read and, if they could, what they understood of the thousand and one advertisements for soap, patent medicines, and mustache wax.

The ferry, black smoke curling from its smokestack, was ready to leave when we reached the dock. Mama would have liked to haggle with the cabdriver about the fare, which she thought outrageous, but a clanging bell gave warning that time was short. We seized our luggage and scampered down the splintery gangway. A toot on the steam whistle sent gulls soaring from their perches on the battered pilings of the slip, and up in the wheelhouse I glimpsed the brawny captain take a swig from a bottle as he picked a course through the motley fleet of rowboats, full-masted schooners, scows, and barges that impeded us.

Inspection disclosed that we had a choice between remaining on deck and sharing a cabin that smelled no sweeter than our hired growler. My sister and I were granted permission to leave Mama alone inside with her thoughts and the luggage while we took in the view outside. We stood together at the stern, watching the turbulent flow of the water, the hovering gulls, and the tangle of tall-masted ships whose rigging spread like spider webs against the patchwork of brownstone, dingy white, and glittering stone that made up Manhattan. Smoke from a hundred thousand chimneys drifted overhead in the easterly wind.

"Do you think we are going to like it here, Nell?"

"I'm too washed out to tell yet. I know I'm going to miss Papa."

"As well as all those boys in the choir who were always making sheep's eyes at you?"

"Ah, I wouldn't give a fig for any one of them!"

"But Mama says that's the principal reason we had to leave. For your sake, she said. To keep you out of trouble on account of ... Well, you've grown up so fast, and everybody calls you good-looking."

Suzanne was born to be a mother's pet or possibly a lady's maid. "That wasn't the real reason at all, you ninny. She just couldn't stand being around any longer after she'd been made to look such a fool and it got written up in all the papers."

My sister began to giggle, and it was infectious. "I can just imagine her stuck there. It must have been a *riot*." It had come close enough to qualify as such.

Mama was a woman of multitudinous talents. She could play the violin, chord a guitar, and sing a sweet contralto. *Mens sana in corpore sano* was a maxim of hers, which explained her taste for roller skating. She could not be satisfied until a rink was built in our own Chicago parish, an undertaking to test the resources of the entire community. Her lecture on "Tortures of the Inquisition" filled St. John's Church hall and added forty-seven dollars and fifty cents to the treasury.

She rounded up all three of her daughters as well as our brother Sammy to return in the audience the following week when Reverend Mr. Irving's subject was "The Crusades." Having two teams of Sunday-school boys sell motto cards was her idea. One battalion ventured forth with "Blessed Are the Peacemakers" and the other with "Love One Another." Rivalry ran so high that they joined in battle on the street, which was left littered with the sad remains of those exhortations. But the money was raised in the end, though it took a month longer than she had anticipated. Toward the end of February, the little wooden arena was ready, its floor covered with fresh tar and layers of sand.

The Methodist minister offered up the opening prayer. Judge Dermot Brennan, two hundred and twenty pounds of him, said a few words for twenty minutes, stressing *in corpore sano*. St. John's Church choir—Helen Louise Leonard soprano—delivered the hymn: "From Greenland's icy mountains, From India's coral strand..." The building felt decidedly chilly to me, a condition that young Joe Katowice, the apprentice engineer, was asked to rectify by piling more wood into the furnace.

Mama spun off onto the floor with Judge Brennan, and fifty or sixty others joined them. All set off at a spanking pace, which continued until the temperature started to rise. Then I observed foreheads glistening and detected the slurping of rollers in tacky tar. The scent of pine blazing in the furnace seeped up through the registers. By nine o'clock the thermometer hung by the entrance registered eighty degrees, and it hadn't finished climbing.

The judge was the first to go down, slithering like a bewildered hippopotamus across the tar. Mama stretched out a hand to help him up, but he was stuck as firm as the lid on a glue pot. She skidded as she hauled and collapsed beside him, a glimpse of white unmentionables showing over her laced boots before sit-me-down, palms, and heels descended in sequence for capture by the melting floor. Her bonnet sat rakishly askew over her eyes. She attempted to release a hand to adjust it, but that was no more possible than a bluebottle's freeing itself from a flypaper.

Those skaters who could still force one foot ahead of the other strove to reach the captives to stage a rescue. There were shouts of "Heave ho!" and "All together now!" but to no avail. They saw derby hats, scarves, and gloves lost to the struggle and found their legs going out from under them to entrap them in the contagious predicament. I had counted twenty-two ladies and fifteen gentlemen caught in a state of adhesion when I heard Mama.

"Nellie! Nellie! Don't just sit there gawking! Come over here and assist me."

"Oh, my dear Mrs. Leonard." It was the judge, dignity gone, spectacles embedded by his left ear. "Can no one obtain a hose or summon the fire department?"

Reaching them was like walking through quicksand with the suction pulling at my shoes. I had no desire to finish appearing like a coon in a minstrel show, so my approach to Mama's hands was distinctly gingerly. The first heave achieved nothing. The second produced an ominous sound of fabric rending. Beside her, where another salvage effort was under way to liberate the unhappy judge, similar strains were audible.

"Just leave me lie," he groaned pitifully. "In the name of decency, let go of me."

Mama had less regard for the consequence in her decision making. "We can be here all night, Judge, if we're too persnickety. Nellie, you hurry away and fetch me my coat."

And thus with a final, determined hoist she was liberated, bequeathing a fragment of black serge from her skirt and braving the smirks of the audience, which detected a flash of starched linen before I could wrap her coat around her shoulders. There was tar all over my fingers after I had unstrapped her skates.

She made a majestic exit, bonnet set straight and eyes fixed firmly ahead, but her pride had suffered terrible hurt. We abandoned Judge Brennan, a monument to modesty, insisting that he would not consent to be extricated until Easter unless the fire brigade arrived in advance of that date.

We scurried home to the little flat that Papa provided as a sanctuary for Mama, Suzanne, and me as fast as our legs would carry us. "Nellie, you show signs of promise. Tonight, you have proved yourself capable in emergency."

The next evening Mama's Golgotha was all but obliterated. Joe Katowice stuffed the furnace with more pine logs, and the rink burned to the ground. But there was no easing of the pain in Mama's heart. She told Papa that she was taking me and my sister to New York City immediately to further my career and save me from perdition.

And so here we were. Mrs. Walker's red brick boardinghouse on Columbia Heights exuded the same air of comfortable middle age as its buxom proprietoress and the King Charles spaniel who patrolled the floors night and day. In the big back bedroom with lovingly varnished woodwork and molded ceiling the three of us shared on the second floor, we could hear steamboats whistle as they plowed up and down the river. From the bay window in the parlor we could see clear across the water to the city.

"Over there," Mama explained with a gesture, "lies Wall Street, wicked Wall Street, the veriest pit of iniquity. That is where they have been scheming and thieving to make their millions and drive the rest of us into poverty ever since the war cry rang through the land."

"Wouldn't you ever like to be rich, Mama?" I knew in advance the kind of answer she would give me, but it was good for her to be teased occasionally.

She drew herself up as straight-backed as any commanding general. "At whose expense? While others went hungry? You are a foolish child. I would not choose to wear the Vanderbilts' collar and squeeze farmers half to death with outrageous freight prices. I could never connive and cheat to corner every ounce of gold and bring the country to ruin like that hideous Jay Gould. My conscience would not let me sleep at night if I had been a Jim Fisk, looting the savings of poor widows and orphans with his precious Erie Railroad and consorting with painted *paramours*."

For an instant I could envisage her as a man, her lean cheeks a blend of the faces of each of those she had mentioned as I had seen them portrayed from time to time back home in the *Daily Tribune*'s smudged engravings. I suppressed a smile. Suzanne supplied the usual gulp that followed her hearing a word such as "paramour."

Mama deserved a little more joshing. "Even if you wouldn't, I'd like to earn lots of money. That's what New York is *for*, a place to make money."

"You misunderstand me, Nellie. I have not said that I should not care to earn. I believe a brain of my capacity merits a certain monetary reward. But I shall earn it, not steal it like those vultures."

"What do you intend to do, Ma?"

She cloaked herself in dignity. "That remains to be seen.

Suzanne should have known better than to ask, "Shall we go out to explore afterwards and look at the shops?"

Mama's smile was forgiving. "You have noticed the piano over there?" The majestic upright had been dusted and polished with more care than the one we girls had been taught on. "Mrs. Walker has been kind enough to say that it may be used for practice. You may accompany your sister, Suzanne, for an hour or so this afternoon. We are in no hurry to see the sights." We kept our pouts and our sulks for each other; it would have been futile to do otherwise.

When we came down into the dining room, the three of us were the only guests. The rest of the boarders, it seemed, were all males, employed somewhere in the city Suzanne and I yearned to visit. Contrary to what Mama's kitchen usually produced, the joint of beef was done to a turn, served with delicious whipped potatoes and a concoction that our landlady termed "Yorkshire pudding," crunchy, crisp but light as a soufflé, topped off with bread-and-butter pudding.

She had done the cooking; a Teutonic servant girl transported the dishes to and fro. "*Sprechen Sie Deutsch?*" Mama asked her. A shake of a flaxen head was the only response.

Mrs. Walker picked a crumb from her bombazine and explained. "From Norway. I find them cleaner than the Irish, but they are inclined to be sullen, I'm afraid. Wages, of course, have gone up since the war like everything else. Ten cents for a loaf of bread, the same for a quart of milk. That girl is paid fifteen dollars a month, which is at least five too much, but what can one do about it?"

"You can blame men's greed." I hoped Mama would not embark on one of her tirades, but she was merciful. "Thank you for welcoming us to your home, Mrs. Walker. I am confident we shall be comfortable here. Now, if you will excuse us, we have things to do."

Suzanne kept her foot on the soft pedal, and I sang *sotto voce.* After a few bars of "Let Me Dream Again," the landlady and her pet came in to sit on the sofa and her lap respectively. Albert, the dog, was named for an idol of her native land, the Prince of Wales. Albert's snuffling was evidence that he, too, liked the music of Mr. Arthur Sullivan.

During most of March, what little sightseeing my sister and I accomplished in Manhattan was done by peering through the dirty windows of streetcars and peeping into tenement rooms glimpsed as we rattled along in one of the elevated trains that raced at perilous speed up and down three of the avenues behind engines spewing sparks and ashes. We saw a city of bewildering contrasts, caught in a welter of change, formless yet perpetually exciting. I had imagined this would be a metropolis of soaring towers, singing fountains, breathtaking perspectives. Instead, it was a gridiron of uniform ugliness, its new buildings of white or yellow stone even less sightly than the old brownstones that were forever being razed.

From our elevated observatory, we could look down on the top hats and feathered chapeaux of the gentlemen and ladies who rode in open carriages behind cockaded coachmen with uniformed footmen standing on the rear platforms. Now and then we plucked up courage to travel with the gentry in the parlor car on the El, which cost an extra nickel. Looking out the windows, we had a totally different view as we sped by windows so close we could have reached out and snatched milk bottles from their place on the sills. Inside those rooms men and women sat huddled over sewing machines, hunched over kitchen tables picking at tin plates with their fingers, sprawled in restless sleep on iron beds. Suzanne was so smitten with this mode of travel that she talked Mama into buying the sheet music of a lovely piece called "Rapid Transit Galop" to expand her repertoire.

Mama's immediate goal was to place me as a pupil, terms to be negotiated, with a teacher qualified to work such wonders with my vocal cords that I might quickly audition for an opera company. Once that had been accomplished, my sister was to be similarly coached for a career with a grand piano. For our initial sortie via ferry into New York City, Mama relied on a referral she had received from the first of the succession of instructors to whose hands I had been committed.

I was not yet seven years old when I was led to weekly lessons from the aptly named Professor Nathan Dye of Chicago, a gentleman of uncertain age, the blackness of whose hair and whiskers owed something to the tinting bottle. His advice to Mama before our departure was to usher me to a Madame Vacari, a lady whose home and studio were combined at an address on Minetta Lane in a backwater known as Greenwich Village.

We discovered that portion of Manhattan to consist of such a maze of dim, meandering, unnumbered streets that even natives had difficulty finding their way. By dint of much questioning and backtracking, we pinpointed the atelier of Madame Vacari in an ancient little low-dormered house which, once we were inside, assailed our nostrils with the scent of asafetida. After the business of introductions and fees had been completed, Mama left me in charge of my new mentor to go off to attend to her own affairs, the details of which she had confided neither to me nor Suzanne.

Madame Vacari, a wizened prune, reputedly had been the toast of Milan, Paris, and London. "The secret of the great voice is not here"—she fingered my throat—"but down below." She prodded me at the point where my corset was laced the tightest. "To create the beautiful tone, we must exercise the dee-a-phray-am. For exercising the dee-a-phray-am we must learn to breathe correctly, in and out. You will remove your dress, please, and loosen your strings." I fumbled to comply with her instruction. "We turn to an implement to help us." I could not conceive what that might be, but apprehension vanished when she held up her parasol.

"You open it slowly, slowly, so, and all the time you are drawing in one big, deep breath of air. Now the implement is open, so you pause and feel the lungs stretching themselves with the oxygen. Then—watch!—you close it very slow, and you *exude*, pressing upward with the muscles of the dee-a-phray-am." At the first attempt, asafetida came nigh to overwhelming me, but I improved as the lesson progressed.

I bore with Madame for two weeks before informing Mama that the lessons were nonsensical and we were frittering away time and two dollars a session. She was persuaded that I was right, and she turned to scrutinizing advertisements in the *Eagle* to find the next tutor for me.

Signor Yaconelli, basso profundo, was also established in what I now knowingly refer to as "the Village"—to be precise, on West Fourth Street, close to the spot where it inexplicably became West Twelfth. He too relied on an implement in his instruction—in this case, a fragment of lead pencil.

"It is very sad, but it is essential to recognize that English must be disregarded as a language fit for beautiful singing. Only in Italian can we throw open wide our lips and allow great, round notes to pour out like a flood." The demonstration he embarked upon rattled the windows in their frames and threatened to jolt a lithograph of Giuseppe Verdi from the wall. "In speaking English, the lips are compressed, and so you mutter. I teach you better. Open your mouth, signorina—wider—as far as you can go. Good!" He propped a cut-off stub of pencil between my front teeth. "We are ready." He turned to the grand piano and, still standing, struck a thunderous chord. "I want to hear an up-scale cadenza. Sing!"

I did not return to the signor. I had been moping around Mrs. Walker's for two days, playing with Albert, when, after a breakfast of tender ham and eggs scrambled with cream and butter, a gleam in the eyes of Mama signaled imminent delivery of a major pronouncement. "Nellie, I believe that we have erred in our strategy. You have been scrabbling about at the foot of the ladder when, of course, the place to begin is at the top. I take it that even your limited reading has acquainted you with the distinguished name of Dr. Leopold Damrosch?"

"Umm—he came from Prussia, did he not, and he writes cantatas?"

"Exactly. We are going to call on him. I have made an appointment. *He* shall be your teacher."

He proved to be a slightly stooped, courteous, middle-aged man with an abstracted manner and the immaculate manicuring of a violinist or physician—in fact, he was both. As soon as the maid had ushered us into his study—"Mrs. Cynthia and Miss Helen Leonard, Maestro"—Mama addressed him in the faltering German she had taught herself at home, so that I could only judge what was passing between them by the increasing firmness of her jaw and the continual pursing of his mouth.

After some minutes she reverted to English for my benefit. "The doctor has said, naturally, that he is extremely busy with the Oratorio Society and the Symphony Society which will be founded this year. But I think I can persuade you, sir. Nellie, let us have your high C!"

Not only did I gulp as audibly as Suzanne ever did, but I sensed to my shame that I was blushing. Clamping my eyes shut, I could imagine Madame Vacari's parasol expanding as I inhaled until whalebone pinched my ribs. I parted my lips, and out it came. He reacted *animato*.

"Very nice. I am grateful to you. Perhaps you would sing for me a little."

I babbled happily all the way back to Columbia Heights. Mama made no effort to restrain me beyond repeating, "There is no knowing what one can attain unless one tries."

For the next few weeks I would gladly have seen my sister's fingers worn raw red by accompanying me, but her enthusiasm burned itself out ahead of mine. Mama impressed upon us the necessity of practicing every morning before she absented herself from the house on undisclosed errands of her own. She would be gone for the best part of the day and again on some evenings, too. Neither of us had the audacity to question her. When she was ready, she would share her secrets. She believed us to be removed from mischief by the fact we lacked the means for indulging ourselves. Papa was sending her one hundred and twenty-five dollars every month to support his three absentees. To that, he added two dollars and fifty cents apiece as spending money for Suzanne and me.

Though we went shopping together on some afternoons when Mama was safely out of the way, from everything we saw and learned Brooklyn impressed us as being so unadorned and parochial that we longed to be off across the river. To our amazement, most Brooklynites made the excursion only when they had to. Manhattan to them was alien territory, hardly the candle that lured this pair of moths.

One May morning I could not bear to be marooned in placid respectability any longer. Outside the open parlor windows a brisk breeze ruffled the water, and it shimmered like sequins on a ball dress. The scent of lilac from the bushes in the front yard drifted through the house. "Suzanne, have you any money?" She was a spendthrift at heart, fond of squandering her allowance on trifles like velvet ribbons and real silk stockings, which she hid in her drawer for fear that Mama would see them.

"Almost a dollar."

"I'll treat then." Watching pennies was another habit acquired from Mama. My one extravagance at this time was buying chocolate and an occasional Philadelphia ice-cream soda. "We're going to the city to spend the whole day."

She was as bug-eyed as a startled fawn. "But what would Mama say?"

"She won't know. She's never back much before six. We'll have gone and returned by then."

"She's sure to find out somehow."

"We'll worry about that if it happens."

My sister enjoyed being led, while I was of an opposite nature. We were ready within minutes with not a word to Mrs. Walker about where we were going, almost skipping along the street in delight.

We goggled at so many things in the city in the course of the day it was impossible to set them in logical order in my mind. We pattered along for blocks of Madison Avenue and Fifth Avenue, craning our necks to admire the spanking new mansions commissioned by the breed of men Mama despised. They stood like private fortresses of granite, brick, or sandstone, with enough balconies, towers, turrets, and minarets to keep you counting them for a good half hour. We stood in awe in front of the most stupendous of them and wondered aloud who owned this huge white marble palace.

A delivery boy with a basket over his arm caught our words. He broke off whistling "Home on the Range" between his teeth to throw a wink sizable enough to crease his cheek in half. "That's Mr. A. T. Stewart's little doodad, paid for out of buttons and bows. Department-store business, which wasn't enough to get him into hoity-toity society. Nobody ever came to call. You couldn't say it broke his heart because he didn't have one, but he keeled over just last year." We thanked him in haste and scurried onward.

We walked farther downtown on Broadway. There, we had heard, was where elegant ladies shopped. A solid mile south of Twenty-third Street was packed chock-a-block with every kind of emporium, large and small, enticing females like my sister with Paris gowns and perfumes, glitter and gold. Such a proliferation of private carriages, from staid victorias to dashing coupés, stood waiting for the customers inside that other traffic had to slow to a walk to gain passage.

We circumnavigated Lord & Taylor's; Arnold Constable & Company; and McCreery's. Lower down, at Ninth Street, we espied a store built of what seemed to be white marble like Mr. Stewart's mausoleum; indeed, it proved to carry his name on every side, but examination showed the façade to be not of marble but ironwork disguised in paint. Suzanne pleaded for money with which to buy some Belgian lace handkerchiefs that caught her fancy, but I was stern with her. Wool for the knitting and thread for the sewing she liked to do were the extent of her purchases.

I greatly wished to see Central Park. Though she fretted about the passage of time, I told her the opportunity should not be wasted. Our feet ached so that I concluded we must ride there rather than exhaust ourselves further. I found the great spread of blossoming trees, mown grass, and tended flowerbeds to be something of a revelation. I had not before been aware of such sharp contrasts. On the edges of the greensward sprawled dejected shanties constructed of tar paper and scraps of lumber, occupied, our driver said, by "squatters" who could afford nothing else.

The spectacle was so preposterous that I preferred to concentrate on the more exhilarating sight of gleaming equipages following one after another along the drives. The matrons' preferences ran to the open landau, drawn by a pair of horses matched both in color and rotundity of girth. Some younger women handled the reins of their own phaetons, with no escort other than a liveried groom perched on the back seat. But the liveliest drivers were the sporty gentlemen who tickled up the willowy beasts harnessed to the curricles, which passed at a speed to bedust every other carriage in the afternoon parade.

It took a tug on my sleeve from Suzanne to cut short my musing. "Nell, I am certain it's dreadfully late. We really should be going." She was right. It was worth the price of another cab to hurry us to the ferry by five o'clock.

We considered ourselves fortunate in arriving just as the hoot of the whistle warned of leaving. I was forced to adjust that assessment after we had made our way into the interior in search of a bench in order to ease our aching feet. Mama was already seated there, with a wearisome look in the droop of her head. Her spirits pricked up, however, as soon as she caught us.

"What have we here? Two fledglings flown from the nest?"

Suzanne's surreptitious nudge told me that whatever excuses were made had to be mine. "Mama, what a surprise! It was such a lovely day we thought we'd enjoy some fresh air and exercise, so we have been walking all over New York City."

"And may I ask what caught your eyes there?"

"We have been educating ourselves, Mama. We have seen some notable examples of new architecture. We looked into the shops without buying a single thing. And what else, Suzanne?"

"We went to the park and watched people drive by. We did nothing wrong, Ma."

"I see. What it amounts to is that you have passed a pleasant day of neglecting your duties to observe how idle people spend their time. I must agree with you; the weather was tempting. Your mother, however, found more useful things to do."

I ventured to ask, "What was that, Mama?"

She seemed to be extraordinarily pleased with herself. "I have affiliated myself with a new organization, not for money, let it be said, but out of principle. In point of fact, I am to preside over one of the branches on what is described as the Lower East Side. I intend to take both of you there very shortly to show you a more important side of life than the frivolities you have witnessed today."

"And the name of the organization, Mama?"

"The name is new, but dedication to human betterment is ageless. We are now called the American Socialist Labor Party."

I could picture her hanged in chains. "But you're a Republican, Mama."

"I have many interests, all nurtured in the cause of progress." I wondered how in the world I could ever break the news to Papa if she decided not to tell him.

II

MY FATHER was a man of such amiable disposition that even strangers usually called him "Charlie" within minutes of being introduced. In or out of his presence, my mother referred to him in the third person as "Papa" unless he had vexed her; then he became "Mr. Leonard." He tolerated this without complaint in much the same fashion as he tolerated all members of his family with the exception of myself. I had no doubt that I alone was the apple of his eye.

From him I inherited an abundance of butter-blond hair, eyes as bright as amethysts, and a skin that was the envy of Suzanne, Jennie, and Ida. Leona and I resembled him in coloring, but she, not I, was regarded as the true beauty among the Leonard girls.

I was the little freckle-faced hoyden who worshiped Papa to the point that I aspired to being remade in his image completely, not doomed to be a female encumbered by stupid skirts and equally absurd restrictions. Like him, of course, I would have eschewed whiskers and kept cheeks shaved clean.

Ever since I could remember, Mama was so engaged in outside undertakings that she was out of the house as often as not. The second to last of the six children, born when she was thirty-two, I was left to the precarious attentions of my three older sisters and an endless sequence of Irish hired girls. They performed most of the cooking. Consequently, never a jar of preserves was put up, and our meals seemed overburdened with salted meat and dried fruit.

Mama had limited time to spare for satisfying my curiosity about how the world could possibly have existed before I entered it. Papa would squeeze me in beside him in his leather wing chair after supper and make amends to the best of his ability, always extolling the talents of Mama.

"Can you guess what she was doing when I first met her in Buffalo? She was working behind the counter in a dry-goods store and enjoying every moment. I doubt whether any other woman in the country had tackled that before. You don't find many of them in those jobs today, but that's all going to change as you grow up, Nellie."

"Then did you marry her?"

"Well, it took a lot of doing to get Cynthia Howland van Name away from the women's literary club she belonged to— she used to win prizes for writing. But after we were married I persuaded her to go to Detroit. I came from Michigan originally, you see, and I found work on a newspaper. There was a little hill I liked to climb to look out across the tops of the trees at Lake Erie and Lake St. Clair. The railroad had been laid along the shore, so there wasn't much to see from there, and the trains and factories made it kind of smoky. So three or four years later we thought we'd move on farther west."

"Before I was born?"

"Quite a while before. You arrived in Clinton, Iowa, in a house we had between Third Avenue and Fourth. You weighed nine and a half pounds, a beautiful baby. That was in December, the month after Abraham Lincoln was elected. The Iowa Land Company had only just founded Clinton when we showed up. When you get to studying history in school, you'll learn about who it was named for: De Witt Clinton built the Erie Canal. It was a natural spot for a town and a drawbridge, right where the tracks were going across the Mississippi."

They held little more substance than a dream, but I had dim memories of newly staked streets and the shrieking of a sawmill that was among the first completed buildings. Wagon wheels that churned up summer dust mired down in winter mud. Once, Papa carried me on his shoulder to the edge of town to show me untouched land that stretched endlessly like a pale-green ocean toward the darkening pink western sky.

"Your mother and I found plenty to do in Clinton, let me tell you. She couldn't wait to see schools and churches opened up before less than half the houses were finished. She set up every kind of committee to push that ahead, even though your sisters and brother were coming along at a pretty steady pace, too."

"Didn't we have a newspaper—our own newspaper?"

"That we did. We went there for the express purpose of starting one up. The *Herald* came out every week, rain or shine. I wrote every word, set the type, and ran off the copies on an old hand press. Then I'd go around the merchants to talk them into advertising. If I came down with a cold or just felt worn down, your mother took over for the rest of the week. And that's about it for tonight. Are you going to read me a bedtime story?"

I could think of means of postponing that as well as more interesting things to talk about than newspapers. "Did you have to fight any Indians, Papa?"

He gave me a hug and a kiss for asking. "Sure as fate, I never did. I'd have lit out faster than a jack rabbit if I'd seen one of those fellers come whooping at me. But '57 turned out to be a big year in Iowa. Up there in the northwest corner at a place called Spirit Lake, the Sioux for some reason or other rode out in a war party and took care of some white settlers who'd done them no harm except move out there. A lot of people were afraid it would likely scare off the immigrants who were needed so badly to help the state grow, but it had no such effect. They kept on coming."

"Did the Indians scalp the settlers?"

"I guess they did. It was a habit they had at the time. Then that same year, the capital was changed from Iowa City to Des Moines, and they revised the constitution to give Negroes the vote. Your mother approved of that, but she was upset that women weren't treated the same way. That will happen sooner or later. . . ."

"Maybe we should have stayed in Iowa if Mama liked it there."

"Our feet got itchy again after she had gotten Clinton licked into shape and the sidewalks were put in. The paper wasn't making any fortune when the war came along and blew everything sky high. Iowa was dead set against slavery, and a lot of boys went away to fight. Not all of them came home in one piece, and your mother earned another feather for her cap by helping open the first soldiers' home in the state. I couldn't have been more proud of her."

"But why did we leave?"

"As I was saying, we both got restless. We had different ideas about which direction we should take, but she won, and we took the train east for Chicago, about a hundred and forty miles away. I sold the paper—I'd had enough of being a publisher—and went into the job-printing business, Knight and Leonard, which is where I'm at now. And where you're at is bedtime. What kind of ride up do you want tonight—a horse or a fireman?"

As a rule, I preferred a horse to a fireman, since that gave me the opportunity to cling tighter to Papa to let him know I loved him. A horse it was on this occasion.

I was too young to miss Iowa. With a trio of other children in the house, I was rarely short of a playmate, willing or not, to whom I could attach myself. A pinch or a poke now and then was one way of letting me know that they regarded me as Papa's spoiled darling. I did not complain, for I was not vengeful. Any manner of attention gratified me, but I could not bear to be excluded. When first handsome Leona and then homely Suzanne commenced private music lessons, I would watch them practice. I was no more than six years old when by imitation I had taught myself "The Bluebells of Scotland" with scarcely a fault.

The recital I gave one evening for Papa proved to be my undoing. Mama had removed herself up to the attic, the quietest part of the house, in a plank-walled corner which she termed "the study." She spent hours alone there when she was at home, usually working on notes for a novel she proposed to embark upon entitled *Failing Footprints, or the Last of the League of the Iroquois*. The occasional faltering she heard in my performance brought her hastening down to chide either Leona or Suzanne, who she thought must be at the keyboard.

She was surprised to discover it was neither of them. "Papa, I was not aware until now that this child has a gift."

"She's been learning some singing in school, then putting in time at the piano when she got home, I guess."

"I had always imagined it was Suzanne who enjoyed that particular Van Name talent."

"Well, Nellie seems to have a good ear, too."

She nodded. "It must be cultivated together with her singing voice as part and parcel of the same. I shall make arrangements in the morning. I do believe she may turn out to be a credit to us." I was added forthwith to Mama's personal projects. My tomboy days were over.

Like ourselves, Professor Dye lived in one of the frame houses which were the predominant style in Chicago. I was glad he was not numbered among the Germans who comprised the greater part of the population, since I knew nothing of their tongue. I was thankful, too, that walking to his classes with Suzanne, whom Mama delegated as my escort, did not take us through those streets of the city that Papa had spoken of where washing hung from window sills and hogs rooted through the trash.

I had not actually encountered any inhabitants of those places until early one Saturday afternoon in the spring before my ninth birthday, when every Leonard save Mama flocked outdoors to join what appeared to be most of the populace in a singular celebration. For the past week Papa, reading aloud from the *Tribune* at the breakfast table, had fed our excitement with accounts of what was to occur. The great transcontinental railroad was within an ace of completion. The tracks of the Union Pacific, thrusting westward, were due to meet up with those of the Central Pacific, heading east, enabling a traveler to journey for 1,175 miles between Omaha and Sacramento without interruption.

Papa, loyal to our city, was overjoyed. It meant, he explained that Chicago's destiny as the transportation center supreme was assured. St. Louis, which had nurtured identical aspirations, must be satisfied with second best. "In next to no time, we're going to see fifty percent added to the value of every stick of property around here. Chicago's got it made."

I could not make out why linking the two systems might not be effected at a more congenial spot than a remote dust bowl in Utah. It scarcely made sense to me to drive a golden spike and drink champagne on Promontory Summit in the midst of nowhere.

"Will those coolies in their pigtails who've been working on the tracks be invited to the party, Papa?"

"Refer to them as Chinese, not coolies, Nellie." Mama spoke from behind her copy of *Harper's Weekly*. "They are no less human than the rest of us."

Papa scratched his chin. "Probably not. John Chinaman won't get to ride the trains too often."

"How shall we know when it's happened, Pa?" Suzanne was itching to watch the parade that was scheduled to start on signal.

"By Western Union. They've strung wire every mile of the right of way. Some feller will jiggle a telegraph key, and we'll be set to go."

Michigan Avenue looked like an anthill swarming in Maytime when we arrived. Leona fingered her curls, hoping to be noticed, but drew not a glance. The only English I heard, unless one included gabbled Irish versions, was exchanged between us as we waited on the few precious feet of sidewalk we had wrested in the crush. Otherwise, it was a babble of German, Italian, and languages I could only guess at—Swedish, Russian, or both? Hungarian, Polish, and Greek? The noonday heat evoked a mixture of effluxes in which could be distinguished the stockyard reek of hogs and cattle, dried blood on unwashed garments, stale beer, cigar smoke, and whiffs of the Chicago River.

On Promontory Summit, I learned afterward, the spike was driven at eleven o'clock, which was to say at twelve by our local time. After a brief interval, we detected the distant blare of brass and thud of drums, and mounted policemen cleared a path down the avenue. In the course of the following two hours I lost tally of how many bands passed before us in ear-splitting exultation.

Soldiers marched and sailors marched. Red-shirted firemen towed a score or more pumpers. Silken flags and embroidered ensigns floated above the heads of contingents from social clubs, benevolent societies, merchants' groups, city councilmen, ward associations, fraternal orders, Sunday-school classes, and the blue-ribboned Band of Hope. There was a surge from the sidewalks as the tag end of the procession approached, and hundreds of citizens ambled in its wake. One of them, with the beery bulk of a meat-cutter, staggered along with a pig trotting after him, tied with a length of string to a foreleg and beset by yapping dogs.

My head ached together with my legs as we turned away for home. Papa let go my hand to buy an "extra" from a bawling newsboy and quickly scanned its front page. "I couldn't have said it better myself. Listen to what it says here: 'Peace hath victories no less renowned than war.'"

As her children grew, so did Mama's roster of chosen obligations. She served as linch pin to a host of charitable institutions, including the Washington House and the Freedman's Aid Commission. She stood like a pillar in the ladies' Leagues of the Northwest. She organized and presided over the Chicago Sorosis, the city's first club for women, and also published its weekly newsletter. She extolled the need of votes for women in public and, in private, of hard labor for me.

An especial interest of hers was the salvation of those unfortunate females who plied their brazen trade on the city streets. In theory, Papa concurred with her view that, in the cause of *mens sana*, nothing existed under the sun that might not be profitably discussed for our benefit, provided that the conclusions we reached came close to her own. In practice, if the topic of fallen women was brought up on the domestic agenda, the lobes of his ears turned pink, and he would excuse himself from the company and leave the room.

I had just walked home from the convent one day when she stalked in from a belated Sorosis luncheon with frost in her eyes. "I have heard distressing news today. The men of the City Council have had the effrontery to draft an ordinance that would turn Chicago into a cesspool of sin."

I did not care to see her angry because it drove her to words difficult to comprehend. "How dreadful, Mama!" Suzanne was up to her placatory tricks.

"For the sake of a few pitiful dollars in license fees, they propose to authorize the opening of houses of assignation. If they have their way in City Hall tonight, we shall all find ourselves in Gomorrah, worshiping evil, lust, and gold. But your mother is determined to stop them. That is her civic duty. If you have questions, ask them now."

Sammy, the perpetual minority of one, saw an opportunity to win attention. "What sort of houses are they?"

"They are factories of a kind, where women are enslaved in a wretched calling, catering to carnality." Mama was not one to make allowances either for ignorance or a limited vocabulary.

"Now, I must leave you children. There is work to do, a petition to prepare. Tell Papa as soon as he comes in that I shall not be here for supper."

I was asleep when she returned that night, but over breakfast she let us share in the afterglow. "With a number of like-minded ladies, I presented myself at the council chamber promptly at eight o'clock, delivered our round robin, and added a few more words on the subject. If ever I saw guilt on men's faces, it was written bold on theirs. Without a vote being taken, victory was ours. Licensed bordellos will have no place in this city." Setting down his coffee cup, Papa recalled having an early appointment awaiting him at the office.

Then on a Friday in a later October, Chicago began to burn. There were those who doubted whether the fire could possibly have grown from an incident so trifling as a cow kicking over a lantern in Mrs. O'Leary's barn at 558 De Koven Street on the West Side, but for two days and two nights we had no sleep.

Two-thirds of our city that housed more than 300,000 people was built of wood, which a long, dry summer had dried into kindling. Mountains of timber for fresh construction were piled up in the lumber yards, where the flames first flickered, then within seconds roared like a demons' choir. The jangle of fire-bells in the distance took us to the front windows to watch a scarlet engine, smoke pouring from its bright brass boiler, go careening down the street behind a team of panting horses, followed within minutes by another.

A neighbor came up onto the stoop with the news. "They say every last one of the yards is burning, but no need for us to fret ourselves. It's way over on the West Side."

Mama cast a skeptical eye on her. "Have you noticed how windy it is today?"

The flames, feeding on themselves and fanned by the veering gusts, leaped over the river to the south and finally to the north side. We stood on the sidewalk with every bucket, dishpan, kettle, and bowl in the house filled with water, fearfully eying the sparks that sailed over the rooftops. We were lucky to have water. Very soon, so much was being pumped in futility onto the uncontrollable blaze that pressure in the faucets died to a trickle. The clamor of bells on engines retreating from the hopeless battle told us it was time to start our prayers for safety.

Papa ran most of the way home from the office with tales of chaos. "I never thought I'd make it. People are all over the streets, thousands of them, carrying bits and pieces of furniture, aiming to get down to the shore, I guess. They say there's crowds of 'em actually out there in the water, hoping that'll save 'em. I've heard about panic, but I've never seen it before."

We spent a sleepless night on watch at the bedroom windows with our supply of precious water, seeing fire brands soar over like shooting stars and choking on the roily smoke that spread across the crimson sky like the clouds of an impending tornado. The next day we heard a thunderous explosion that set us wondering whether a gasworks or an arsenal had blown up. Only later did we know the cause, after we read accounts of the fires' fury, the pillaging, and the orgies that had accompanied what seemed like Judgment Day: Gunpowder had checked the conflagration on the South Side.

The second day became a second night of fear before rain fell to douse the flames in the north. The waterworks that stood there were in ruins along with the streets around them. The prairie that reached to the far edge of the city was then within an inch of burning. Mama took the rain to be God's handiwork.

It was said that one hundred thousand people lost their homes by the time the embers were doused. More than three square miles of Chicago was destroyed—close to eighteen thousand buildings and property valued at $196,000,000. Loss of city records made it impossible to count the number of dead. This was easy to believe when Papa took some of us to inspect the smoldering debris, redolent with odors whose origin was best left unknown. One category of victims claimed the energies of Mama. The razing of innumerable houses of ill repute increased the misfortunes of the unfortunates. The police hauled off the hapless creatures by the dozen as they walked the blackened streets in areas that had escaped destruction.

"What those girls deserve is shelter, not prison," Mama exclaimed, proceeding to repeat herself in written appeals that duly appeared in the newspapers. Far from content with limiting herself to words on paper, she announced open house for fellow citizens who shared her concern.

Suzanne could not contain her curiosity. "You shan't invite one of those women, shall you, Ma?"

"Who else can provide us with a firsthand account of how sorely they are treated?"

Business affairs at Knight & Leonard engaged Papa that evening, but any of us children who so chose was free to linger at the top of the stairs to watch. Sammy and I sat side by side as staid gentlemen and sedate gentlewomen arrived one by one and two by two with a common air of righteousness, to be escorted into the parlor by Mama. Time had gone by, and she had already called the meeting to order when the doorbell jangled again.

I scampered down to admit the latecomer. In appearance, the girl was not unlike Leona, but of paler complexion and slighter in stature. Her dark-circled eyes blinked in the gaslight, and her fingers trembled. We exchanged uncertain gazes for a moment before she spoke. "Does Mrs. Leonard live here?" I said that she did. "Please God she'll excuse me for being late, but I was detained."

Mama swooped out into the hall. "I fear I do not remember your name."

"I'm used to being called Maggie Mooney, ma'am." Mama helped her off with her heavy shawl and took her to meet the company. I went back to sit with Sammy.

His breath tickled my ear. "She's one of those, isn't she? She's a hoor."

"What if she is? She's sort of pretty in a way."

"Yeah, I guess so. It isn't right to have her in the house, though."

"Why not? Mama must have invited her."

"It still isn't right. They're wicked women, with paint on their faces and smoking cigarettes and such like."

"You don't know everything. Everybody doesn't have to think the same way you do, just because you're a boy."

"I didn't say they did. You ought to have learned about sin from those nuns at the convent. They'll tell you the difference between right and wrong."

"I wouldn't go by what they say. They've never been out in the world, and that's where I want to go when I'm grown. I'll decide for myself then what to do."

Our voices must have risen as we argued. Mama's forbidding face appeared around the parlor door. "That will be quite enough. You are disturbing us. You may go to bed. Good night."

The evening's outcome was the founding of one more enterprise consecrated to a worthy cause. At its next gathering the Good Samaritan Society, chaired again by Mama, voted unanimously to establish a hostel for the fallen and appointed a committee to suggest how to provide the needed capital. Its third session produced a well-to-do German lumber merchant, recently a widower, who offered his forty-room mansion as a shelter. Mama proposed the vote of thanks.

She kept so many irons warming simultaneously in the crucible of her brain that it was impossible for anyone to foretell which would glow next into white heat.

She was overcome at present by the appeal of putting pen to paper and thought to record her impressions of the great fire and its consequences in the guise of fiction. *Failing Footprints* was set aside in favor of a fresh manuscript. Perhaps she explained to her club sisters how her chosen title fitted the work in hand, but she omitted to do as much for any member of her family. Eventually, she did discover a publisher willing to risk issuing *Lena Rouden, or The Rebel Spy*, but I read no more than the title page of the copy she gave me.

Whenever Mama's mind was in a state of flux, those of us around her were likely to feel the goad of change. She concluded at this time that I had been exposed long enough to the dubious influences of Mother Church. What she prescribed for me now was finishing school so that the last vestiges of the hoyden might be erased and the principles of *politesse* instilled. I was accordingly entered into the Park Institute, which I attended without enthusiasm, since beautiful manners, which figured large on the curriculum, struck me as being of less utility than a cool head.

In almost the same breath, she announced a turnabout in the career she intended for me. Professor Dye had long since given way to a Professor Gill as keeper of my vocal cords. He had been supplanted by Mr. Carl Woolfson, who envisioned me not in opera but as a shining star of oratorio on the concert stage. I was too shy to ask how long it would take to attain such eminence and who was to support me meanwhile.

Papa's resources were ebbing away. The fortunes of Knight & Leonard had fallen into decline in common with those of most businesses throughout the country since the autumn of '69. Mama knew exactly where the root of the trouble lay—in the machinations of Jay Gould and Jim Fisk in their plot to corner every available ounce of gold and so rocket up its price to make more millions. That September's "Black Friday" ruined half of Wall Street, and she condemned "goldbugs," as she berated them, to eternal damnation.

Though she did not discriminate between them, I thought Fisk, always plump and smiling in portrayals of him in the press, considerably more attractive than skinny little Gould, his partner in the Erie Railroad. As she explained their scheme, they had to be sure the United States Treasury would not release any of its stock of gold to break the monopoly they were planning. Fisk courted President Grant by inviting him aboard the *SS Providence*, flagship of a steamship line of which Fisk was a kind of admiral. I liked to picture him in the uniform he designed for himself. He pleaded with the President to set higher prices for the precious metal, but Mr. Grant's response was only to light another cigar.

The two conspirators turned to another method of influencing Washington by allotting $1,500,000 worth of their hoard to the name of the President's brother-in-law, Abel Corbin; it cost him nothing, and he would reap the profits when gold prices soared. "Oh, they were shrewd, that pair, and Corbin was venal," Mama sputtered.

The President did direct the Treasury to slow down its sales, but his brother-in-law urged him so vehemently to cut off the complete supply "that even the unsuspecting idol of our nation smelled rotten fish." Jolly Jim Fisk made the rounds of Wall Street, dropping hints of an imminent harvest to be reaped by buying gold. Mama fished a clipping from the *Herald* from her reticule, where she preserved it as ammunition, and had me read the account of the day the market collapsed. "As the bells of Trinity pealed forth the hour of noon, the gold on the indicator stood at 160. Just a moment later, and before the echoes died away, gold fell to 138."

I paused. "Why was that, Ma?"

"Because Mr. Grant roused himself at last, just as he did at Shiloh, and ordered the Treasury to sell gold and keep on selling gold until the goldbugs' wicked plot came to naught." I went back to the clipping. "Over the pallid faces of some men stole a deadly hue, and almost transfixed to the earth, they gazed on vacancy. Others rushed like wildfire through the streets, hatless and caring little about stumbling against their fellows...."

Mama retrieved her fragment of newsprint. "Had I been there in the crowd that set out to find them, I would have hunted down Gould and Fisk wherever they were skulking and then been glad to watch those goldbugs hanged."

Chicago was already suffering from the blows of one Black Friday when the second Friday set our metropolis ablaze. Further hurt was inflicted on the likes of Papa, who could prosper only when his customers prospered, too. The Park Institute's fees were higher than the convent's; corners would have to be cut somewhere.

When we met in family conference, Mama supplied a surprising solution. "Nellie must have the opportunity to demonstrate that she is capable of applying herself to her music without further aid from a teacher. We can dispense with Mr. Woolfson. She will practice, on her own responsibility, at least once a day."

Papa was as much taken aback as I. "But, Cynthia, she is doing so well. Why, after that Chickering Hall recital for the Good Samaritans, she got her name into the *Tribune!* She would be heartbroken. We can certainly find some other way to keep our heads above water without sacrificing Nellie."

"I shan't mind at all, Papa, if it—"

"You are interrupting, Nellie. If she practices—and I trust you will ensure that she does—little harm can be done to her prospects. Besides, I have something else in mind."

His sigh was barely audible. "What is it to be this time?"

"Nellie takes after my grandmother on my father's side." Mama's lineage provided her with two hundred years of references to fall back on, dating to a marriage conducted at sea, according to her account, by the captain of the *Mayflower* and including two great-grandfathers who fought under General Washington. "My grandmother might well have attained renown as an artist had she lived long enough. Nellie has the same deft hand with a brush."

"But why swap horses? Painting lessons for her will cost as much as singing."

"Not entirely right, Mr. Leonard. Madame St. John is a fellow member of the Sorosis. She has exhibited her oils both in Boston and Philadelphia. I have already asked whether she will assent to instructing our daughter, and she has agreed as a personal favor to me. I showed her some of Nellie's watercolors. She was favorably impressed."

I reported to Madame St. John every Wednesday afternoon at four. I continued to duplicate the scenes I had attempted most often before and could render best: lily pond with green frog; imagined impression of Mount Vesuvius in eruption; imitation of Landseer's "The Monarch of the Glen," in which my stags invariably resembled sheep adorned with hatracks.

The daubs I had been churning out at Madame St. John's behest proved to have a not insignificant part in effecting another change of course. Before parting from Mr. Woolfson, I had promised to appear on the program he was assembling for a concert devised as an advertisement for himself.

I sang rather well in my opinion and also in that of two attendant reviewers. A certain Madame Schoenburg, previously known to Mama only by hearsay as a distinguished musical mentor, read the published critiques and decided she and I might profit from a mutual attachment. She approached Mama.

I was not present at their *tête-à-tête*, but I was encouraged by the result. Madame Leonard, although flattered by the lavish praise for her daughter, regretted that present pecuniary circumstances prohibited music lessons for her. Madame Schoenburg, however, ascertained that the daughter was receiving instruction in the visual arts from Madame St. John. If the pictures were of sufficient quality to merit hanging in Madame Schoenburg's salon, she would be delighted to take me on as a pupil, free of charge. For the price of one blurry stag, two lily ponds, and a pledge of more œuvres to follow, I was worked harder than ever before. Now I had to begin committing complete scores to memory in readiness for the day I was acclaimed a prima donna and Madame Schoenburg could bask in my glory.

Meanwhile, Papa had been casting around for a lifeline to save Knight & Leonard from foundering. One winter evening a week or so before my sixteenth birthday he entered the house with a rare look of satisfaction on his often melancholy face. "Cynthia, I believe we've turned the corner, or will very soon. We're going to start printing books. Knight and I struck a deal today."

Mama, for a change, accorded him all her attention. *Lena Rouden* had yet to find a publisher. "What kind of books, Charles?"

"Well, I'd like us to handle work that I can be proud of. Our first job will be the speeches of Robert Green Ingersoll. The colonel's in town to deliver one tonight, and we met him today, a mighty impressive man."

Mama's upper lip curled. "Ingersoll, the lawyer of Croesus. Ingersoll, the anti-Christ with faith in nothing but his own willfulness. Ingersoll, Charles Darwin's American bulldog."

Suzanne the peacemaker put down her sewing. "What's he like, Pa?"

"Heavy-set feller in his forties. Sincere, I'd say. Speaks his mind."

Mama could not be deterred. "He preaches the gospel of atheism, Suzanne, a clergyman's son who spurns God, and your father admires him."

"I happen to think just about the way he does, if you want to know." I had not seen Papa so riled up before. "I like Tom Paine, and so does he. He believes in Darwin's evolution, and so do I. What do you really believe in, Cynthia, except your own high and mightiness?"

Sparks burned in her eyes. "If your faith is the same as his, then you believe in nothing. I do not believe that monkeys maketh man, except perhaps in the case of Mr. Ingersoll and yourself, Mr. Leonard. I also believe that I can no longer live under the same roof with you."

She set out the next morning before breakfast in search of apartments for herself and her share of the family, which she insisted be divided out of fairness, as she said, to all. Suzanne elected to live with Mama. I would have chosen to remain with Papa, but I was overridden.

"Nellie is at an age where she is in dire need of a mother to watch over her. She appears to have forgotten the words she used to recite to me from her school reader: 'Be not like the peacock, proud and vain, on account of your beauty and fine clothes, for humility and goodness are always to be preferred to beauty.' But *I* remember."

She was close to the truth. Sometimes in the night when I knew my sisters were asleep beside me and I felt certain that Sammy in his room and Mama and Papa in theirs were, too, I crept out into the upper hall to stand before the mirror that hung there. Had Suzanne in turn done the same? I doubted it. Leona? I was confident she had. Mama? Never. By candlelight, I stood and examined myself, first the face, then inch by inch down to the waist, where the walnut frame cut off the view. Finally, I would set down the candle to move a chair in closer, climb up on it, praying for it not to creak, and lift my nightgown up about my waist in order to complete the inspection. I had no fault to find with what the mirror showed.

Mama pressed her argument. "Only selfishness could lead you to keep her with you, but I suppose I must expect selfishness now as always." He could not parry that thrust. Leona would keep house for him, and Sammy would stay on with Papa. I vowed that I would call on him every day.

While I suffered the pangs of parting, Mama suffered in a different way: She missed having her attic den in which to retreat with her thoughts and take up *Falling Footprints* again. So far as I could tell, Suzanne did not suffer at all. Knight & Leonard completed a first printing of Mr. Ingersoll's oratory and anticipated further orders.

I spent a miserable winter, occupying myself all week by learning and practicing the soprano part in *Lucia* together with three more scores and singing in St. John's on Sundays. Mama's time was taken up in raising funds for the skating rink. Then came the night of her shame, and we were flung into the throes of packing. The one man I had ever loved was still Papa, though one pimply fellow member of the choir whose tenor voice showed signs of cracking into an uncertain baritone insisted that I accept a new autograph album as a memento. The first entry was already inscribed:

> Go where glory waits thee,
> But while fame elates thee,
> Oh, still remember me!
> When around thee dying
> Autumn leaves are lying,
> Oh, then remember me!

Papa came to Van Buren Street Station to see us safely aboard the Lake Shore & Michigan Southern parlor car that would carry us without changing onto the New York Central tracks at Buffalo. He blamed his sniffles on a cold in the head, but I made no effort to disguise my tears.

III

*L*IFE IN BROOKLYN subsided into unrelieved monotony. I practiced for not less than two hours every day lest Dr. Damrosch should be disappointed with me when I went for my weekly lesson. I daydreamed of how, when, and whether fame might find me. I calmed my fears of being doomed to failure only when I pulled up a chair for breakfast, dinner, and supper at Mrs. Walker's invariably tempting table.

Suzanne had more to busy herself with than I; she had found that our fellow guests appreciated her doing their mending, and she was spreading word among local drapery stores that he services as a dressmaker were available at a modest charge to interested customers. I was so bored that I should have been happy to accompany Mama on her political excursions or wherever else it was that she went, but I was not invited.

Singing expanded my rib cage; Mrs. Walker's cooking had a corresponding effect elsewhere. I was being rounded out at such a rate that I wondered whether I should forego a dish now and then. Mama would not tolerate it. "How dare you say such a thing? You are tall, and your figure is like a goddess'. Whoever heard of a scrawny prima donna? Don't talk such nonsense again."

Suzanne snickered. "Nellie would have us stay over a restaurant and live on fumes from the kitchen."

No opportunity had been accorded for me to see for myself the dimensions of any woman on the New York stage. I pined for another carefree jaunt to the tantalizing city to witness a performance in one of the old theaters around Union Square or in one of the new ones risen farther uptown on Broadway. Mama, however, ruled that buying tickets to any form of entertainment would be wicked extravagance.

The theater, by her assessment, had fallen on evil days. *Uncle Tom's Cabin* was one of the few plays of which she approved in principle, though she had not actually seen it in all the years it had been staged by a hundred different stock companies. *La Traviata* was excluded from my repertoire because its heroine was no better than she should be. I slaked my thirst for divertissement—or was it only aggravated as if by sipping sea water?—by listening, eyes a-pop, to accounts of theatrical delights sometimes delivered at supper by another boarder.

Mr. Riley, a paper-collared bachelor, clerked for Mr. Chauncey Depew, who, I was given to understand, was the envy of all for the quality of his tailoring and his position as general counsel of the Vanderbilt railroads. Mr. Riley bought $1.50 tickets at half price in cigar stores, which obtained them *gratis* for displaying in their windows the lithographs advertising current attractions.

From him I learned about Lester Wallack's playhouse at Thirteenth Street, whose reputation for productions of elegant comedy had extended as far as Chicago. "Ah, if only you were an actress and not a singer, Miss Leonard, you could appear there, and with your looks you'd be on the high road to a fortune. Or at the Booth, where they've got three balconies and machinery in the basement to lower half the stage and then hoist it again with different scenery." Mama, two places down the table, scrutinized him as critically as though he were expressing a kind word for the opium habit.

I gushed. "Of course, we went to plays all the time in Chicago." Untrue; never once. "But I am wondering which actresses are the most popular in New York City. I'm sure they must all be beautiful, but what of their proportions? Do audiences prefer them stout or slender? What do they wear? How much do they earn?"

Mr. Riley was too busy concentrating to notice Mama. "Well, most of those you saw in Chicago would be the same as we see here, but going on tour. As for money, Wallack's used to pay a hundred dollars a week to favorites like Mrs. Hoey, but they get half as much again nowadays. What do they wear? A lot or a little, depending what's called for and how much they want to show."

Once upon a time I would have blushed, but no more. He leaned in an inch or so closer. "They usually have more clothes on than they did the first time I ever went to a theater, which was ten years ago. That was at Wood's Museum, close to where Wallack's stands today. The Lydia Thompson Burlesque Company. They were all English girls and as well built and fair-haired as you are. Lydia was the boss, and then there were Pauline Markham, Ada Harland, and another one—I forget her name—who sang."

"What else did they do?"

He winked. "Wore tights. It caused a sensation."

I was dismayed to sense that my cheeks threatened to glow. "Tights are still the fashion at Niblo's Garden, too. You know what they say—legs never go out of style. I saw *Around the World in Eighty Days* there last year."

Mama intervened. "And what, may I ask, does an audience pay for these titillations?"

"Only fifty cents, ma'am, Perhaps you and the two young ladies would care to join me one evening? You'd enjoy it."

"Do you really think so?"

She found less abrasive company in Mr. Cartwright, who was employed on the New York *Tribune*. We had suspended our attendance at any church now that her ardor was apportioned in equal parts between the Socialist Labor Party and the doctrines of Mary Baker Eddy. Mrs. Eddy's impatience with established forms of religion was shared by Mama, and until she was farther along toward her goal of organizing a Science of Life Club in New York, we spent Sunday mornings with the waxed flowers and rubber plant in Mrs. Walker's parlor. The boarders either stayed in bed or went to Sabbath services. Like our landlady, most of them attended Plymouth Church, where Dr. Henry Ward Beecher and his flowing gray locks retained an unimpaired hold over the congregation. He had lived down accusations of having seduced one lamb of his flock, a worshipful Sunday-school teacher, Mrs. Theodore Tilton. I was as frustrated in my desire to behold the persuasive pastor as in sampling Niblo's Garden.

Sundays were an improvement over the other days of the week. There were the gentlemen guests to converse with, and in the evenings I had an audience of them to sing to. It had become almost a tradition for the Leonard girls to entertain with a musicale—principally old ballads like "Twickenham Ferry" and "The Kerry Dance," which always evoked a welcome round of applause.

On a subsequent Sunday, Mr. Riley, who had come down as usual fifteen minutes after Mrs. Walker had rung the gong, touched my arm to draw me into the hall after the dishes had been cleared away. Suzanne was busy with needle and thread; Mama had retired to our room on her own affairs. Mr. Riley's *sotto voce* was pitched for my ears alone. "I have an urgent and personal question to put to you, Miss Leonard. How would you like to appear on the stage, and I don't mean this year, next year, some time, never, but perhaps next week and with money in your hand for doing so?"

He bewildered me. "Of course, I should be delighted, but I confess I have no idea on earth what you are talking about."

He gushed apologies. "Allow me to explain. After we went to Tony Pastor's last night, some friends of mine and me dropped in for a rarebit at the De Soto on Bleecker Street. All kinds of actors and managers go there, you see, and you can pick up a lot if you listen. I just happened to learn that Mr. Edward E. Rice is going to be looking for people like you right here in Brooklyn, starting tomorrow morning."

"What has that to do with me?"

He ran moist palms over mousy hair, which gleamed with a heavier than usual anointment of pomade, no doubt in honor of the Sabbath. "Do you know who Sullivan and Gilbert are?"

"I thought everybody did. I sing songs by Mr. Arthur Sullivan, and he wrote the music for *The Sorcerer* while Mr. William something Gilbert supplied the words."

Astonishment. "I guess you know as much as I do about that, then, but Ed Rice is famous in the theater, too. He puts on shows all over the country, and he's putting on the new opera by Sullivan and Gilbert, their latest. He wants people to sing in the chorus."

I skipped over the question of what Mama would say. "How could he know anything about me?"

"He doesn't yet. You have to go and sing for him, and then he'll engage you. I'm certain he would."

"Where would I go?"

"To a hall not far from Brooklyn Tabernacle. You walk three blocks past there and turn. I'll take you there if you want me to and introduce you like I was your manager."

With Mr. Riley as guide, there would presumably be no problem in reaching the place, though I should have to let him understand that he must expect no return for his kindness. Dealing with Mama would be a different matter, but I'd jump that fence when I came to it. She had long since disappeared on her daily rounds before it was time to leave to meet Mr. Rice. I had become so permeated with tedium in my present subsistence that I would gladly work without pay if he showed the least interest in me. I fancied I might even don tights like the boldest of coryphées and spin pirouettes for him if I had to. Like any Johnny Reb, I was ready to secede.

For the sake of making conversation on our walk, I asked Mr. Riley how he proposed to explain away his belated arrival at his desk. "Oh, I'll just say I swallowed a dirty oyster for supper." So I had nothing to be concerned about in that respect. Neither had I as the rest of the morning developed after he had approached Mr. Rice as cheekily as though he had been dealing with him as an equal for the past fifty years.

"What are you going to sing for me, young lady?" He chewed on a frayed cigar as we stood together on the bare stage. I turned to the pianist below, interestingly pale, perhaps ten years my senior, wearing a velveteen jacket and soft, dark hair to his shoulders. "Do you know 'Let Me Dream Again'?"

"I do, and I know you, too. You're Helen Leonard."

No one had told him my name. How could he already have learned it? "I heard you in Chickering Hall when we were doing another show in Chicago. I conduct the orchestra for Ed. Harry Braham's my name. Some people confuse me with my father, Dave. He's in the same business. You won't have any trouble. I remember your voice. Beautiful."

That also described his playing. After the rippling bars of the introduction, confidence welled up inside as the notes poured from my throat. Mr. Braham cocked an eye at Mr. Rice to see if he'd had enough after the first chorus, but his cigar waved us on. I was accepted on the spot for the chorus of what the posters pasted up at the end of the week proclaimed as "original nautical opera by Sullivan and Gilbert—H.M.S. *Pinafore or The Lass That Loved a Sailor.*" The five dollars a week I was promised would be more money than I had ever before received on a single occasion.

Mr. Braham, taller than I, walked me to the door, with stumpy Mr. Rice sulking behind us. I glanced at the portion of the score I was given to learn before commencement of rehearsals and discovered it to be a barely legible scrawl. Mr. Braham supplied the explanation.

"It saves Ed money the same as paying nothing to the authors does. Can you guess how many versions of the *Pinafore* will soon be performed in New York? We'll be number six, there are two more to come, and not a nickel goes to England for the men who wrote it."

"Are all faithful to the music and the words?"

"Nobody bothers about that except Gilbert and Sullivan so long as people buy the tickets, and I think we'll sell plenty. Everybody's going to be humming and whistling the *Pinafore* before long. I'll see you here in the morning."

I thanked him, advised Mr. Rice that he should tarry no longer, and made my way back to Mrs. Walker's. Before I confronted Mama I would dash off a note to Papa and study my lines. I had best not let her see them. I did not want her to be inflamed more than necessary by such lyrics as:

> *Hardly ever swears a big, big D—*
> *Then give three cheers, and one cheer more,*
> *For the well-bred Captain of the Pinafore!*

As soon as she had walked into the house and gone to our room to wash her hands, I slipped up to deliver the lines I had concocted for myself. "Mama, I have found employment. Isn't that wonderful? I am to sing in an opera."

She dabbed a corner of the towel around her mouth. "Well,

now! Every day brings its surprises. Are we to thank Dr. Damrosch for this? You were not content for me to make the necessary overtures?"

"He doesn't even know about it. I am really quite old enough to begin looking after myself, which is what I did today."

"And which of the operas is it?"

I gave her an abridged edition of events, including the courtesies of Mr. Riley, but without referring to Mr. Braham. "So you are talking about *comic* opera? And not the masterworks of Mozart or Donizetti but rather the jingles of a burlesque ridiculing Queen Victoria's navy? Your name will have no mention in the program, of course, and your voice will be lost in the chorus. You would be wise to think again, Miss Leonard."

I could not tolerate her in this mood. "I have done enough thinking to last me a lifetime. Practice, practice, practice, and I won't have you ding-donging at me as you did at Papa. I am going to appear for Mr. Rice, and there is nothing you can say or do to stop me."

To my amazement, there was no answering fire. Instead, she stared so long and hard at me that I felt almost a stranger. "You are much like myself when I was a girl, headstrong, self-willed, bent on having her way. You will find the paths you tread do not always lead to happiness, whatever they may be. But if you develop your brain along with your determination as I have done, I shall be satisfied."

We seldom exchanged kisses within our family, but now I touched my lips to her forehead, at a loss for anything further to say. She hesitated briefly, then gave my hand a quick pat. "What do you plan to tell Dr. Damrosch?"

I had not thought about that. "Perhaps I could write to him, since I shall have no time to continue with any more lessons."

"That would be cowardly as well as discourteous, Nellie. You should speak to him."

In triumph, I could afford to be lenient. "Very well, then. I'll see him once more."

I waited until the end of my hour with him to let him know our association was to end. His face puckered as though with a twinge of pain. "If your decision is made, there is no use trying to unmake it. When we are young, we sometimes fail to choose wisely at first. At your age, I began to study medicine at the University of Berlin. But it was the wrong choice. I was ignorant of what joy meant until I turned to the violin to make music, which was what my nature demanded of me. I ask only one thing more of you. When your experiment in the theater is over, search your heart to see if that is how your talent should be used." It was easy enough to promise that I would.

I bounced out of the house to go to rehearsals, taking a few deep breaths to keep rein on my elation, then abandoning the attempt as the songs of the *Pinafore* echoed within my head. Harry's forecast was surely accurate; nothing in the world of melody could be more appealing than "And you may all be Rulers of the Queen's Navee!" and the rest of the songs. The costumes rented for the chorus were darned in places but entirely decorous, and I took the greatest delight in wearing a sort of sailor suit, topped by a jaunty straw hat with a ribbon on one side. I formed an instant friendship with a girl named Amy Leslie, but what caused me increasing excitement was the presence of Harry Braham.

I had come out on top in my first test of will with Mama. I was off upon the sea of theatricals, pursuing a course of my own charting. Next, I must have someone to share in my enchantment, no matter if I had to pit myself against my mother for a second time. I resolved to fall in love. The man I selected for attention was Harry Braham.

The secrets of romance would have to be learned by doing. Like my sisters, I knew something of the theoretical aspects of biology from Mama. In warmth of feeling, I had no experience apart from affection for Papa. First, obviously, Harry must be made to take note of me above every other lady in the company. I began by feigning to be puzzled over how to give the correct inflection to certain phrases sung by the chorus. We intervened, staccato, during a passage dominated by our Captain Corcoran, splendid with his epaulettes, sword, and cocked hat: "And I'm never, never sick at sea!"

Chorus: What, never?
Captain: No, never!
Chorus: What, never?
Captain: Hardly ever!

Chorus: He's hardly ever sick at sea!

A model of diffidence, I approached Harry, who straight-way offered to coach me when work was concluded for the day. It was as simple as that. "What, *never?*" "Hardly ever!" became passwords exchanged between us long before one heard them on everybody's lips and encountered them repeatedly as a standard jest in the newspapers.

We made a dusty boxroom behind the stage our first trysting place. He led me there one November evening shortly before the Edward E. Rice version of *H.M.S. Pinafore* was due to open its run at the Brooklyn Academy of Music, not to be confused with its more illustrious Manhattan namesake. His pretext—that he needed help looking for an extra music stand—was discarded the moment we were closeted inside with the door shut.

"Have you ever been in love, Nellie?"

The emphasis I gave to my reply was that which we had re-hearsed together. "No *never!* And you?"

He answered in kind. "Hardly ever! But would you believe that I am now?"

"I think I might."

He stretched out a finger to touch a ringlet of my hair. "Bright as gold, and a skin like silk. Has anyone ever told you what a marvel you are?"

"Hardly ever. Except you."

He knew where his arms should go as he folded them around me. I was ashamed at how awkwardly my hands clasped his back. His lean nose pressed into mine at his first attempt at a kiss and again when I tilted my head in the same general direction as his in an effort to resolve the quandary. Then finally lips were settled against lips, and we heightened each other's passion with our tongues. I had not realized how hard it would be to breathe. But before very long, I had the hang of it, and we were kissing like the dickens. The taste of his mouth seemed every bit as sweet as this new victory.

I still clung to him after his arms had fallen away and he strove to compose himself. "Have supper with me somewhere."

That would mean a subsequent accounting to Mama for my absence. I was not ready to rejoin her in battle yet. I wanted to enjoy for as long as possible the knowledge that I was in love and not dilute the knowing by talking about it to anyone but him. Harry Braham was *mine*, a precious, private treasure.

"I think I ought to go. We can come back here tomorrow."

"May I take you to your lodgings?"

"Not all the way. To the corner, if you wish."

"Is there nowhere close by where we might go?"

"Not tonight. A boardinghouse is a poor place for us." It struck me that I knew so little about him that I had no idea where he lived. I asked.

"Behind my own front door on Washington Square. Would you like to see it? Can you come?"

"You don't mean now?"

"I do, but I know you can't. Soon?"

"After we've opened. It will be easier then."

Before we parted, I discovered an additional pleasure. Embracing in the shadow cast by a tree made love an extraordinarily private affair even though on a public street. I was so late in knocking at Mrs. Walker's door that I wondered whether I should go to bed hungry, but she served me pork pie and pickles in the kitchen. Love, I ascertained for myself, can sharpen the appetite.

In the little looking glass outside our door, I reassured myself that, so far as I could tell, no signs of change showed in my face. Then I entered, fingers crossed. My luck held. Thoughts for things to come preoccupied her, not events of the day. A book lay unopened on her lap; the name of its author, Henry George, was new to me.

"Nellie, I have been guilty of neglecting you, and I must make amends. How long ago it is since I promised to let you see where I devote some of my time! We shall go together on Sunday for you to make the acquaintance of my political friends."

I had nourished the hope of somehow escaping to Harry that day, but it was not expedient to say so.

"Beyond that, I have been debating once more with young Mr. Cartwright. I am persuaded of his sincerity, though I question his conclusions. He will be happy, he says, to conduct me to those homes of which he spoke when all of us were discussing selective breeding as a means of improving the state of mankind. Do you remember?"

"Of course I do, Mama." I wondered whether she would judge Harry as physically or morally fit for parenthood should they ever meet.

"That also is to be done on Sunday. I should like you with me for both our sakes. Will you come?"

It was strange that instead of demanding, she asked. Was it a portent that she accepted the fact that I was a grown woman? If true, she deserved encouragement. "I shall be glad to, Mama."

Mr. Cartwright did not approve. When she broached the subject of my enlistment for the expedition, he harped on forever about the danger involved. He would be safe enough, and so would an indomitable dowager when they ventured into the somber streets he had in mind for her edification. But a young girl? A platoon of policemen might be required for her protection.

Mama had the solution. "As a child Nellie always hankered after being a boy. This shall be her chance to dress as one. We can put her into trousers, dirty her face, and pull a hat over her hair. It will be too dark for anyone to notice the difference if she keeps a still tongue in her head."

His objections withered away. He offered a shapeless cap and an old suit of his for my disguise. When I tried the garments on, they fitted well enough with sleeves and cuffs rolled back, though between the front buttons the jacket was somewhat tight. "Look, Mama! I'm playing Shakespeare. What's it called—where the girl wears her brother's clothes?"

"Nellie, child! What has happened to your memory? *As You Like It*, of course."

The costume went with us in the timeworn valise when we set off from Mrs. Walker's with our guide. The elevated railroad took us downtown after we had disembarked from the ferry at 34th Street. Mama led the way up the stairs of an ancient brownstone to our first stop. A crudely lettered cardboard on what might once have been the library on the second floor supplied its present identity: "American Socialist Labor Party and Reading Club. Visitors welcome."

The language of the sign was English, but German prevailed in the babble of voices inside. I had been prepared to see the walls painted a revolutionary red; in fact, they were slimy green.

The bookshelves bulged with tracts, pamphlets, tomes, stuffed in higgledy-piggledy. Mama thrust herself into the throng that filled the room with conversation and tobacco smoke to extricate one by one those fellow members whom she wished to introduce to Mr. Cartwright. They were scrubbed and in their Sunday best, and the air immediately surrounding them was scented with the tangs of their trades, this one with printer's ink, that one with malt, another with the aroma of fresh-rolled cigars.

While the rest bobbed their heads and beamed at Mama and Mr. Cartwright, a plump-chopped, close-cropped printer closed in on me. "The look in your eyes tells me you do not understand what they are saying. If you please, I will address you in English, although German is our official language. You are the daughter of Frau Leonard?"

A quick smile was more than sufficient to encourage him to continue. "Most of us here are new to this country. We come because we are—how do you say it?—at odds with Karl von Bismarck-Schoenhausen, who now terms himself Prince. He does not care for Socialism, and we do not care for him. He is for imperialism and *Kulturkampf*; I am for the other Karl, who wrote *Das Kapital*." He laughed until he threatened to choke on his own jest.

"*Ja wohl!* Enough of that. Your mother bears with us Prussians, but she believes it would be contrary to reason to make a revolution here unless it is in English. Perhaps she is right. She is respected because she works so hard. She is not like some other comrades."

The tips of his generous mustache curled with scorn. "We are infested with bourgeoisie. Some come here to preach that temperance is the cure for evil everywhere. We have gottamn Greenbackers telling us, 'If only the government would print more money, we pay off all our debts and live in paradise.' Idiots! Then the poor starvelings who still slumber arrive because it is raining outside, and what do they do? They spit on the floor!"

I could understand his words, but not their meaning. I was thankful to catch a nod from Mama, signaling the time for my transformation. I retreated after her to ring the changes in the presidential cubbyhole—a sewing room in more tranquil days? I ambled along with her limping on one side and our increasingly tense pilot on the other as we made tracks for Grand Street. He clutched the valise with my discarded clothing in it. I trusted that the length of the trousers would hide my shoes.

I had not foreseen that the curb would be lined with peddlers' pushcarts beset by peasant women who, shawled against the vapors of the night, shopped by the smoky glare of kerosene lanterns, fingering every morsel of food before it went into their baskets. A swarthy Italian, bandanna knotted around his neck, revolved the handle of a hurdy-gurdy. Everything seemed so festive that under my breath I picked up the tune, with variations: "Buffalo boys, won't you come out tonight... to dance by the light of the moon?"

But no moon shone in the turgid sky. After leaving Grand Street, our path was lit for the most part by delicatessens' steamed-up windows, crammed with piles of smoked herring, cheeses, hams, jars of spices, and honey cakes, or by the saloons, where an opening door let loose a medley of coarse voices, clink of glasses, rattle of dice.

Mr. Cartwright's morale was sagging fast. "I should have been happier if Jake Riis could have joined us. He knows his way around far better than I do. But unfortunately he is working at the paper tonight."

More turning down ever dingier streets brought us within earshot of the whir of machines as it drifted through broken glass panes in the tumbledown buildings that closed in on us from both sides. Mama shook her head in sadness. "There is no need for you to tell me what that is. Sweated labor. Whole families doomed to earn a pittance for sewing the seams and buttons and ribbons on the clothes we put on our backs."

Our nostrils were clogged with the stench of dirt and decay compounded by the stink from splintery barrels of garbage overflowing onto the mud we trod and the emanations from leaky gas pipes. A tousled urchin, legs bowed like parentheses, scurried past trailing beer drops from the bucket he was carrying to whatever served him as home. The whiff of petroleum left in his wake spoke of somebody's sterling effort to rid him of lice.

The lingering scent prompted Mama to interrupt her stride and with right hand upraised declaim, "Bring me my spear: O clouds unfold! Bring me my chariot of fire."

Mr. Cartwright ventured the attribution. "William Blake?"

"Correct. It is clear to me that this city needs the same cleansing by flame that we had in Chicago. Even before our fire, the poorer classes there were seldom exposed to such squalor as this, and after all the rebuilding, they have never been so well off as now."

"I am of the opinion that slums are a natural product of industry, subject to the same law of supply and demand. When people keep pouring into the city looking for work and a place to live, they have to be squeezed in somehow, so the landlords take what were once good, big houses and make them over for half a dozen families or more. Then, of course, you have more modern tenements, crowded back to back to save space on a block."

"And there they live if it can be called life without daylight, heat, or hope."

"Not without hope, Mrs. Leonard. It was hope that brought most of them here, and it keeps them at it, trying to learn the language, working in sweatshops, dying as poor as when they arrived, but always in the hope that their children will have it better."

"Meanwhile, we know that darkness, dirt, and disease breed crime and discontent, so we build hospitals and prisons instead of tearing down the slums, and the poor children drop out of school because they've no boots to wear and they must be chained to the same treadmill as their parents."

I wondered whether the picture was quite as dark as the two of them were painting it. "Doesn't New York have any laws against that sort of thing?"

He gave a sour smile. "Certainly. The first one has been in the books for ten years and more. It says every house has to have city water and be kept clean and in good repair. No cellar dwellings unless the ceilings are at least twelve inches above the ground."

"Then why on earth doesn't somebody do something about it?"

Mama's hand touched mine. "Child, you have so much to learn. I believe I am right in saying, Mr. Cartwright, that the law was passed in the reign of Boss Tweed, who deserved to die as he has in prison. It was a sham, devised to hoodwink the poor souls whose votes he bought every election day to keep him and his gang in Tammany Hall, robbing the city blind until a book-keeper exposed them to—was it your newspaper, Mr. Cartwright?"

"No. The New York *Times.*" His voice was as low as his spirits. "It's bad here, as you can see, in winter, but it gets worse in hot weather. The flies swarm, and typhoid breaks out, and dray horses collapse on the street, and half a week can go by before the carcasses are hauled away to the glue factory."

I suddenly trembled and not from the cold. "Mama, let's go back. I hate this place."

She whispered as he and I did now. "We owe it to ourselves to stay awhile longer. Are we to go inside any of these buildings, Mr. Cartwright?"

"Perhaps for Miss Leonard's sake, we might visit only one. I have been there before with Jake." She would be content with that, she said, but she planned to return alone at a later date. I kept hold of her arm while we walked on, and I felt Mr. Cartwright's hesitant hand on my elbow.

I could never recall afterward how long it took before we were hurrying through a narrow alleyway under rows of laundry lines strung above our heads. In total darkness we groped our way up an exterior flight of trembling wooden stairs, fearful that we might trip. The reek on the landing was the clue to where the water pipes and other necessary plumbing lay.

The room was lit by a candle, guttering in the top of an empty wine bottle set on a crate that had once brought oranges from across the sea. The walls were a patchwork of faded white-wash and peeling plaster. Here and there in the wainscot rags had been stuffed to fill holes that rats had gnawed. A string of garlic and another of onions hung over the cold and rusty iron stove. On a shelf above the old boards that served as a bed stood a china statuette of Mary Immaculate and a flickering nightlight in a blue glass.

On the pile of gray straw that constituted a mattress, a woman stirred with a puny baby cradled in one arm, half covered by her long, unkempt black hair. In a mound of rags on the floor beside her, more children huddled together for warmth like mice in a nest. It was not possible to count how many.

The mahogany-hued little man in a tattered shirt and patched trousers who had opened the creaking door at Mr. Cartwright's tap broke off his coughing to smile in recognition of his visitor, but his sable eyes were wary. Once again, I could not make out a word of the patter that was spoken between them. Then our guide sketched in the background.

Angelo and his wife were Sicilian-born, "among the poorest of the poor," according to Mr. Cartwright; their five children were all native Americans. What work he could find was as a laborer for the *padrone* whose scows carried refuse to dumping grounds at sea. He had been washed overboard in a squall last week and suffered pain in the lungs as a result of the dunking. He was praying that the Virgin would bless the city with early snow. City Hall hired men by the hundreds to clear the streets, and shoveling would be less likely to leave his family fatherless.

Our host continued to cough and nod simultaneously throughout Mr. Cartwright's explication, but Mama took to blinking back the tears that welled. She fished into a pocket for her purse, and Mr. Cartwright covered her half dollar with one of his own as we exchanged our good nights for a *buena notte*.

I had imagined the worst to be over, but I was mistaken. We were threading our way back to Grand Street when a doorway ahead of us burst open and a cluster of women came streaming out to gather under a nearby lamppost. Two of them stopped to face each other, shrieking like angry parakeets, while the rest, joined by some raucous males, formed a rough circle around them, effectively blocking our path.

One of those within the circle was a slender young girl whose silk blouse had been ripped from her shoulders. The other was heavier and older, dressed in purple satin that also showed evidence of recent rough usage. Both were rouged and carmined, both shrieked curses the like of which I had never heard, both were armed with—daggers? Not quite. In the yellow light I could see they were long hatpins, flashing as they jabbed at each other.

The men among the spectators cheered for their favorite. "Give it to her, Little Mame." "Get her where it tickles, Sheeny

Rose." The younger of them was quicker on her feet, the older more determined to draw blood. The girl grabbed the other's improvised stiletto in an effort to force it aside for her own lunge, but she failed. The steel was too smooth to be grasped in her fingers. As the woman retrieved it, she jabbed it swiftly forward, clear through the palm of her opponent's hand. But Purple Satin took a moment too long to crow with delight at her mastery. Torn Blouse's hatpin drove an inch or more into her plump chin.

A whistle shrilled somewhere. In the gibbering that broke out among the spectators, I heard, "Here they come!" and "They'll have the nippers on us if they catch us." The street was emptying more rapidly than it had filled. The three of us were left alone for a second in sight of the two combatants. The encounter was over. One made a fist of her right hand to check the bleeding; the other wiped the trickle of red from her jaw with the sleeve of her dress. Then each hoisted her skirt to her knees and scurried back to the doorway from which they had come.

Mr. Cartwright thought it prudent for us to hurry off, too, before the police arrived, possibly to delay us with their questions. None of us spoke a word for the longest time after that. On the entire homeward journey we made no reference to what we had witnessed in the course of this night after taking our leave from the SLP.

I had formed a new resolution. I lacked further desire to sample poverty and degradation in any form. The poor, I concluded, would be with us through eternity, and I had nothing to contribute to their salvation. I intended Harry to make me his wife without delay.

IV

*H*E COULD SET my imagination ablaze as deftly as he flicked the head of a match to light his cigarettes. He had such dreams for the two of us. I remember him asking one day, "Who do you think the theater really belongs to?"

"You mean where we're rehearsing?"

"No, you goose. The *theater*, the whole profession of putting on shows."

"The landlords who own all the buildings?"

"Wrong. Not even warm."

"The producers and managers, then."

"Strike two."

"I know. The audiences who pay for the tickets."

"You're out. The theater belongs to the actor, and that covers the actor as poet, director, musician, scene designer—everybody who's an artist like you and me."

"I'd never thought of it like that."

We sat together on a mildewed leather trunk in our backstage haven. He slipped an arm around my waist. "I grew up thinking that way. I didn't want to be nothing but Dave Braham's son, living in his shadow, doing the same things he does—lead a band, write a little song, make a little money, run around like a chicken looking for a handful of corn."

"What do you want to do, sweet?"

"That's easy. I intend Harry Braham to be the most famous name in the musical history of America."

[54

"And it will be, too."

"Maybe, but there isn't a lot of competition. Why do you think Ed Rice does Gilbert and Sullivan, and most of the shows in New York and every place else are brought in from Europe? It's because there isn't any up-to-date American music worth singing. And do you know why that is? Because every student who can afford the training goes to Germany to learn how to write it."

"Did you?"

"I wanted to. Mr. David Braham said money was too tight, then he bought himself a new piano. I didn't forgive him for that until I realized how lucky I was. I can write real American music and you'll be singing it one day."

"Oh, yes! I'd love to. Have you started yet?"

The frown was make-believe. "Do not doubt me, fair maiden. I've torn up most of it. I'll show you one or two songs I think are good enough. I might even compose something just for you."

"Can I be your inspiration?" I was only half pretending.

"I think you are already."

"Kind sir, you flatter me."

"Don't smile. When you're an artist as we are, you create the whole world over again. People come to the theater to learn what things like love are really about. But you can't write the music for it or sing about it unless you yourself know what it is. We can teach each other if you want to. We can make Gilbert and Sullivan look like nothing compared with you and me."

"I want to so much I don't know how to say it."

Coaxing him into proposing marriage had turned out to be no job at all. I cultivated the art of loving as I polished my tiny role in the *Pinafore*. I learned how and where to be embraced and how to return his kisses until our hearts raced in unison. He provoked feelings in me such as I had never before experienced. I longed for the moments we fitted into every day when I would feel his hands on my face and arms and through the fabric of my dress. The impulse was strong to entice him into extending his caresses, and I should doubtless have taken the initiative had it been necessary to stir him further, but his ardor needed no arousing.

I agreed without enthusiasm that the ceremony should wait on the opening of our performances. When that evening came, I suffered none of the terror that supposedly attends a professional fledgling. I was too preoccupied with watching Harry, clad in a somewhat worn suit of tails and wearing a set of rhinestone studs in his shirt front, as he flourished a masterful baton over an orchestra that played either *forte* or *fortissimo* from curtain up to curtain down.

But for adoring him, I might have suffered disappointment over the deficiencies of this debut of mine after a dozen years of preparation for it. The rounds of applause that followed our finale could in no way be interpreted as meant for me when so far as the audience was concerned Helen Leonard was an anonymous nobody.

On Tuesday, December 4, in the third week of our run, I reached nineteen. I had news for my friend Amy in the chorus dressing room that evening. "Today's my birthday—and that's not all. I'm married, and nobody but us knows it." The justice of the peace sought out by Harry had taken the matter so casually that I almost resented him; his wife had obliged as witness.

Amy smirked. "Harry Braham?"

"How on earth did you guess?"

"Holy Moses, love must be blind! Anybody with ordinary gumption could see you two mooning over each other. Where are you going to live?"

"In his apartment on Washington Square. Isn't that elegant? All kinds of rich people for neighbors."

Amy knew her way about the city. "Depends which side you're on. The north's awful fancy, the south isn't at all. Does your mother know?"

"Not yet. I'll let her know tomorrow."

"Tomorrow? Oh, I see. Will you go on working until—well, if you have a baby?"

"Harry doesn't want me to go on working. Ed Rice can get somebody else easily enough."

"He isn't going to like doing that, breaking in a new girl."

"Who bothers about him?"

"Can I see your ring? You did get one, didn't you?"

"I should think I did! I can't wear it yet, though." I opened my purse. "Look. It was Harry's mother's—solid gold, and that's a diamond. It's too big for me, but we'll get it fixed."

When the performance was over that night, Harry and I found a dark corner of the deck behind the ferry's pilot house out of the wind and kissed our way across the river. For similar reasons, I saw nothing of the streets we passed through in the cab. We ate a good supper of honest spagetti, kneaded, rolled, and cut on the premises in a basement known as "Maria's," letting go of each other's hands only to manipulate fork and spoon.

A strand of pasta decorated Harry's chin after every mouthful just like Papa's. I supplied the same service as for Papa by dabbing Harry clean with a napkin.

I was too elated to pay attention to the entrance to the apartments, the stairs going up, or our home itself except for the narrow bed with brass headboard and a silk shawl for a spread, concealed behind a faded damask curtain. By rights, I ought to have brought at least a nightgown and my toilet things, but taking them would have aroused Suzanne's suspicions before I left Mrs. Walker's that morning. I could dispense with a trousseau tonight as well as with a dowry and any honeymoon for the present. My ring, which I took from my purse and slipped onto my finger, would do for all three. He was about to touch a match to the gaslight, but I checked him. Darkness would be best this first time.

I was glad to have had enough seasoning in making costume changes so that I did not fumble with buttons and tangled bows. When I had finished my task, I unpinned my hair and then, resting on my hands, lowered myself across so that our faces were enclosed in its yellow length like a tent. For the first minutes, I found it possible to preserve a sense of detachment and record impressions to remember. The coils under the mattress jingled. Every breath I took brought the scents of maleness, more potent than I had imagined they would be: brilliantine; the Chianti we had shared at supper; the "Richmond Gem" cigarettes he smoked whenever he was nervous; and the acrid-sweet fragrance of his skin that increased as our excitement mounted.

I recalled afterward that he singled out not only my physical attributes for praise but also my responses. I had prepared myself for a degree of pain, but his gentleness was such that the discomfort was of no consequence by comparison with the pleasure. After that, my recollections blurred. I was aware only of a kind of hunger fulfilled at last and an ambition appeased.

I could not venture to guess how much time had passed before he disengaged himself to turn onto his back and place his hands together under his neck on the pillow. "How are you going to tell your mother?"

"I thought I would see her in the morning. Will you come with me?"

I was glad that he hesitated before making his reply. If he had consented immediately, I should have known that his courage exceeded mine, and I should not have liked the discrepancy. "Maybe it would be best for you to talk with her first, Nell. I can meet her later. I'll let Ed know what we've done if you like."

The bargain was struck. Then we returned to our explorations of each other until he fell asleep, and I composed myself to do the same within the confines of what I suddenly recognized to be a none too comfortable bachelor's bed.

Waking early was not difficult. I rubbed the cramp out of my arms, sluiced my face with cold water from the jug on the washstand, dressed, and left him, still sleeping. I let myself out and walked downstairs with a finger crooked to prevent the ring from falling. Pigeons were the only other inhabitants sharing this hour of the morning on Washington Square. On the far side stood the mansions of the rich. So we resided on the unfashionable south. It mattered no more than the murky sky that promised rain or even snow.

A church bell tolled seven. I resisted the temptation to cross myself automatically as we had been encouraged to do in the convent. The night had not been spent in sin because I was a married woman. I must stretch out the time, however, before I braved Mama, since I did not wish to make explanations to anyone but her and, if need be, Suzanne.

The downstairs rooms were empty when I let myself into Mrs. Walker's. I trod delicately to the second floor, opened our door, and paused just inside. Mama was alone with the morning newspaper, which she put down on her lap as she removed her spectacles. "I trust you spent a happy birthday?"

So irony was to be her weapon today. "Yes, I did, thank you, Mama."

"Come closer, Nellie. I want to look at you." When I had done so, she rose and stared deep into my eyes. "I can see that you did. And he enjoyed himself, too?"

"I don't know what you mean." Our conversation had scarcely begun, yet already I was allowing her to demoralize me.

"The man with whom you evidently passed last night. Dissipation tends to show itself in a woman's eyes."

I extended my right hand and pushed the ring back into place. "We were married yesterday. See?"

Her face was as set as a paving stone. "Have I the pleasure of knowing the man?"

"Not yet, but you will. He's an extremely gifted musician. He conducts our orchestra. Mr. Harry Braham."

She turned the name over on her tongue like a pebble. "The real name perhaps being Abraham? John Braham was a renowned English tenor in my youth, born of Jewish parentage. Drury Lane, Milan, Genoa, Leghorn, Venice—he sang in all the places I intended for you. Is your husband's family aware that his bride is a Gentile?"

"He hasn't told them yet." And I should not be there when he did, if I had my way.

"If you bear him a child, they will want it brought up in their faith. Have you considered that? What precautions are you taking?"

The questions stung like darts piercing my skin. "I want to have his baby. I don't care about precautions. I don't give a hoot about anything except that he loves me, and I love him."

Her mouth softened. "Poor airy, fairy Nellie! What an ignoramus you are! Do you expect me to approve of what you have done so impetuously? You have wasted your talent, and now you are jeopardizing your chance of happiness. I can do no more than wish you *bon voyage*."

I refused to be softened into weeping. "Will you come and visit us?"

"I think not. If the time comes when he wishes to be introduced to me, or for me to meet his family, I shall be available."

At that, I lost the urge to cry. I delivered a peck of a kiss on her furrowed forehead and, simmering with indignation at her loftiness, flounced out of the house before I met anyone else. I would wait for Harry at the academy.

I soon grew accustomed to life on the more obscure side of Washington Square after Mama had my belongings sent over. I learned how to fit myself into the bed, which we promised to replace as soon as we had money to spare, and how to move my husband to passion when he arrived home tired or out of sorts. I taught myself the rudiments of cooking on the little gas stove in our tiny pantry, which filled with smoke whenever I fried a chop.

I had not counted on loneliness when I withdrew from H.M.S. *Pinafore*, while Harry was kept away from me for the most forlorn part of each day. As soon as Papa received my letter with tidings of my married status, he offered to increase my allowance, but I suspected that printing the works of Mr. Ingersoll and others had not proven to be the windfall Knight & Leonard had hoped for. My reply painted our present circumstances in rather more glowing terms than they deserved. Harry would be grieved, I wrote, were I to accept money from Papa, who should perhaps save up to make the trip east to see us as soon as he possibly could. Mama, whose word was her bond, was a stranger to Washington Square, and Suzanne followed her example. I was as stubborn as either of them. We did not exchange letters, and Harry said nothing about his parents to me.

For the first time in my life, I read the newspapers as assiduously as Mama. Harry had been in the habit of taking Mr. Pulitzer's *World*, but I preferred Mr. Bennett's *Herald*. In the early weeks of matrimony it unfolded the story of the ferment in the city attendant on the presence of Gilbert and Sullivan in person. While I sat in solitude, impatient for Harry's homecoming, I devoured every detail, which was a mistake, since it sometimes led to melancholy. I would find myself humming the *Pinafore* songs and reflecting that some people must have made a name for themselves despite a lowly start in the chorus.

The journal noted that the managers of the various New York theaters who were pirating the *Pinafore* had audaciously chartered a fleet of steamers, festooned them with flags of both countries, and sent them to welcome Gilbert and Sullivan off Sandy Hook when they arrived from England aboard the *Bothnia* with their impresario, Mr. Rupert D'Oyly Carte. Ed Rice was not mentioned as a participant in the gesture, which I thought typical of his niggardliness.

Bands on deck had pounded out Mr. Sullivan's melodies and choruses shouted Mr. Gilbert's lyrics to make themselves heard above the dinning of steam whistles, but Mr. Gilbert apparently was not to be placated. He was so outraged by the pirate producers' theft of his *libretti* that he threatened never to compose another if the Yankees were going to pilfer it.

The *Herald* devoted whole columns to the two Englishmen. Mr. Sullivan "keeps a monocle dangling over one eye while the other twinkles merrily at you." Mr. Gilbert "is a fine, well-made robust man...with the brightest and rosiest of faces, an auburn moustache, and short 'mutton-chop' whiskers, tipped only slightly with gray, large and clear blue eyes, and a forehead of high, massive, and intellectual cast." I saved and stored away some of the pages as a doleful substitute for ever meeting the gentlemen.

Mr. Gilbert had disembarked protesting that his latest opera was far from completion, but the *Herald* was not deceived. It quickly established that his pretense was a ruse to thwart fresh thievery. The libretto was ready, but Mr. Sullivan was slaving day and night in his hotel to compose the music for *The Pirates of Penzance, or The Slave of Duty*, which was due for a star-spangled opening at the Fifth Avenue Theater on New Year's Eve.

I conceived the errant fancy that if I could succeed in having either one of them hear me sing, a miracle might be wrought, rewarding me with a place in the chorus. The *Herald* named the hotel in which they were staying. I presented myself at the desk in the lobby and asked that my name by announced to either or both of them. The reply was sent down by Mr. Carte. It said, in essence, "Go away!" I scurried off, meek as the mouse that lurked in my pantry. I would have failed, anyway. I had abandoned my practicing on our wedding day. There was no piano in our dwelling that was parlor and bedroom combined with pantry attached. Harry had little time for coaching me. But if I could not appear on the stage, could I not at least sit in the audience with Harry? Arms around him, I posed the question as soon as I had let him in some minutes after midnight.

"Dearest, every ticket must have been sold long since. Besides, its going to be a very refined affair. I wouldn't wish to take you there unless you were the most beautifully gowned lady in the whole theater."

"It says there is to be a matinee on New Year's Day and another on Saturday. May we go to one of those?"

"We have the same thing in Brooklyn. Ed's hoping to fill the house on both days."

"You could say you were sick and miss just one performance."

"I should not want to risk it. I need to stay on the right side of Mr. Rice. It might not be easy to find somebody else to work with."

One of the matters in which I was instructing myself was the subject of disappointment. I should be qualified for graduation very shortly. I settled for reading about *The Pirates of Penzance* instead of watching it performed. I pitied poor Mr. Sullivan when, in the last week of December, the musicians he was to conduct went out on strike, demanding more pay because the score was "like grand opera." I shared what I felt sure was the Englishmen's exultation when the *Herald*, on New Year's Day, acclaimed their latest endeavor as "a palpable hit" and proceeded to describe the dazzling appearance in the stalls of Mrs. Alva Vanderbilt, Mrs. Caroline Astor, and one of Mr. Leonard Jerome's three daughters. I preserved that clipping, too, with the others under the lavender sachet in the drawer in the sideboard I reserved for myself.

It would be misleading to depict all those days in terms of disillusion. Harry enjoyed taking me to a number of his old haunts on Sundays, when he was spared the necessity of journeying to and from Brooklyn. One such place was Charlie Pfaff's cellar café on Broadway close by Bleecker Street. Harry told me that Walt Whitman had once held court in an alcove there. That was before the war and before paralysis compelled him to retire as an invalid to New Jersey.

Harry was forever urging me to dip into his copy of *Leaves of*

Grass, but I had little interest either in poetry or the controversy the book stimulated. I was much more intrigued by his account of another customer of Pfaff's he remembered. Her true name, he said, was Jane McElheny, but she chose to be known as Ada Clare, and people called her "the queen of Bohemia."

"I often saw her down here. You're the only girl I ever met who was better looking. She had blue eyes like you and golden hair, but she cut hers short and *she* smoked cigarettes. By the time she was nineteen, everybody was talking about her. She wrote poems about love, and the magazines published them. Some of them—well, I wouldn't like you to read them even now. Then she went on the stage, and that didn't improve her reputation."

I reached across the table to stroke his hand. "She was like you in something else, too. She also fell in love with a piano player, a man even more distinguished than me."

"He could not possibly have been, my sweet."

"Louis Gottschalk was. He knew Chopin in Paris, and when Gottschalk came back to give recitals here in New York, the ladies fell all over him, including Ada. But there was one difference between the two of them and us. They never did get married."

"Did she have a child?"

"That's the sad part of it. When she told him she was going to, he gave one last concert before he sailed off to the West Indies. He wanted nothing more to do with her. She went to Paris, which was where her son was born."

"Don't you dare go off anywhere when we have our baby!"

"I promise. Not even to Brooklyn."

When the changes in me told me that I had conceived, Harry had gone not to Brooklyn but much farther away, touring with the Ed Rice company. I felt extra joy because a baby to care for would alleviate my loneliness. There would be a crib and who knew what else to buy, of course, but expense we could ill afford must be managed somehow. I decided not to write to Harry lest my letter should fail to catch up with him, and I was reluctant to commit my secret to a telegraph operator. I would tell Harry the moment he walked in the door.

He came home days sooner than his itinerary had called for. He looked unusually pale and drawn as he set down his bag and his music case, and his eyes were as bitter as his voice. "Ed Rice called it quits before we hit Chicago. We ran out of steam, that's all. Nobody wants to hear second-rate Gilbert and Sullivan when they can get the real thing for the same price. The two of them are blanketing the country with companies of their own— Philadelphia, Baltimore, Cincinnati, Chicago, and I don't know where else. I'm out of a job, Nell."

I saved my news for as long as I could. Then the queasiness that attacked me on waking each morning prompted Harry to ask questions to which I had to blurt out the answer. His lips were trembling as he kissed me. We began learning other lessons together, the exercises that poverty imposes, which were more painful in their way than the stretching of limbs in gymnastic classes.

He tried to break himself of the cigarette habit and, when he was unable to, substituted the "Sunshine" brand at twenty for a nickel for the more expensive "Richmond Gem." I took my shopping basket to Grand Street and picked up the art of haggling with pushcart peddlers as adeptly as any immigrant woman straight from Castle Garden. My first venture into that bedlam of a marketplace brought memories of the night when we had passed through there on our explorations with Mr. Cartwright. Throughout the months when I was with child, I had a recurrent dream. I found myself in the Sicilian garret, lying on straw like the mother we had seen while Harry wracked his lungs with coughing until blood filled his mouth. I grew as slim as I imagined Ada Clare must have been.

He surrendered his rhinestone shirt studs to a pawnbroker, and my wedding ring followed suit some weeks later. I asked whether his family might help a little until his search for work was successful. He had abandoned hope of securing a new position conducting an orchestra. He looked only for an opening in some restaurant that entertained with piano music or a string band.

"I met my father on the street a while ago. I meant to tell you. I told him about us. I couldn't ask for money when I left him because I knew what his answer would be. He called you a name they use on Hester Street. Do you know what *kurvch* means? It means a harlot."

As yet, vestiges of pride prohibited contact with Mama. But I wrote and rewrote the few lines I addressed to my father until I was satisfied with every nuance:

My darling and very own Papa: Greetings from old New York and congratulations to the first gentleman of Chicago! It is wretched of me not to have written before, but I am sure you will forgive. Taking care of a house without a servant keeps a girl busy, but you are in my thoughts all the time, and I waited so as to be certain about the surprise I have for you. That's the reason for my congratulations. You are to become a grandpapa! So there is a multitude of things to shop for, and I shall buy something special in your name for—him or her? Guess what he will be called if it is a boy! I promise to write again very soon. Meantime, I send all my love.

I used to question afterward whether we could have survived through spring into summer without the fifty dollars he forwarded by return. To that we added the few dollars Harry earned by substituting now and again for the tipsy pianist in a Hungarian trio that played in a restaurant on MacDougal Street. The long weeks of waiting were hard on both of us. We had only limited comfort to afford each other when my size made the bed too small for two and he resorted to sleeping on the floor. But at the worst, we rarely missed more than one meal a day, though the landlord's patience wore thin in spite of the smiles I tendered him some weeks in place of rent.

We kept his roof over our heads, however. My son was born in the bed with the brass headboard while Harry paced the room on the other side of the curtain, lighting one Sunshine from another. Amy Leslie, a constant visitor, provided the midwife, whose touch was as kindly as her Russian accent was thick.

Charles Henry Braham's name was ready for him at the moment I realized that he had been delivered into the world alive and felt his presence across my stomach, where the midwife, with a muttered prayer, had laid him. He weighed so little that I had to reassure myself with fingers on his damp curls to be certain he was there at all. Harry could not be persuaded to pick him up for fear of damaging him in some fashion. I thought to postpone his christening until he had grown a trifle sturdier, but his progress was slow. After his feedings, he whimpered so much that Amy recommended paregoric to soothe his distress.

It was she who clinched my decision to seek employment for myself again. I had turned the question over in my mind innumerable times already. Harry's objections were barely worth listening to when he brought in nothing more than his meager earnings with the trio. Unless we could do better, we were condemned to our present hopelessness.

Amy had the right idea. "Nobody has to know you've got a baby. With your voice and your looks, you can find yourself an evening job, singing in a café. I'd be glad to go the rounds with you, calling at places."

"I dare not leave Charlie with him. He's afraid even to touch the baby."

"So why not lay out half a dollar and hire a girl so you and me can shop around."

I never could determine where the blame lay. On Amy for making her suggestion? On me for my haste in accepting it? On Harry for his refusal to have any part in caring for his own son? Or on the Irish slattern who was left in charge of Charlie for an afternoon?

She was alone in the pantry, huddled in a corner with arms locked about her head keening when Amy and I returned after a fruitless round of calls. Her whimpering drew me to her the instant after I turned the key in the front door. Harry had gone —to notify the police, as it developed. I could get no sense out of her, so I ran to the bed, where I had left Charlie in fitful sleep.

In the end they declared it an accident, and no charges were laid. By Harry's account, the girl's fumbling had thrust a pin into Charlie's navel as she changed him into clean toweling. She claimed it was the paregoric that Harry dosed him with too massively in an effort to control the convulsions. Which of them lied made no difference to my son, who in death looked even tinier than on the day he was born.

I stayed long enough for the ambulance to come and carry him away. I knew Amy would attend to all other arrangements.

Then I said no more than "goodbye" to Harry and walked down the stairs and on and on through the sultry night toward the ferry.

Sometimes the rising of the October sun or the pigeons' cooing on the ledge outside the window dispersed the shadows of dreams, and at the moment of waking it would seem that I had lived nowhere else since we left Chicago but here in Mrs. Walker's back bedroom. Mama still slept under a mobcap, propped up against goosedown pillows in the single bed, lips fluttering as she breathed. Suzanne and I shared the double bed, lying back to back and as far apart as possible in our respective territories of the mattress. I suspected that she feared contact with me would contaminate her purity.

Our landlady set as fine a table as ever three times a day, and I felt uneasy when she watched me pick away at the dishes served by the freckled Scot who had replaced the surly Norwegian. The boarders remained the same, save for Mr. Cartwright, who now worked for the Philadelphia *Press* and resided in that city. The explanation Mama concocted for my absence was generally accepted: I had been away in Chicago visiting family, she said, and, having been taken ill there, forced to delay my return.

A glint of skepticism appeared occasionally in Mr. Riley's narrow eyes. He currently sported celluloid, not paper, collars; continued to boast of the friends he had in the theatrical profession; and pressed invitations on me to accompany him to any show of my choosing. Though I persisted in declining, refusals had no more effect on him than rain on a duck's feathers.

On the night I fled back to Mama and sobbed in her arms, I had fully intended to pursue Amy's plan for me the following morning and start anew as a singer in some local employment. However, I withheld word of this from Mama as she tucked me into her own bed. "You will sleep better here, child. Be sure to remember your Shakespeare and 'knit up the ravell'd sleave of care.'"

After hours of wakefulness, I fell into such torpor that it was noon before my eyes opened and I experienced a weakness similar to giving birth. The next day, it was all I could do to dress myself. I had not foreseen that Mama would come with me to meet Amy, or go with us to the Church of the Transfiguration, or stand with us by the spaded earth in a remote corner of the burial ground. I saw no sign of Harry Braham.

Neither had I expected the forbearance Mama showed when I clung to our quarters at Mrs. Walker's like a sparrow fresh out of the egg and fearful of being forced to take wing. I heard no "I told you so," no lectures, no demands for me to practice again. I lived in idleness for weeks, and for the first time I could remember, Mama condoned it.

The wounds to my esteem slowly healed by themselves, inflicting twinges as other scars do as they form over physical injuries. My appetite awakened, and I shed all hesitancy about sitting down to Mrs. Walker's cooking. By November, I was taking to the piano for perhaps half an hour each afternoon of my own accord and singing to amuse myself.

Mrs. Walker found me passing time in this manner one day. "I am pleased that you're looking so much better. Now I wonder if I might ask a favor of you. Mr. Riley wants to have a musical evening on Sunday to entertain some of his friends. He'll be glad to pay for all the extras, he says, and he'd be ever so grateful if you would give them a song or two. Everybody else would, too, I'm sure. What do you say?"

My first inclination was to refuse. The voice remaining to me had lost much of its power. I doubted whether I should ever again recapture the joy of letting it soar and seeing in the faces of those who listened the joy it brought them. I was content with seclusion and weary of challenges I lacked the strength or will to contest. And yet, how pleasant it would be to hear applause once more, to win not sympathy but approval for oneself! Perhaps it was worth the risk.

"What songs do you think they would like to hear from me?"

"You couldn't do better than sing some of those old English ballads you used to do with your sister. They always set me thinking of when I was a girl living in Twickenham by the Thames."

Suzanne consented to play for me, but Mama let it be known that the SLP had more pressing claims on her than any musicale.

I was jumpy as a cat all Sunday morning and afternoon as I washed my hair and pressed what had to be called my best dress. Suzanne, a living advertisement of her skill with her new sewing machine, went down immediately the first visitors arrived. Nervousness and the wish to make a more stately entrance prompted me to remain in our room until Mrs. Walker tapped and whispered that in five more minutes the gathering would be ready for me.

Mr. Riley waited at the foot of the stairs. "There's a very prominent friend of mine who's aching to hear you. He'd be charmed to make your acquaintance. Just a minute." He darted off into the parlor and returned with a little man plump as a partridge whose hair, eyes, and mustache all matched the black of his well-filled suit. "May I introduce a dear pal and lover of all mankind, Mr. Tony Pastor?" Observing his coloring and his Neapolitan manners, I concluded that a "Pastore" dangled somewhere on his family tree.

We had done no more than exchange pleasantries before Mr. Riley seized Mr. Pastor and myself by a hand apiece and dragooned us into the parlor. After a tedious introduction from our host, who clearly had been sampling too much spiked punch, I placed myself beside the piano, closed my eyes, drew a deep breath, and for the sake of Mrs. Walker set off on "Twickenham Ferry."

A sense of well-being increased with every bar I sang. The handclaps when the song was finished were merited, I thought. Next came "The Kerry Dance." Words and melody were so familiar and I felt such confidence that I let my eyes linger on the faces of the listeners.

> *O, to see the Kerry dancers!*
> *O, to hear the piper's tune . . .*

Mr. Riley gazed at me as if I were an unwary chicken and he a marauding fox. Mr. Pastor tapped out the tempo with his fingers on the gold watch chain that stretched across his waistcoat. After the encores that were demanded had been completed and the hurrahs! had died down, the chubby little Italian stumped up to me.

"Sing two songs a night like that for me, and I'll pay you thirty dollars a week. What do you say?"

I was so inculpably naïve that I had no idea who he was. Mr.

Riley promptly furnished a brief but fulsome biography. This was the Tony Pastor whose name was emblazoned all over his theater of varieties at No. 585 Broadway, right across the street from Niblo's Garden. He was still an entertainer in his own right as he had been ever since '47, when he made his debut at Barnum's Museum on Ann Street. He was, Mr. Riley averred, "the dean of the profession."

Mama had spoken in the past about "variety." She said it amounted to nothing more than an imitation minstrel show, made up of jig-dancing and men and women in lampblack shouting vulgarities to lure patrons into smoke-filled drinking halls where these revels were staged. "Is alcohol served in your establishment, sir?"

I feared his shirt front would explode from his indignation. "Never a single drop. For ten, twenty, thirty cents I provide the finest in comedy, dancing, music. I make my people famous. Nobody is ever ashamed to come to Pastor's. I am a good Catholic. I clean up everything to make it decent for high-class customers. You see for yourself when you work for me."

"I shall have to ask my mother first."

"Tell her you're going to visit a friend. Sing your songs and get back before she knows it. I'll make it thirty-five dollars a week." I said I would let him have my decision in the morning, but I had already decided. I needed the money, and being occupied would help erase memories of the past eleven months.

The outside of the building was garish, the interior opulent with Turkish carpets and plush-covered chairs. His office, where a marble Madonna vied for attention among a host of plaster cherubim, might well have suited King Humbert of Italy himself. Mr. Pastor suggested that my name was perhaps too sedate for a singer in variety. I thought a change would do me good in the pursuit of forgetting. He produced a board on which was chalked a wide choice of pseudonyms. Did I like the first of them, "Lillian Anderson," or perhaps the last, "Marion Russell?"

"Nothing there impresses me as quite appropriate, sir, but if we may put two of them together, I should like to be known as 'Lillian Russell.'"

"*Bene, Bene!* You shall be Miss Lillian Russell, the beautiful English ballad singer, starting tonight." But I had no suitable gown to wear. "Buy yourself something magnificent but discreet and pay me back, ten dollars a week."

I stepped out from the wings that evening after my mentor, in white tie and collapsible opera hat, had introduced me with a fanfare from the orchestra. I had a new, white, forty-dollar satin dress with a high, square-cut neckline, a new name, and hope abounding.

V

ONE OF THE MANY fictions invented in later years
had it that I was garlanded with laurel that very first night.
It was an engaging fable, circulated within a profession which
subscribes to the creed "Success is a rare paint; it hides all the
ugliness." The fact of the matter was that to Tony Pastor I
represented a gamble at long odds. He had greater expectations
of a young St. Louis girl, Florence Merton, who appeared on
the same bill.

She had freckles, a large mouth, and a voice infinitely more
commanding than mine. The musicians came close to being
drowned out when she roared her medley of popular Irish and
Scottish ditties, while I was too shy to do more than sing softly
of trysts "down by the babbling brook" or "where the old mill
stream splashes."

Yet when Florence rapidly vanished from public life, in my
heart I knew why. She behaved on stage with the boldness of a
woman of the world, although in her personal affairs she was a
model of rectitude. By virtue of my upbringing and eyes which
retained a virginal luminosity no matter what Mama claimed, I
appeared on the other hand to be unsullied by the least breath
of wickedness.

An anonymous writer for *Harper's Weekly* touched on the
paradox of Flo's disappearance and my own burgeoning career.
"Her companion, however, soon set the whole town talking about
her sweet blue eyes and the exceptional beauty of her face.... It
soon became apparent that she was a girl of extraordinary possibili-

ties.... The fame of the new singer spread through the town."
That was palpable truth. I opened on Monday, November 22,
rather less than two weeks before my twentieth birthday. There
was plenty of money in circulation with the building of even more
miles of railroad tracks proceeding apace, and Pastor's was always
packed. By Christmastime, few theatergoers were unacquainted
with the name of Lillian Russell.

A chance line in a newspaper about this alter ego was my cue
to inform Mama that I had dissembled in telling her I had been
going off each evening except Sunday to help nurse Amy, allegedly suffering a lingering but undiagnosed ailment. Mama instantly reverted to the goad she used to be. "A pretty success!
A success of bright eyes and rosy cheeks, and how long will it
last? The only success that counts is this." She applied a sharp
knuckle to my brow.

Mr. Gilbert and Mr. Sullivan had sailed for home months
since, leaving behind a fund of Gilbertian witticisms which the
Herald chronicled from time to time. One of them centered on
a lady of a breed I was learning to recognize: Their eyebrows
soared when they heard I sang at Pastor's. It seemed that this
member of the species, cornering Mr. Gilbert at a New York
reception, had babbled on about Mr. Sullivan, whose music,
she said, reminded her of "dear Bach." She wondered what Bach
was engaged upon at present. "Is he still composing?"

"Well, no, madam. Just now, as a matter of fact, dear Bach
is by way of decomposing." I admired a man with a sense of
humor. I still hankered to meet Mr. Gilbert.

Instead, I was busily rehearsing the score of *The Pirates of
Penzance*, which half the country already knew by heart. In this
case the words were not Gilbert's but Tony's. He was a mite too
honest to stoop to outright piracy, but he rated it fair game to
produce a burlesque of the opera bouffe that audiences never
tired of. Far from being hidden in the chorus, I was cast this time
as Mabel, ingenue of *The Pie Rats of Penn Yan*, wooed by starry-
eyed Frederic, an apprentice buccaneer bent on reformation of
his character.

My comeliness won applause every night, not my ability. As
a performer, I was left in the shade by a fat, perennially jolly
Canadian girl whose mother had induced Tony to place her on

the stage. From the start, May Irwin caught the fancy of the street boys who crowded the gallery. She could wring laughter from any line or crack jokes to convulse the house. For instance, "Your lifeline shows you are going to die of starvation."

"Shipwreck?"

"No, boardinghouse!" Mrs. Walker would not be amused.

In the yellow glare of the hissing coal-gas footlights, I moved as stiffly as a mechanical doll, envying May as she told about the poverty-stricken Irishman who declined employment as a deep-sea diver. "Are you too scared?" Not at all. "Aren't the wages good enough for you?" That was not the problem. "What is it then?"

"I never could be happy in a job where I couldn't spit on my hands."

The gallery loved her, while the dudes in the stalls ogled me. I thought myself fortunate to be under the wing of Tony Pastor, who as a matter of policy forbade male admirers to loiter around the stage door. May sparkled again as the Countess in the next travesty at Pastor's, which made fun of the Frenchman Edmund Audran's *Olivette*. I felt less conscious of being overshadowed, since I had a scene in which, dressed as a boy, I was encouraged to dance a rollicking sailor's hornpipe.

Mr. Pastor's watchfulness and my own squeamishness concerning masculine companionship resulted in the circulation of a rumor which pleased neither one of us: Lillian Russell was letting praise turn her head. One item of published chitchat had it that "If the young lady does not allow adulation to conquer her ambition and elevate her too high in her own esteem, she will become a bright and shining light on the lyric stage." How very much like Mama!

When *Olivette*'s run ended in April, Tony farmed me out under the contract I had signed with him. The excuse he made was that I might improve my capabilities as a performer by working for Willie Edouin, who was a comedian of sorts, in the company he was putting together to travel west as far as San Francisco. I had no cause to quarrel with Tony. I could be reunited with Papa for an hour or so when we changed trains in Chicago.

He had not changed at all, though a housekeeper managed

for him now that Leona was married—Mrs. Ross. He continued to dream of the day Knight & Leonard would blossom as a major publishing house. He regretted that some reliable agnostic were not installed in Washington, D.C., instead of a picture of piety like James Garfield. His taste for westering had grown if anything; he would have dearly loved to accompany me to California.

Then I told him as much as I could bear to relate about his grandson. "You should not let bitterness taint your life, Nellie. You'll find someone else one day. Don't be scared to take another chance."

"I'll be more careful next time, if there is a next time, Papa." I tried to make him take the fifty dollars I had saved to repay him for his act of salvation, but I should have known that he would be bullheaded. I refrained from telling him about an undertaking I had given to Willie Edouin before we took the train from New York. In *Babes in the Woods*, with which we were to regale San Francisco and numerous other cities, I would play the Fairy Queen, wearing purple tights—I who had been raised to believe that, except on a roller-skating rink, ladies kept their ankles concealed in public places. I was afraid that, even by sympathetic Papa, tights would be misinterpreted as a mark of depravity.

After the Edouin troupe resumed its journey, I endeavored to dissipate the sadness of parting from him by first watching and then joining in the sessions of poker with which my companions filled the tedious hours between the three stops a day we made for meals. If I were to expose my limbs to an audience, I might as well take one more downward stride and improve my acquaintance with what Mama called "the devil's playthings" and barred them from our house. I liked the single-minded concentration that poker demanded of one.

For the rest of the time between dawn and dusk, I gazed moodily out the window, hoping for a glimpse of Buffalo Bill Cody, the ghost of Kit Carson, or one of the other heroes of a hundred dime novels and a dozen tawdry plays. But as far as the horizon, the western plains contained no hints of romance. Along the track, carcasses of buffalo massacred by hunters and Sioux for bounty money lay rotting or picked clean to the bones by jackal or carrion crow. Rivers ran brown with mud from land cleared of trees but as yet bare of grass. Smoke curling from mounds of sod that studded the prairie farms told that these, incredibly, were settlers' homes. Raw new towns consisted of as many tents as of flimsy frame houses whose false tops on single stories did nothing to correct the illusion that by tomorrow morning they would be gone.

San Francisco, thank heaven, looked much more substantial, though I was told that in the previous generation it had been destroyed by fire five times in three years. I thoroughly enjoyed following in the footsteps of lovely Helena Modjeska, who had trod these same boards of the Bush Street Theater, playing a lovelorn concubine in *Adrienne Lecouvreur*. Where she had bared her soul, I displayed my legs and gave thanks that the summer weather was warm enough to ward off any chill.

Far away from Tony Pastor's solicitous defenses, I was a target for the attentions of any number of men whose fortunes flowed from the Ophir and other mines of the Comstock Lode across the mountains in Nevada—more than $30 million worth of silver a year, or so it was said. On the whole, I preferred Comstock millionaires to the other whiskery gentleman of that name who, as chief beagle for both the New York Society for the Suppression of Vice and the Post Office Department, energetically prosecuted what he deemed to be immorality. I prayed that the notoriety of my tights and the disgraceful high-laced boots that went with them would not extend over the three thousand miles separating me from Mr. Anthony Comstock. I wished to be pure as a snowflake in his puritanical assessment.

Had I been less fastidious about responding to affection, my theatrical career could have been advantageously terminated then and there. My wedding ring remained with the pawnbroker unless he had already sold it. Benefit of clergy and a new wedding band were included in some of the proposals the gallants of San Francisco made to me, always with a diamond or a gold nugget or two proffered in advance. I thought it would be uncivil to refuse these gifts and unwise to accept the donors' invitations. I had no particular relish for ex-prospectors whose horny hands could scarcely grasp a pen to write a check on their bursting bank accounts. All too often their new finery was unable to mask the smell of unwashed armpits.

Our stay in the Baldwin Hotel was not altogether happy or

our evening performances uniformly boisterous. Early in our run the city was electrified by news of the dreadful attack made upon President Garfield as he walked in Washington's Union Station. For the next seventy-nine days, our spirits and box-office receipts rose and fell together as he alternately gained and failed. We read of his doctors' bafflement as they poked and probed his lungs, liver, and abdomen for the assassin's bullet. I saw an illustration of Alexander Graham Bell seeking for it with his electrical listening device.

We were heading eastward, performances concluded, when we heard that the White House had a new occupant in Chester Alan Arthur. Charles Guiteau's pistol had finally achieved his purpose. He deserved to be hanged, the murderous frog of a Frenchman.

I returned to Brooklyn so weighted down with the mementos of San Francisco that had been pressed into my hands that I deposited my new jewel box with a bank for safe storage, out of sight of Mama. I also kept to myself an enlightening lesson I had brought back from my travels: The taste for riches can be as habit-forming as the acceptance of poverty. Before setting out for California, I aspired to earning a living and forgetting the past —nothing more. Now, mindful of my few valuables sitting in that vault, I was after as much money as I could make—certainly more than the $50 a week that Pastor offered me for the coming season.

What the situation called for was a manager, I realized later, and I hadn't one. Mr. Riley dropped hints as wide as a barn door that he would be more than happy to serve, but his intentions, as always, obviously ranged beyond that, and I would sooner have become Mrs. Buffalo Bill than Mrs. Riley. Surely a daughter of Cynthia Leonard could handle her own affairs, financial or otherwise. I set about finding a producer who assessed my value above $50.

John A. McCaull boasted the title of colonel, as did half the men past the age of forty whom one met in those days. He claimed to have fought for the Confederacy and nobody questioned his word. He spent more on costumes and scenery than on his players, but he was willing to pay me $60 a week, and his Bijou Opera House stood almost spang in the middle of what everybody had taken to calling the Rialto, that portion of Broadway reaching from Madison Square at 23rd Street to Herald Square at 34th.

To stroll along the Rialto always brought on an interior tingle. Theaters, close to a score of them, lined both sides of this elegant stretch of the avenue, with the spaces between them occupied by scintillating bars and ornate hotels. As each day darkened, lamplighters came padding along on their rounds, turning on the jets in the streetlights with their long poles and igniting the gas with the tiny flame that flickered atop the pole. The ceremony signaled the start of a spectacle that rippled my spine. The sidewalks overflowed with a sea of people pouring in to see the shows, while gleaming carriages waited in line to deliver perfumed ladies and top-hatted gentlemen under the glittering marquees. More and more theater foyers and hotel lobbies shone nowadays with Mr. Edison's marvelous incandescent bulbs, which made the arrival of the audience a tableau in itself. The patrons at Pastor's dressed as they pleased, but the Bijou was one of the more fashionable playhouses where formal attire was *de rigueur* in the boxes or orchestra seats, which was a source of gratification for me.

I wore no tights but a skirt as D'Jemma and had the title role in Mr. McCaull's *The Snake Charmer*, but the stellar attraction was supposedly Madame Selina Dolaro, imported from Europe and managed by D'Oyly Carte.

After suave Mr. Oily Carte's brusque treatment of me during the dark times of Washington Square, it was pleasant to win acclaim rivaling that of his client. The notices without exception were adulatory. Lillian Russell was "pretty as a posy," said one of them, and another, "Her fresh beauty, pleasing voice, and natural grace charmed the audience." I heard nothing from Harry Braham, though his father was churning out songs played by every hurdy-gurdy in the city.

David Braham was the father-in-law of Ned Harrigan as well as *in absentia* of myself. The rowdydowdy comedy team of Harrington and Hart—"The Nonpareils," as they billed themselves— had just spent a reputed $100,000 on remodeling the old Globe at No. 728 Broadway to house their farces. Braham senior led the orchestra and composed the music; Harrigan wrote the lyrics.

I invariably flinched every time I heard "The Salvation Army," "McNally's Row of Flats," or one of their hundred other jingles.

Reading and rereading the critics' opinions of D'Jemma sent caution flying. I had no cause to doubt that my future was assured. Henceforth, I must dress up to what was expected of a theatrical comet. While my evenings were spent at the Bijou, afternoons were devoted to the Ladies' Mile farther south on Broadway past Madison Square where I had once window-shopped with Suzanne. I could not resist the bijoux in the jewelers' windows or the satins and velvets on display at McCreery's, which I ordered by the bolt to be made up by a dressmaking house, Bloom's, highly recommended by Amy Leslie, another recruit to the McCaull Opera Company.

The first dress to be completed, of closely cut chiffon with matching hat and parasol, so delighted me that, like a fool, I wore it to show my sister and Mama. "How could you?" cried one. "What has come over you?" demanded the other. "Is it paid for?"

"No, but it soon will be."

They found me guilty on two charges. I was altogether "too hoity-toity"—Mama's words—for my own good; I had disgraced my sister's reputation as a seamstress and taken bread from her mouth.

I recoiled from their verdict. "Do you imagine it has been easy for me to continue here with you all this time, to cross and recross on that repulsive ferry every day, waiting for the stupid bridge to be opened? Don't you consider that I deserve a little gratitude for that? Are you never going to say at least that you are pleased or perhaps even proud of me?"

"Control yourself, Miss Leonard. You are throwing a tantrum."

"What if I am? I'm going to make some changes in my life so I can throw a tantrum whenever I choose to, whether you like it or not. I can't live under the same roof with you." Somewhere in memory, I heard an echo of Mama's voice on the night she quit Papa. Did the urge to leave home run in families like the coloration of eyes and hair?

The elegant and artistic Hotel Lafayette on 9th Street just off Fifth was the place for me. Some people called it "the French pension," though I certainly would not. This was where celebrities lived or dined, especially those whose fame had been won in opera or on the boards. The whole neighborhood had an air of cultural distinction, and the closeness of the library endowed by the first John Jacob Astor from the profits he made from the fur trade with the Indians and then in his real-estate transactions was a convenience when I wanted to borrow books.

I rather regretted the fact that the uncertainties of our profession rendered it impossible to accumulate such fortunes as his. Instead of renting the best room I could afford in the Lafayette, I should have preferred to be moving into one of the splendid new mansions that were arising farther uptown. Though the block-long brownstone palace of William Henry Vanderbilt between 51st and 52nd did resemble a hotel, I could have been happy there if I'd had the $3,000,000 it cost to erect it.

In my heart, I envied the rich whom Mama despised. I should have liked to be one of them, no matter if their millions had come from selling shoddy uniforms to the Union armies, bribing Congressmen, double-dealing with the carpetbaggers to buy Southerners' property at knockdown prices, fleecing homesteaders and Western Indians. I used to watch their fancy carriages rumble over the cobblestones of Fifth Avenue on their way up to Central Park, thinking to myself that, given the chance, I'd show off in such style that they would be put in the shade.

But living in the Lafayette had its own compensations. Here in the company of other women in my profession I could appear in public without raising eyebrows if I decided to wear rouge and face powder, which Mrs. Caroline Astor would not condone among the ladies she admitted to her holy of holies at Fifth and 34th Street. The hotel lobby was filled throughout the day with idlers hoping for a peek at the likes of Ada Rehan, John Drew, Mark Twain, or the overrated Madame Nordica. In an impish mood, I would ascend the central staircase, lifting my skirts an inch or two higher than necessary and smile to myself as men's eyes popped at the sight of a silk-stockinged ankle.

At this juncture my career developed a leak, which brought it sinking earthward. Though *The Snake Charmer* ran to full houses until December, I was far from being besieged by calls from other managements. After an idle Christmas, I succumbed to Mr. Pastor's beckoning and resumed work for him—at $50 in wages, which was an improvement over a zero figure when bills were starting to mount. I had already been forced to reach an accommodation with Mr. Bloom, whose charges were fully three times more than what would have been reasonable, but he offered to await payment at my convenience.

Pastor—or rather his tame actor-author, Jacques Kruger—had turned his hand to parodying the latest of Gilbert and Sullivan's triumphs, *Patience, or Bunthorne's Bride,* which was currently being filched by several New York producers and also playing in D'Oyly Carte's brand-new London theater, the Savoy, which we heard to our disbelief was lit entirely by electricity in place of gas. ("All very well, but it'll never catch on," Mrs. Walker's darling, the Prince of Wales, was reported to have commented on opening night.)

I portrayed Patience herself, the untutored village milkmaid with whom the yellery-greenery poet, Reginald Bunthorne, falls in thankless love, according to the original text. In ours, Bunthorne was transmuted into a theater manager, but Pastor's customers looked for humor that was broad rather than crisp. The reviewers' rapture spurred me to approach him for a raise in pay. Not only was I put off, albeit with avuncular expressions of good will, but I was burdened in addition with studying a new part in yet another burlesque that was to follow *Patience.*

"Let's see how you fare in *Billee Taylor* before we talk about fresh terms for you, Lil." I wondered whether Pastor the penny-pincher appreciated me, and Amy supplied the answer: He did not.

Billee Taylor, music by Edward Solomon and book by Harry Stephens, was yet another English import plundered by our theatrical privateers, but this was no concern of mine. I had as one costume a satin sailor suit that showed me to advantage, causing one ecstatic critic to rhapsodize that Lillian Russell "looks like Venus after her bath." Mr. Solomon himself, in town for the run of the genuine production, called at the stage door, asking to see me.

I was hesitant at first about having him admitted to my dressing room in case he berate me for the impudence of my performances, but when I did so, he entered carrying a bouquet of hot-house roses, which I was delighted to accept. I was surprised that a man so surprisingly young—he must still have been in his mid-twenties—should have gained renown as a composer so soon on both sides of the Atlantic. The politeness of his manner impressed me as much as his fair complexion and chestnut brown hair, which belied the usual swarthy caricatures of those of the same ethnic origins.

I let three weeks elapse before reintroducing the subject of my finances to Tony Pastor. Fingering the crucifix that dangled on his watch chain, he hemmed and hawed about the temptations that would beset a girl of twenty-one possessed of money to burn. He implied that only regard for my soul kept him from granting my request for more money. "You know what they say about beauty being its own reward? There's a mountain of truth in that."

I had reached the point where, without greater income, I should have to part with some of my San Francisco souvenirs to satisfy my creditors. I decided that a show of strength would subdue the sanctimonious Mr. Pastor. I did not appear at his theater that night or any night afterward, confident that within a week he would run begging to me. But it did not happen that way. He closed *Billee Taylor* and replaced it with some other underrehearsed piece. I would never again knuckle under to Tony Pastor.

One of the jewelers on the Ladies' Mile bought the smallest of my California diamonds. The proceeds were enough to keep the bill collectors temporarily at bay and take me to Chicago to visit with Papa.

I returned to New York resolved to dip no more into my scanty treasure trove. I had a contract with Pastor that remained unfulfilled, though he made no effort to enforce it, and another with McCaull, which gave him first call on my services whenever he had a script in hand. But it was imperative to have cash coming in immediately without waste of time on unpaid-for rehearsals. I hastily signed a third contact with Bothner, Hirshy & Company for one hundred and fifty almighty dollars a week to play Phoebe once more in another stolen rendition of *Patience* at the Bijou, rented from McCaull, who was off on tour with *The Snake Charmer.*

There ensued such wrangling that I was driven halfway to distraction. McCaull reappeared to escalate the rent on his theater to the level of 50 percent of the price of every ticket sold. A rival producer promised me $250 a week to appear in a new show. Bothner, Hirshy promptly agreed to match that figure, which, combined with the landlord's extortions, jettisoned them into financial straits, and I pocketed the $250 only once before they closed. But a different iron had been heating in the fire. With three other members of the cast whose thinking coincided with mine, I saw no reason why managements should forever get away with making most of the money. We would be managers ourselves.

A second diamond of mine followed the route of the first to stake my share in our endeavor. A newspaper paragraph about us brought Mama to my hotel under a flag of truce. "I compliment you, Nellie, on your enterprise. It is one thing to perform in operetta but quite another to succeed as an impresario. This will be a golden opportunity for you to develop business talents. I shall be glad to assist in whatever way I can." And thus she added theatrical affairs to all her other hobbies, as alert as Anthony Comstock for any hint of vice in our guileless production.

She approved of our plan to employ ourselves and the rest of what had been the Bothner, Hirshy company in a continuation of *Patience*. She liked what she saw and heard when she attended rehearsals. I was astonished to catch her humming:

> A *Japanese young man,*
> A *blue-and-white young man.*
> *Francesca da Pimini, niminy, piminy,*
> *Je-ne-sais-quoi young man!* . . .

She voiced grave reservations, however, about our choice of venue. "Surely you could have found a less tainted place than Niblo's, with its reputation for unabashed sensuality." But Niblo's was available where other playhouses were not. The rental appeared to be within our means, and I set foot inside its doors for the first time as a director, not as the intended flame of Mr. Riley.

Perhaps our facsimile of Gilbert and Sullivan was one more

than the market would bear. Evening throngs still flowed up and down the Rialto, but most of them passed us by. The *Dramatic Mirror*, which Mama had added to her perusing, infuriated her with its glib accounting for our failure: "*Patience* was managed by a woman and, yet more absurd, by a flighty and flattered woman." What mattered to me more than the insults was the fact that my jewel box had been rifled to no purpose.

Its depletion continued unabated through that summer of '82, compelling me in the fall to gulp down my pride, bow my head in pretended penitence, and make peace with Colonel McCaull, who with Southern courtesy had been huffing and puffing, "If Lillian Russell doesn't abide by my contract, I'll take damned good care she doesn't abide by a contract with anyone else."

It was to be the mixture as before: $150 for eight performances a week; Bijou Opera House; Gilbert and Sullivan, this time a four-year-old work of theirs which unaccountably had been overlooked by the pirates who flourished on the Rialto. *The Sorcerer's* fanciful plot told of the confusion wreaked in a village when Alexis, son of Sir Marmaduke Pointdextre, orders doses of a love philter for all who dwell there so that they may share his bliss over his forthcoming engagement to Lady Sangazure's daughter Aline. I, of course, was Aline, whose sip of the potion brewed by John Wellington Wells ("a dealer in magic and spells") unexpectedly arouses her passion for the parish vicar.

The costumes ordered from Messieurs Godchaux surpassed even McCaull's exacting standards for excellence. During fittings at their premises on Clinton Place, the couturière whispered a suggestion through a mouthful of pins that I should provide the audience with a special treat by wearing two dresses bought on my own account. I fell into her trap and was billed for $495. One more diamond pawned at Lindo's fetched $300. "You must not worry your pretty head about the balance, mademoiselle," said the wily dressmaker. "Take as long as five years if you like, and meantime, run your fingers over this bolt of camel's hair, just in today...."

The papers praised my opening-night "charm" and "sincerity," which had to be interpreted as a tribute to some emerging histrionic ability, since I felt the presence of neither quality. I had never before suffered the ignominy of laboring for a man I detested, and this for a salary humiliating to my ambition and inadequate for my needs. It may have been the inclement weather or, probably, sheer aggravation that robbed me of my voice early on in our scheduled run. The doctor I consulted found a temperature, diagnosed the case as possible typhoid, and prescribed medicine every four hours.

The doughty colonel, taking my nonappearance on three consecutive evenings as a sign that I was playing games with him, repeated his threat to take steps to bar me from working for anyone whatever if I broke my contract with him. To my shame, I scampered back to his fold, only to be reduced to further croaking after a night or two of singing.

During the next two weeks of absence from the Bijou, rumors spread that could have had their source only in this latter-day Simon Legree. I was malingering; I was trying to shake him down; I was paying the inevitable penalty for a life of dissipation. Mama moved in to take care of me and man the defenses with a letter to the *Dramatic Mirror:*

It is not unusual for singers to be troubled with bronchial affection, and Miss Russell is subject to trouble of this kind in damp, unwholesome weather. She has never shirked her duty, but on the contrary appeared in her role even when she could not do justice to herself in singing. After her first attack, she returned to work much too soon, which was the occasion of her present illness. I am happy to state she is mending, and we hope will soon be able to assume her duties.

—Cynthia Leonard

The vapid little physician who had been treating me was sent packing after a single exchange with her. "Tell me, Doctor, what is the fluid in this rather generously sized bottle that my daughter has been taking?"

"It is for the relief of her cough and a mild sedative for her chest pains, less habit-forming than opium, I assure you."

"I am not unfamiliar with the orthodox pharmacopoeia as well as with the homeopathic materia medica. It is codeine, is it not, in dosages big enough to stagger a horse?"

"Codeine is the medication of preference in cases such as Miss Russell's."

"I trust your capabilities, Doctor, but not your school of medicine. You are obviously an allopath whereas I am a believer in homeopathy. I quote a classical text: 'It is only by means of the spiritual influence of a morbidic agent that our spiritual vital power can be diseased, and in like manner only by the spiritual operation of medicine can health be restored.' Miss Russell's recovery requires only a millionth part of the tablespoonsful of the physic she has been swallowing on your advice. Please let us have your bill. Good day to you."

His sucessor had me on tinctures so diluted I might just as well have been sipping water. The year ended, another spring was on the way, and I was no more able to sing than I had been in November. I was too sick to receive the stream of well-wishers who came rapping on our door, but Mama relayed their sentiments to inspirit me, and our quarters were constantly replenished with flowers, baskets of fruit, and gifts of wine. The reporters haunted us. One cadaverous scribe called regularly at midnight to ascertain whether it would be in order to publish the obituary he had prepared in next morning's *World*.

I concluded that I should indeed have succumbed if only from ennui had it not been for Edward Solomon. He was the first to visit me after the fever had dropped and I was no longer plagued in fitful sleep as I had been by nightmares of tenements, painted women, and my Charlie. Mama had an engagement at her Science of Life Club that day; Annie the maid let him in. He had an armful of daffodils, narcissus, and jonquils for me, and his manner was as breezy as the March day outside.

"I thought I'd drop in to see if I could cheer you up a bit. You must be going absolutely mad, cooped up here week after week. What can I do to help put the roses back in your cheeks?"

"Would you play for me? I'm starved for music. I hope to resume practice before the end of the week."

"How do you know I can play? Perhaps I use a dulcimer or a penny whistle."

"Something about you says you can. But nothing too lively, please, to tempt me to skip right off this sofa, which would be contrary to doctor's orders."

"I'll do something special, dedicated to you. First of all, tell me the funniest thing that has happened to you in the past week."

That was not difficult in my present airy mood: the call from the reporter who was so eager to see my death notice into print. "Perfect! Now listen." My visitor opened up the piano's lid. His fingers combined "The Dead March" from *Saul* with "Oh, Susanna, Don't You Cry for Me" to such comical effect that before he had finished I had twinges in my ribs from laughing.

Teddy had the peculiar gift of being able to express everything in an improvised medley or melody of his invention. He urged me to pour out my woes to him, and he transmuted them into frivolity as his hands ran over the keys.

He came every day after that, always optimistic about finding me alone, though Mama's schedule was unpredictable but bearing up nobly if she or other friends were with me. Even then he could communicate as if in private simply by sitting down and keeping up a quiet keyboard commentary on all that transpired around us. At first, he won Mama's favor by accompanying me as I labored to restore my singing voice, but her suspicions of him were sprouting before she satisfied herself that my recovery was complete, and she resumed life on Columbia Heights. Now I was my healthy self again, my blood raced at the very thought of Teddy.

He was altogether different from any Englishman I had known in the past, considerate of my feelings when most of them treated a woman as if her only interests were saucepans or bedsprings. I felt soothed by his courtesies as well as by the touch of his hands. He was always quick to open a door ahead of me, to help me on as well as off with a coat, to take my arm when we crossed a street, to insist that I choose where we went and what we did together. He liked to button my gloves for me and kiss my wrists in the process, kneel on the floor to lace my boots with a similar treat for each knee. He was, in other words, my idea of a perfect gentleman, my Sir Lancelot.

From the little he said about his family, I gathered that he was the only son of the owner of one of the grander London theaters, a self-made man who wanted Teddy to have the best of everything. Perhaps the reason my new lover was such a model of gallantry was that he had escaped being sent to the usual boarding schools, where boys of his race were unwelcome. He had, he said, been "educated privately" by tutors who, like his father, were impressed by his musical talent.

He made his debut when he was fourteen in a recital on his father's stage, with his mother turning the pages of the score as he played a little Beethoven, some Czerny, and a great deal of Liszt. The applause he received convinced his papa to arrange a series of Sunday concerts for Teddy, advertise them in *The Morning Post*, and give his son 10 percent of the gate for spending money. "It was all rather plain sailing after that. Various people wanted me to write music for their shows. They thought I was the boy genius, another Mozart. The world, as they say, was my oyster, and it has been ever since."

"The girls must have adored you."

"They used to tell me I looked like Franz Liszt."

"You still do." I caressed his hair where it curled on his velvet collar.

Since *The Sorcerer* continued to cast its spell at the Bijou, I thought I would celebrate regained health, restored appetites, and a rapturous new romance by rejoining the company for its final week. Aburst with vitality, I was ready for anything when I sailed in on McCaull. I could take him on along with a troop of cavalry without any help.

"I'll be glad to have you back, Lil, but it's going to run me into money, getting the costumes fitted for you. I can't pay you a nickel more than two hundred."

"Make it four."

He spluttered like a bonfire in the rain. "Are you raving crazy? What are you trying to do—crucify me?"

"A flock of little birds tells me that the day I appear on your stage I'll pack the house. They'll be standing on line around the block to buy tickets after everything they've read about me in the newspapers."

"If I sell every seat every performance, I can't afford you."

"Then I'll work for a percentage to make it easy for you."

"You know I don't give percentages. I'll tell you what I'll do. Sign for the two hundred and promise me you'll do my next show, *The Princess of Trebizonde*, at two-fifty, supply your own costumes."

"Three-fifty for *The Sorcerer*, four hundred after that. There isn't a producer on Broadway who'd offer me less if they knew I'm available, starting now."

"Lil, let's compromise. Two-fifty for *The Sorcerer* as well as for *The Princess*, and I'll pay for the costumes."

"I'm underwhelmed. Let's say three hundred for one, three-fifty for the next. If I can't sell out every performance, then only three hundred for *The Princess*, but you'll have to show me your books to prove there's an empty seat, and you buy the costumes, no matter what." He was so cagey about how much he made that he would have hired a blind man as a bookkeeper if he could have found one.

The deal was struck on my terms, contract signed on the spot. I had a parting word for him. "By the way, I have just the man for your conductor for *The Princess*. He knows Offenbach better than his own mother. His name is Teddy Solomon." The job was his when we opened in the new Casino Theater, a Moorish-style fantasy at 38th Street.

Colonel *Götterdammerung*, of course, had his own method for making sure he obtained a *quid pro quo* in whatever he did. I had to pledge that I would be at least polite to the dudes who clamored to be introduced to me when those dudes chanced to be stockholders in the McCaull Opera Company, handing cash to the proprietor on his promise to "make them solid" with us women who worked under contract for him. They got short shrift from me. There was only one man I wished to have commerce with.

Nobody had brought me greater happiness than Teddy. I lived in a state of elation, jubilant and carefree, as though inhaling whiffs of a dentist's laughing gas. Teddy was in turn amusing, provocative, loving, demanding. It delighted me to have my emotions played upon as deftly as he rendered a Liszt or Chopin. He could inspire the gentlest desire, to be satisfied with a sedate kiss, or a fire that fed on itself until he had quenched it.

We saw much of the town together before *The Princess* began commanding our evening hours. I was curious to see Mrs.

Langtry, who with her troupe of players was drawing the crowds into the Fifth Avenue Theater with *Pygmalion and Galatea*, written by Gilbert before his association with Sullivan. On this, the Jersey Lily's first descent on our country, the statuesque English import had created as much commotion as the fireworks shot off to celebrate the opening at last of the Brooklyn Bridge. It was common knowledge that her current Lothario, chinless Freddie Gebhard, had traveled with her every mile of the two-month tour she had just concluded. We clucked like a hen house at laying time about the possible effect this would have on her erstwhile master, the Prince of Wales.

Teddy escorted me to her dressing room one afternoon. She reclined on a sofa in an exquisite silk peignoir, toying with a string of the most magnificent pearls. Her form, shoulders, and skin were worthy of their reputation, but I was pleased to notice that her years—at least nine or ten more than mine—showed in a certain puffiness about the eyes.

She received me like an empress, and Teddy actually stooped to kiss a beautifully manicured hand, which she thereafter raised with the utmost delicacy to stifle a yawn. I was on the point of asking whether she cared enough about America to wish to live here when she broke in. "Do you play cards, dear?" I allowed that I did. "Then pour yourself a glass of something. Poker, shall we say—aces and deuces wild?" Before she let it be known it was time for her to bathe, she had relieved me of twenty-three dollars, Teddy of five.

Infatuated, I bought new clothes and new jewels, heedless of the cost or the future day when the bills would be presented. I wanted us to live in splendor, sinful or not, so I signed every contract put before my nose—there were five or six of them—provided the promised price was right. He would devote himself to me and the writing of operettas, I would devote myself to him and the singing of them, beginning with *Virgina and Paul*.

Clouds gathered in the autumn sky. Every day the creditors closed in tighter. Managers learned that, far from having exclusive rights to my talents, they could look forward to only a share of them at some uncertain date, and hints of recourse to the law began to multiply.

Teddy was more insouciant than I. "There's no earthly reason why we should go on being pestered to death here, you know, my sweet. We can do *Virginia and Paul* just as well in London. They'll love you over there every bit as much as I do. Shall we go and take Harry Stephens and his wife with us?"

Perhaps it was my maid who let slip an incautious word after I sent her with the money to buy four steamship tickets. Whatever it was, the *Dramatic Mirror*, failing to extract confirmation from Teddy or me, sent a man over to Brooklyn to interview Mama. "Nonsense! Lillian or her maid Annie would certainly inform me of any intention to take a step like that you suggest."

We four voyageurs had little thought for Mama or *The Princess of Trebizonde*, which was still in mid-stride. Early one June morning, my darling and I engaged a carriage to hurry us to Jersey City to take refuge in a hotel room and elude immediate legal interference for the next few hours. Mr. and Mrs. Stephens met us in time to sail aboard the *Lydian Monarch* at half past three o'clock.

~ VI ~

*T*HE STEAMSHIP crept into the Liverpool docks in a morning haze so murky that, for all our eyes could discern, our captain might have turned about in mid-ocean to disembark in New Jersey. I had looked forward to being in a land whose every inhabitant spoke English by contrast with polyglot New York, where fully half the people were immigrants and mostly unintelligible to me. Nevertheless, I had to rely on Teddy to translate the gibberish of the porters who, with much tugging of forelocks, got us and our luggage safely aboard the train for London.

Compared with the mammoths of our country, the locomotive was a mere toy, yet the plush comforts of our cozy firstclass compartment exceeded those associated with Mr. George Pullman, and the roadbed was reassuringly smooth all the way. I passed the time in similar fashion as on the trip to California, playing bezique with Teddy and the Stephenses or staring through the window at a sunlit landscape as trim as a park, but now with Teddy's arm about my waist and his lips occasionally nuzzling my ear.

London wore a veil of pearl-gray evening mist. Gas lamps glowed like silver moons as a hansom cab trotted us to the accommodations which a letter in advance from Teddy had reserved for "Mr. and Mrs. Solomon" in Chelsea, a few steps around a corner from the River Thames. Though I fell into bed weary from travel that night, Teddy's caresses soon banished fatigue, and we celebrated what we both felt confident would be an imminent British triumph for both of us.

[92

In those first weeks, I found London a mass of contradictions. The main thoroughfares were kept better swept than in Manhattan, yet the helmeted "bobbies" allowed one to be badgered by beggars, which the police would not condone on Broadway. The *hauteur* of the superbly costumed ladies who frequented the West End stores surpassed that of their American counterparts, as did the obsequiousness of the coachmen who brought them to the doors and the assistants who danced attendance on them inside. I gathered that here an actor or actress, save perhaps Mr. Henry Irving, enjoyed no more prestige than a black-faced minstrel.

Society ignored the like of Teddy and me, and I had been wondering whether I might meet Queen Victoria! But she, it seemed, never showed herself in her capital city. I would have settled for an introduction to the Prince of Wales; however, at present, he also was an absentee, being off on a bachelor's jaunt to what the English referred to as "the Continent."

The company Teddy and I shared reminded me of the cast of *Patience*. The darling of most of the men was the Irish show-off, Oscar Wilde, whose few published verses I had not been tempted to read. During my plunge at being an impresario, he had been sent to New York by D'Oyly Carte as a kind of walking advertisement for *Patience*, whose Reginald Bunthorne was quite obviously Oscar. Like him, his languid fellow aesthetes walked the Chelsea pavements sporting green carnations and prattling about beauty being the essence of life, whereas his female followers with their pallid, skinny faces and shapeless robes provided proof to the contrary.

The theater booked for *Virginia and Paul* was something of a revelation. Its manager, John Hollingshead, who had first united Mr. Gilbert with Mr. Sullivan, had installed a restaurant, previously unknown in any London playhouse. He had also started the custom of Wednesday and Saturday matinees, though none of us in the profession had cause to give thanks for that. He had scarcely a gaspipe anywhere on the premises of his Gaiety. He insisted on the musicians and stagehands being as well rehearsed as his actors so that ears would not be assailed by sour notes or audiences kept drumming their fingers between acts. But for all that, I was repelled by the scrambling of the mob for seats in the pit and gallery that was taken for granted in otherwise orderly London. On the Rialto, they had learned to stand patiently in line for admission, a practice that could well have been copied here.

On the other hand, I wished some Manhattan eating place had served dishes as succulent as those our housekeeper prepared. Mrs. Walker had instilled in me an appreciation of roast meats, fresh vegetables, and luscious desserts. Our Mrs. Tuttle outdid her with her steak-and-oyster pies, jugged hare, saddles of lamb, raspberry fool, angels on horseback, and the Lord knew what else. The monthly accounts were a testimonial to the quality of her cooking. She was expensive, but surrendering an item of jewelry now and then to make ends meet was well worth it, even if I did need Teddy's help to lace a corset.

Unfortunately, no rush for seats in any part of the house materialized after I opened as the heroine of *Virginia and Paul* in July, with Teddy wielding a gilded baton in the orchestra pit. Where New York critics could be curs snapping at a performer's heels, their London colleagues were veritable hyenas. To a man, they poured scorn on what one of them derided as "the songs of Solomon." Another took exception to my making my entrance wearing my most treasured ornament, "a brooch," as he described it, "with the name of the companion of her flight conspicuous in brilliants." A third inflicted the cruelest cut of all. In physical proportions, he jeered, I was "not the figure for London." I wished them all to perdition when we had to post early closing notices, count our losses, and lick our wounds.

Teddy's next recourse was to take me to call upon an old acquaintance of his who had expressed interest in his prowess. (Mama denounced both Teddy and his music as "trashy" in a blistering note I received from her.) We went to see Arthur Sullivan—Sir Arthur since last April. After hearing me run through one or two of his compositions I had his endorsement for the latest operetta—he vowed it would be the last—that the team of Gilbert and Sullivan devised. I was to be the principal with the title role in *Princess Ida, or Castle Adamant*, due to commence its run at D'Oyly Carte's Savoy Theater next January 5—Sir Arthur, as usual, was burning midnight oil and gulping black coffee to complete the score on time. Mr. Oily Carte and

I both conveniently forgot our previous arm's length encounter, and a contract was concluded between us. I then achieved the long-standing aspiration of mine and went into rehearsal under the direction of Mr. Gilbert himself.

One more temple fell. He proved to be a tyrant with the bearing of a drill master and the sting of a wasp. The entire company trembled in fear of him. The rules he set were as strict as in a convent. Men dressed on one side backstage, women on the other. No stranger was admitted through the stage door. Visitors, even Teddy, were barred from the dressing rooms.

I should have foreseen what lay in store when one aging actor bridled at being hectored by this autocrat with the blazing blue eyes, whose disposition, I suspected, had been further soured by envy of his partner's knighthood. He had taken the old trouper through the same pages of the script twenty or thirty times without remission before his victim complained. "There is no need to continue, sir. I know my lines."

Gilbert's roar would have stopped a bull in his tracks. "Yes, but you don't know *mine*."

"No, sir, I object. I have been on the stage quite long enough—"

"Quite." The poor fellow was discharged on the spot.

At first I did my best to please my tormentor, and he indulged me, or so I thought until I construed the true meanings of his repartee. When Teddy's presence was forbidden backstage, I resented having one of the male principals slip an arm around me and address me as "my American beauty," and I carried a protest to Gilbert.

He guffawed. "Never mind, my dear, never mind. He couldn't have meant it."

When I overheard the woman who dressed me criticize my character, I went back to him to ask for her to be replaced. "What did she actually say?"

"She was gossiping with the doorman and I heard her distinctly. 'She's no better than she should be.'"

"Well, you're not, are you?"

I was trapped into answering, "Why, of course not."

"Ah, well, then that's all right."

I found the differences in the way the language was spoken

on this side of the ocean perplexing. He would mount the stage
beside me, instructing me to copy his every intonation. "The
audience won't know what the devil you are saying. Your pro-
nunciation is the American one. It will be more satisfactory if
you speak in the usual English. It is not 'tomayto' or 'eether' or
'cahn't' or 'neether.' Listen to me." The tips of his mustache
would vibrate as he mouthed the words as he wanted them
spoken.

He mocked me as his libretto mocked the emancipation of
women, which was a movement we Americans took more to
heart than most of our sex over here. Princess Ida was a "mighty
maiden with a mission" who, seeking sanctuary in distant Castle
Adamant in preference to marriage with Prince Hilarion, accepted that

> *Man is coarse and Man is plain—*
> *Man is more or less insane—*
> *Man's a ribald—Man's a rake—*
> *Man is Nature's sole mistake!*

Mama would probably apply the lines to everyone in trousers, but I excluded Teddy, for one, from the slurs. The more
I saw of Mr. Gilbert, the more I was persuaded that the passage
fitted him like a glove. For instance, it was hard to break the
custom of standing stage center when I sang, which enraged him.
"Why are you posing there like a marble sepulchre when I told
you to stand over here?"

"Mr. Gilbert, I have always been used to taking the center of
the stage in opera."

"My exquisite Miss Russell, this is not opera. It is only a low
burlesque of the worst possible kind. For God's sake, do as I tell
you!"

Relations between us grew so strained that I asked if I might
speak to him in private. He promptly invited me to his new
house in Harrington Gardens, Kensington, which turned out to
be the most handsome I had entered since stepping ashore at
Liverpool. A footman led the way into an enormous paneled
library with windows of stained glass and electrically lit lanterns

suspended by chains from the molded plaster ceiling ten feet above the Persian rugs on the parquet floor.

I was welcomed with a fond pat rather far below the waist. He treated other actresses in the company in the same fashion, though he was reputed to resist further temptation and to be devoted to his wife Lucy, who was not present for the showdown. "We can make ourselves comfortable here. It's really quite a nice house—telephone, central heating, bathroom on every floor." It came close to what I had in mind for Teddy and me when we had the money for it and had disentangled ourselves from the tentacles of the law.

"Sit yourself down." I was relieved to see there was no chesterfield in the room, only embroidered armchairs, one of which I took while he swung his slippered feet up onto a footstool in front of another. "I suppose you have come to tell me I am an ill-tempered pig? I am, of course, and I glory in it."

"Not exactly that. But you hammer at me so in front of everybody that I despair of ever being able to satisfy you."

"You might make a start, my dear, by being on time for re-hearsals. Ten o'clock means ten o'clock, not whenever you have finished powdering your nose. You have been late twice already, and I insist on people being as punctual as the postman. Not that mine is any marvel of diligence. I've had to complain about his dilly-dallying to the Postmaster General."

"I didn't feel well on those two mornings."

"We may pity though not pardon thee. Do you know who said that? William Shakespeare, *The Comedy of Errors*, Act One, though in my professional opinion all the claptrap he wrote should be kept off the boards."

"Anyway, we've gone over every line and every bit of business until I feel like a fool repeating myself."

"Then we can talk on equal terms."

I was slow to catch the implication. "I beg your pardon?"

He kicked up his heels in glee. "I accept your apology."

Patience was wearing thin now. "Can we stop beating around the bush and talk sense for a moment? I want to please you, but I won't be browbeaten. I'm not some chit of a girl in the chorus to be pushed around."

"Oh, definitely not. It would be a ponderous undertaking."

"Will you be serious? It isn't funny."

His eyebrows collided at the bridge of his nose. "You are quite right. It is not. You, Miss Russell, are not unlike those compatriots of yours who fought George the Third. You have courage, but you lack discipline. Incidentally, you also sing better than they probably did. But when you work for me, I must ask you to curb your democratic instincts and do as you are told."

"And if I refuse?"

"If you do not comply with my wishes, I shall apply to the courts for an injunction to prevent your performing in the play at all, whatever your contract stipulates."

I did not wait for the flunky to show me to the front door, which I shut with a slam that would have rattled the windows in a less substantial house. On waking in the morning beside Teddy, my insides churned. I sent excuses for the third non-appearance in a note carried by a cab driver, but Gilbert swore afterward it was not delivered to him. His letter to me came by special messenger the same evening. "Your services being no longer required for *Princess Ida*, your contract is hereby terminated forthwith. I will refrain from further comment and content myself with stating that you should not doubt I have consulted my solicitors on the subject." My replacement—what irony!—would be a certain Leonora Braham. A relative? I did not know.

It was my turn to find a lawyer and instruct him to bring suit for breach of contract. The damage claimed amounted to a tidy five thousand pounds. I could not afford to let anyone but Teddy know that in any event I should have been compelled to walk out on *Princess Ida* before the end of her run if she enjoyed the success anticipated for her. I was carrying his child.

After the tightest of lacing could no longer conceal the fact of my condition, I avoided being seen outside our apartments except after dark, when a thick veil and a voluminous coat, unbearably warm in sultry spring weather, provided a disguise, and Teddy would choose some distant haunt for us to go to for an outing or a meal. In spite of precautions, however, a whisper reached that disgraceful weekly journal, *Town Talk*, which published a scurrilous snippet saying, "The joke goes that Mr. Edward Solomon and Miss Lillian Russell are to be married by the special consent of her distant American spouse."

We devoted endless hours, days, weeks to discussing our predicament. No matter what we did, fresh scandal could probably not be averted. Worse than that, my little cache of jewels was near depletion, and Teddy's income consisted only of the trickle provided by payments of performing rights to his music.

"If you don't want the baby, Lil, I'm sure there's somebody in London like the woman who ran that brownstone on 52nd Street and cut her throat in the bathroom after Anthony Comstock had her arrested. What was her name?"

"You must mean Madame Restell. But I do want our baby. If I didn't, I should have turned to hot baths and cold gin. That has worked for some girls. You haven't changed your mind, have you?"

"Whatever you want I want. I've been wondering whether we can find somebody to marry us."

What harm could be done when I was already over my head in lawyers, being sued in New York and suing in London? I wished our child to be spared by all possible means the stigmata of illegitimacy. Harry Braham was three thousand miles away, and I had no thought that I should hear from him again. If exchanging formal vows with Teddy would help spare our baby future misery, I would postpone worrying about the consequences.

The ceremony, conducted in a dusty registry office by a trusting clerk, was as mundane as an appointment with a hairdresser. I gave my name as Helen Louise Leonard and, as we walked out the door into May sunshine, felt content that I had stronger claim to being the veritable Mrs. Solomon. Happily, in those days the imperfections of printed photographs made them a poor means of identifying anyone other than the queen, her family, and Mr. Gladstone. After two experiences, I came to the conclusion that marriage was essentially a matter of bodies and souls united, not signatures put on a scrap of paper.

My new husband's affections were enhanced. He made every allowance for my increasing cumbersomeness and showered me with expressions of his love when I had swollen to a size too large for the physical act. Our talents seemed to resume their growth like plants watered after prolonged parching. He undertook to coach me once more, endowing me with a voice not like a girl's but a woman's, reflecting an indefinable depth of sentiment. I was better than I had known I could be when shortness of breath forced me to suspend the practicing.

Meanwhile, my dearest Pygmalion was completing the score for his latest operetta with the leading role tailored for his Galatea's new-found range and tonal richness. If he could contrive it, *Polly, or the Pet of the Regiment* would celebrate both the arrival of our baby and the triumphal return to public esteem of the parents.

Dorothy Lillian Solomon was delivered without complications in our home during the summer of '84. With her strong jaw and brown hair, she bore greater resemblance to her father than to me, though we adored her equally. She was left in a wet nurse's care when rehearsals began at the Novelty Theater. My solicitors were in the throes of reaching a settlement with Mr. Gilbert's and Mr. Carte's. The fact that I was not to be trifled with may have impressed itself upon Polly's producer, who treated me with proper respect.

Most of the news I had from the country to which I hoped to return some day came from Papa. The absence of any mail from Mama indicated that she had once more given me up for lost on hearing of my dubious marital status. Though he made light of it, I gathered that Knight & Leonard had been hard hit again in the wake of the financial panic that infected Wall Street that spring. He attributed the trouble to the machinations of Eastern bankers and the weakness of President Arthur. The government, Papa said flatly, needed a good housecleaning. "Those Republicans have ruled the roost too long; it's time to throw the rascals out."

Wonder of wonders, Mama was to offer herself in November as a mayoral candidate to cleanse New York City of vice. She was the nominee of something called the National Equal Rights Party, which was even putting up a *woman*, Belva Lockwood, for the Presidency of the United States! I vaguely recalled that Lawyer Lockwood had long been an apple of Mama's finical eye.

I had a vision of her emulating Belva by riding a tricycle along the avenues of Washington, D.C., clad in crimson stockings.

Polly and I were greeted with instant applause from the commencement of our joint appearances on October 4. The critics kindly committed *Virginia and Paul* to oblivion and ranked Teddy's latest achievement above *Billee Taylor*. We would be established at the Novelty for a minimum of two months. At the dressing-room party, elation carried me sky high without the champagne that everybody else indulged in.

Before October was over, I received fresh tidings from New York. There was at least one glaring inaccuracy in the account contained in the clipping forwarded by Amy Leslie, but it was obvious that the man I thought of only as my ex-husband knew something of my circumstances. Mr. Harry Braham was suing for divorce, "defendant now living with Solomon as his wife and has borne a son." Putting in an answer would be a waste of time; being rid of him would clear an encumbrance from the path. I was intrigued to note that after the London papers picked up the story, more tickets to *Polly* were sold than before. Notoriety was clearly no handicap in the career I was relaunched upon. It was preferable to succeed as a sinner than languish in uneasy virtue.

Suddenly, I was a valuable commodity where before I had reconciled myself to being only Mrs. Solomon. Of the numerous contracts dangled before my nose, I chose only one involving an American theme. In a pale bronze makeup, I would portray Princess Pocahontas in a show of the same name at the Empire Theater, risking my wigged head to Indian Chief Powhatan's papier-mâché club eight times a week.

Pocahontas scored a minor victory. We lasted long enough for me to pay off most of my debts and lay the foundations of a new bank account. We might have done better had not the whole town been buzzing in expectation of another Gilbert and Sullivan spectacle. D'Oyle Carte had made peace between Sir Arthur and the brute. *The Mikado, or The Town of Titipu* was taking shape behind the guarded doors of the Savoy, where the brute was lashing the cast more cruelly than before and reducing his male lead, little George Grossmith, to drug addiction, according to gossip.

March 14 would be opening night, and the house was sold out weeks in advance and for weeks to come, Teddy said. I did not care to work forever in a city whose playgoers accepted Mr. Gilbert as a deity or to witness his fresh glory. With Teddy, Dorothy (whom we pet-named "Daughtie"), and a nursemaid, I set sail for New York ahead of the date.

There were no bands playing or fireboats spouting fountains of water to greet us, but then there were no process servers or sheriff's men either—the nonsense about broken contracts had been forgotten while I was away. Even Mama came down to meet our boat with a smile for me, a nod for Teddy, and a pat on the bonnet for Daughtie. "I am pleased to see you looking well, Nellie, after your vicissitudes. I have read of your progress in London. Success must agree with you. I trust that it will not elude you in your native land."

It was all I could do not to fall back into the patterns of childhood and answer meekly, "Yes, Mama." Instead, "But you have been spreading your wings, too. Imagine—mayor of New York! I was disappointed for you."

"Eighty-four votes. A frustration, but also a beginning. Mrs. Lockwood intends to try again, and perhaps I shall, too. If only women had the ballot, it would have been a totally different story. But our day will come, never doubt." For a moment, I almost pitied her. She was close to sixty years old, and success, by my standards, was a stranger to her. Yet failure did not daunt her. In that respect, she was worth looking up to.

Teddy and I established our menage in a cozy apartment, which we proceeded to furnish with a degree of luxury, at 58 East 9th Street, a sentimental choice, since it stood within a minute's walk of our old rendezvous, the Hotel Lafayette. It was a pleasure to dine there and see heads turn, a sign that I could regard myself as having passed over the threshold to fame, though not yet placing myself in the same category as the sculptor Auguste Saint-Gaudens, for example, who was another habitué of the place. With a settlement from D'Oyly Carte to tide us over, we were in no particular hurry to go to work again. I was delighted to be home, especially when the flurry of talk about my divorce had died down at the same rapid pace as the various managements' snarls about taking me to court.

I should not have dreamed of signing again with McCaull but for the fact that he was willing to restage *Polly*, which meant only a modicum of effort for me and with Teddy as the orchestral maestro. Back we went into the Casino, whose reputation as a temple of operetta and stamping ground for gilded young gentlemen had sprouted in our absence. The dudes arrived early and departed late at this haunt on 38th Street, wearing silk hats and carnations in the lapels of their truncated black jackets, cut in the style invented, it was claimed, by the Prince of Wales himself. Some of them came laden with flowers to toss across the footlights—still old-fashioned gas—at a favorite, others to order bouquets of more unwieldy proportions for an usher to carry up onto the stage. Few evenings passed without my being embowered in these tributes. Orchids, gardenias, roses, and coal gas were the remembered scents of those days.

The bucks of Gotham, young and old, lusted for introductions to any "Casino girl" with or without payment of a fee for the privilege. The three of us whose names were ultimately due to appear in the blackest type and brightest lights—Pauline Hall, Isabelle Urquhart, and myself—held ourselves aloof from the Champagne Charlies. (I could write that name without a pang now that I had Daughtie.) They must satisfy themselves with members of the choruses, many of whom were happy to trade their favors for a twenty-dollar gold piece, or its value in cheap jewelry. During the intervals, the more elderly Casanovas exchanged tales of emeralds and diamonds, carriages and pieds-à-terre which they lavished on their targets, but I was as yet a novice in that phase of our profession, having Teddy as my beloved.

The zeal of the roués in their search for evening nectar had been inflamed rather than cooled by the latest effort to purify the city. To date, my personal experience of life in night town was confined to the one indelible excursion with Mama and Mr. Cartwright. I had seen little of Sixth Avenue beyond its intersection with Broadway at 33rd Street where the Manhattan Theater stood, but I knew the label, "Satan's Circus," applied to that avenue by Dr. DeWitt Talmadge, who preached in Brooklyn. I also knew the reputation of such dens as the French Madam's, The Haymarket, and The Cremorne. I had an abiding curiosity to look in on some of them, but I hated to walk under the cacophonous elevated railroad tracks. I could not expect Teddy to squire me. His scruples, and the disdain he had in common with most of his race for promiscuous unchastity, made him a model of propriety outside our circle of two.

The same considerations—the elevated and my husband's squeamishness—kept me from touring the Bowery, whose saloons and dives were so notorious that we had heard of them back in Chicago. I was equally inquisitive about them, though the only evidence of public sinning I had actually witnessed was provided by the ladies of pleasure who, fashionably garbed and carrying telltale parasols, paraded Broadway from Canal Street to 23rd, eying the males. These "night chippies," as they were called in the theater, usually loitered outside the lobbies at exit time without interference from the police, who, it was understood, did not go unrewarded for their tolerance.

But their indulgence had been interrupted by an outcry raised in the churches after one bishop pointed out that "there are more prostitutes than Methodists in New York." A total of seventy-four madams had recently been carried off by paddy wagon, and the Casino girls were much sought after in accordance with the law of supply and demand.

A peek through the spyhole in the curtain before it was cranked up on *Polly*'s opening night disclosed a dwarf of a man with an enormous, bald, pear-shaped head seated on the center aisle in the front row beside an imposing brunette. He was such an oddity that I turned to my tenor to inquire about him. "That's little Abe Hummel, the lawyer." The name rang a bell so clear that it momentarily left my knees trembling. Howe & Hummel, attorneys at law, 89 Center Street, had been retained by one thwarted impresario at the time of my flight to Jersey City.

The tenor's whisper dispelled fear that I was in for fresh harassment. "Little Abe draws the line between business and pleasure. Howe and Hummel are defending all the brothel keepers the cops took in, but he's here to enjoy himself, not to slap a writ on you. If he likes your singing, he'll get up and dance. I've watched him do that before."

I heartened myself with another peep. His head looked like Humpty Dumpty's, adorned with a masher's mustache. Farther along in the same row I saw another grotesque. Fat men had been in fashion since Grover Cleveland was elected last fall, weighing in, the papers said, at two hundred and fifty pounds. The leviathan I spotted, who overflowed onto the seat on either side of him, must have bested the President by forty pounds. The smile on his jowls gave him the appearance of a cheerful bloodhound, but even more astonishing than his tonnage was the glitter from the dozens of diamonds that encrusted his shirtfront, cuffs, and fingers.

"You've no need to tell me who else is out there. It's the man they call Diamond Jim Brady, as large as life and twice as shiny."

"Seeing is believing," my tenor chirruped, and we took our places as Teddy's musicians neared the end of the overture. Abraham Hummel's shifty brown eyes drilled into me throughout the first scene. At the close of a stylish solo, he *did* desert his seat, so help me, to skip into the aisle and prance about in patent-leather toothpick shoes with what appeared to be elevated heels, calling, "Bravo! Bravo!" and ignoring cries for him to sit down.

Mr. Brady had his own method of expressing his regard. The flowers delivered to my dressing room were accompanied by a little gilded cardboard box and a card in careful, Spencerian script: "Please accept this little doodad as a mark of esteem. I hope to have the honor of meeting you soon—James Buchanan Brady." I had the unset stone which the box contained appraised by a jeweler the next morning. It proved to be a genuine small diamond that would do very well as the start of a new collection. I would buy the rest myself. I was not eager for the company of a man as gross as this, whose bulk evoked feelings of guilt when I had to admit I was not as slim as I used to be.

The formula of music by Solomon and singing by Russell increased our fame and our financial security through the summer and fall. Daughtie learned to say a few words and gurgle the first notes of what I could distinctly recognize as "Baa, Baa, Black Sheep," though Teddy swore it was pure imagination on my part.

He was engrossed in another score, featuring a heroine saddled with the unlikely appellation *Pepita, or the Girl with the Glass*

Eyes. Harry Stephens, who had rejoined us in New York for the purpose, provided the libretto, a peculiar cross between Gilbert's satirical creations and Mary Shelley's *Frankenstein.* I was the beauteous daughter of crabby Professor Pongo, who manufactured musical automatons. When his mechanical soprano breaks down, I must take her place, and then—but why continue this nonsense? I thought the music delightful and the words ridiculous, but the audience reveled in it.

One morning at breakfast Teddy opened a letter with a Queen Victoria stamp on the envelope, read it through once, twice, then crumpled it into a ball that he stuffed into his pocket. I was surprised, since we customarily let the other see all correspondence. "I'm sorry, my sweet, but I'll have to go over to London as soon as I can. There's some business about royalties that needs my attention. Someone's been cheating us."

The new Cunarder *Aurania* was sailing the following morning, and Teddy secured a suite of the staterooms advertised as "bridal chambers." I helped him pack, but he wanted to spare me the pandemonium of the piers. I saw him into a rented carriage with a parting kiss through a window, and Harry went with him to the ship. The first violin would conduct in Teddy's place at the theater until his return.

That was the last contact I had with Edward Solomon. A message from him transmitted by the Atlantic Telegraph Company reported his safe arrival. There was nothing further. He had promised to let me know where he was staying as soon as he had found a hotel, but he sent no word of that. I expected his first letter would tell me. I had reconciled myself to waiting long days before it arrived. I kept watch from a window for the mailman to enter the street and raced into the hall whenever the letter box rattled, to be crushed when there was no envelope in Teddy's scribble.

The seeds of fear for his health and safety began to sprout, but I did what I could to calm myself. Perhaps bad weather at sea was delaying deliveries, or perhaps the letter was lost somewhere along the route. I felt so utterly helpless not knowing where to reach him that there were nights when I cried myself to sleep, beset by anxiety and frustration in equal parts.

It took Harry Stephens to supply the explanation. He presented himself at East 9th Street while I was still in bed one morning. I asked Fanny Corcoran, our maid, to brew fresh coffee, slipped on a negligée, and went out to greet him.

His face was as long as Anthony Comstock's. "I had a letter today from Teddy. He wanted me to give you his love and have you read this." It was a scrap from a London newspaper. Lily Grey, "serio-comic and burlesque artist," declared that "my age being sixteen and Mr. Solomon's eighteen," she had been married to him at Bow Street registry office on March 15, 1873. "Teddy's been arrested for bigamy," Harry said, and he started to cry before he let himself out.

I walked slowly into Daughtie's room, where she lay chewing on a woolly toy sheep, ready for a nap. I picked her up, hugged her, and returned her to her crib. In the parlor, I took out a pack of cards and laid them out without faltering in a drawn-out game of patience. The irony of it was too much for tears. I felt no anxiety for Daughtie. I could provide for her. I supposed that one bigamist deserved another, which was a thought so wry that I came close to a smile. But why had he not told me about Lily Grey? It would have made no difference to us. Men were so impostrous that I wondered whether I could bring myself to trust any one of them again.

What I should do was to pay a call on Abe Hummel this very afternoon.

$\sim$ VII $\sim$

$\mathcal{A}$ SIGN thirty feet long and surrounded by electric light bulbs identified the premises as "Howe & Hummel's Law Office," and this intelligence was repeated on the plate-glass windows of what evidently had once been some kind of store. They occupied the ground floor of a red-brick edifice on the corner of Leonard Street, an ideal location for them, standing directly across from the Tombs, from which they had to extricate a large proportion of their clientele from time to time.

I had some notion of what to expect as a devoted reader of James Gordon Bennett's *Herald*, which related in great detail the cases involving Howe & Hummel.

It was presumably the need for dependable legal counsel that prompted the *Herald* to picture Mr. William F. Howe and Mr. Abraham Hummel in the most glowing terms as defenders of the downtrodden, including Edwin Booth, John Drew, Nat Goodwin in his matrimonial adventures, and Ada Rehan, as well as less illustrious patrons such as Mother Mandelbaum, queen of fences, Abe Greenthal's Sheeny Mob, Steve Brodie, the Bowery's aquatic saloonkeeper, and the Valentine Gang of forgers.

Since I had not waited to make an appointment, I was distressed to discover as I alighted from the cab that a half-dozen carriages lined the curb outside 89 Center Street. Nevertheless, deciding to take my chances, I pushed through the door into a dismally shabby reception room that opened straight off the sidewalk. A wizened clerk in a suit so old it gleamed like a starling's plumage was opening a wall safe, which so far as I could ascertain contained nothing more confidential than a coal scuttle. After he had carried this over to refuel the iron stove at one end of the chamber, I gave him my name and asked for Mr. Hummel, then followed his instruction to take a seat.

I lowered myself with caution onto one of the splintered pine benches that lined the walls, comprising the only furniture, and discreetly inspected the score or so of fellow supplicants. I gave a gracious nod across the room to an actor I recognized under a well-mangled fedora as having appeared with me in *The Snake Charmer*. The florid-faced stalwart clad in expensive serge next to him could be only a banker or Wall Street double-dealer. The extreme emaciation and yellowed cheeks of his neighbor spoke of addiction to the opium houses of Mott Street. There was one plug-ugly whom I judged to be as familiar with a bludgeon as Charles Dickens' Bill Sykes and another whose finger rings and paunch denoted either a bookmaker or a Tammany heeler. The solitary other female was dressed with such artistry, from the aigret feathers in her hat to the rhinestones on her shoe buckles, that she could have been the French Madam in person. I kept a tight hold on both my purse and my emotions.

Further speculation about the nature of the company was punctuated by the entry of a man of impressive girth with a head as shaggy as a bison's and walrus mustaches, dazzling to the eye in the number of diamonds he sported, which were surely the equal of Jim Brady's. My suspected drug addict rose to his shaking feet to have a word with him. "Mr. Howe, sir, if you could spare me a moment—"

"You'll have to see my little Abe" was the only response he was given before the senior partner disappeared through an inner door, trailed by an aroma of bourbon whiskey and the ancient clerk.

I was settling down to kill more time when the old retainer reappeared to announce that Mr. Hummel was awaiting me. The glowering of the audience compelled me to proclaim as grandly as possible, "I have an appointment," before moving on into Little Abe's sanctum.

The office was almost as austere as the reception room, though here coals in a brazier in the fireplace supplied the heat and the wall beyond him was plastered with inscribed photographs of actresses.

"Howe and Hummel never keep beauty languishing. Let me guess the reason for your call. You have come to see me about Mr. Solomon."

I expressed astonishment at the accuracy of his surmise. "We have our sources in London, Paris, New York—everywhere, in fact, where there are, shall we say, gleanings? I could not begin to tell you how many young ladies we have helped because we were instantly aware that they had been seduced under promise of marriage, suborned, or wronged in some equally actionable fashion." He flicked invisible motes of dust from the sleeves of his immaculate black suit.

"Members of your profession—or is it a calling?—have also spoken of you. Mr. Pastor is an old acquaintance of ours. Do you see this?" He toyed with a gem-studded matchbox bearing a death's-head with diamond chips for eyes that was attached to his watch chain. "Made of virgin gold dug from the Colorado mines by Mr. Pastor in a forgotten chapter of his career. What are your wishes regarding Mr. Solomon? Have the whole thing over and done with?"

I fumbled to find the right beginning, but no long exposition was necessary. "I came to you for advice on that. You see, there are certain complications."

"Namely, status vis-à-vis Braham at time of marriage to Solomon? You may spare us the painful details, dear lady. They are no secret to us. I observe no weeping. Am I to take that to signify courage, or is it determination?"

"Both—or neither. I don't know. I am confused just now. Resignation is probably what I really feel."

"As a bachelor, I am upset by tears, but I hope they would be on tap if Howe were to put you on the stand. Hee! hee! You know the motto of our clients—'Millions for defense, but not a penny for tribute.' Are you in want of money?"

"Not from him. He has none to speak of, anyway."

"We should be able to wring out of him whatever he has if you want it. No more than an affidavit, perhaps, redeemable on payment of five, ten, fifteen thousand dollars or equivalent in pounds sterling. Concealment of preexisting matrimony with

Grey. *Ergo*, Russell deceived into form of marriage constituting unwitting criminal conversation. Fascinating case."

"What is 'criminal conversation,' Mr. Hummel?"

"In common parlance, adultery. But he's already charged with bigamy. I shall have to ask Howe whether he knows what English law prescribes as the penalty, though it would be better to know the judge. It always is." This time, he tapped his teeth instead of his cheek.

"If I did want a divorce, would there be difficulties?"

"Difficulties? None at all. Very easy in Indiana or Illinois, assuming you have a spouse to dispose of. An annulment might serve you better. Are you in a hurry to find a new husband?"

I shook my head. "Twice bitten, forever shy, Mr. Hummel."

"Very good. Witty as well as pretty. But beauty, you know, has a habit of fading, which cash at five percent avoids. What about support for your child?"

"I can take care of her. I don't want her name dragged up in another scandal. I shall go on working, naturally."

"I see, I see." He fished a long Cuban cigar out of the humidor that stood on his desk beside a wooden plaque with the legend "We reckon hours and minutes to be dollars and cents." He applied a match from his gold box and puffed smoke toward the grimy ceiling.

"You ask for advice. Here is it, free, *gratis*, and for nothing, but don't tell all your friends you found Abe charitable today. There may be other times when you can pay a bill. I advise you to forget about *Pepita*, drop out of sight for a while, then find some engagement away from New York until the Solomon business has blown over. Stay away from lawyers except Howe and Hummel. No annulment, no proceedings whatever at present. In other words, you could still be a married woman in most everybody's opinion. That can keep you out of trouble from other sons of bitches. If you need a man to take you around, choose one who'll give and go on giving without asking much as a reward."

I should need time to mull over his proposals, but at first hearing their rationality was impressive. "Have you anyone in mind as a protector for me?" I placed a mental bet at short odds that he would offer himself.

"Jim Brady. I surprised you, didn't I? Tee! hee! Now you must excuse me, dear lady. My partner will be over in Pontin's back room on Franklin Street with a bottle of fizz on the table, waiting to see what the day has brought us." I received a squeeze on the forearm and a parting word of counsel. "Watch out for pickpockets as you leave." He was still chuckling as his door closed behind me.

I put the first of his recommendations into practice that evening by sending off a note to the theater, pleading indisposition; my understudy could play my role. If any tangle developed with the management, I had confidence in Little Abe's capacity for unraveling it. I suspected that he had already been busy when the maid brought in an envelope, hand-delivered while I was breakfasting in bed the following morning. I remembered the cursive writing before I read the card inside: "May I enjoy the pleasure of escorting you to supper this evening if you are feeling well enough? A telegram or telephone message to my office, 26 Cortlandt Street, would greatly oblige—Yours truly, James Buchanan Brady."

I was not ready to cope with him yet. There were too many other things to dwell upon. I had woken in the night, chilled in spite of the covers, and reached for the warmth from Teddy. The realization that he would never be there again had swept me with sudden apprehension. I had lain awake, listening to the far-off clock of Grace Church ring out one hour after another, with alarm on a stampede through my veins. What if I could not earn a living for myself and Daughtie? I had as yet little to fall back on in the way of finances and no one to turn to in disaster apart from Papa and possibly Mama. The notes I could produce in my throat were all that separated the two of us from poverty (and a memory of night town struck hard at that moment).

Our only resource must be conserved with the utmost care. Never before had I suffered fear for the loss of something I had taken as much for granted as the color of my eyes. I rose and, in the bathroom, gargled for a good ten minutes with lemon and glycerin, vowing to repeat the exercise at least twice every day.

I instructed the maid to summon a Western Union boy to

take my regrets to Mr. Brady. I would remain in seclusion until such time as a suitable part came my way to carry me from Manhattan in accordance with Little Abe's recommendation.

It seemed that I was to be permanently saddled with memorizing lines written by the Englishman I despised as much as any on the face of the earth. The brutish Gilbert and his long-suffering associate were churning out one nauseating success after another. *The Mikado, Ruddigore*—was there to be no end to their harvest? The only comfort lay in the fact that the monster had to go on yearning for a knighthood to match Sullivan's.

The irony of it was that managements considered me ideally suited for singing those tongue-torturing lyrics. I would have preferred almost anything else—other than donning tights again—to joining James C. Duff's Opera Company, preliminary to departing for the Pacific Coast to play Phyllis in *Iolanthe*, which Messieurs G. and S. had sandwiched in between *Patience* and *Princess Ida*.

But I must work, and nothing else was on offer, so I made hash of my self-respect.

Who could look after Daughtie while I was gone was a puzzle. The solution came from a most unexpected quarter. Suzanne had entered into what she thought of as the holy state of matrimony during the time I was in England. She brought Mr. Robert Westford, an amiable young draper, for my inspection soon after the news of Teddy had become common knowledge. I anticipated a somewhat cool encounter, marked by gloating on her side, yet our reunion developed otherwise. Generous impulses were emerging in my sister. Nothing would do but for her to take Daughtie in with them in the house they were buying on a mortgage in the county of Queens, an unknown wilderness so far as I was concerned, though they assured me that the air was wholesome there. "It will give Robert and me the chance to try a different kind of practicing from what you and I used to do, Nell. We plan to start a family of our own. Please let Dorothy come stay with us."

I boarded the train in Grand Central Station, content with the arrangement but in a persisting state of wonderment at the changes marriage had wrought in Suzanne, whose appearance had improved along with her disposition. But I had the looks, the kudos, and hope of riches. I should make do with those in lieu of the happiness so evident in her.

The vocal cords of the entire company benefited from the moist atmosphere of San Francisco, and we grew accustomed to nightly ovations. The nabobs plied me once again with keepsakes for my jewel box and bore me off to after-theater parties at the Cliff House or the Poodle Dog. Some of them wearied me when, as one magnum of champagne succeeded another, they harped on about the price of silver.

So far as I could gather, they were kept in constant uproar by the government's refusal to buy their silver and coin it into dollars which would be equal in value to gold. I was forever being told that they were being ruined because the Eastern bankers wanted all debts paid only in gold, not in silver or the greenbacks in use since the war. I tried to explain that I, as an example, chose to put diamonds or gold pieces away in my strongbox because their worth would not decline as that of silver had done over the past years, thanks to the enormous outpourings from the Comstock Lode. But I was not listened to. Faces flushed, fists hammered on tables, and glasses were smashed. More than once, I left a table unnoticed to return to my hotel.

After the harangues about "bimetallism" to which I had been exposed, it was like a reprieve to be back in Manhattan in time for Easter, which fell early in March that year. I bought a princely perambulator for Daughtie, as my sister and brother-in-law would bring her home on the Sunday morning, and we would all parade in our finery on Fifth Avenue.

The throngs who in later years turned out to make the day a festival of fashions were less numerous in those days, and the plutocrats who hungered after special distinction had barely started to flank the avenue north of 42nd Street with their palaces and chateaux to create a veritable millionaires' row. Jay Gould had built his mansion on a far corner of 47th Street and Collis P. Huntington, once a peddler in California, his yellow castle at 57th Street.

A healthy glow lit Daughtie's chubby cheeks as she ran into my arms. Suzanne had cut and sewn a beautiful light wool coat for her not unlike the one she had made for herself. Robert was dressed to kill with gloves, walking stick, and a gleaming silk hat. We had only compliments for each other's good taste as we set out and only one complaint to utter: The weather was unseasonably warm.

Ordinarily, the avenue was quiet and free of crowds at all hours of the day. Carriages rolling over the Belgian blocks took the householders to their offices, then their ladies to and from the shops, and finally brought the gentlemen home again. There were few males in sight—a patrolling policeman, a cab driver, deliverers of groceries, coal, and ice, and that was about it. But today the sidewalks were jammed with processions of people taking in the sunshine and first scents of spring as they strolled beneath the still-bare branches of the trees. We even spotted straw hats on some male heads and parasols shielding the pale complexions of the distaff side.

Outside the Stewart house, I pointed out the bright orange tips of early crocuses to Daughtie, who had an immediate desire to leave the buggy her uncle was pushing and be allowed over the rail to pick some for me. Now and again we were trailed for a block or so by someone who recognized me, but this was done with faultless courtesy and caused a stirring pride rather than resentment. As usual, the swarm was thickest by the ramparts of the Egyptian Reservoir, where the horse-car bells jangled on the 42nd Street crosstown line. On the crest of the massive stone walls, a rare turnout of men and boys dangled rod and line in forlorn hope of hooking a bass or trout, descendants of those with which the city's water supply had been stocked in the distant past.

Our original resolve had been to make the reservoir our terminus and turn back there, but Suzanne amended the route. "It's such a pretty day. Let's go on up and take a look at St. Patrick's Cathedral. I haven't been there since the spires went on." Those finishing touches were of such recent date that neither had I seen the effect nor, needless to say, been inside the place. Since Daughtie was all for extending our excursion, we continued our path up the avenue, alert for the stage coaches transporting the lowlier worshipers to mass and the broughams with liveried servants on the box which carried the affluent faithful.

We were standing in a press of sightseers, craning our necks to admire the chiseled tracery on the granite pinnacles, when I heard a growl in back of me. "How d'ya do, Miss Russell? It's a pleasure to see you again."

I turned around. "Why, Mr. Brady! What are you doing here?" The group of us was immediately encircled by gawkers. The diamonds were at a minimum today, confined to a single stone little bigger than a pigeon's egg on his ring finger, a saucer-sized cluster attached to a gold chain and worn like a flower on his lapel, and a third gem that sparkled in the handle of the Malacca cane on which he leaned his weight.

His voice sounded as though it issued from some hollow in the depths of his monstrous frame. "Well, I tell you. I ain't been in there on these knees. I gave up that stuff as soon as I got too old to be dragged in as an altar boy, and now I'm a real old sinner, past anybody's saving."

So there was humor in the man. I introduced him to Suzanne and Robert, and he gravely extended a massive paw to Daughtie, who looked to be having difficulty deciding whether he was as comical as a clown or awesome as an ogre. After some brief words of small talk, he squinched up his eyes—in diffidence or was it to shade them from the sunlight? "If you got nothing better to do this evening, perhaps you'd all join me for a bite of something— the little one, too, provided it ain't too late for her."

Robert quickly begged off, citing the uncertainties of a return to Queens at a belated hour. A moue of disappointment flickered across Suzanne's lips. I excluded Daughtie as being too young for excitement long past her bedtime and was about to make excuses on my own behalf when Jim Brady's wattles drooped forlornly over his bow tie. I changed my mind; I had nothing planned for the evening. "I'll come. Will you call for me at, let me think, eight?"

His mouth was so lost in the drooping cheeks that the smile was almost indiscernible. We bade him *au revoir* and headed for East 9th Street and an early meal for all of us before the West-fords departed and I tucked Daughtie away for the night.

I had not been out in New York with any man since Edward Solomon disappeared. I scented the water I bathed in, had Yvonne dress my hair, chose a demure satin gown that complimented my eyes, perfumed myself, added pearls and a ring or two, and was ready as the new ormolu-cased clock in the salon struck the hour.

He was equally punctual; the doorbell rang as the last of the chimes faded away. I hesitated to suggest that he remove his velvet-collared topcoat and come in, since I was barely acquainted with him. It was not until I had agreed that we might proceed to Delmonico's at 26th Street and he had deposited the garment with the cloakroom attendant there that he was revealed in gaudy glory akin to that I had glimpsed at the Casino.

An impeccably clad *maître de cuisine* bowed a greeting as we entered the *salle à manger*. My companion grunted, "Evening, Charlie. How's your father? We was going to eat across at the Brunswick, but I thought it was time to give you a turn." I caught the allusion. The kitchens of Lorenzo Delmonico and his son, who owned the place, competed with those of their competitors on the other side of Fifth Avenue. Legend claimed that a gourmet could starve to death on the street like a donkey confronted with two equally tempting bundles of hay, incapable of deciding which restaurant to patronize.

"Your usual aperitif, Mr. Brady?" Charles cooed after we had been conducted between ranks of pivoting heads to a table in the best part of the room, able to see all but afforded some privacy of our own by the fronds of an immense potted palm.

"You know me. Always the same—lots of orange juice, fresh squeezed. What's it going to be for you, Miss Russell?"

Orange juice could not possibly be to blame for his gargantuan bulk. "I'll have the same." At the imperious snap of Charles's fingers, an underling attired only a shade less splendidly than the master came scurrying over with a crystal pitcher brimming with the stuff, while my host buried his bulldog head in a menu of newspaper-page proportions, contained within velvet-covered board, which Charles had handed him.

Brady interrupted his devotions when our glasses had been filled. "Nothing stronger for you?"

"Never. I was carefully brought up."

Was it surprise that he showed? I could not tell. Every expression was camouflaged by fat. He raised his glass. "Here's how!"

"Here's Hummel!"

He had drained his glass at a gulp and replenished it before any waiter could reach our table. "Speaking of bringing up, you was different from me, then. I was born and raised over Dan Brady's saloon, corner of Cedar and West Street. My name was the only fancy thing I got. Dad was a Dem, and the party had just picked James Buchanan to run for President in '56." He wheezed with what I concluded was laughter. "It could have been worse. I might have been Franklin Pierce Brady, 'cept he lost out to Buchanan."

The menu enticed him again. Reminiscing was suspended until he had gone down the list from Little Neck clams to *fromages variés*, proceeding via *potage tortue verte*, whitebait, *filet de boeuf madère*, *selle d'agneau de Central Park*, and *côtelettes de ris de veau à la parisienne*, with accompanying vegetables.

I speculated that prolonged admiration for bills of fare had taught him the French for interpreting them, but I was curious about his background. Our captain-waiter had departed for the kitchen, leaving me wondering how I was to stow away this heroic order, when I pursued the subject. "How old were you when you quit school, Mr. Brady?"

"Jim to you." If he reckoned on a matching gesture, he would have to be disappointed. I was uncertain at the moment whether I wanted him as a friend. "I had enough of school and the saloon, too, when I reached eleven. Dad had been dead about four years, and Ma took up with another feller, John Lucas. He made me work as hard as my brother, who was another Dan, older than me. Sweep the floor, mop up the slops, run buckets of beer, and I don't know what else. Lucas turned the place into nothing more than a lowdown waterfront dive. We seen him slip knockout drops in sailors' suds and draw money when they was shanghaied. The one thing I liked about Lucas was the free lunch he kept on the counter. But you don't want to listen to me rattle on all night. What are you doing with yourself?"

"Duff wants me to do another season with him, but I'm not sure about that." There was no point bringing up the bone of contention between us. Mr. Duff was eager to put me into tights, which could be drafty in the backwoods as well as undignified for a woman who could hold her head above the shoals of creditors without showing her legs. Abe Hummel might have to be sicked onto him.

Two questions intrigued me equally: How had Jim Brady, an illiterate Mick whose written prose nevertheless had a touch of Lord Chesterfield, actually made his money, and would he have another gift for me tonight? As soon as each course was put on the table, he attacked it with such gusto that conversation was limited to the lulls between them when one pitcher of juice succeeded another.

"After you left school, what happened?"

"My brother Dan went first. Ran away and landed a job as bellboy at the St. James Hotel on Madison Square, a high-class place. He was thirteen. I hung on for three months, then he come to bring word there was a berth there for me, and I skipped out after him." The rumbling I detected could have been the result of amusement, his gorging himself, or an inexcusable *faux pas*. "I was a big boy even in them days. I was put to work cleaning up the bar, but the order went out to keep me away from the free lunch. Whenever I got hungry, which was all the time, I'd go down to the eel market at Catherine Slip by the Battery, where they sold 'em by the foot, to sample a few, then up to South Street for a couple of dozen oysters at a penny apiece. Ah, those was good old days, when you couldn't have been no more than a kid."

It was close to eleven when the last nibble of *fromages variés* with assorted crackers had been disposed of. The whalebone about my middle was constrictive. The outside air had grown strangely heavy and damp, and rain was falling. He sucked in a great breath as we waited for the doorman to hail us a hansom. "Smells like it did in January. I was out West on a trip, looking for railroad business. Next thing you knew, the snow was coming down thick and heavy, and two hundred people was gone. Little children, some of them, on their way from school. Damn near broke your heart."

He sat like a self-conscious schoolboy as far apart as possible in the cab, which he kept at the curb while he hurried me, without a touch of the hand, upstairs to my front door. "Don't mind if I ask you why you come out with me tonight?"

"Why did you ask me to?"

"That's an easy one. Because you're a beautiful woman, the best looker I ever seen."

"And you're a rarity yourself—you have a kind heart."

At the compliment, he shuffled as awkwardly as a dancing bear. "I brought something for you." He reached into an inner pocket and extracted a small cardboard box of a sort he had sent before.

"I won't accept it."

"Go ahead. It's well meant. No strings attached."

"I should hope not, but it's still no. You have not offended me, I think I could like you, and I hope to see you again. Now I'll say good night." He raised his silk hat with a flourish I imagined the Emperor Franz Josef could copy to advantage.

It was not any sound but the lack of it that disturbed me from sleep in the morning. I missed the rolling of wheels and the clicking of heels under my window. Even the sparrows had stilled their chirping in the trees on the street. I got up and looked out. Monday, March 12, and overnight snow had turned Manhattan white. I found Daughtie perched on the window ledge in her room with an arm of Mrs. MacDonald, my housekeeper, around her as she reached out in glee to catch the swirling flakes blown by a blustery wind.

After the usual five minutes in a cold bathtub for the sake of muscle tone, I drank a tumblerful of water as hot as I could stand in the interests of my digestion, not entirely recovered from last night's marathon. Daughtie took breakfast with me, and I had poured myself a second cup of China tea when the maid announced Mr. Brady.

He was stamping feet encased in Congress gaiters on the doormat in the hall, swaddled in a buffalo robe and bearskin cap with flaps elevated over his ears, looking twice his normal supernatural size. Against a wall, a brand-new red sled reposed. "Last one left in the store," he gasped, crimson-cheeked. "Thought your little girl might like to take a ride."

"How very kind! I'm sure she would, and so would I. What's happening outside?"

"Coming down heavy, and getting colder. Looks like we're in for a bad one. The horsecars have stopped running, and the

El ain't going to hold out much longer. Cost a sawbuck for a cab to go down and close the office and fifteen to get back."

"Then let's be off and out while we can." I hurried to put on my warmest clothes, highest boots, and thickest scarf and had Mrs. MacDonald do the same for Daughtie. The moment we stepped out into the carpet that had hidden the front steps overnight, a gust threatened to knock Daughtie off her feet. I grabbed her, and Jim, with a mumbled "Excuse me," seized my free arm in a grip so fierce it almost hurt.

At least a foot of snow must have covered the deserted street already, but the wind was so strong that it had blown patches of sidewalks bare. The air was filled with blowing flakes and crystals of ice that tingled on our faces. We could see no farther than the corner at Fifth Avenue, where two or three hardy souls, muffled up to the ears, crept or slid over drifts waist high. All we could hear was the wailing and blasting of the gale.

I felt a glow of exhilaration on my cheeks and saw the same on Daughtie's. Jim's tiny eyes were crinkled with similar pleasure, and the blanket of white accumulating on his furs made him look so much like a polar bear that I stopped to grab a handful of the stuff to pelt him with. Daughtie chose me as her target for bombardment before I lifted her onto the sled, and she set off behind Jim, who began puffing as loud as a grampus.

He called over his shoulder. "You having fun?"

I slogged on faster to overtake him and slip an arm through his. "Wonderful, glorious! Daughtie, too. She's never seen anything like this." She was encouraging him as one would a dray horse, clicking her tongue and shouting "giddy up."

"You warm enough?"

"Yes, thank you. And you?"

"Like a Turkish bath."

We pushed on to the corner, where a fresh delight awaited Daughtie. She clapped her mittens together in joy as a plow went by, drawn by a span of five horses whose breaths rose in a cloud of steam indistinguishable from the hoary showers which the angled blades sent cascading over us.

Jim tried to no effect to paw some of the layers of crystals off the two of us. "The avenue don't need clearing first. They ought to be concentrating on the firehouses. The wind's treacherous."

I had to shout to be heard. "You're an old sobersides. I think Daughtie's getting cold. We'd best go back, Jim." As we turned, we saw a tree crack in half, its tip slowly tilting under the weight of the burden on its branches. The effort of walking and hauling the sled took its toll of Jim. His chest was heaving by the time we approached the Lafayette. Over his protests, I insisted that we go inside for a while before we proceeded on the last steps of our journey.

No doorman was on duty, so we deposited the sled by the entrance before Jim sank into an armchair in the foyer, pulled off his cap, and closed his eyes. In less than a minute, he was on his feet again. "Got to see if I can reach my ma. She's home with her nurse on Lexington Avenue." I went with him as he ambled toward the telephone, regretting that as yet I had not had an instrument installed in my apartment. A succession of "Hello, Central"'s achieved nothing. "Wires must be down. Miss Russell, let's be going."

It was the moment to adjust our relationship. If we were to be friends, I would treat this bighearted mountain of a man as a brother. "No more 'Miss Russell,' please. I was christened Helen Leonard—'Nell' to you."

We shared in tugging the sled the rest of the way home. Since we had set out from there, another two inches must have been added to the sparkling quilt that was choking the city. There was no sign of letup, and the bite of the wind on the skin bespoke a temperature dipping close to zero.

I wished I had brandy to offer him after we had disposed of our wrappings and he stretched out on a sofa in the salon which his every movement set acreaking. Daughtie was popped into a hot bath, and when I returned from toweling her, he was sound asleep and snoring.

I asked Mrs. MacDonald to delay luncheon until he awoke, then apologized for the skimpiness of the juice from three oranges, which were all we had in the larder. He attempted once more to find a cab, passing cart, hack, or vehicle of any description, but the storm had cleared the street of everything. We could do no more than settle down before the fire, listening to the ice rattle against the windowpanes, and amuse ourselves with some hands of poker. I was certain I won because he allowed me to.

It was a peculiar, pleasant day. We whiled away a little time with the slides on a stereopticon. He lowered himself ponderously onto hands and knees to play bear with my enchanted daughter. He mumbled a request for me to sing "The Kerry Dance," his particular favorite. He devoured most of the leg of lamb that the housekeeper roasted, and I knew, of course, that he left the table hungry.

But humor did not desert him. "A Scotchwoman can best an Irish when it comes to cooking. Reminds me of the story they tell up in Michigan. Paddy Murphy went ice fishing, they say, and all he brought back was a fifty-pound hunk of ice. Mrs. Murphy put it on the stove and damn well drowned herself." He gurgled over his joke. "You got a nice place here, Nell, for your little girl. That's another difference between you and me. When I go home, there's nobody there but Ma and the nurse, and we don't always get along too good."

We accepted the inevitable when he returned from a look at the street and the weather: three feet deep now, still snowing, and drifts taller than he was. For lack of a spare room, he made himself as comfortable as he could on the sofa again with a pillow and two blankets. Before I retired to bed, I peeked around the salon door. I watched him fold his clothes carefully over a chair and lower himself onto the cushions in his bright red flannels.

Tuesday morning was a repetition of Monday. No milk, no mail, nothing stirring, though before the morning was over a shivering boy came along the street hawking copics of the *Morning Journal*, which I had not read before, with howls of "Special snow sheet—icicle edition—one cent." Mrs. MacDonald went down for one and brought back extra tidings she acquired from him. My favorite newspaper was not available because a thirty-foot snowbank blocked Herald Square. In uptown sections of the city, rescuers werc digging for victims buried and lost.

The *Journal* filled in some of the gaps in our information. New York was cut off from the world by a blizzard that had struck from Chesapeake Bay up to Maine. Every railroad line out of the city was blocked, and the last telegraph wire had gone down overnight. The toll of dead and tally of property damage was yet unknown, but rumor said that fifty people had been killed on the Third Avenue El when engineers, half blinded by the snow, had run two trains into each other head on. Homes and factories had burned like tinder while firemen struggled in vain to approach them by whipping their horses along deserted railroad tracks. Perhaps the most ominous words were those of the forecast: "The weather for today will be cold and stormy."

Tuesday was different in some ways. The sense of elation was gone. I worried about how long the food would last when Jim's appetite surpassed any three men's. We stayed marooned in a beleaguered city, waiting for a turn in the weather because we could do no more. He struggled to the Lafayette to attempt to call his home on Lexington Avenue, but the telephones were still out of service. Otherwise, it was more poker, more songs, more stereopticon, more peering out the windows for a glimpse of the sky that remained invisible.

It began to clear on Wednesday morning. We were reduced to toast, a few strips of bacon, and black coffee or tea for breakfast, and Mrs. MacDonald was praying that the coal wagon could get through before our supply was gone. Jim's cheeks were as bristly as a hog's—Edward Solomon's spare razor had long since been thrown out with the rest of his belongings. But our unexpected lodger decided to go down and hunt for a cab to get on his way.

"It's a funny thing, Nell, but I've enjoyed every minute of it, and I ain't going to forget."

I had an impulse to risk scraping myself against his jowls, but I overcame it. I did not want to upset the little applecart that we had put together in the past forty-eight hours. I had learned a lot about Jim and liked much of what I saw in him.

VIII

*H*E HAD SPENT four years as a bellboy at the St. James Hotel, catering to other people's pleasures. It was easy to see he had not lost the habit. I could visualize him as a moon-faced Irish lad, bulging out of his brass-buttoned uniform, hard put to lay hold of enough food to satisfy his appetite or the attention for which he was equally famished. He counted himself fortunate in escaping notice from the Children's Aid Society. "Once they nabbed you, you'd likely end up on some farm and be sweating out in the fields all day without a nickel to show for it. They said it was for the good of your soul."

At fifteen, he was taken under the wing of a patron of the St. James's bar who must have been attracted by his grin, his muscle, or both. "Mr. Toucey was with the New York Central, a dandy dresser like most of 'em in the head office there—they all wanted to look like Chauncey Depew."

Jim was enticed into a job as a baggage-smasher at Grand Central Terminal, the old building along Hudson Street. "I figured railroads was the place to make your fortune. Old Commodore Vanderbilt was the only man in the country worth more than twenty millions of dollars by the end of the war, and every day going to work I'd spit on my hands for good luck as I passed the statue of him that stood in front of the terminal, with bronze steamships and locomotives and railroad cars and anchors all over it. If he could do it, maybe I could, too."

Mr. Toucey—he always sounded like a character from the pages of Charles Dickens as Jim described him—encouraged him to study bookkeeping and penmanship in evening classes at Paine's Business College on Canal Street. (So *that* was where the Spencerian script and curlicued signature came from!) As a reward eighteen months later, Jim was appointed ticket agent at Spuyten Duyvil, a flag stop across the Harlem River from the tip of Manhattan in the barrens of the Bronx. Between trains, he added another string to his bow. Professor Edison had been a telegraph operator before he started making millions with his patents. Jim would follow his example.

"When I was up there, I done the only dishonest thing in my life. One Sunday morning, counting up Saturday's take, I found as I was ninety-five cents short, which was a lot of money for a young feller making three dollars a week. Then a Kraut steps up to the window talking double Dutch; says he wants five round-trips to some place up the Hudson where his German band is going to play the old oom-pah-pah for somebody's picnic. I charged him for round trips, but I gave him one-ways. Day after that, he comes back hopping mad, but I make out I can't understand him, so he gets tired of hollering and goes away. That night, I took what was left over from the little swindle and ate a good dinner at Smith and McNell's." My mama would have taken the deception as early proof that Jim was well equipped to become a railroading man.

Two years later, he was brought back to the head office as a clerk for Mr. Toucey and for fresh classes at Paine's. "In '77, I was making fifty a month as chief clerk and spending most of it on new clothes—stove-pipe hat, double-breasted frock coat. Now I aimed to look like Mr. Depew along with the rest of 'em. When I went down to the Bowery with a few pals on Saturday nights, some of the girls would give me the eye but I wasn't interested in them kind of women."

"How old were you then, Jim?"

"Twenty-one."

That was the year Mama brought us to New York, and I was sixteen. I had fancied him to be at least a dozen years older than I, but his size was misleading. I wondered if he had ever had a romance, but the question must wait until we knew each other better.

"Then I made the mistake of trying to do my brother Dan

a good turn for the one he done me at the St. James. I got him a clerking job in the general office, and he got to milking the petty cash. When Mr. Toucey caught him at it, Dan said he was doing it for me, to help pay the debts I'd run up, which was a pack of lies. Anyway, the outcome was we both got the bullet, though as things turned out that was the best thing Mr. Toucey could have done for me."

At the time Harry Braham and I were married, Jim started out as a salesman, again at Toucey's doing. He didn't care to chance having Jim enlist with Jay Gould and pass along Vanderbilt railroad secrets to the obnoxious little man who was angling to make another fortune by churning New York Central stock, which he was already doing with the Union Pacific.

"I would have drawn the line at working for Gould, but I didn't let on to nobody about that. I knew he was out hunting for Western Union and the New York El, too, but one night I seen him with his guards, pacing up and down the sidewalk on Fifth Avenue, coughing so hard he was spitting blood. I was pulled up kind of short at the sight of him. I asked myself whether I'd ever want to get like him, and the answer was, 'No, sir, I would not, not at any price.'

"Toucey had a friend in Charles A. Moore of Manning, Maxwell & Moore who sold equipment to railroads, including the Central. The company had just taken on a brand-new line, a portable handsaw with a blade hard enough to cut a standard steel rail. Nobody else had anything like it. You got to remember that, after iron went out of style and steel came in, if you wanted to shorten a rail, it had to be shipped back maybe a hundred miles or more to the machine shops, where they sliced 'em with a big power saw. Mr. Moore, he talked to me for an hour, took a shine to me, and I was hired—no wages, only straight commission."

No salesman worth his salt would dream of setting off on the road without a diamond ring. It was as important to him as his sample case and price list. Jim had $200 squirreled away. He spent all of it equipping himself despite the grumbling of his mother, who was running a lodging house on Washington Street for Irish girls fresh off the boats. Jim paid $90 for the one-carat ring that twinkled on the little finger of his right hand.

"I had to show my customers I was prosperous whether I was or not. Nobody buys nothing more than a Bible from a feller who looks to be on his way to the poorhouse. You might say I got bit by the diamond bug. I love 'em. I love the shine in 'em. I can't get too many. If you're going to make money, you got to look like money."

He was the right man in the right spot at the right time. Jim Hill; Collis P. Huntington; E. H. Harriman; William Henry Vanderbilt, who inherited from his father, the Commodore; Jay Gould—everybody was laying more track for a total that promised to stretch for 100,000 miles crisscrossing the country.

"Selling come easy to me. I could talk the lingo to the section bosses, roundhouse mechanics, shop foremen, front-office clerks. After work, I'd have 'em up in my hotel room, swilling booze while I stuck to root beer. Sometimes, they'd pass out cold, and I'd let 'em sleep on the floor. But I got a lot of information out of 'em and made a lot of friends, which was what Mr. Moore had told me to do for a start. Then good old Jim set his sights on the purchasing agents."

He was soon carrying the full line of the three M's catalogue—running gear, brake rigging, handcars, switch stands, undercarriages. "Hardest part of the job was making out the orders. I got writer's cramp, I'm telling you, and the commissions kept piling up untouched because I was living off the company. Anything extra I needed I could win playing faro or shooting craps in a smoking car, but I'd sooner play for diamonds than for cash, and I spent a lot of my winnings buying 'em."

"What made you do that? Didn't you have enough already?" We were sitting in my salon a few days after the March storm.

"There ain't no such thing as enough where diamonds is concerned. I'm still collecting, and I'll go on doing it. Soon as we got into a new town, the others would make off for the nearest saloon, and I'd look for the local pawnshop, asking to see the rings. Then uncle and me would do some horse trading. Whatever he said the price was, I'd offer half. If he said no, I'd walk out and go back another day. Sometimes we dickered for months, but eventually I'd get the best of most bargains. Then I'd have him take the stone out of its mount and sell the mount right back to him as old gold. Let me show you something."

He pulled out a wallet so swollen that an oversized pocket had to be tailored for it in his suit. Out of one crocodile-skin compartment tumbled a heap of faceted stones, which he spread onto a table. All were diamonds, pink, yellow, and white, flashing cold flame under the gaslight, some of them half carats, others jewels the size of his well-chewed thumbnail.

I could only gasp. "Pick 'em up, Nell. Hold 'em up and see 'em shine. Ain't they a pretty sight? Five thousand dollars' worth there in your hand, and I got dozens more at home. I'll tell you a secret. I show 'em the same way to customers if they treat me like one of your ordinary, run-of-the-mill peddlers. I learned a long time ago as how diamonds open doors for you."

"You really are Diamond Jim. Did you invent your own name to get noticed, too—like a sort of advertisement?"

"No. Markie Mayer done that. He traveled in cotton goods for H. B. Claflin; stubby little feller, crackshot at pinochle. It happened four years ago in Cincinnati. A bunch of us was getting together one Saturday afternoon in the old Burnet House, and I showed up late. 'Anybody seen Diamond Jim yet?' Markie says. They didn't know who he was talking about until another one pipes up, 'You mean Brady, the big moose who never touches a drink?' 'He's the one,' Markie says. 'Diamond Jim Brady, the pawnbrokers' curse.'"

He sorted through the pile for the largest stones, holding them up one by one between thumb and forefinger to assess their quality with a glitter that matched theirs in his deep-set blue eyes. When he was satisfied that he had found the finest, he passed it over to me. "This one's yours, Nell, a little memento for a good Samaritan. I'll get it mounted for you." It was by no means his last gift for me or his final act of kindness.

A sense of frustration drew us closer together that spring. He was ambitious for more money and a secure reputation as the best salesman alive in America, which he felt could not be achieved working for Manning, Maxwell & Moore. I was in the midst of squabbling with Jimmy Duff over being pushed into tights, and we had reached a state of deadlock. I had an additional reason for declining to wear them: My legs were becoming decidedly sturdy. He held me to my contract and had his attorneys start proceedings to bring me to heel.

Abe Hummel agreed to appear for me. Lillian Russell's photograph had been given pride of place on his wall, and his arm went around my waist whenever we met, whether in his office or at the parties he gave in his brownstone on West 73rd Street. I had every confidence in my perky little friend's expert knowledge of theatrical law, but the case had to await its turn on the court calendar. Meanwhile, I was at a loose end, unwilling to work for Duff, yet restrained from signing other contracts.

Jim and I were back in Delmonico's for another fourteen courses from oysters to a box of chocolates when he had a suggestion to offer. "What do you say to taking a trip with me for a couple of days, or longer if you like? I'd be proud to have you with me, and you might enjoy getting away."

Why not? Daughtie would be happy to visit her Aunt Suzanne again. I found doing nothing wearisome. Jim could be trusted to act as a gentleman. My virtue if not my reputation would be unimpaired, and what actress could worry unduly about her reputation? I had no objection to devoting two weeks or more if necessary to our excursion. What I had an especial fancy to see, I told him, was the actual construction of a railroad at the farthermost point of its tracks. Nothing could have pleased him more than the opportunity to introduce me—show me off? —to some of the wildest land in the West. We would go, he declared, to Montana Territory, which had been betwixt and between for four years while the Congress dawdled over admitting it as the forty-first state of the Union.

James Jerome Hill was laying rail across Montana, pushing what he would rename the Great Northern line closer and closer to his goal, which was Puget Sound, and Jim Hill was a man after Jim Brady's own heart. "Hill's Folly," as Eastern newspapers called it, was being built without government help either in loans or land grants, unlike the millions of acres handed over to the Union Pacific, Central Pacific, and Northern Pacific, the last of which had been running trains into Montana for half a decade.

"I was out there last winter, Nell, in his private car with him. It was snowing like all get out, and a crew was out there half froze, trying to dig six feet of it off the track. He got out, grabbed a shovel and sent them poor stiffs inside one after the other to thaw out over cups of hot coffee. I've done him a favor or two in my time. Maybe he'll do one for me."

While I outfitted myself with suitable clothes for the trip, which were all to be charged to him, my Jim got in touch with Jim Hill. Yes, he would be happy to make his private car available on condition that he could spend five civil minutes with Miss Russell. The five minutes developed, of course, into supper hosted by Jim Brady at the Lafayette.

With an empty socket where one eye had been, Hill struck me immediately as a honest-to-goodness frontiersman—old lion's mane of grizzled hair, gray beard, and smoldering fire in his good eye. He laid his cigar aside only to shovel in a mouthful of food or rasp out a few words of conversation.

"I don't have to tell you, ma'am, that I like Jim Brady. I liked him the first time he ever got in to call on me. I wouldn't see him for a week, but he came back every day to squat in my outer office. Finally, I went out. I said, 'What in the name of the eternal do you mean by camping out here?' Cool as a cucumber, he replied, 'I've been waiting to tell you, Mr. Hill, that you can go straight to Hades.'"

"And I could see myself being tossed out the window like that telephone I heard tell about as you once ripped clean out of its moorings. But I tell you, Nell, one hour later, I had a contract off of him for five million dollars."

"If you want to take a look at how we're pushing along in Montana, you and Jim can ride in my private car."

But his ceaseless search for more financing detained him. We had his traveling hotel, ten rooms of it, to ourselves and its staff of servants for the journey westward. The car rode smooth as glass on its set of sixteen wheels, no matter how rough the roadbed. We each had a suite of beautiful, miniature rooms to ourselves, comprising parlor, bedroom, and bath, in which the corners of each piece of polished furniture were padded as a precaution against hard braking should longhorn or Indian wander onto the rails. Electrical fans cooled the air if the sun beat on the windows; porcelain stoves warmed us when evenings grew chilly.

At first, we tended to sit together in splendor on the observation platform, watching from wicker chairs as the landscape rolled away behind us. "God, Nell, ain't it grand?" It most certainly was. After we'd drunk our fill of scenery, we stayed in the salon. *Pilgrim's Progress* kept company with *Fox's Book of Martyrs* in the bookcase. We took turns examining copperplate illustrations of Christian thrusting his sword into Apollyon and heretics being fried at the stake after Jim had looked in vain for any volume by Mark Twain, the only things I knew him to open apart from dime novels.

The chef was busy at all hours in the kitchen, and we dawdled half the day away in the dining room from breakfast—steak, chops, eggs, flapjacks, hominy, and cornbread—on through dinner, with mid-morning oysters and afternoon sandwiches to tide us over between meals. Since our pantry wall was made up of built-in iceboxes, even fresh orange juice always appeared on the menu. We consumed it by the gallon, in vain hope in my case that it would work magic and hold down the avoirdupois.

When we were not busy stretching our digestive systems, he talked to me, talked as if nobody before me had ever really listened to him, always with the look of an anxious puppy in his eyes lest he was boring me, which he never did, always crediting pure luck for taking him where he was.

"I just happened to be in the right place at the right time, with the war being over and a lot of big men outside of Dixie having money to burn building more railroads. I didn't have no family to tie me down, so I could rove around as I pleased, doing a job of selling. I told you once as it come easy to me. That wasn't strictly true at first, anyways. I was nervous as a cat mixing with people who had better brains than I'll ever have, and whenever I got nervous I started to eat, plateful of food that helped me forget what we used to have on the table when I was a kid —mostly potatoes and maybe a bit of fish on Fridays.

"My dad, God bless him, used to blame the English for all our troubles, saying he'd had to leave Ireland because everybody there was starving to death. Then things began to pick up for us when he got on the right side of Tammany Hall and opened up the saloon. But every Christmas he'd give Ma a fit when he'd raise his glass before he sliced the turkey and give a toast: 'To Queen Victoria, God damn her.'

"Funny, but I didn't take after him. I don't know as I ever

hated anybody in my life. You hate somebody, and he hates you, and I don't care for that. Respect people, I say, and they'll respect you. I never picked a fight with nobody either. I was so big in school I was afraid I might kill 'em. What I liked to do was play round ball in the evenings on West Street. I had a good eye for it, but I got to be so heavy I wasn't much of a runner.

"I don't believe I've ever envied people either. Everybody's entitled to make as much as they can and hold onto it if they want to, though Dad was always preaching, 'Share the wealth; the rich has a duty to help the poor.' I guess a bit of that did rub off on me. I can't pass a beggar on the street.

"I didn't envy men who was a cut or two above me, but I tried to copy 'em. Not the fellers who was born into money, because they look down their noses at the likes of me, but the ones who made it themselves, the hard way, like Jim Hill, who started with nothing at the age of eighteen in a place called Pig's Eye on the Mississippi River—it got to be known later as St. Paul. Then there's Carnegie. Come over from Scotland as a lad and went to work when he was thirteen as a messenger boy for some telegraph company in Pittsburgh. He had it harder than me, but he saved his money and made his millions. And what about old Cyrus McCormick, who died in '84? He was close to forty before he was selling more reapers than he could make, one hundred twenty dollars apiece, thirty bucks down and six months to pay. But Philip Armour made two million in ninety days because he guessed ahead of time when Johnny Reb would be done for, and he bought barrels of pork at eighteen dollars and sold 'em for forty."

I could not understand how he came to be so well acquainted with men who were only names to me.

"I like to read about 'em, Nell. I figure I ain't got a hope of stacking up their kind of money, but I'm doing all right, and so long as I keep pegging away and not being greedy, I won't starve. One thing I've learned from them is to be independent. You got to work with yourself in mind, not have some other feller sitting on top of you, telling you what to do."

Endless miles of scrub and pine, sprouting green wheat, empty plains and awesome gradients brought us at last by the banks of the Missouri on a graceful curve around Fort Benton, which stood perhaps a mile away. I inquired why the tracks by-passed that community.

"Jim Hill's doing. He asked 'em for a right of way free of charge last year. Town fathers said, 'Nothing doing,' so he left 'em out in the cold and the same time taught a lesson to Cascade, which'll be coming up as our next stop. They was in process of incorporating there, too, and when they seen what happened to Fort Benton, they give him a dandy piece of property scot free, spang through the middle of the town park, because *they* wasn't hankering to die of stagnation. He's done worse. Back at Way-zata, Minnesota, when they complained about the din his switching engines made all night, he tore down the station there, moved it east and called it Holdridge."

Cascade looked the way I imagined an army camp would on the eve of battle, a dust-covered confusion of horses and wagons, men and machines, boxes and packing crates. Without pulling into the depot, we were shunted onto a siding under a fluttering banner which, roped between two poles, was inscribed with a legend in straggly red: WELCOME LIL RUSEL. The sentiment appealed to me if not the spelling. The park had disappeared altogether under the maze of steel rails.

News of our impending arrival had obviously been telegraphed ahead of us. Jim was confident that visitors would be descending on us at any minute now. I rushed into a new tweed suit, which seemed tighter than when it had been fitted, Spanish leather boots, a rakish sombrero, and pearls. Jim emerged into the salon to join me, calmer and far more glorious in a spotless Prince Albert coat and stove-pipe hat, and adorned in his traveling kit of rings, studs, and cuff links.

The bass drum of an approaching band attracted me to a window. A cornet, trombone, harmonica, and two fiddles picked up the beat as the parade neared the car. It was a remarkable motley turnout of the nations, not forgetting a handful of pig-tailed Chinamen in faded blue cottons who shuffled along in a solitary group of their own. There were contingents of gaunt women, pushing baby buggies or clutching onto older children, and other females whose garish gowns marked them as soiled doves. Freckled Scotch, blond Scandinavian, and rubicund Irish faces provided an odd contrast to the black African and mahogany skins of representatives of the Mediterranean races. Bits of wood and cardboard waving aloft echoed the greeting of the banner overhead.

A certain amount of jostling at the entrance heralded the visitation of the welcoming committee, alike in their masculinity and haircuts that evidenced hasty calls at a barbershop. An elderly man with a gilt chain of office around a freshly scrubbed neck burst in first, removed his derby, and announced himself as mayor of the town. He was rudely interrupted and nudged aside by a second member of the party, an angular gentleman with military mustache and revolver strapped about his waist under a natty Norfolk jacket. His accent gave the clue to his origins.

"Hold on for a minute, Mayor; you'll have your turn later." Then: "I salute you, Miss Russell, in the name of Mr. James Jerome Hill, who has delegated me to attend to your every need. How splendid to see you! Allow me to introduce myself. I'm Chalmers, Peter Chalmers. I saw you in London in *Polly*, and marvelous you were."

I trusted the vacuous smile I gave him would conceal my disdain as a round of handshakes was concluded and I negotiated the stepstool to find firm footing on the gravel spread between the ties below. At my appearance, a ragged cheer broke out from the swarming throng, punctuated by the rattle of firearms discharged into the heavens in a burst of enthusiasm reminiscent of a Chinese New Year on Mott Street. Flinching for a moment at the thought that Geronimo and his Apaches might be on the loose again, I received a comforting touch on the shoulder from Jim, who was standing behind me.

Under a navy-blue sky speckled with pure white cloud, the breeze was so keen that I caught my breath, causing our English chaperon to clasp my arm. "It's the altitude, you know. We're thirty-three hundred feet up, according to the surveyors, but you won't be meeting them. They're a hundred miles in advance of us, staking the route and, I dare say, keeping an eye out for the confounded redskin."

On his signal, half a dozen subordinates, Hill's men to judge by their pistol belts, shoved the crowd into a semblance of order. I beamed in turn on the stationmaster, the machine-shop superintendent, the dry-goods merchant who doubled as postmaster, the undertaker, the principal saloonkeeper, and an assortment of others, all in Sunday best redolent of mothballs. A shy little girl whose blond curls struggled to escape from a dimity bonnet presented me with an armful of the rose-red blossoms that had been new to me until I had remarked on the multitudes of them flowering along the tracks that brought us in. Another cheer erupted as I stooped to kiss her and ask their name. "Bittersweet," she murmured and burst into tears.

Chalmers resumed his irritating hold to help me up into an ill-used wagonette, over whose horses' ears circled a variety of flies, green, blue, and black. "Not quite what we're used to in England, eh? But it's the best we could do, I'm afraid. We've drained every livery stable dry, renting horses and wagons to move the gear out to the front line."

Flanked by Jim and the excessively attentive Englishman, I was driven through streets where drab tents outnumbered dwellings of wood. With Jim Hill's dollars as fertilizer, Cascade, founded five years ago, was growing like the proverbial mushroom, as the land sharks' billboards testified. On one teeming thoroughfare, a black bear cub chained to a tree advertised a restaurant where meals were served *alfresco* on tin plates which appeared to be nailed to the long plank table. I perceived a shirt-sleeved waiter swabbing them off with bucket and rag.

A board outside one pavilion of flapping green fabric designated it as a hotel. I was curious to peek inside, but it took a minute or two to persuade the hifalutin Chalmers of the advisibility of doing that. He frowned even more heavily at the prospect of Jim's coming, too. "You must remember this isn't Broadway, Mr. Brady. Some of them would be at you like bees after honey to strip off those decorations of yours." However, Jim avowed he would take his chances and lumbered after us as the disgruntled agent preceded me into the tent in search of the innkeeper.

The interior was chockablock with tiers of beds, vaguely resembling a railroad sleeping car in the draw curtains on brass rods that provided a modicum of privacy. The resemblance ended there. Army blankets—no linen—had been flung at random over paillasses laid on raw lumber. Trampled earth constituted the only floor. The atmosphere was thick enough to slice, a mélange of perspiration, acrid cigar smoke, the fumes of stale beer and rotgut whiskey. Even Jim's diamonds lost most of their gleam in the sickly light filtering through the canvas overhead. Though it was late afternoon, the restless stirring of bodies and the clearing of windpipes could be heard behind some of the bunks.

I was aware of someone watching me when Chalmers reappeared to report that the boniface had evidently taken off for the nearest groggery. Then a curtain was pulled back, and a grimy ruffian with a bottle in his left hand swung himself down and staggered toward me.

"You'll do for me, darlin'. I got money to pay for you." His right hand thrust a roll of bills toward my face. "How much?" He tipped the bottle to his lips, presumably as a prelude to extending it to me.

I could be something other than a hot-house orchid at a time like this. "Bug off, you festering sore."

Jim moved next. He swept off his hat and slashed the rigid brim of it across the bridge of the creature's already battered nose. He swayed backward, stumbling over a tarnished cuspidor, spilling greenbacks and bottle onto the brick-hard ground. I considered that adequate treatment for his impudence as he sprawled there, groaning, but the liegeman of Queen Victoria thought otherwise. He strode over to kick him and apply the butt of his revolver with such force across his skull that it left the poor sot unconscious.

"That should take care of him. I shall see to it that he's locked up immediately. I do apologize, Miss Russell, but we can't take chances here, you know."

"Weren't you somewhat harsh? That really wasn't necessary."

He appeared surprised. "One can't deal kindly with scum, I regret to say. Shall we be on our way?"

I begged off. I had tasted enough of Cascade to last me for the rest of the day. But there was to be a banquet for me, Chalmers protested. Without pressing for details, I pleaded that a headache compelled me to retreat. Falling prey to typhoid did not appeal to me. Jim and I could rely on the kitchen and the chef in our hotel on wheels. We went aboard to eat as heartily as ever. We heard curiosity seekers prowling outside on foot and on horseback during the evening. Jim saw to it that all doors were secured and shades pulled before we settled down with a deck of cards.

Chalmers called at a comfortable hour the next morning to conduct us closer to the battle zone. Before our departure, Jim slipped a derringer in a coat pocket, which he believed went unnoticed, but he had no occasion to employ it. Providentially, he also had the chef make us up a generously stocked picnic basket.

Hill's agent and hirelings had cordoned off a row of benches in a work train shuttling reinforcements to the railhead to maintain the advance of several miles a day that their master clamored for. I gathered that, depending on their efforts, each would earn between $2.50 and $4.00. Once again, they were men of every age and derivation, similar only in burliness of build and shabbiness of clothing. They peered at Jim and me like hawks until the locomotive chugged into a peculiar, portable camp in whose shacks, Jim said, the labor crews bought food, items of clothing, liquor, women, and the opportunity to squander their wages at the gaming tables.

Like Barnum, Bailey & Hutchinson's circus, these emporiums were loaded onto flatcars at regular intervals and rolled on along the newly laid rails, to be set up again within easy reach of their clientele. Chalmers suggested that we sample the commissary's cuisine. Today's bill of fare, he said, would in all likelihood be the same as yesterday's and tomorrow's—deer meat, hard tack, beans, and coffee. Jim and I opened up the picnic basket and left the Englishman to his own devices.

Some miles still separated us from the spearhead of the incursion. We covered the gap by perching on little seats in front of the boiler of a pilot-engine whose every inch of steel and brass had been hosed and polished in our honor. Chalmers rode on the footplate with the engineer.

With a blast on the whistle, we were off down the track, wheels clicking with a clock's rhythm over the interspaces where fishplates joined rail to rail, sparks streaming from the smokestack behind us like a comet's tail, wind threatening to kite the hat from my head. I discovered I could peer down over the coupler and, as they flickered beneath us, attempt to count the sleepers laid at precise intervals across the graded soil. I whooped with delight at this novel mode of transport.

Jim beamed as broadly as if he had invented railroading overnight. We rattled past a water tower with a wave to the men who were painting it and chugged over a trestle bridge with a glimpse of the coulee below. "Having a good time, Nell?"

"It's a wonderful way to travel. I love it." I started to sing, and he added bass harmony in a voice as deep as a well. *I've been working on the railroad, All the livelong day* ... Watching the rails converge on us, gleaming in the sunlight, I found my brain spinning. The immense trees on either side that suddenly changed into rock scored by blasting, which in turn became abrupt banks of graded earth already dotted with bittersweet— everything blurred out of focus before my eyes, and I felt imagination take wing.

It seemed that, if I let my thoughts expand, I could capture the entire land in the lens of my mind. Somewhere far behind lay one shining ocean and beyond the virgin forests ahead stretched the Pacific, which these tracks would reach one day. Across the curve of the globe in between stretched the enormous land of cities and striving, plains and prairie, riches and poverty, rivers and mountains that was America. I was an integral part of it; it was part of me. The steel I rode upon bound us together in a mysterious union, which brought me abounding joy.

The rest of the excursion was anticlimax. We climbed down off our roosts when only a few more lengths of rail remained ahead. We watched teams of sweating mortals grapple with the steel that would span the continent, transferring it from flatcars to the wagons that would carry it ever farther, using the grade for their road. The men turned to goggle at us until the ganger cursed them back to work. Jim took me to see two toilers with arms as thick as thighs operate a Manning, Maxwell & Moore saw. Then he couldn't resist leaving me alone with Chalmers, whom I promptly snubbed, to make himself known to the gang boss. I had the pleasure of hallooing to him as he levered himself up onto a handcar, seized one handle while his newfound informant grasped the other, then set off puffing and pumping along the track, diamonds sparkling, hat jammed on head, coattails flying.

The moments when I could command an exalted view of my country stayed sharp and clear in my memory. It might fade somewhat in the course of time, but surely never disappear. The mixture of squalor and arrogance I had witnessed out here meant nothing in comparison. I had much to reflect upon as we turned about to leave the frontier and commence the long journey east.

My day in court followed shortly after our return. Though he was coy about saying so, Abe had obviously applied his maxim about the benefits accruing from knowing the judge rather than the law. The gallant jurist quizzed me from the bench for only a minute or two before sustaining my objections, nullifying the contract with Duff, and dismissing the action. I clipped the anonymous verse one journal published in commemoration of the victory.

> There was a young lady named Russell
> Who wouldn't wear tights 'neath her bustle
>   Cause it gave her a cold,
>   Where cannot be told,
> And she and Jim Duff had a tussle.
>
> Then Jimmy, the young man, he sued her,
> Rather tough for a person who'd wooed her,
>   But you can't quite explain
>   The regrets in the brain
> Of a man who finds out he don't suit her.
>
> The judge was a sort of Golightly
> And treated the matter politely;
>   Made a speech against tights
>   And gave Russell her rights,
> While Jimmy went home very quietly.

I personally went home in a state of jubilation, which was further inflated before the week was out by overtures from another impresario. Dapper little Rudolph Aronson was manager of the Casino, "gilded temple of golden youth," as some journalists chose to dub it. Free-spending lads and even more charitable graybeards flocked to the temple in such numbers to ogle the girls on stage that he had little difficulty finding Wall Street backers for his productions, which in their costumes and settings were lavish to the extreme.

He had endeavored in the past to enlist me in his light-opera company, but our haggling over money had always led into a cul-de-sac, a cause of regret to me, for he was a stickler on the subject of decorum, condoning no hanky-panky with male visitors in the dressing rooms on the pattern of McCaull's tousled management.

The publicity attending my triumph in court evidently impressed Mr. Aronson. He came up with a contract promising an unprecedented $20,000 for a season as his prima donna. Experience had taught me the value of tarrying before signing. I had Abe draft an additional clause, stipulating that under no circumstances was I ever to be required to put on tights—my lower limbs were now of truly substantial measure.

Rudolph did not balk. Soon I was in rehearsal for Chassaigne's delightful operetta *Nadjy* and never in better voice. It was quite remarkable, as Jim observed, that an assured income was more soothing to the larynx than any amount of lemon and glycerin. He, too, was in a mood to celebrate. A rotund, pintsized Englishman had put him on an assured road to riches, and Jim could not wait to acquaint me with the technicalities involved.

Sampson Fox, president and principal owner of a business called the Leeds Forge Company, had come to New York from Yorkshire, England, seeking a representative to sell the railroads here a piece of equipment that bore his name. The Fox Truck, made entirely of pressed steel, promised to revolutionize the manufacture of freight cars. A truck, as Jim expounded to me, was the cradle beneath a car to which were attached the wheels and coil springs that supported it. I was chagrined to be told that in this respect the British innovation was far superior; American trucks were built of wooden beams bolted together.

"Their eyeballs are going to pop straight out of their heads when they take a gander at this new gizmo, Nell. I got a signed and sealed agreement with Fox to be his exclusive agent.

On each and every one of them trucks I sell here or in Canada, you know what commission I make? Thirty-three and a third percent, that's all!"

Tickets for my *Nadjy* opening went on the auction block, which was a custom of those days. Abe paid $200 for three, Jim $150 for a pair to accommodate himself. At the close of the first act, as the curtain rose and fell repeatedly to permit me to take my bows and throw kisses in all directions, a platoon of ushers came staggering down the aisles, weighted down by enormous baskets of flowers and floral pieces which they piled up around me until the stage looked like a botanical garden.

I rejected all invitations but Jim's that night. We glorified ourselves within the marble walls of the Hoffman House, where the portions served were as generous as the renowned free lunch on its bar. Our fellow diners—Manhattan blue bloods, Thespians, Tammany sachems, and the sporting element—rose to applaud our entry, myself in an iridescent white gown and Jim in his usual blaze of diamonds. Before the evening was over, I had one more jewel for my vault. He asked for not so much as a kiss, though he received one just the same on the end of his pudgy and impossible nose.

IX

I OUGHT TO have been far more careful about pre-
serving the paragraphs, entire columns, and—yes!—whole
pages concerning me that the newspapers and magazines printed
when I was in my prime. As it was, some well-wisher would
usually snip out the particular story and forward it to me. I'd
read it, then tuck it away in a drawer, always promising myself
that tomorrow I would start keeping a scrapbook to gloat over.
I let the published compliments accumulate until they left too
little space for my gloves, at which time I would discard them
and begin all over again.

That Irish firebrand, George Bernard Shaw, said in later
years that an artiste should remember only critical notices and
ignore the eulogies, but that was part and parcel of his absurd
radicalism. I preferred to recall the words of those reviewers who
wrote in terms of "exquisite voice... blond loveliness... superb
revelation... queenly walk... the most golden woman in the
United States." One odd sentence stuck in its entirety in my
mind: "She has again vindicated her claim to be the most conspicuous figure on the American Stage." Precisely what was the
meaning of that?

In retrospect, I believed there was a simple explanation for
my perpetually putting off the task of assembling all those
articles. The quality of the productions in which I appeared,
one after the other, did not impress me. I was caught up in comic
opera of a type in which only the soprano lead was of importance.
Practically no dramatic ability was called for, and I yearned to

sing as a prima on the stage of the new Metropolitan Opera House, which a corporation of men of the mark of Gould, Pierpont Morgan, Whitney, and one of the Vanderbilts had erected in yellow brick and terra cotta on a site bounded by Broadway, Seventh Avenue, 39th and 40th Streets. The distinguished Madame Marcella Sembrich had made her debut there in *Lucia*—what else?—and my old mentor, Dr. Damrosch, was temporarily installed as manager.

I hesitated to approach him, for I had been negligent about practicing. I consoled myself by counting my jewels, totting up my meager bank account, and dining with Jim, feeling no urgent need for more demanding male companionship. It was a source of quiet amusement for both of us to hear that gossips were calling us lovers. At first, I used to ruffle his hair and tease him in private over this. "Why, there wouldn't be room for me on your lap, you old gorilla!" But his girth and his sensitivity on the subject grew hand in hand, so I stopped joshing him.

"I ain't the loving nor yet the marrying kind, Nell," he said one day. "I wished I was. I don't much care for females as such —only for a lady like you."

"Have you ever—you know, gone with a woman?"

He nodded, glumly. "A few times and paid through the nose for it, too. I felt rotten afterward, though. I got the idea they was laughing at me."

Nadjy lasted for an impressive two hundred and fifty-six performances. Papa came from Chicago to see one of them and was the first to rise at the close of every scene to lead the applause. To the end of his days, he missed not a show of mine, the sweetheart. He was fond of quoting a line of Dr. Samuel Johnson's: "Nothing can make a town so fond of a man as a successful play." Making allowances for male bias, I agreed with the observation. Jim put the same thought in a phrase I heard time and again from him: "God, Nell, ain't it grand?"

Rudolph Aronson immediately prepared a new Casino presentation which had me hailed as "unquestionably the queen of comic opera" in spite of my scorn for the lyrics. The vivacious music of *The Brigands* was Offenbach's, the librettist none other than Gilbert. To cleanse the sour taste from my mouth, I went out most nights for after-theater supper with James Buchanan Brady.

His career was steaming along like the Vanderbilts' Empire State Express. By threatening to introduce the first Fox trucks to the Pennsylvania Railroad, he sold a hundred of the things to his old pals of the New York Central after demonstrating that they would bear twice the normal load on the run to Albany and back. Then, as anyone who knew him would have guessed, he went to the Pennsy with word of the rival's latest equipment and earned an order for enough trucks to outfit two hundred and fifty new cars that were being assembled in Pennsy shops.

Once the rest of the railroads learned what was afoot in the East, he was deluged with appeals from presidents themselves to let them in the door. "I got such awful cramps in my fingers it's a job to pick up a knife and fork, but I'm making close to fifty dollars on every blessed truck."

At the outset, he employed the same brand of salesmanship as a quack doctor peddling bottles of Kickapoo juice, warning that the rarity of his goods demanded fast action from the customers. In this instance, he was not exaggerating. The trucks were being put together not by the Leeds Forge Company but in a blacksmith's shop Jim found on a back street in Illinois' so-called "Steel City," Joliet, forty miles from Chicago. Business was so brisk that within two years the acorn had burgeoned into an oak—the Fox Solid Pressed Steel Company, with three great buildings covering some two and a half acres and presses that could turn out for $15 apiece the items for which Jim charged $120.

He was simmering one night when he called to collect me. "That damn fool Moore asked if I wanted to leave and go full time with Fox. I told him straight, 'Why in hell would I when I got every railroad in the country eating out of my hands? Don't you know I can sell 'em millions of dollars' worth of your stuff if I promise to steer some trucks their way before some other outfit gets 'em?' I'll be God-damned if I'll quit now!"

Like John Paul Jones, Jim really had not yet begun to fight. Mr. Andrew Carnegie was causing trouble for the Fox manufactory. The granity little Scotsman's enormous steel works on the Monongahela at Homestead, Pennsylvania, had such a grip on the market that prices, like marionettes on strings, jumped more or less at his command. Fox decided the time had come to look for a steel mill he could rely on. Jim figured he could arrange that if all his expenses were paid for.

He patroled the Hoffman House bar, with the lunch counter to sustain him between sittings, until he found two susceptible Wall Streeters, whom he talked into buying the moribund Carbon Steel Company of Pittsburgh on his pledge that Fox would take everything its furnaces poured. Jim underestimated Carbon Steel's capacities under new management, but nothing fazed him. He went to call on John Warne Gates, who had only recently finished setting up the American Steel & Wire Company, and signed him up to buy the surplus.

"Bet-a-Million Gates is some sharpshooter, Nellie. Started in my line of business, selling barbed wire down in Texas. Now his new company's capitalized at ninety millions of dollars. There's no place else in the world a feller can rise as fast as that." His belly jiggled with glee. "He don't know I'm paying myself a nice little commission on every ton we sell him."

Jim was advancing along the road to considerable wealth, and I was fast becoming "a voluptuous goddess—the idol of this generation" if one was to believe a proposal of marriage penned on his return to Cleveland by an unknown gentleman who claimed to be an intimate of John D. Rockefeller. The number of similar communications received in the mail both at home and at the theater was growing apace. They were all ignored.

Jim had three different expense accounts to draw on—Manning, Maxwell, Moore & Fox, and Carbon Steel—and very nearly $100,000 on deposit, he told me, in three different Manhattan banks. He would not hazard a guess at the market value of his trove of gems. "I never seen the need to add up what they cost. I buy 'em because I can afford 'em. No appraiser's ever had his fingers on 'em, and I don't mean to sell any. They're my pets."

"Are you sure every one of them is the genuine article, not an imitation?"

I had shocked him far more than if I had defamed his mother. "Well, you got to understand I know my diamonds." He unbuckled the miner's belt he had taken to wearing lately to carry his portable collection now that it had outgrown his wallet. He tipped out its contents. "Just hand me any one of 'em, large or small." I played this game charily, shunning the biggest stone, since that would in all probability pass any test, picking over the stock until I detected one with rather less shine than the rest.

"Here. How can you be certain this is real?"

"Easy." He levered himself up from the chair in which he sat and ambled to the window to write "James Buchanan Brady —1890" in large, flowing script on a pane. Every future home I had bore his mark on it, appropriately dated, in the same style.

Clothes, servants, daughter's upkeep and so on kept my bank account puny, but the safe-deposit box did not rattle so emptily as in the past, and I had an arrangement with the *National Police Gazette* by which I shared in the proceeds of that weekly sheet's promotion of its "Hall of Fame." Its publisher was another Fox —Richard Kyle—who was another of Howe & Hummel's clients. Abe introduced me to him. For ten cents a time, his readers could send in for sepia photographs of his "Hall of Fame" celebrities, a list that included Queen Victoria and President Benjamin Harrison, the little red-whiskered gnome whom Papa accused of having stolen his last year's victory over Grover Cleveland. Steve Brody and Buffalo Bill Cody were on offer, too, as were Mrs. Langtry and doughty John Lawrence Sullivan, the Boston Strong Boy, who had reigned undefeated as world heavyweight champion for the past eight years.

Abe's Mr. Fox lost no time in getting to the point. "We sell our pictures by the thousands. They hang 'em in bedrooms, hallways, barbershops, pool parlors, political clubs, you name it. You could go like hot cakes, and I'll give you a split if you cooperate."

"What am I expected to do?"

"Well, actresses come in three poses—costume, tights, or bust showing."

"What did Lillie Langtry opt for?"

"Costume."

"And which do you find sells best?"

"Tights or bust showing."

"I'll try the latter." Tights, after all, were so vulgar, and I had a bosom to be proud of.

Jim had the cash and I the fame. We pooled our resources to give New Yorkers something to talk about as we disported ourselves in the livelier parts of town from Longacre Square to The Haymarket in a show of our own producing. It was good business for both of us. The more attention I could attract, the higher my price could be raised on tomorrow's contracts. Jim's reputation as a celebrity fanned his customers' eagerness to have dealings with him. Fame was ever the spur for all breeds of horse.

Along the Rialto, gaslight was slowly flickering out, replaced by Edison's electric lighting, while the Wizard himself, by all accounts, was holed up across the Hudson in Menlo Park, wrestling with the impossible—a device for making pictures move which he called "the Kinetoscope." Some wag labeled my beloved stretch of Broadway "the Gay White Way," and the label was sticking. Jim was bent on having himself acclaimed its king and I its empress.

He had a palace earmarked for us, a lobster palace, to be sure, but that was in keeping with one of our especial gustatory pleasures. Rector's was more than a restaurant; it was a shrine for big spenders indifferent to the cost. Charles Rector used to drive horse cars on Second Avenue before he opened a seafood place in Chicago and, as Jim said, "parlayed fifteen cents' worth of oyster stew into a tankful of jack."

At Jim's urging, Rector opened up somewhat removed from the Rialto proper, between 43rd and 44th streets on Longacre Square, from which the livery stables and attendant flies that once flourished there had vanished under the northward march of progress; it would be renamed *Times* Square when that newspaper built its tower on the south side and moved out of Park Row.

Rector's long, low, dun-colored building was identified only by a green griffon, electrically lit, on its façade. Further advertisement was unnecessary when, as dusk fell and again after the theaters closed, the approaches were clogged by shining equipages and hansoms awaiting their turn to discharge passengers at the restaurant doors.

Without flattering ourselves, Jim and I took credit for helping to make Rector's an American institution. During the season, we made our entrance there at least one night a week. I would wear a hat of cartwheel dimensions and a gown of shimmering silk with a train that susurrated prettily as I moved; Jim, his ornaments that lit him up like the Milky Way, with a huge stone in his scarf glowing like a locomotive's headlight. A gypsy fiddler would meet us at the carpeted stairway and play us to our reserved table in the green-and-gold main dining room on the lower floor, the "inner circle" as it was known, from which outsiders were excluded unless the *pourboire* they had for Paul, the headwaiter, met with his satisfaction. Jim knew all about Monsieur Paul Perret. "He's got to pull down forty thousand a year in tips, and half of that every Christmas."

"But that's fifteen thousand more than the President of the United States."

A flashy wink. "You betcher."

As Paul led the way down the center aisle, under the canopy of crystal chandeliers that was reflected in the mirrored walls, conversation at the other ninety-nine tables would stop, heads veer, and cutlery remain in motionless hands. Such homage deserved a gracious bow to left and right from me and a wave of a dazzling finger from Jim. This was his domain and a source of peculiar power. A stranger in town who had cultivated Mr. Brady would not be kept dithering for admission to the inner circle if Jim slipped an advance warning to Paul. Rector's was one of Jim's best calculated investments in friendship and hard cash.

Sometimes the proprietor would sit with us while we ordered. "You're in the company of the finest twenty-five customers we've ever had, Miss Russell" was a standing jest as Jim scowled at the menu, ready to have a tablecloth-sized napkin tied about his neck before taking care of perhaps four dozen Baltimore oysters, a dozen crabs, half as many giant Maine lobsters, a three- or four-pound steak, and a tray of French pastries.

"Do you know how much orange juice you got through the last time you were here?" his protegé asked him on one notable evening. "Three gallons."

"Make it four tonight, and squeezed fresh, mind." To the accompaniment of the tzigane band's melting violins and rippling zimbolon, I did my utmost to match him in the comestibles department without always succeeding. As an attraction for other customers, we were undoubtedly worth a score of gypsy orchestras.

As the 1880s made way for the Nineties, the puffery we had contrived for ourselves in the press and by word of mouth paid off handsomely. Now I could demand a bigger income than the President's from Aronson—$35,000 a year to be exact—and he made no bones about meeting the figure or accepting Abe's "no tights" clause in the contract.

Rudolph perennially tried to outdo himself in theatrical splendor. As his next extravaganza, he revived *The Grand Duchess*, music again by Offenbach. Rudolph's intention was to enchant New York with extravagance from the moment of my entrance, furred in ermine, riding in a sleigh behind two ponies in a blizzard of white confetti, to the final curtain, which found the Duchess of Gerolstein secure in the embrace of the second tenor after assorted choruses by French men-at-arms and hairy Russian muzhiks.

Though the astronomical salary bolstered morale, it did mischief to my voice. Thinking about the flow of dollars that would soon come pouring in left my throat dry, and gargling was no help. I had been too lax. I must place myself in the care of an operatic coach.

Signora Louisa Cappiani was a sturdy daughter of Italy who boasted of having shipped in an army of relatives and was looking forward to bringing over reinforcements after Ellis Island opened at the end of the year; I wondered how many would end up among the Black Hand murderers of policemen. Emotion coursed through her like a spring torrent. If I pleased her with an exercise, she would clasp me to her ponderous breast in much the same way as I had seen women of her race prepare to cut a loaf of bread. If I faltered, she would beat her fists against the same portion of her anatomy with cries of *"Dio mio!"*

"For the Offenbach, it is necessary to be naughty and—how you say it?—*chic*. In these things, unhappily you are not too strong. But the voice is now very good and the figure—*bellissima!*"

At the first act's end on our opening night, she caused a greater stir than Abe Hummel ever had. Swathed in scarlet and with a flower in her tousled black hair, she darted out of her seat to make for the footlights, clutching an arrangement of perhaps four dozen roses, wired in place in a substantial container. "*Brava, Russell, brava!*" and, taking aim at my midsection, she let fly. Before I could get wind back into my sails, the ushers had pounced and were carting her off toward a side exit. I had to flag Jim in the front row to intervene and save her.

A day came in the course of our run—one hundred and forty-five performances before we went on tour—when I was conceded almost as much space in the newspapers as the Sherman Silver-Purchase Act that proved so useful to my Comstock Lode devotees. I was invited to sing for the President, not in the White House but from my dressing room in the Casino. The American Telephone & Telegraph Company was suddenly anxious to popularize long-distance calling. Though I was not among the quarter of a million clients across the nation who allegedly had instruments in their offices or homes, I was first choice for the demonstration.

I was given to understand that the enthusiasm I showed was not shared by the intended audience of one on the receiving end. Mr. Harrison's fervor for all forms of innovation lagged far behind his suspicions regarding them. Electric light switches were not for him; he always had a servant handle them. But he grudgingly consented to the undertaking, and early in the next week an elaborate apparatus crowned by a large metal funnel was duly installed for me—a hazard, I might say, when it came to changing costume. The event was set for a Thursday evening between the first and second acts. The orchestra filed up from the pit onto the stage, where it could be heard clearly enough through my open door. The audience was hushed into silence, the line to the capital cleared, the introduction made, and I burst into the *Sabre Song*, which resounded tinnily in the horn.

No equipment had been provided to enable me to hear the President's response, but I was happy to get a complimentary telephone for East 9th Street and a thank-you note on White House stationery, signed in a spidery scrawl "Benj Harrison." The flurry of excitement created by my debut over the wires brought further solicitation to participate in what most of us regarded as a passing fad. In the past decade, Professor Edison's "phonograph or speaking machine" had progressed from its conception as a cylinder covered with tinfoil and cranked by hand. Now a wax cylinder was turned by wound-up clockwork.

I received a message from him—over my new telephone, of course—saying that he wished to visit my apartments "to bottle up your voice." I declined. I could ascertain no valid reason why total strangers should hear me perform other than those who were prepared to buy tickets at the box office.

I played the Duchess of Gerolstein for so long I wearied of the enterprise, most particularly of the ponies, whose toilet habits were not to be depended upon. I was not sorry to be done with it.

Jim and I resumed the display of ourselves around the town. I joyfully indulged myself at the table again, having been down to half rations during the past months of performing. Rector's had lost none of its appeal in my absence, but as time went on we spread our patronage farther afield. We ate at Delmonico's, the Brunswick, and Bustanoby's new Café des Beaux Arts over on Sixth Avenue, famous for wines which the *sommelier* could not tempt us into sampling. For pre-dawn breakfast to round off the night, we went to Jack's, where neither kitchen nor bar ever closed and most of the waiters looked capable of going a round or two with their compatriot, John L. Sullivan.

Milk wagons were jangling along Sixth Avenue when we came out of Jack's one pale pink morning. A hackman I recognized as Gashouse Sam stood by on the curb by his woebegone steed. He generally liked to make an early start by bamboozling tipsy out-of-town night owls into taking an overpriced ride to see the sunrise in Central Park. He tipped his decaying top hat. "Day to you, Miss Russell, ma'am, Mr. Brady, sir. Time for some shut-eye? Welcome aboard."

Jim burped as he sank back into the scratchy horsehair upholstery. I had heard the thought before and would hear it repeated *ad nauseam* by others, but at the moment it seemed to encompass the truth. "It's a helluva good life, Nell, if you don't weaken." He began humming "Little Annie Rooney" but had dozed off by the time we reached my door.

These were prodigious times if one lived with the comforts of Manhattan on tap and had the appetite and means for enjoying them, as we did. The businessmen who constituted Mr.

Harrison's Cabinet had the good sense to take care of their own kind and therefore of the nation. Though Mr. Morgan held himself aloof from Washington, D.C., he was the busiest of them all, exerting his influence to bring harmony between rival railroad barons and dickering with Edison to gain control of the electric light industry.

Some people—Mama for one—had nothing better to do than rant about the "evils" of those institutions we had recently been taught to call "the trusts," which, she claimed, forced up the price of coal, steel rails, and I forget what else. "Bellyachers" was Jim's word for the grumblers. "All their damn fussing's not going to change a thing. They ought to get wise and appreciate that money makes money and always wants more. Nothing they can do to stop it."

Of course, the smaller men at the distant end of the scale were not overlooked. Sixty million dollars a year voted by Congress in benefits for war veterans, their widows, and orphans put plenty of cash into circulation, yet every time she visited me, Mama, the Socialist stalwart, rambled on about the "poverty-stricken farmers," the "downtrodden sons of toil," and the "poor immigrants." To my way of thinking, the "poor immigrants" were robbing native Americans of their jobs.

There was a superabundance of fresh eating places for Jim and myself to explore. The current boom in construction seemed to result in another fancy restaurant or magnificent hotel opening its doors every week. Mansions and apartment buildings were rising in such number that the entire face of the city changed season by season. Heaven alone knew what wonders to expect when New York fulfilled what we believed must be its inevitable destiny as host city to "the World's Columbian Exposition of Arts, Industries, Manufactures, and the products of the Soil, Mine, and Sea," as an Act of Congress provided for to mark the fourth centennial of Columbus' discovery of our remarkable land.

On many an evening, the path of pleasure took us to the magnificent new Madison Square Garden on the square at East 26th Street. The grimy old structure owned by Phineas T. Barnum which had once occupied the site had held no attraction for me. I was not interested in his circuses and wild animal menageries or even in General Tom Thumb. This latest building, on the other hand, offered every kind of refinement, at bargain prices, too, which was a surprise, considering how much of Morgan's money was invested in it. Fifty cents bought one blanket admission to the theater that was housed there, the music hall and the roof garden, though one paid more at the Fourth Avenue entrance to see the horse show or "Mile-a-Minute" Murphy race against Major Taylor on the banked wooden track of the six-day bicycle contests.

The roof garden was a haunt of Jim's and mine, with Saint-Gaudens' notorious statue of Diana the Huntress pirouetting in her bronze nakedness at the apex of the Spanish-style tower overhead. Her nudity did not bother me half as much as it did the professional bluenoses, who were forever howling to have her hauled down, but in my opinion she would have been better off with a little more weight on her bones, and Jim agreed.

He marveled at the changes time had wrought on the surrounding landscape. "I can remember when all this was the New York & Harlem's Union Depot—tracks all over the yards, big roundhouse just about there, engines clanging and smoking twenty-four hours a day. Then when the old Commodore built Grand Central, somebody put up a place called the Hippodrome. There was a sign on the gates when they was building it: 'Men wanted; no Irish.' I was only a kid, but that got my mickey up, and one night I wrote underneath it, 'Whoever wrote this wrote it well, for the same is wrote on the gates of hell.' The old Hippodrome was a lot of fun. You could fork out two bits and see 'em make pretend they was fighting the Battle of Gettysburg."

Once or twice, young Stanford White stopped by at our rooftop table; he was the architect who had designed the new Garden, and he had an apartment somewhere beneath Diana's groin. Jim had struck up a friendship with him somewhere along the line. Stanny was equipped with good looks and an eye for the ladies. He received no encouragement from me.

The small boy who still survived in Jim under the layers of avoirdupois could not resist Buffalo Bill's Wild West whenever it came into town. I suppressed my desire for more legitimate forms of entertainment on display in the Garden's theater. I could have watched Edward H. Sothern, leading man of Daniel Frohman's company, every night, sword in right hand, cloak flung over his left arm, as he dueled in *The Prisoner of Zenda*. Instead, I would go with Jim, holding a cambric handkerchief over my nose to spare it from the dust of the tanbark that arose in clouds as Colonel Cody astride a white bronco galloped after Indians, stagecoaches and buffalo, while rifles and revolvers kept up a drumfire fit to deafen you. I was, of course, in a minority. Every seat was invariably taken, and the air was thick with the scent of popcorn and exploded cartridges.

After another production, *Poor Jonathan*, Rudolph Aronson and I came to a parting of the ways. I knew he had a problem on his hands in that the number of seats available in the Casino made profits on his lavish productions hard to come by. But sympathy must not impede my career or stay me from approaching him in September for a salary increase even if dividends for his backers were a thing of the past and he was in trouble with Wall Street. I had been paid my $35,000 long enough. I told him I was worth an extra $10,000. He offered half of that—$750 a week.

I temporized. "Very well, then. In that case, please prepare a new contract. I will call to sign it next Thursday."

I had raised such a song and dance to Jim about staking out the claim I felt I had on Aronson that I was ashamed for not having been firmer. Somewhere in my heart, I envied Jim his knack for fattening his bankroll without working himself to death. After thinking over what I had said to Aronson, I took steps to remedy the situation.

I returned to his office on the appointed day and spoke up before he could. "I have signed already."

"I don't understand. The agreement is right here on my desk, ready for you."

"I mean I have signed with Mr. T. Henry French for twelve hundred dollars a week and a share in the receipts."

There was no meanness in Rudolph. "What am I to say but congratulations? I wish you all the success in the world." I had not divulged the complete story. Besides reigning supreme as prima of the Lillian Russell Opera Company on French's guarantees, I was to be given 15 percent of the proceeds from the sales of everything in the theater—tickets, souvenir photographs, chocolates, refreshments, sheet music, even the charges leveled for use of the cloakrooms.

Who else could have achieved this for me but Little Abe? I murmured "tee, hee, hee!" to myself all the way home. Jim had it in mind at first to commemorate my coup in usual style at Rector's, but I chose otherwise.

It was a matter of principle with him to furnish a customer with whatever he asked for apart from one of his shimmering "pets." Be it a banquet, a case of champagne, seats to a theater or prize fight, even though championship bouts had been declared illegal and his barroom comrade, John L. Sullivan, once arrested for his part in one—Jim supplied them all. (He mentioned in passing that every cent of the Boston Strong Boy's winnings went to pay for his defense in court by Howe & Hummel.)

When his visitors craved the excitement of gambling, with the sky the only limit, he took them in most instances nowadays to Frank Farrell's place, which had opened up a few steps away from the Waldorf Hotel, a recent appearance in splendor on 33rd Street. I had a fancy for illicit amusement tonight. Farrell's it had to be.

"But you don't see real ladies there, Nell. I've bumped into Jamey Bennett, young Pierre Lorillard and Willie Vanderbilt, but the women they bring in with 'em ain't in your class."

I had seen Bennett only once at a distance, coming out of his house on West 47th Street on one of his rare visits home from Paris. I could not understand how he could abide living among the French even if he was blacklisted by the upper crust after he jilted Edith May and was horse-whipped by her brother Fred to teach him better manners. Bennett's response was to call him out to duel with pistols on the Delaware–Maryland line. My favorite *Herald* was owned and edited by Jamey at arm's length by way of the American Cable Company, which he founded with John W. Mackay.

Lorillard was only a name I saw in the newspapers. Who was he? "He's a fly boy, Nell. His old man makes his millions from the family business—snuff and tobacco—and the kid spends it.

His dad's a plunger, too. Remember his horse Iroquois won the Derby over in England a few years back?"

I shook my head. "Well, that's one bunch that don't live up to what people say about rags to riches in one generation. Cigars and cigarettes—perhaps I should have got into that line of business."

"Which Vanderbilt is Willie? Is he the one who said, 'The public be damned'? I get them confused."

"Naw, that was his father. This one's the old Commodore's grandson—one of 'em, anyways; owns that Frenchified house up on Fifth Avenue. He's a sport with the girls, too."

"I think all the fine gentlemen you know at Frank Farrell's are due for a surprise. If what I hear is true, he serves a free buffet supper there every night. Why don't we try it?"

He groaned in torment. "Nellie, you'd be out of your league. Some mighty high rollers goes to Farrell's. I've known a feller win more than two hundred thousand simoleons playing two nights in a row, then lose it all back plus eighty thousand more. That kind of gamble ain't for you and me. The fellers I take in there, they use their own money, and I mostly stand by and watch 'em."

I was not going to be deterred. "Then that's just what I'll do." It rankled, to be honest, to think that he would not be flattered to have me on his arm anywhere on the face of the earth. I won. In all my fall finery, I stepped from a rented carriage—the first of my very own was on order—onto the sidewalk outside what the cognoscenti referred to as "the House with the Bronze Door." Possibly as a cure for his dejection, Jim glowed even more brightly than usual.

Stanford White, the lady killer, had drawn the plans for remodeling and decorating the premises that housed Frank Farrell's at an outlay of half a million dollars. Stanny and Jim were drawn together by some bond as deep as a submarine cable that was difficult for me to fathom. One was born rich, the other black-Irish poor. One was a college man, the other educated in the school of hard knocks. One gleamed like patent leather; the other was as well scuffed as an old shoe. Yet they got along as famously as Mr. Lord and Mr. Taylor, and Jim never tired of telling me how his bosom friend was making over the face of New York.

The Metropolitan Club on the corner of Fifth and 60th was an example of his handiwork, designed to calm Morgan's rage after the Union Club refused membership to one of his partners. The Washington Arch was a White creation, like the Century Club, the Whitelaw Reid mansion, the new Tiffany building, the University of New York, and Pennsylvania Station. Jim relayed some of the problems Stanny was encountering in converting the William C. Whitney house on East 67th into a private museum with gates from a Roman palace and a ballroom made up of bits and pieces from some French castle. I drew my own conclusions about what he was doing to the moral standards of the city.

He was a married man with a son at Harvard and a house at No. 121 East 21st Street, but he kept his bachelor apartment under the loins of Diana the Huntress. Whatever favors Jim did for him—I suspected that girls were involved—they were repaid in full at a party there. I heard not a word about it, naturally, from the guest of honor, but one of the maidens had a sister who was friendly with a contralto in my opera company, who found the tale much too titillating to keep it to herself.

Jim and ten other specimens of manhood were invited to gorge themselves at supper. Then for dessert waiters carried in a gigantic cake from which one red ribbon dangled, to be handed to Jim, along with eleven white ones for each of the other men there. My friend's pull on his extracted some young hussy in her birthday suit who climbed onto his lap to tease him. The ten other guests complained they had been cheated until the ever-charming Stanny clapped his hands to summon eleven more creatures, all in the same state of undress and equally willing to please.

Curiosity more than anything drew me to Farrell's massive door, genuine Italian Renaissance, installed to the rear of the foyer and sturdy enough to withstand assault from raiding police axes. After passing inspection by its muscular custodian, I found myself in a room as decorous as I imagined any gentlemen's club to be. The hush was broken only by the soft clicking from the roulette wheels and the calls of the croupiers, rehearsed in what passed as French, "Fate *votre jeu!*" Haze from Havana cigars floated low over the heads of the players, clad to a man in evening dress, with tail coats predominating over dinner jackets. I was the only woman present. My self-esteem dipped a degree or two when my entry caused only a momentary flicker of interest. On sight of us, the proprietor sauntered over to offer a perfunctory handshake with a gleam of cynicism in his eyes.

Jim remained ill at ease. A nudge from him directed my attention to a squat, exceptionally built disciple of Lady Luck who was standing by one of the green-topped tables. "Big Bill Devery, chief of police. Never has to pay for a chip, but he's a sore loser. Watch him when we go in for supper. He'll eat like a hog."

The game was a novelty to me. Counting thirty-eight little compartments on each wheel, including a single and double zero, I caught on to the fact that there was a steady percentage in favor of the house, but even with Jim's muttered coaching it took a while to get the hang of the play. Meanwhile, Captain Devery's stock of blue chips was slowly melting away.

Finally, I gathered the significance of the black and red rhombuses, the *pair* and *impair*, *passe* and *manque* imprinted on the cloth, and I was ready to take the plunge. I would let Jim buy no more than a hundred dollars' worth of the little ivory disks that could ruin an incautious life every bit as effectively as opium or alcohol. I began prudently with a minimum stake on *pair*, since it struck me as appropriate for the two of us. The croupier chanted, "*Messieurs*—ah, beg your pardon, ma'am. *Messieurs et* Miss Russell, fate *votre jeu!*" Nineteen came up, to pay back my investment, doubled.

After several more ventures of the same chary nature, some fruitful, others not, I was no better off than when I started. Jim was counting the minutes to suppertime. Devery, his evening's quota lost, had left with a scowl and a curse. So far, I had experienced less excitement here than in going shopping for a set of dishes. Perhaps I had been too circumspect. I must screw up my courage and try *en plein*, placing the maximum permissible stake on only one number.

But which? The patterns of play followed by some of those clustered around the fickle wheel denoted a system. Tonight, however, everybody's wins and losses balanced each other more or less like the rise and fall of a tide. Then inspiration prompted me. Twelve hundred dollars a week would soon be arriving from Henry French. Twelve was the luckiest number in my career to date. I reached out toward the designated rectangle on the green baize cloth; twelve *en plein* could multiply my outlay a dozen times.

"*Rien ne va plus,*" the croupier droned, and the tiny ball commenced its circling. It slowed, and so did my breathing as I reached out behind me to clutch Jim's hand. I thought the wheel would spin forever before the ball that momentarily represented the entire universe stopped—at *twelve!* I subdued the desire to turn and kiss Jim, but a gasp escaped from me. The trace of a smile crossed the croupier's sallow cheeks.

I played twelve again and won again, stayed out for the next two spins (third time lucky), then reentered the game on the same number for another harvest. A uniformed servant announced the serving of supper and within an instant Jim had my arm to steer me by the quickest route to a knife and fork. Suddenly, bells began to jangle the alarm. He exploded. "God damn it to hell, that son of a bitch Devery's done it again." Gentlemen players who in the heat of the evening had discarded their coats retrieved them from the backs of their chairs. An exodus through the doorway at the back of the room got under way while the croupiers sat calmly covering the wheel and sorting chips left behind by the fleeing guests. Farrell came to stand by his bronze door, on whose outer side fists could be heard pounding.

Jim was of ideal weight to clear a path for us amid the exiting throng. "The bastard's pulled this trick before. Gets mad if he don't win, then shows off by hollering for his coppers. He knows he won't catch nobody." He had taken the precaution of scooping up my stack of chips for cashing in at a later date.

I couldn't think where we were heading. "Don't worry your pretty head. Frank bought the house next door." Upon our arrival outside, I had assumed the building to be some sort of mercantile establishment. Other fugitives faster on their feet than Jim had already pulled aside heavy velvet draperies in a further room before we got there. At the threshold of the door now revealed in one wall, a cluster of patrons shoved and pushed to gain egress.

One portly character with a chewed cigar in his rat-trap mouth and three diamonds in his shirt front was clawing his way to the front of the mob, evidently having abandoned the cards or dice that were the attraction in other rooms of Farrell's.

Jim reached out to tap him between the shoulder blades. "If it ain't Johnny Gates, keeping ahead of the competition as usual. I'd like to have you meet a good friend of mine. This here's Miss Lillian Russell."

The cigar swiveled. "That so? If you're looking to get into a poker game tomorrow morning, drop by my office. You too, Brady."

I bestowed my most seraphic smile on him without saying a word. We were holding up the line, as those in back of us did not hesitate to proclaim. *Move it on there... Cut the goddamn cackle... Who's the dish with Diamond Jim?* I kept the smile switched on.

The exit was none too wide for me, and Jim needed some shoving from the rear to squeeze through. We and our fellow escapees were in a house empty of all furniture, but a series of dim lights showed the way to the front door. Down the street, police wagons stood waiting for the fast-disappearing catch. We turned in the opposite direction toward the Waldorf, strolling along without a hint of concern despite the fact that all hats and coats had been abandoned in flight. They would be safe with Farrell, Jim declared; he would collect ours in the morning.

"You done pretty good tonight, Nell. I reckon you picked up a couple of thousand."

"That's what I figured. I guess we got out just in time."

My winnings would go toward paying for something else I wanted—a new home. I had outgrown East 9th Street. At my next address there would be such style that it would put any London mansion in the shade; no Louis Fourteenth Street junk for me. I pictured a drawing room done in pale blue to complement dark mahogany furniture, with a cozy corner where I might lounge on a divan, submerged among soft pillows. Oak would be best for the dining room, with dark-red velvet draperies. My sitting room—white and gold—would be upstairs, where I could practice in private, accompanying myself on the grand piano set by one of the windows. My boudoir should be on the same floor: a brass bedstead draped with India silk, satin ribbons on the bolster, and mirrors on every wall. The bathroom? Virginal white tiles, porcelain, and rugs, with stained-glass panes. Daughtie and guests on the third floor; servants' quarters on the fourth.

Achieving it all might run me into debt again, but surely any store would be delighted to enjoy my patronage. If I ran desperately short, I could always try my luck once more.

X

I JOINED in the fashionable migration seeking peace and quiet in what we called the West End, which meant west of Central Park and north of 59th Street. My four-story brownstone was one of a new row on West 77th Street between West End Avenue, where much more lavish residences were rising faster than on any other city thoroughfare, and Riverside Drive, a favorite spot for a spin with a horse and rig through the narrow but beautiful park laid out along the Hudson River. The West End had a distinct tone of exclusivity. The nearest station of the Ninth Avenue El was at a sanitary distance, and the cable cars on Tenth were well out of earshot.

Down to the blue lights in the bathroom window, the interior was furnished almost exactly in accordance with my ambitions. I saw no call to compromise on quality, though the final bills appalled me; the furnishers and contractors would simply have to be patient. Two more servants were engaged to make up a total staff of four, and before long I was in readiness to declare my dwelling open to guests.

Charles Rector was prevailed upon to cater the buffet for my first formal party, held not long after Grover Cleveland trounced Mr. Harrison at the polls to win office for a second term. I engaged a string trio to play at the rear of the drawing room, where a second pianoforte had been installed by the Chickering people, who sold it to me at cost and on long-term credit. I had Bridget, the house maid, roll up the two tiger-skin rugs that normally covered the parquet there in case some of my guests chose to dance. Jim helped with the tally of those to be invited. Acting as host in anybody's private house was a novel experience for him. His mother's hostility to his companions of either sex was such that he dared not take them home.

In view of my years—I was thirty-two—and my professional experience, I was surprised by the prickling of nervousness besetting me as I prepared to dress for the soirée. Calming myself with a spell of gargling, I fell into a fit of indecision over which of three new gowns to wear before settling on the silver lamé, which would go best with one particular necklace Jim had bought for me. I had little fear that any woman this evening would outshine me. The list of about four dozen in all had been restricted in the main to ladies older than I, other than one or two girls from the opera company, brought in as companions for males arriving alone.

I walked through the downstairs rooms, rearranging the flowers for the dozenth time, unlocked the dining-room cabinet —it was fashioned to resemble a keg—that contained the liquor decanters for those who wished to help themselves to something more vigorous than champagne, then found I had time to spare before Jim was due. I asked the trio to provide a background of Strauss and composed myself on the pastel-pale silk cushions in the dim light of my cozy corner. Taking a jeweled holder from the Spanish guitar that had been rather cunningly converted into a miniature storage chest, I lit up a Melachrino. I was still puffing contentedly when Bridget announced "Mr. James Buchanan Brady," and he entered in a blaze of light.

He ignored my extended hand. "I'll be damned. How long have you been making a chimney of your nose."

Airy-fairy Nell replied, "Oh, for a week or so. Can I tempt you?"

"No smokes for me, thanks. I always thought cigarettes wasn't becoming for a lady."

"You're an old prude in so many ways. Lillie Langtry smokes. Sarah Bernhardt smokes. Why shouldn't I?"

"It's going to ruin your voice, that's why."

"What nonsense! It doesn't do a bit of harm. Besides, it soothes my nerves. Try one. It won't kill you."

"You can't bet on it. I got to be careful of my health. I don't know what's come over you. You keep it up, and you're going to smell like skunk cabbage."

"I'm growing up, dear Jim. Your namesake, Mr. Duke of the American Tobacco Company, wants to put my picture on some of his trade cards—I forget the brand. That means more money, you know."

"I never would have thought you'd stoop to that, Nell." He went on muttering until the first guest arrived and I returned my holder to its hiding place. Nat Goodwin was invariably an early bird, purportedly so that he could make his pick of the pretty girls he hoped to find at a gathering like this, a number of whom he eventually married. He was equally renowned as bridegroom and male lead, but Nat, thin as a willow stick, did not appeal to me.

The rooms began to fill up nicely. Circulating through them, I found myself cornered by Bet-a-Million Gates and his ever-present cigar. "My old woman begged off. I came off second playing baccy and got home at five o'clock this morning, so she ain't speaking to me." If he anticipated organized gambling tonight, he was doomed to disappointment. But when sleet pattered against the windows, he coaxed some of my visitors into wagering with him as to which silvery drop would be the first to trickle down to the putty, so he was kept happily occupied.

The musicians had turned to *Ta-ra-ra-boom-de-ay* when Jim approached me with a distinguished old codger in tow, corseted to judge by the slimness of his middle and sporting a fluffy set of gray mutton-chop whiskers. "Miss Russell"—Jim was Lord Chesterfield in public—"I'm real pleased to present somebody we've all heard a lot of, Mr. Chauncey Depew."

The voice had the timbre of a violoncello. "And, if I may say so, I have heard much of your wonderful charm and genius, my dear, all, to your credit, of course. I trust I may add you to a long roster of friends which has included all of our Presidents, commencing with Mr. Lincoln, who was one of the most delightful of hosts."

"I am flattered, Mr. Depew."

"My friends call me Chauncey, as the Prince of Wales most graciously did—when was it?—in '60, I believe, when I had the honor of being among the deputation that escorted him from the Fifth Avenue Hotel to the ball at the Academy of Music. He had trouble squeezing his hands into his white gloves, as I recall. I was younger then, of course, only four years down from Yale and about to enter the New York bar. The Commodore, Cornelius Vanderbilt, used to drum into me, 'Railroads are the career for a young man; there is nothing in politics.' He was one of the most remarkable men our country has produced. It has been my good fortune to meet with more or less intimacy many outstanding men in every walk of life, but I think the Commodore was the most original. He was endowed with wonderful foresight, grasp of difficult situations, ability to see opportunities before others, to solve problems, to hold fast to his convictions—"

"And put you on the ladder that led up to being president of the Central." Jim was applying encouragement to his golden calf when surely none was needed to spur his talking.

"But not, alas, to the Presidency of our country, although that vista did stretch before me at the '88 convention in Chicago. Mr. Blaine was in Scotland, but he made his presence felt. I was prevailed upon to withdraw to clear the path for little Ben Harrison, who was nominated on the eighth ballot. In addition to his persuasiveness, Mr. Blaine exercised another extraordinary gift, which is said to belong only to kings: He never forgot a face or a favor. There was talk of my becoming Secretary of State, but the post went to him, as we all know. I tell myself that I might have done better than little Ben last November and kept Cleveland out of the White House."

Jim attempted to wrest a minute or two for me. "She and me took a trip west not so long ago and had a look at Jim Hill's new road out in Montana."

I was poised to tell of the effect a ride on the pilot-engine had on me, but Chauncey steamed on, unheeding. "A singular personality is our Mr. Hill. You and I, James, might describe him as a diamond in the rough, though he obviously subscribes to my view that there are greater rewards to be won in building railroads than in running them. Railroads—the arteries of travel, commerce, and trade! Growth follows the rails, our cities prosper, villages blossom into great manufacturing centers. Yet the Granger states, and especially Iowa, are hostile to railway management and railway men. They pass laws that are practically confiscatory of railway securities."

Most of this was above my head, but I tried to contribute a word or two. "I'm an Iowa girl myself, but I agree with you that—"

It was hopeless. The cello played on. "New York City, too, has not always remembered how intimately bound is its prosperity with that of the great railroad whose terminal is within its city limits. I have from time to time had to iron out certain differences with our legislators in Albany..." Chauncey Depew, I hurriedly decided, would not notice the loss of half his congregation. I slipped away to chat with less voluble guests, remembering for a moment how my swain of Brooklyn days, the unlamented Mr. Riley, had worshiped this windbag.

The evening went off to my satisfaction, on the whole. Favorable comment was passed on the appearance of my rooms, the performance of the trio, and the excellence of the repast. Succumbing to requests for a song, I obliged with a contemporary ditty, "My Sweetheart's the Man in the Moon."

When champagne corks popped and the Rector's waiters filtered among us, I accepted a goblet myself and, under Jim's disapproving gaze, took a further step in a new direction. I concluded afterward that I preferred the taste to the fizziness; I would equip myself with a gold swizzle stick I had noticed in Tiffany's for stirring out future bubbles.

One of my guests and her husband showed up belatedly, as I had expected. Mrs. Charles Armstrong, born Nellie Porter near Melbourne, Australia, had opened at the Metropolitan, which caused heartburn if I thought too long about it. After hearing Madame Melba, as she liked to be known, in what was already one of her most famous roles—*Lucia* again and more heartburn— I had appraised her voice as more liquid than mine and her face more homely. As to our respective ages, I had the advantage of a single year.

In the drawing room, she and I flung ourselves into each other's arms in the practice of our calling. I begged her to sing for us, but she claimed she could not risk it so soon after concluding a performance. Thereupon, the assembly urged me to repeat the little candied melody I had just delivered. Competitive spirit billowing within, I completed the song with a potent and effortless high C.

When the applause had died down and I had refused an encore, Mrs. Armstrong drew me aside. "Have you ever totted up how many times you hit high C?"

"Seven or eight times a performance when I am engaged."

"God's truth! How many performances a week?"

"Seven. Then I practice at home every morning. What do you say to *that*?"

"You must be off your nut. An audience doesn't value anything they get so cheap. Take my advice and give them no more than two a night. They'll think a lot more of you."

Possibly, she was right, but I was not prepared to put her recommendation to the test. It was all very well for a prima donna to talk. My career had taken a different turn. The public reckoned on Lillian Russell chirruping like a lark, parading like a queen, and retaining a string of lovers. I had to delight my following on the first two counts and conceal the actuality that under all the trappings I was Nellie Leonard from Clinton, Iowa, devoted mainly to Daughtie, Papa, the memory of my son, and Jim in that order of precedence, with some grains of affection to spare for Suzanne and my incorrigible mother. Whether I could be measured as "good" by her generation's standards, I was not prepared to ask myself, but I certainly knew the meaning of discontent, and I was peculiarly fascinated by sinfulness in others, so long as it did not impinge on my own sanctimony.

This became evident a week or so after the party. Jim and I had dined at home. We sat by my fireside, he engrossed in a work entitled *Rocky Mountain Al, or Nugget Nell, the Waif of the Range,* being the week's issue of Beadle's Dime Library, and I in Mark Twain's *A Connecticut Yankee at King Arthur's Court.* The telephone brought a call from Nat Goodwin. The gist of it was that he had become enamored of my contralto, a slip of a thing named Ruby Paxton. She was panting to savor the night life of New York. They would deem it a pleasure if Jim and I would savor it with them.

"May I ask where you plan on going?"

"Harry Hill's." I was aware of the reputation of that so-called concert saloon on Houston Street east of Broadway as a popular hangout for bibulous visitants to the city from the loftiest to the lowliest social strata. The place was known as "a reputable vile house," and the long-submerged curiosity to inspect a nest of wickedness immediately bobbed to the surface. Yes, I said; we would meet Nat and his current inamorata there within the hour.

As I might have guessed, Jim balked. "Aw, that ain't a place for you. You wouldn't like it there. It's got no class. It's a den of thieves and harlots."

I had every confidence in his ability, should the occasion arise, to sell music boxes to deaf mutes, but his negative arguments rolled off my back. "How do you know? Have you been there?"

"In the course of business, I have. Some customers of mine make a beeline for the place. Harry's got a ring staked out in one room where his lads have a go at each other."

"Do you ever run into trouble?"

"Not as I recollect. If he spots a dip or a shakedown artist doing anything on the premises 'cept have a drink or take a turn around the floor with one of his hookers, he tosses 'em out on their ears."

"Then there's no more to be said about it. We shall go, but we'd best try not to make ourselves too conspicuous if that's possible."

It was not difficult to hold sway over Jim Brady. He might fret and bluster, but not for long. He would say, "I'm willing to compromise," but it meant capitulation. I ascribed his surrenders to the fact that he had greater need of me than I of him. Despite his magnitude and physical strength, he was a comparative mollycoddle, but I was no less fond of him for that.

He paid off the cab outside a ramshackle frame house, two stories high, illuminated by a large gas lantern with red and blue panes, the most brilliant light on the block. There were two entrances to Harry Hill's. "Women gets in free, but you're going to come in with me through the gents'." Admission cost him twenty-five cents a head.

Whereas Stanny White was cultivating a taste among the rich for cupolas on their rooftops and colonnades in their halls, Mr. Hill's establishment was loyal to the disappearing era of spit and sawdust. But instead of the general murkiness I had anticipated, a row of chandeliers lit the ground floor as bright as day.

Most of one side was taken up by an extensive bar, behind which I shuddered to recognize myself in *National Police Gazette* sepia. The imbibers were as mixed a bunch as gathered in Abe Hummel's waiting room. At a guess, Harry Hill was host tonight to lawmakers and lawbreakers, pimps and panders, peddlers of drugs and vendors of votes.

A sandwich-and-oyster counter occupied much of the opposite wall. Since Nat and Ruby were not in sight, Jim shepherded me toward it. "What do you say we have a few while we're waiting?" The counterman's spotless white apron reached to his ankles. He promptly dipped into a barrel of Malbecs and shucked one open to tempt me. A squeeze of lemon rendered it perfect. We tackled a dozen apiece, and now that his equanimity was being restored, Jim punctuated his gulping with snatches of song:

> *The herring loves the open sea,*
> *The mackerel loves the wind;*
> *But the oyster loves the quiet tide*
> *For it comes of a gentle kind.*

"How about that, Nell? Got a job for me in your opera company?"

"I'll put in a good word with Barnum and Bailey. You sound like a hungry seal." He ordered two more dozen to honor the launching of a dubious new career.

The tall, poker-straight individual who sauntered up was itching to be introduced, if I were any judge. Jim moved to intercept him. "Evening, Doc. Seen anything of Nat Goodwin?"

"Why, yes. He went upstairs a few minutes ago. I don't believe I've had the pleasure—"

"Some other time." I was rapidly convoyed toward a narrow staircase leading to the second floor, where the faint strains of a polka and the beating of footwear on bare boards told of livelier entertainment to be had. Jim was muttering to himself. "He's a disgrace to the medical profession, a qualified man like him working for Harry Hill to make him look more respectable." The idea of a saloon having its own house physician tickled me, however.

The dancers were cavorting in the space between a small stage and another bar, whose customers were required to sit at wooden tables. A sign on the wall spelled out the rules of the establishment:

No loud talking

No profanity

No obscene or indecent expressions allowed

No one drunken and no one violating decency will be permitted to remain

No man can sit and allow a woman to stand

All must call for refreshments as soon as they arrive

And if a man does not dance, he must leave

Not every female in the hall seemed worthy of the chivalry specified by regulations. There must have been a hundred of them, in the arms of a behatted partner, sipping drinks by the bar, or sitting demurely against the walls, awaiting an invitation. Some cheeks still wore the flush of youth, others the war paint of the demimonde.

We found a table and abided by dictum number six by calling for two root beers, which were promptly brought by a waiter-girl in an exceedingly low-cut bodice and abbreviated skirt whose bare legs were encased to the knee in black boots. I spotted Nat and Ruby on the floor, with a minimum of distance separating them, and they came to join us as soon as the pianist stopped his thumping of the keyboard.

Ruby was aglow with her exertions. "Oh, Miss Russell, I'm having such fun!"

For a moment as I glanced at her, I felt my age and grew a mite peevish. "I wouldn't have too much fun, Ruby, if I were you, or you might end up like some of those creatures by the wall."

Jim's eyes narrowed under his hat brim. "And quite a few of them goes on from there to swallow an overdose of carbolic and finish in potter's field."

Nat's arms arose in a tragedian's despair. "Listen to them! A couple of spoilsports, and the night's still young. We'll have to cheer them up, Ruby, my love." He turned to beckon a waiter-girl. "A bottle of bubbly, darling, as quick as you can."

Just then, a thickset bull of a man with trimly parted dark

hair and a wrestler's shoulders took the floor. "Attention, ladies and gentlemen, if you please! Pray silence for the concert which is about to commence—you girls over there, quiet down! Order your refreshments now, and order them again between the acts." I surmised, correctly, that this must be Harry Hill in the flesh.

We were treated to "Down Went McGinty" by a raucous baritone, Pat-and-Mike jokes told by a red-nosed comic clad in bottle green, glimpses of the petticoats of a high-kicking sou-brette, and an abridged version of Hamlet's "To be or not to be" soliloquy delivered by a mournful down-at-heel mummer, during which time Jim stuck to root beer and I, with my swizzle stick, shared in the first and then a second bottle of what was purveyed as vintage champagne.

I had recollections later of endeavoring to teach Jim the in-tricacies of a reverse turn in the waltz and of Harry Hill walking over to inquire if I would consent to "oblige with a song." I knew he would have been too polite to press the point, but Nat, with a hiccup, leaped to his feet and proposed that the four of us unite as a quartet. After a resounding introduction from the owner, we proceeded up onto the stage and, while Nat waved his derby like the minstrel man he once had been, we warbled in harmony:

> Where did you get that hat?
> Where did you get that tile?
> Isn't it a pretty one?
> Just the latest style ...

We were too absorbed to keep an eye on our table, where I had left my gloves and foolish Ruby her purse, but not Harry Hill. The instant we were finished, to a thunderous round of applause, he shoved his way over to the head of the stairs. There he grabbed one hastily departing patron, spun him around, and flattened him with a left hook to the side of his chin. "He'll know better next time," Harry Hill murmured as he returned gloves and purse to our possession and sent over more champagne and another stein of root beer.

Sharp at midnight, in observance of an unwritten canon of

the house, we had to leave; the place was closing. Someone suggested we finish the night at Bill McGlory's Armory Hall. When Jim's jaws snapped tight and he borrowed a cudgel from Harry Hill, I tingled with the thrill of incipient danger. Even the huskiest male who entered McGlory's alone risked being dosed with knockout drops, robbed, stripped of his clothes, and committed to the gutters of Hester Street, or so it was said.

We huddled together behind fat Jim as we approached the "concert hall" through a long, black hallway. We were led by a clubfooted doorman to a balcony overlooking the dance floor, or more accurately crowded into one of the booths of the balcony, all of which could be enclosed behind curtains for private enjoyment with an accommodating companion or two from McGlory's barnyard. Below us, waiter-girls in various ranges of undress threaded through the entwined dancers whose faces without exception would have been adjudged sufficient evidence for committing them to appointments with the electric chair in Auburn prison now that hanging had been declared out of date. I noted one curiosity: We were in the heart of the ghetto, but no Jew was to be seen anywhere in the hall.

A number of the tray-bearers seemed to have strangely cropped hair under their bonnets, though cheeks and lips were carmined and eyebrows black with mascara. Jim answered my question dejectedly. "They're boys, dressed up. McGlory caters for everybody." Nat, who had eavesdropped, was on the verge of whistling for one of the youths to come up for closer inspection, but Jim restrained him.

I was grateful for that. My head was spinning from the general rankness of the atmosphere and the chatter of unknown seekers after vile excitements. Jim led me out. They were welcome to whatever folly they chose to indulge in. I had personally seen enough to last a lifetime. It could have been imagination, but I thought I saw Captain Bill Devery going in the door as we left.

I paid more attention to my morning *Herald*'s accounts of the doings of Dr. Charles H. Parkhurst after that night. Last year from the pulpit of Madison Square Presbyterian Church he had denounced the rulers and the police of our city as "a lying, perjured, rum-soaked, and libidinous lot" who "shield and patronize iniquity," making New York "a very hotbed of knavery, debauchery, and bestiality." Mama snipped out the original report of his Sunday sermon and mailed it to me with *Hear! hear!* inked across it in red. Then, with a young parishioner and a hired detective, the pastor set out to explore the dives and brothels to gather affidavits to prove his case against Tammany and the police department. What followed made more sensational reading than any work of Beadle's Dime Library. To be sure I missed none of it, Mama continued to send the articles as they were published, peppering them with her crimson comments.

The delvers into sin paid five trollops three dollars a head to perform "a dance of nature" for their edification. (*Scandalous!* scribbled Mama.) They called at the Golden Rule Pleasure Club, where the sight of simpering catamites attired similarly to McGlory's young men sent Dr. Parkhust fleeing down West 3rd Street. (*Sodom on Hudson!*) At Paresis Hall (*memorable name!*) on Fourth Avenue the investigators marked a police captain among the visitors. And when the pastor's pet Society for the Prevention of Crime sent agents to Essex Market Court to testify against bawdyhouse-keepers in the area, they had to run for their lives, chased by a hostile mob. (*The heart of man is the place the devils dwell in!*)

There was serious thinking to do about Daughtie, who would be ten this coming summer. I did not want her exposed to the moral climate of this fair city. She must not share in the mode of living I had to adopt for the sake of my profession. It would soon be time to resume my travels, and Suzanne, a mother now, could not constantly be burdened with caring for her niece. Wrenching as the decision was, I judged that the nuns could provide the best home for Daughtie. We parted from each other with tears on both sides at the Convent of the Angels in Fort Lee, New Jersey, just across the river, yet it seemed to lie at the farthest corner of the universe.

The decision had to be taken in something of a hurry. From the first day of May onward, I was to spend sixteen weeks in Chicago. New York's reputation for vice and civic corruption had disqualified it as host for the Columbian Exposition. Now the city that was still home for Papa was being transformed, one year behind schedule, into a wonderland, and I was billed as a stellar attraction, along with other marvels of American ingenuity, including Bell telephones and Cyrus McCormick reapers, George Ferris' revolving wheel and Little Egypt's rotating navel.

I could not contemplate visiting with Papa for that length of time, and the prospect of being cooped up in a hotel dismayed me. Instead, I rented a house on the South Side, which had lost its social eminence when the Potter Palmers built on the north.

When Mama was informed of my commitment, she had an indulgence to ask. "If it is not inconvenient, Nell, I should like to accompany you to Chicago. I shall try not to be in your way."

"I shall be only too happy. We might even find the opportunity to sit down together with Papa."

"It may surprise you, but that is one purpose I have in mind. Neither he nor I is getting any younger. Possibly, the years will have increased his understanding of me. However, there is something else that draws me to Packingtown."

"Which is?"

"The Woman's Building. For once, we have not been overlooked. Mrs. Potter Palmer has quite graciously intimated that I should be welcome at the dedication ceremonies. Considering the vast holdings her husband has in real estate, she is remarkably enlightened."

"I shall have a bedroom at the house ready for you, Mama."

"That will not be necessary, thank you. Mrs. Potter Palmer has offered accommodations in the Palmer House, unaccustomed as I am to hotel luxuries."

She protested at first about riding with me in a Pullman car, preferring, she said, to travel with the servants in coach seats, but she was converted after the tickets were bought. Jim was unable to leave his business affairs for the May Day opening; he would be out later. In only one respect was our journey identical with that which had carried Mama, Suzanne, and me to New York more than sixteen years ago: Mama brought along her hardworn copy of *Science and Health.*

On the evening of our arrival, April 30, Mama greeted Papa almost cordially when they both dined with me in my rented house, and she accepted a hesitant kiss from him. Time and distance had raised a barrier of shyness between them. I encouraged them to destroy it with small talk to keep them away from politics or religion, inflammatory subjects, as I remembered all too clearly from the past.

How greatly Chicago had improved since the fire, she said, and wasn't State Street supposed to be very grand these days? It was indeed, he said, and the exposition, which had cost six million dollars to build, was bound to magnify the city's stature. Gosh almighty, he had ridden most of the way here on one of the new electrical streetcars!

She was not sure, she said, that Chicago would escape the trouble that lay ahead for America. Neither Democrats nor Republicans paid attention to the needs of the farmers and the laboring classes. Was Papa aware that Mr. Eugene Debs's American Railway Union had already acquired 150,000 members?

I could foresee what was coming, but there was nothing I could do to avert it. Her tone grew shrill. "Class war is brewing in America. Ten days before your Mr. Cleveland took office, the Philadelphia and Reading Railroad went into receivership with debts of over one hundred twenty-five million dollars. Mark my words, we are going to witness mass unemployment, crueler poverty, and the stirrings of revolutions in this country before the year is out."

Papa pushed aside the melted remnants of his strawberry ice cream. "If that comes about, and I don't say it will, you can't blame Cleveland. It's the Republicans who boosted the tariffs, looted the Treasury, and spent money right and left. A billion dollars in a single session! And who got the real benefit? You know as well as I do, it was the trusts."

"I can tell you, Mr. Leonard, who gained nothing whatsoever, and that is the women and the average workingman." I stopped listening to them. They went at each other for the rest of the evening until I pleaded that I must have an early night to ensure my state of health tomorrow. I gave Papa a photograph of Daughtie in convent uniform; Mama already had its match. He said he would escort her to the Palmer House on his way home, and I was happy to see them toddle off together, bickering to the end, but perhaps the mysterious nature of affection might turn that into some kind of bond between this odd variation of Jack and Mrs. Sprat.

Fretful clouds scurried across the sky as my rented coachman drove my open carriage through the entrance gates of Jackson Park. At the edge of Lake Michigan there had risen a pristine city of white marble palaces (or were they stucco and painted wood?) replete with colonnades, tessellated pavements, gilded spires, and enchanting gardens in gorgeous bloom. In a man-made lagoon that served as a reflecting pool for a mammoth statue of the Republic, gaily hued electric launches were moored, ready to take part in the festivities for President Cleveland, who was slated to appear at eleven-fifteen to inaugurate what the program described as "four centuries of progress, enlightenment, and civilization."

A vast assemblage of people had already clicked through the turnstiles—a quarter of a million before the day was over, the newspapers reported. They wandered in a state of awe and some confusion over the bridges, up and down the maze of broad promenades between allegorical figures of stone (or perhaps plaster) and pavilions dedicated to agriculture, machinery, manu-factures, and electricity. Not an inch of space remained vacant in the concourse in front of the huge, white-and-gold domed Administration Building, where the President was to speak from a red-carpeted dais.

He had arrived earlier and was closeted out of sight within when I entered at the rear, to be led to my appointed place on the platform that stretched behind the dais. There, tier upon tier in a solid phalanx, sat the most prominent personalities of the American continent—statesmen, soldiers, scholars, and merchant princes; governors, senators, and congressmen; jurists, artists, and churchmen. Commingled with them were delegates from every nation of the earth—foreign blue bloods; grandees from far-off Asia clad in the quaint robes of the Orient: European magnificos in picturesque court costumes laden with the orders of chivalry.

And Nellie Leonard was one of the company, exultant to be a free citizen of the greatest among commonwealths!

From this elevation, the uncovered heads below us resembled an ocean of skulls. A crash of martial music from the six hundred bandsmen massed at the rear of the platform announced the beginning of the ceremonies with "The Columbian March," composed especially for this day. A hush fell over the multitude. In the throng were to be seen Egyptians, Arabs, and other exotic aliens in multicolored garments and even a sprinkling of Indians in feathers and paint. The balconies, porticos, and rooftops of the surrounding buildings were also crowded with spectators. The more venturesome among them had climbed to giddy heights and, perched on turret and parapet, they looked like pygmies no bigger than Tom Thumb. I feared for them as they abandoned all thought of safety to add their voices to the cheers for the corpulent figure who, escorted by members of his official family, made his way to a chair behind a small rostrum on which rested an electric button. The incorruptible Mr. Cleveland's girth, I concluded, owed much to his well-known fondness for beer, but for all that he was less adipose than Jim and rather handsome in a black morning coat.

The performance was mercifully concise. I could hear not a syllable spoken by anybody, a handicap shared by everyone but those immediately in front of the dais. I watched the President flap his arms as if in pantomine, then press the button to send the grand old American flag up a staff in the center of the courtyard. On either hand, the banners of Castile and Aragon unfurled in the wind; fountains spouted; whistles screamed; a flock of white doves took wing over the ornamental waters; and cannon boomed in a twenty-one-gun salute.

A cousin of Spain's Duke of Veragna (a descendent of Columbus), one Pedro Colon y Bertodano, if I had his name correctly, lost no time in attaching himself to me as the platform emptied and some seventy of us followed Mr. Cleveland and his partner, Mrs. Potter Palmer, into noontime breakfast served on the building's third floor. Formality was foreign to the scene. With few exceptions, we sat where we pleased to sip champagne and work through consommé, soft shell crabs, roast tenderloin, broiled snipe and bacon, strawberries, and coffee for those who cared for it. There were certain advantages accruing from the presence of a hearty eater in the White House. Señor Colon was kept too busy to do much more than cast melting glances in my direction.

When the meal was over, Mr. Cleveland arose to retire for a good, lazy smoke in the sanctum of a Palmer son who was president of the fair. An aide summoned me to shake hands with our country's leader in the corridor. He had just lit up a long cigar when a uniformed attendant ordered, "Put that out! No smoking allowed in this building today." Mr. Cleveland responded with democratic alacrity. "I can brave the wrath of the Tammany tiger, but of a Columbian guard, never! Now, Miss Russell, we can have our little chat."

"Sir, if you will excuse me, I promised to attend the dedication of the Woman's Building, and time is running short."

His walrus mustache curled up in amusement. "So you're one of our gracious hostess' kind, are you? It would never do for a lady to desert her cause. I'm going to take a turn around the exposition in a while. Perhaps we shall run into each other then."

Mrs. Palmer marshaled a parade of like-minded ladies to a rank of carriages, and guards jostled a right of way through the crowds for us. At our brief journey's end, we found a swarm of women fighting to gain entrance to their mecca, faces flushed with excitement, dresses torn, bonnets crushed in the melee. Our convoyers' bluff services were required again before we were squashed through the doors.

I came upon Mama standing by a curtain of palms and ferns only moments before she stepped out with the contingents making up the grand march around the auditorium. Her eyes were bright, and her gray head nodded in approval of this manifestation of our sex's advancement. "Do you know that Queen Victoria has sent over some of her own needlework, Nell?" If that impressed Mama and Mrs. Palmer, it left me no more than lukewarm.

We opened with a prayer and a recitation by an Amazonian Englishwoman and closed with a woman preacher's benediction. In between times, Mrs. Potter Palmer roused her audience to red heat. "The moment of fruition has arrived. Of all existing forms of injustice, there is none so cruel and inconsistent as is the position in which woman is placed. Urged by necessity, she has demonstrated that her powers are the same as her brother's." I felt my own temperature climb as I flourished my parasol and cheered.

With our redoubtable shepherdess and a handful of other ladies, I caught up with the Presidential party when, concluding a thirty-minute tour of the manufactures pavilion, it was heading for the electric boats.

"Get aboard, Miss Russell," called Mr. Cleveland, who was the first to step down into a launch. "Sit here in the stern by me." Then, referring to his Secretary of the Interior and his Vice President, "Come on, Hoke, and you too, Adlai. There's room for you in the bow."

"Get in with all that weight aboard?" Mr. Stevenson's eyes roved over the stern. "Guess not. I'm afraid we'd sink."

"Pshaw. Your few pounds won't make any difference. Get in!"

The water did rise perilously close to the gunnels, but we whirred pleasantly around the lagoon until Secretary Smith remarked that Mr. President should be thinking of returning to Union Station for a five-o'clock departure. He had a final question for me. "What are you going to be doing here?"

"Singing, sir, five times a day on the midway."

"Anything in particular?"

I had to smile. I guessed what the crowds' first choice would be. " 'After the Ball,' I imagine, sir."

"I shall come to hear you when I return in the summer with Mrs. Cleveland. Now I must ask you to excuse me."

I rather liked the jovial fat man whom the Republicans called "His Obstinacy," but I could never be converted into a Democrat.

XI

*I*F THE GALE warnings emanating from the East were to be believed, the ball might well be over when it had barely begun and the exposition compelled to close its gates before the month was out. I had only Mama's sermonizing about the wickedness of capitalists to thank for my escaping the consequences of the crash that was to topple Wall Street. Gambling in stocks and shares held no appeal for me. Otherwise, I should have been tempted like a host of others to take a fling with the National Cordage Company, a great favorite with speculators when it declared a 100 percent dividend and its price went to 147.

I had been appearing for four days at the Columbian Theater in the Midway Plaisance to crowds whose size compared favorably with those desiring to ride on the Ferris wheel, witness tamed Apaches attacking a simulated stockade of white sharpshooters, or sidle in to admire Little Egypt's diamond garters and undulating abdomen. Though my repertoire included arias from *La Cigale* and *Giroflé-Girofla*, I was not mistaken about the song most often called for.

After the ball is over, After the break of morn ... On May 6, National Cordage collapsed with such impact that it shook the very foundations of national prosperity. I congratulated myself on my foresight in retaining my savings in gold or diamonds and went on singing five a day without conserving a single high C.

After the dancers leaving, After the stars are gone ... The bankers and promoters were not alone in having their fingers sorely burned. Unprecedented casualties were suffered by im-

petuous innocents who had given thought only to the market's
rising, never to risk of its fall. Yet the Jackson Park turnstiles
continued to click as busily as before.

Many a heart is aching, If you could read them all... It was
odd to be swamped with requests for a number whose composer,
Charles K. Harris, was on the way to earning $100,000 from its
performances.

Many the hopes that have vanished... The cause of the
trouble the country was in appeared to be a scarcity of gold, so
far as I could comprehend the heart cries in the financial pages of
the *Daily Inter Ocean* and other local newspapers. There was
no shortage of silver money or greenbacks, but everyone like
myself who laid hold of a gold dollar tucked it away in a vault,
in a stocking, or behind a chimney. Then in June, Queen Victoria's Indian Government stopped coining silver, and the fat
was truly in the fire after this act of British perfidy. Now a silver
dollar was worth less than sixty cents in gold. A run on the banks
by creditors at home and overseas demanding only gold in payment of debts drove five hundred of those institutions to ruin,
and thousands of commercial concerns fell like so many dom-
inoes.

After the ball! Some at least of Mama's recent prognostica-
tions, which I had dismissed as absurd, were coming to pass. The
poorer classes of Chicago had probably never been better off
than during the first two or three years after the fire. Generous
aid, over and above gifts of food and clothing, provided barracks
and temporary housing for them, tools for workmen, and sewing
machines for their wives, while the city was rebuilt with amazing
rapidity. Now the new metropolis of brick and stone from which
wood was all but barred, larger and wealthier than hitherto,
showed distressing evidence of the hardships America suffered.
I found it scarcely possible to walk anywhere without being
accosted by jobless beggars and homeless tramps.

I worried over Jim's financial welfare. The railroads on which
he relied were in dire straits, with thousands of miles of track
being abandoned to weeds and weather. Every week seemed to
bring fresh failures—among them the Erie, the Santa Fe, the
Union Pacific, the Northern Pacific—until seventy in all had
gone under.

A telephone call from him revealed how unwarranted was my anxiety. "I'm coming out next week. I been scouting around all over the country, trying to rustle up orders, but business is dead as a door nail. Till Mr. Cleveland gets this muddle straightened out, Mr. Brady's going to shut up shop. I got another little doodad to bring you, by the way."

"You shouldn't do any such thing at a time like this. You ought to be looking after your money."

Over the humming wire it was easier to catch his bellow of laughter than his words. "Don't upset yourself, Nellie. The nest egg's safe and sound, and there ain't nothing wrong with the country that can't be cured. Say, did you hear about Jim Hill?"

"What's that?"

"The Great Northern reached Puget Sound, and he's got the only railroad to survive in real good shape. Only competitor west of Fargo was the Northern Pacific, and now he's got the whole pie to hisself. Nell? Can you hear me? I got another good one for you. Take a listen to this." In barroom basso, he started to boom:

> "After the ball is over,
> She takes out her little glass eye,
> Puts her false teeth on the dresser,
> Locks up the bottle of dye . . ."

I interrupted, giggling. "That's quite enough. You're going to have me in stitches every time I have to sing the silly song. But I can't wait to see you, Jim. I need protection from the wolves. Guess who joined the pack the other evening—Mr. J. P. Morgan!"

"What did that old buzzard get up to?"

"He came to my dressing room with his red nose gleaming and imagined I'd never refuse to have supper with him, but I did."

Jim and I exchanged fond *au revoirs*. I withheld from him an account of how royally I was being snubbed by those who pretended to higher social standing than I. Probably to humble me after my turn around the lagoon with the President, Mrs. Potter

Palmer made sure that I did not meet a chit of a Spanish *infanta* or a sulky Austrian archduke who arrived with their retinues at the exposition, the princess to turn up her nose at everything she saw, the princeling to beg off when it came time for luncheon at a café called Old Vienna. Mrs. Potter Palmer and her clique of Armours, Fields, Leiters, and McCormicks steadfastly declined to invite me into their homes. I suffered limited pain from their discourtesy, but I lost patience with these fine-feathered ladies with the scent of the packing house, machine oil, and dry-goods stores only recently dispelled from their dyed hair.

The snobs ganged up to embarrass me when I attended the running of the Derby in Washington Park one Saturday afternoon. I chose a suitably sportive dress with leg-o'-mutton sleeves, a diamanté stomacher, and three rows of ruffles at the hemline. I was driven straight to the clubhouse, looking forward to placing a successful bet or two with a little help from Lady Luck. I encountered hostile stares from members' wives and daughters, overshadowed completely by Miss Lillian Russell. I was better dressed and better-looking than any of them, and I had dared to apply a touch of makeup to round off the effect.

One woman in an absurd feathered hat that looked as though she had shot it before breakfast seized her insipid daughter by the hand and ran cackling to the president of the racing association who was en route to welcome me. "She is an *actress;* this is no place for her." One might have gathered that the roof was about to fall in.

I had less distasteful things to do with precious hours of leisure than create a scene. The rising sounds of discontent from the crowd that packed the grandstand and pressed against the rails made me aware that the program was being held up by these impossible females. I was bracing myself to take my leave with all the dignity I could muster when the president approached wearing a nervous smile. Would I mind very much if I were seated in a box in the grandstand?

"I shall be only too delighted to do whatever you ask. We must not keep thoroughbred mares champing at the bit, must we?"

He took my arm rather too fondly, I thought, as I swept

out, taking my time about it. The *alfresco* throng took up my name, and several gallants plucked carnations from their button-holes to toss at my feet. The first cheers grew crescendo. My brief stroll became an impromptu procession as dozens of sports fell into step with me, oohing and ahing. A smile, a stately nod, a wave of a hand were all the reward they asked. I foresaw that at any moment they would have me up on their shoulders to afford the less fortunate a better view.

Someone was hurrying into the box with a bouquet of roses when I seated myself there, leaning forward to let the sunlight catch my face, since it could withstand such illumination and the audience would appreciate it. The president marked my card for me and handled all arrangements for the bets I placed. Between every race, the box drew admirers as honey lures bears. In all, I backed four winners that afternoon and felt that I had walked off with the entire program. In the newspaper lists of those in attendance, Miss Lillian Russell outdistanced Mrs. Potter Palmer.

The fair was still young when a man who announced himself as Fred Hall called at my dressing room. He was a partner, he told me, in the publishing house of Charles L. Webster & Company, which a few years ago had distinguished itself by issuing and selling in vast quantity the memoirs of General Grant and of Pope Leo XIII. Mr. Hall brought an invitation from another partner in the firm, more illustrious than himself. Wonder of wonders, Mark Twain wished to make my acquaintance! "He say he'd rather see you in the flesh than the shade of Ulysses S. Grant in full-dress uniform or any Pope on his wedding day," Mr. Hall remarked wryly. An appointment was duly made for me to present myself at the Great Northern Hotel.

My fantasy had pictured our country's best-read author as perennially clad in cream-white suit and gambler's necktie. When I saw him, he was in bed, wearing a rumpled nightshirt, drugging himself with whiskey from a decanter on a bedside table, puffing on a black cigar between paroxysms of coughing, and talking a blue streak, hardly able to contain himself until Fred Hall had effected the introductions and left us.

"At the age of fifty-seven and doubtful of making fifty-eight,

I was smitten with curiosity to see whether you were the Venus you're purported to be. The mountain was asked to visit Mohammed because there has never been a time that I have been able to look at even the outside of a theater without a spasm of dry gripes. As for the inside, I know next to nothing about that, for I have seldom had a sight of it or ever had a desire in that regard which couldn't have been overcome by argument."

"Would you call me Venus?"

"If I wouldn't, you'll pass muster in a country in which the entire population is purblind in the matter of beauty and, exclusive of women, rotten as far as the dollar is concerned. What do you do at the fair?"

"Sing for a living."

"I fancy that even the aboriginals flock in for an eyeful and an earful. I decided, against my inclination, to make it easy for you."

"By doing what?"

He coughed so hard his white mane shook like a mop before he drew again on his cigar and resumed. "By scheming to buy and exhibit here the certified bones of Cristoforo Colombo himself, excavated from the cathedral in Seville where they were laid to rest at last. But the deal fell through, which made one more failure. I expected it, but as the bride said the next morning, I didn't suppose it would be so big."

I ignored his crudity. "May I inquire what brings you here, Mr. Twain?"

"Not *what* but *who* is the question, and the answer is my brother Orion, whom I once mistakenly regarded as a businessman, and poor little Hall, who is wholly incompetent. Orion pines to be hired as correspondent for the fair by the Keokuk *Gate City*, which is a newspaper if you can bring yourself to believe it. As for Fred, he is still cosseting the rich to invest in our moribund endeavors as publishers of mortal works of biography and backers of Paige's typesetting machine that succumbs to the blind staggers every twenty-four hours. I have tried myself to sink a hook into Carnegie and ease $100,000 out of him at five percent, but he turned around to try to hook me into a plot to entwine England, Ireland, and Canada into the American union. I couldn't borrow a penny. What he had to toss me was a crumb of advice: 'Put all your eggs into one basket and watch that basket.'"

"I always had the impression that you were—well, a millionaire. I recall an article in the New York *Herald*—"

He spat into a bedside cup. "That daily issue of unmedicated toilet paper! By February of '86 we were worth five hundred thousand dollars, 'we' being defined as the Charlie Webster Company, named for a nephew of mine who is a victim of neuralgia in the head. We should have been worth a deal more if our books had not been cut-rated by John Wanamaker, that butter-mouthed, Sunday school, slobbering sneak thief now of Philadelphia, presently of hell. Then Charlie felt the call to exercise his judgment and commercial acumen, and today the whole business would not fetch a dollar and a half. I emptied into the till twenty-four thousand which I had earned with the pen, lost my house in Hartford, and am currently a pauper." He poured himself another dose of whiskey. "There are two times in his life a man should not speculate—when he can afford it and when he can't."

I was taken aback by the bitterness of the man whose talents deserved to have been better rewarded. I reached out to render a sympathetic touch to a pale, gnarled hand. Hawkish eyes pierced mine. "I can stand considerable petting," he acknowledged. "A body forgets pretty much everything these days except his visions of the poorhouse."

The only book visible in the room was an ancient one, Mrs. Gaskell's *Cranford*, but it prompted a question designed to divert him. "Are you working with the pen at present, Mr. Twain?"

"For the first time in twenty years, I am compelled to be a full-time writer. The sawbones say one lung is permanently damaged, and with rheumatism in my north hand, every pen-stroke gives me lockjaw. I am teaching myself to use my south." He pushed back the sleeve on that side. "My biceps have the tone of an oyster wrapped in an old rag, but the spasm of virtue afflicts me. I accept my own implausible argument that sickness is a figment of an excitable imagination. I am writing or intending to, leastways. Just what evolves remains to be seen."

A glance at the tiny diamond-set watch I wore pinned to my blouse disclosed that it was close to time for another concert.

I endeavored to cheer him before I disappeared. "You sound a little like me, almost a believer in Christian Science. There's a member of my family who—"

His voice was a rasp. "I regard Christian Science as the Standard Oil of the future. When we contemplate Mrs. Eddy and what she has achieved, it is blasphemy to longer deny the Supreme Being the possession of a sense of humor. In the same way, the political and commercial morals of the United States are not merely food for laughter—they are an entire banquet."

I was careful to apply a parting pat not to his right but to his less sensitive left hand. He had some final words of sour wisdom to speed me on my way. "Remember, Miss Russell, that this is a world where you get nothing for nothing, where you pay value for everything you get and fifty percent over, and when it is gratitude you owe, you have to pay a thousand. Gratitude is a debt which usually goes on accumulating like blackmail, so I'll be done with it in this case by thanking you once and no more for coming."

When the secret was revealed years later, it was inconceivable that the manuscript this cranky, tormented old man had been working on was *Personal Recollections of Joan of Arc* and its so-called translator, "Jean François Alden," was in fact Mark Twain.

His views on gratitude pricked like a burr under a blanket. I could not rid my mind of the subject during the weeks of waiting for Jim. As I ran through the catalogue of those I felt obligated to, he stood out virtually alone. T. Henry French and my $1,200 a week from him was a thing of the past. His letter claimed that he had consistently lost money as my sponsor and gave notice that due to unforeseen circumstances arising out of the national crisis et cetera, the contract was terminated.

If only I'd had a percentage of the take at the Columbian Theater, my welfare would have been guaranteed. Never a seat was empty at any performance. The crowds in Jackson Park never thinned. The exposition management was optimistic that paid admissions would exceed the 20,000,000 mark before the gates were finally closed in October. Yet the news from Washington was invariably bad.

Mama had returned to New York, and I was not too unhappy

over that. She and Papa would probably never see eye to eye, but there was hope they would not again lose touch with each other completely.

The constant talk of crisis depressed me, and Mark Twain's broodings about the poorhouse were infectious. I began to feel frighteningly insecure. Perhaps I should look for a third husband to provide shelter in the storm. First, of course, I had to be legally rid of the second. I resolved to make that a priority as soon as I could sit down with Abe Hummel. Jim, I knew, would be crushed if I remarried, but that couldn't be helped. What was it Mark Twain had said? "Gratitude is a debt which goes on accumulating like blackmail." He was right; I had to purge myself of a sense of indebtedness to anyone.

Jim came out to spend a month in the Palmer House and a small fortune on our pleasure. I said nothing to him about my forebodings. Most evenings he sat in the front row in expectation of my company, which I did not deny him. Somehow, my uneasiness communicated itself to him, and he seldom failed to bury his disquiet under extra helpings of food. Whenever I ate with him, I followed suit.

We gorged ourselves for four weeks. Corn was our especial downfall: corn on the cob, dripping with dairy-fresh butter; corn sautéed in heavy cream; corn pone; corn fritters; corn chowder; corn pudding; corn muffins. He was forever coming up with another restaurant that served the luscious yellow kernels in a different fashion. We must have gone through half the crop of Illinois and Iowa combined that season. We would pit ourselves against each other to see who could put away the most ears at a sitting. The outcome did not vary. He would push his chair back from the table and slap his paunch. "I'd say that for a woman, you done damn well." I vowed to myself that the day would come when I bested him.

He bought more "little doodads" for me, but, kind as he was, I had no more relish for him than for the man in the moon as a partner in matrimony. He also shopped for an oil painting or two with thought of laying the foundation of another kind of collection. Limited as my knowledge was of this branch of the arts, I doubted whether large canvases of French women in teasing wisps of veiling gamboling across landscapes dotted with crumbling castles would be appropriate anywhere except in a saloon.

He was as tickled as I was when rumor unearthed a suitor for my hand. Before the exposition opened, a skinny, saturnine hustler who went by the name of Florenz Ziegfeld had been commissioned to go to Europe to import talent for shows on the midway. His most impressive discovery was a German goliath and professional strongman whom Ziggy promptly undertook to manage as a sideshow attraction. Eugene Sandow, who could snap chains and bend iron bars like so many stalks of rhubarb, became my alleged Lothario. The guile of Ziggy, who knew the value of headlines, was not hard to discern.

I let him talk me into meeting his candidate. I rated Sandow as uninspiring as he was overpowering, but the press, egged on by his zealous manager, immediately spun cobwebs of speculation extolling the eugenic compatibility of beauty and brawn. *Town Topics* hastened to seal the match. "The giant has given audiences to a number of beautiful Chicago girls within the last week or so, and as he has managed to quite capture most of their hearts, why not the airy and erstwhile fairy Lillian's? . . . The couple would look simply magnificent marching up the aisle of the church together."

Jim took the printed word more seriously than I. He had to seek corroboration of my sentiments. "You'd come straight out and tell me, wouldn't you, if there were anything behind all this damn flimflam?"

"I wouldn't dream of marrying that German wiener if he could pick you and me up in one hand and carry us back to New York."

When I did get back, I had a talk with Abe. Proceedings to annul my seven years' dead marriage with Edward Solomon were begun on September 8. Not surprisingly reporters came a-running. I was ready for them in a rainbow-tinted silk kimono, fastened at the neck with a four-carat diamond clasp and with a glib explanation for the step I was taking. It was necessary, I claimed, because I wanted no confusion about some real estate in which I was investing.

A scribe from *The Sun*, J. P. Morgan's favorite daily, was impertinent. "Rumors that have preceded you from Chicago suggest a more romantic reason."

"Nothing of the kind, I assure you. I do not intend to marry." Perhaps I had gone too far; I must retreat a pace. "I do not intend to marry until my stage career is over. Someone who does not love me started those reports. They are untrue. I merely want this question of my legal status settled."

Nothing was heard from Edward Solomon. On November 16 the annulment was granted by default, and I was free again. I had expressed no more than the truth to the scribe from *The Sun*. I did not intend to hazard my career in a new liaison with any man. I could manage quite well, thank you, without the fleshly pleasures of a bouncing mattress, though not so easily without those served on the dining table. A good meal never troubled my digestion, but the memory of how I had been deceived by Solomon soured my stomach. I would give no further thought to him or credit him with any role in the source of my greatest happiness, Daughtie. Jim shared in celebrating my liberation from a blackguard of a husband, but Abe had reservations about the prudence of the whole procedure. Whatever opinions Mama had, she kept to herself, thank heaven.

I had additional cause for rejoicing. Apprehension at the prospect of being included in the swelling ranks of the unemployed was dispelled when a new team of theatrical producers beckoned. Mr. Lederer possessed the experience and Mr. Canary half a million in ready cash, which he hoped to see multiplied on the Rialto. Together they were leasing the Casino, my old stamping ground, whence Rudolf Aronson had been driven by his continuing financial shortfalls. I signed with them to reassemble the Lillian Russell Opera Company and appear in *Princess Nicotine*, whose plot bore a resemblance to that of *Carmen*, though the score was less taxing than Bizet's.

Town Topics' attention was concentrated elsewhere than on my voice. "Lillian will return to the Casino. She has parted those scarlet, rapturous lips of hers and said so. She will expand and heave, throb, bloom, and fascinate in our own vicinity."

At the price of splitting his party, the President had achieved delayed victory in his efforts to release the country from the grip of the silver barons, and a mood of euphoria briefly prevailed in New York, ensuring a full house on our opening night, November 24. One old habitué of the temple of gilded youth was overheard exclaiming, "That delicious creature is the incarnation of peaches and cream."

Shortly before Christmas I was awarded a new leading man. The program listed him as Don Giovanni Perugini, his birth certificate as John Haley Augustin Chatterton of Michigan, aged thirty-nine. His credentials were impressive. Not only had he sung at the Casino at the time of its birth but also in opera with beloved Adelina Patti. His tenor was *robusto* like the Metropolitan's incomparable Jean De Reszke's, his manner charming, his dark eyes irresistible, his taste in dress exquisite.

We made as pretty a picture as any playgoer could wish to see, I in gowns whose allure matched those of the Aronson era, he in three brand-new outfits, including a white bridal getup with gold clocks embroidered on his hose. He was a bachelor, and I was single again. He seemed compliant with my wishes and, except in the matter of vocal ability, unlikely to compete with me.

The kisses called for by the libretto grew more realistic as affection bloomed between us. It was a novel exhibition of romance. In the role of Chicos, he smothered me with love; offstage, innate delicacy allowed him to go no farther than brush my fingers with his lips.

Jim was appalled to hear that on New Year's Day I would take Jack to supper at Rector's at my own expense, since my salary greatly exceeded his. "What's gotten into you, Nell? He ain't nothing but a larynx on legs. He's out to use you, nothing more."

I laughed at him. "Do I detect green envy in your usually ruddy cheeks? Do you happen by any chance to be jealous?"

"Jealous? Of a three-dollar bill? You got to be kidding."

"He has one thing lacking in you, James Brady, and that is refinement, and another, which is good taste, and a third of which you know nothing whatsoever—spirituality."

"Open your eyes, girl. He's putting on an act. He wants to climb on your back to serve hisself. A feller like him thinks there's nobody matters in the world 'cept number one."

"You are insulting my intelligence. I know what I'm doing.

So far as I'm concerned, Jack is an ideal man. We have every-thing in common, which is something else you fail to under-stand. We are *artistes*."

"Wait till he has you singing his tune. You're going to be sorry, Nell, God help you."

Rector's effervesced with excitement when Jack and I ap-peared on the night of Monday, January 1. The gypsy fiddler's bow hesitated for a second over the strings at the sight of us, but suave Charles greeted me as though my new beau had been bringing me here since Sherman marched through Georgia. At every other table, cutlery lingered in mid-air between plates and jaws as usual, but a hiss of whispering replaced the customary moment of silent admiration.

I had braced myself by putting on a dazzling new gown, which I splashed generously with diamonds, and a Paris model hat that cost $50 at Schlesinger & Mayer's in Chicago. Jack, possibly for similar motive, had been liberal in his use of cologne. A magnum of champagne added further fortification, but joyful as I was at the stir we were creating, for once I felt uncom-fortable under the stares of some two hundred inquisitive people. It made the oysters seem unwieldy as whales, my fork a derrick, my mouth like Kentucky's Mammoth Cave.

The embraces of Nicotine and Chicos were the talk of New York during the week that followed. The ink-stained hounds from Park Row came to quiz me about our plans. I received them with Jack at my side.

It was pointless to be evasive. "Signor Perugini is a gentle-man, a dear, good fellow, and he has asked me to marry him. I am only a woman, after all, and these rumors have both an-noyed and hurt me. I hope my marriage will put an end to that sort of thing."

He was gallantry itself. "This is the first time I have been engaged. When a man of my age falls in love, it is the genuine thing. My wife—ah, that is to say she who is to be my wife within two months; I wish it were now. My sweetheart and I are very happy. We shall devote ourselves to *opéra comique*. I say 'we,' but it is Miss Russell that is the one. I put myself in the background."

He was too eager to please, in fact, for us to bide our time until Palm Sunday, the date we had originally chosen. I was sufficiently sentimental to wish for a ceremony conducted in my drawing room with a houseful of guests and a string quartet playing Mendelssohn, but Abe ruled it more expedient to be married in Hoboken if I insisted on going through with it. I accepted his counsel but jeered at his quibbling.

No more than a dozen of us ascended into hansom cabs on West 77th Street one brisk Sunday noon at the end of the month. Jim was not invited, but George Lederer was there, undoubtedly gratified by the publicity we were generating, and so was Mama. She had to be taken aside and assured that I was fully aware of what I was undertaking, though in light of subsequent history it should be recorded in my favor that on the previous night I had known a sleepless hour or so of doubt.

Standing before a justice of the peace, we heard the not unfamiliar vows repeated. We returned to my house for the wedding breakfast, served by Bridget at what would otherwise have been suppertime. Mama found it inconvenient to stay on.

Since Jack showed no eagerness to retire as the evening wore away, I concealed my own feelings and suggested to George and some others that we might as well enjoy a friendly game of draw poker. I was soon completely absorbed, having found myself on the first go-around blessed with four-of-a-kind in spades and an odd heart. Fortune attended me. An hour or more later, when I was some two hundred dollars ahead, my new husband yawned himself to bed.

George intimated that he was willing to call it a day, but I dismissed that as a show of unnecessary politeness. He deserved a chance at revenge, so I lit another Melachrino, and the game continued. By the time three o'clock struck, I had augmented my winnings by another fifty dollars. "Why don't you boot us out, Lil?" he asked.

I had to say something frivolous and concealing. "I wouldn't think of it. I always play cards on my wedding night."

But now there was no detaining him or the rest. I bade them good night, emptied the ashtrays and went upstairs in a state that blended expectancy of pleasure with a certain detached curiosity as to how I would respond in a physical association to which I had been a stranger for so long. I roused my bridegroom from his slumber, but the effort was for nought. He protested, "I love you too much to defile you" and fell asleep again. I remained undefiled for the rest of our married life.

Neither of us was in the best of humors at the breakfast table, but he was the more petulant. "I didn't like the way some of those people here last night kept looking at me. You'll have to be more careful about whom you invite to our house. And the maid is consistently insolent to me. She will have to go."

"But Bridget is a treasure. She's been with me for years."

"Oh, so you care more about her than about me?"

"Not at all. I suppose I could manage without her if you would help around the house sometimes when you've nothing else to do."

"I hope you're not suggesting I become your housekeeper. Or would you like that so I'd be out of the way and you'd have the applause to yourself every night?"

I would have been willing to meet him more than halfway in all these matters had he proven himself a husband worthy of the name, though I ought to have realized the truth and left him that same afternoon. We had momentarily patched up our disagreements by then. Bridget had brought sandwiches and tea to the second-floor sitting room while he went off down the hall "to change," as he said. I expected him to reenter in a smoking jacket. What he wore instead was a peach-colored tea gown with a short train and cascades of lace.

"What do you think? It's from Paris. I bought two more like it for my trousseau."

Laugh or weep? I did neither. I determined to live with him as a sister and maintain at least the appearance of happiness before the world. He was all too willing to move into the best guest room. Each evening as the last curtain fell on *Nicotine*, I would hasten to invite friends or even foes in the cast to come home to help ease the tension. One of them was brawny Marie Dressler, my stage mother and stalwart ally, whose ferocity scared Jack.

She would stop by my dressing room to deliver malicious reports on his latest aberrancy. He had counted on his name being displayed outside the Casino in the same size as mine and was furious when George refused to take the hint. He preened himself in front of mirrors, and Marie would mimic his smirking in a forlorn attempt to raise a smile from me.

His thwarted ambition to be co-billed made him spiteful even on stage. It was not easy to sing when I was constantly being thrown off balance by muttered threats and whispered curses. One night Marie caught his comment after a solo of mine, delivered while he clasped me in his arms: "You were off key again, you brainless bitch."

It was her turn to growl under her breath. "If you ever say that again, I'll throw you into the bass drum." When the curtain fell, she grabbed a stage brace of heavy iron and took after him as he scampered to his own dressing room. Before he would leave it for the second act, he demanded that the stage manager provide him with two scene shifters as bodyguards to protect him from her.

I endured this farce of a marriage for the sake of my fellow players and the salary I was drawing, all of which would have been suspended if my contract were broken, but the humiliation of it all was hard to bear. I had taken him as a husband expecting him to be overwhelming in his attentiveness and not unduly demanding of physical satisfaction. Yet I was totally denied the pleasure of enticing him if I were in a mood for a little sensuality and turning him away if I were not. I was a woman spurned.

After every Casino performance had been filled by throngs eager to see the foremost sweethearts of the American theater, *Nicotine* met with a similar response in Baltimore, Washington, Pittsburgh, Philadelphia, New Haven, and Boston. Then the Lillian Russell Opera Company traveled the same route with a revival of *Giroflé-Girofla*, some of us as discontented as the unemployed rabble of Jacob Coxey's "army" who, I feared, would pare down our Washington audiences on the day they marched up Capitol Hill. I was not sorry to hear that after the police went to work with their truncheons, many a marcher's head was as sore as his feet.

At the Hotel Stanton in Philadelphia I realized that I could stand it no longer. A shortage of rooms put my darling and me together in the same suite. He left his sticky, scented hairdressing on a sofa, staining my skirt when I sat down. When I snatched up the open pot, he clawed at me as he thrust me toward the open seventh-floor windows. I managed to grab a hairbrush, applying enough blows to force him to desist. He turned and sped through the door with a last whack of the posterior to help him.

His end had come and gone in that moment. I made up my mind to do two things: Set down the facts on paper in a statement for the New York *Herald* and resign from Lederer & Canary.

He threw a tantrum for a *Tammany Times* reporter who followed up publication of my painful story by going to interview him. With streaming eyes and sniffs from a vial of smelling salts, Don Giovanni Macaroni resorted to deliberate slander. "Do you know what she did to me? Why, sir, when we had to share apartments, she took all the pillows; she used my rouge; she misplaced my manicure set; she used my special handkerchief perfume for her bath; she always wanted the best mirror when we were making our toilets whether for the theater or the street, and she usually got it. She's a desperate character for all her smile is sweet for the public."

The reporter put in a kind word. I was probably well-meaning, he said, and like many of my sex, I may have failed to consider in advance the price of an apparent bargain.

From a pouch carried inside his sock, Don Giovanni produced a powder puff to mop his cheeks. "Don't talk to me about sex. I don't think this is a question of sex. It's a question of right and wrong. You must publish a contradiction of what Lillian said. I want you to say she laces and wears false hair and is horribly made up and is not the least bit pretty off the stage."

"Third time lucky" was evidently a maxim that did not apply to me. I was at liberty from both employment and a parody of a husband, facing an action for breach of contract from Lederer & Canary, and, of all things, a suit for alimony from him.

I had also learned that Jim had found another girl, younger than I, on a vacation trip to Old Point Comfort, Virginia, and was talking of her to friends as the one he intended to marry.

XII

MORE URGENT MATTERS called for concentration than Jim's dalliance with some Southern
belle of whom I knew not so much as her name. Unless he should
bring her to the door, there was little chance of our meeting, for
I was virtually imprisoned in my own house, my every exit
dogged by a robust employee of the New York branch of Pinkerton's Chicago detective agency.

They were there in consequence of a new contract I had
entered into without first tidying up affairs with Lederer &
Canary. The offer from the firm of Abbey, Schoeffel & Grau was
too tempting to be turned down merely because my previous
sponsors were being disagreeable. Henry Abbey, one of our foremost operatic impresarios, was the original lessee and manager
of the Metropolitan, with Maurice Grau handling the business
end of things. Poor Henry lost $300,000 on that venture, but
now that the entire building had been reconstructed after the
fire of '92, they were both back in office, presenting Melba as the
great attraction.

I was baited by their intimating that, if first I went to
Europe under their management, my heart's desire would at last
be fulfilled on my return: They would book me to grand opera
at its temple in Manhattan. Through some oversight, word of
the plan escaped. Lederer & Canary obtained an injunction to
restrain me from sailing, so here I was, besieged within my own
four walls.

But for the ingenuity of Little Abe I might have been trapped for weeks. He was in an advantageous position in that both my past and present employers were clients of Howe & Hummel. He responded to a beseeching telephone call by showing up in my drawing room. He lightened the atmosphere by demonstrating how deftly he could pick the pockets of my tailor-made suit, which had an abundance of them in conformity with the latest fashion, then got down to brass tacks.

"How important is it to you to go to London?"

"Abe, how can you possibly ask? It is all part and parcel of the arrangement that will finally make me a prima after these long years of struggle. Why, I am to do what dear, departed Dr. Damrosch always envisioned for me—sing Marguerite in *Faust*, Elsa in *Lohengrin*, and in front of thirty-four hundred people! There could be no more fitting tribute to his memory."

"It won't bring him back, will it? Tee! hee! But tell me exactly what the Pinks do to keep tabs on you." I explained how four sentinels watched by day and one by night.

"That one's your ace in the hole. Here's what you do."

I followed his instructions to the letter by packing in readiness on the eve of an ocean sailing, again from Jersey City. Bridget made a willing accomplice. In the early hours the next morning she crossed the street to approach the sentry with a tale that I had gone to bed, leaving her to invite him into the kitchen for a sandwich and any refreshment of his choosing, and there was John Jameson whiskey in the house. I could hear two Hibernian brogues blending together before she plied him with a tot after surreptitiously adding drops from a small bottle that Abe had sent around by office messenger. He guaranteed that recriminations would be suffered by nobody, since a Pinkerton man known to drink on duty would be fired instantly.

Our guest's snores signaled time for departure. A hug was Bridget's recompense when she slipped out to wish me a temporary farewell. While I was out of the country, Abe would see what devilment Chatterton was brewing and would also referee the dispute over my future, notably by talking Lederer & Canary out of trying to have me jailed for contempt if I risked appearances in England.

Besides the promise of imminent renown, there were other advantages to being on Abbey's team. Henry Irving and his love

Ellen Terry had come over at Abbey's direct invitation to be-witch New Yorkers in Alfred Tennyson's *Becket*. For my debut at the Lyceum Theater in September, I was given by way of return the use of Ellen's dressing room and of Henry's salon for receiving visitors. I thought her charming and him affected with his fantasies of one day receiving a knighthood from the queen, which put him in Gilbert's fawning category so far as I was concerned.

The brute himself did not show his face, but Sullivan called, to enthuse me with a proposal that I sing the leading role in an operetta he had thought of composing. *Peg Woffington* was to follow sometime after *The Grand Duke*, for which the brute was to write the lyrics; their on-and-off relationship was tempo-rarily on again. *Peg Woffington*, alas, proved to be still-born; Sir Arthur was laid to rest in St. Paul's Cathedral before his task was done.

Artistically, the operetta for which I was currently engaged was a disappointment. *The Queen of Brilliants* lacked a third act when rehearsals began, which militated against a polished production, and the scenery was more memorable than either the melodies or dialogue. But socially I was lionized (or perhaps "lionessed"?) even at a pinnacle of London Society, in the man-sion of Lord "Natty" Rothschild, the first Jewish peer of the realm, and in the presence of the Prince of Wales.

The evening came about as a result of a request made of me by his American friend, Mrs. Ogden Goelet. When Mrs. Goelet sought to inveigle me into entertaining His Royal Highness, she obviously had not learned that the threat of prison overhung my head. I was mightily curious to see him at close quarters, so I set my fee below that of Mademoiselle Guilbert, asking only $2,500, which worked out at approximately five hundred pounds. I laid down only one condition. Wild horses could not drag out of me a note of the warble that was catching on as quickly here as it had back home. I refused to trill about Mamie O'Rourke tripping the light fantastic on the sidewalks of New York.

Happily, I was told that Lord Rothschild's honored dinner guest would like nothing better than to be regaled with arias by Tosti, which meant some tedious hours of practice in advance. The prince's companion of the evening was the heiress Lady

Frances Brooke, who had replaced Mrs. Langtry in his affections —a vivacious face, I thought, but her frame was a trifle underweight.

He was as plump and finely plumed as a pheasant and a model of guttural graciousness to me. "Goot evening, Miss Russell. You are verry pretty, with a most delicate fair skin, which is not always the case among your American compatriots." I found the meal appetizing but the portions on the skimpy side. He talked in the main about his yacht *Britannia*, the shortcomings of his racing stable, and a new grandson (I caught the name of David) without once mentioning his wife.

His applause was as perfunctory as everyone else's, but he appeared to appreciate Tosti and urged me to stay on in England; he was not specific about his reasons. When we ladies retired to the drawing room and the gentlemen turned to cigars and brandy, I was amused to discover that female aristocrats were little different from women in all walks of life. Pert young Lady Brooke asked what kind of face powder I employed, whether my hair was naturally golden, how I kept my complexion wrinkle-free. What they wanted from me was not the viewpoint of a patriotic American but beauty recipes.

I did not stay in England long enough to receive overtures from the prince, if that had been his plan. A cablegram from Abe brought glad tidings: Lederer & Canary had accepted $30,000 from Abbey, Schoeffel & Grau to cancel my obligations. *The Queen of Brilliants* was to be transferred to New York. Chatterton and Abe had not been in touch.

I found the city in a condition of turmoil bordering on the hysterical. Some of us who had enjoyed the uninhibited pleasures it offered to those able to afford them were suddenly afraid that our way of life was doomed to extinction in the forthcoming election for mayor. Like any native, I had become totally accustomed to take news of raids, graft, and the shenanigans of Tammany and the police department in my stride when I perused the morning paper.

But the philosophy of live and let live, it seemed, was wearing thin. During the months of my embroilment with the Chatterton creature, odium drenched Manhattan. Like an enraged watchdog, Dr. Parkhurst had worried the merchants of the

Chamber of Commerce into demanding that Albany investigate bribery and corruption in New York. Boss Tom Platt, the Grand Old Party's grand old man in the State Legislature, seized on the chance to bedevil Boss Richard Croker, Irish immigrant, suspected murderer, and self-made millionaire who reigned in Tammany Hall. Mr. Platt ordered a committee established under one of his docile Albany senators, Clarence Lexow, and before long scandal began to pop like corn in a hot skillet.

I was glad that in my absence Bridget had saved each day's copy of the *Herald* to allow me to catch up with developments lying in bed of a morning. Captain Bill Devery's name cropped up repeatedly in print. It was he who assigned Captain Max Schmittberger to the West 30th Street precinct, covering the Tenderloin, which extended north to 49th. He dropped a broad hint to his junior to go slow on Georgiana Hastings, whose quiet house in the area was patronized by millionaires, Tammany sachems, and justices of the courts. Ignoring the cue, handsome Max went looking for one judge to sign a Lexow Committee warrant for Georgiana's arrest. He unearthed him in the midst of a personal *tête-à-tête* with the madam herself in her sacrosanct oasis.

Max Schmittberger was clearly a vessel of wrath. Senator Lexow and his three eminent counsel would have gotten nowhere without him—or without his schoolboy son, whose playmates teased him about reports concerning his father that appeared in every journal. One day at the dinner table the lad asked the captain if the stories were true. Schmittberger's response was to take to the witness stand and tell everything he knew.

As a trustworthy newcomer who bought his way into the force in accordance with the usual scale of charges, he had been put to work collecting protection money from keepers of saloons, gaming houses, and brothels, distributing the proceeds among his colleagues and superiors and retaining a portion for himself to pay off the price of his appointment: A patrolman's job cost $300, a sergeant's $1,600, a captain's as much as $15,000.

Following him as a less willing witness came Inspector "Clubber" Williams, so nicknamed on account of his boast, "There's more law at the end of a club than in any courtroom." To the committee he bragged, "I am so well known here in New

York that car horses nod to me mornings." He showed more reluctance to speak of his three-story townhouse, his bank accounts, his yacht, his Connecticut acreage, or the sources of his income, earned, he avowed, by speculating in real estate among the Japanese.

Though the inspector was evidently as crooked as Pearl Street, I gave him credit for valor the morning I read of his invasion of Bill McGurk's on the Bowery, popularly known as "Suicide Hall."

I had once been so ingenuous as to confuse McGurk's with McGlory's, but now I knew how fortunate we had been to have looked in at the latter enterprise after our evening out with Nat. McGurk's second-floor bordello was the most iniquitous in the city. His "cadets" recruited innocent girls with promises of marriage or a place in the chorus of a Broadway show. I shuddered to remember days of boredom in Brooklyn when, but for Mama, I might have been susceptible not to the first but possibly to the second proposition.

A recruit to McGurk's was kept imprisoned by his ruffians, broken in for her trade, then subjugated into accommodating as many as sixty men a day. Many an unfortunate would find surcease only in self-destruction. The horse ambulance would collect her body from the gutter outside for transportation to an unmarked grave on Hart's Island, its progress heralded by the only mourning bell, and "natural causes" would be listed as the explanation for her end.

Clubber took a battalion of fifty of New York's finest for the assault on Suicide Hall. They arrested sixty young women and two hundred and fifty men, transported them to Eldridge Street police station for booking—and, to the jeers and catcalls of the riffraff who watched outside, saw them forthwith released on bail so that the girls would not lose any work. I was not quite sure that Inspector Williams deserved the loss of his job in the department, but I had no sympathy for Captain Devery, who, after his day on the stand, suffered the same fate.

I was mulling over the issues one morning when Bridget came bustling in to announce the presence of Jim Brady in the front hall. I had her bring him into my sitting room, while I put up my hair in a ribbon, applied a touch of perfume, and slipped into a robe. I found he had a suitably sheepish sag to his cheeks.

"Such a surprise! What brought you in?"

"I come to apologize for staying away. I brought you a little something to say I'm sorry." He thrust into my hands a jeweler's box whose contents required no guesswork.

"A peace offering?"

"You could call it that. We both made fools of ourselves, Nell—first you, then me."

"I certainly did. I didn't know about you."

"Biggest tomfool you ever laid eyes on."

"The girl from—where was it? Virginia?"

"You got it."

"What went wrong? Do you want to talk about it?"

"I didn't come to cry on nobody's shoulder."

"I'd like to know."

"Well, this is how it was. I seen her at Old Point Comfort, at a dance in the Chamberlain Hotel. A feller from the Baltimore and Ohio was staying there, and he introduced us; he knew her ma and pa. I took her out a few times, and we got along fine. Then I had to come back to New York on business, and her ma must have got after her, saying as how I wasn't good enough for her, which I wasn't. But I went down again to call at their house once or twice after that, not knowing the welcome mat wasn't out. Then the letters I wrote started coming back unopened, and I got no reply to my telegrams. I finally has three fellers from the office go down to find out what's gone wrong. Hears nothing from 'em for close to two weeks, then they shows up and tells me they've tracked her down to the Asheville Inn, North Carolina. Her ma and pa was with her, and they're not letting her out of their sight. But like a goddamn idiot I took off down there just the same. Couldn't see nobody but the mother. She turns out to be the toughest customer I ever come across, and that was the end of it. Now hark at me confabulating on without even telling you her name."

"I don't want to hear it. But tell me one more thing. Did she love you?"

Misery oozed into his eyes. "I dunno. She said as she did at first. Maybe nobody don't without I'm giving 'em presents. What about you, Nell? Does that apply?"

I stroked his sleeve. "Let's be friends again and leave it at that."

He sighed. "You can't win 'em all." He asked to hear no more on the subject, but the restoration of peace between us called for a banquet for two that same night. He explained that our reunion would of necessity also involve parting for a spell of several weeks: He was taking his younger sister, who worked with the nuns, to see the sights of London and Paris. I was not ready yet to face the crowd at Rector's again after the nonsensical flaunting of Chatterton there. Tonight, Louis Bustanoby would have our patronage.

Louis's earringed violinist and the *maître* himself steered us to the Café des Beaux Arts' best table. Donning his diamonds seemed to have raised Jim's spirits. "I'm glad to see you ain't been pining any pounds away, Nell, since your bust-up."

"What of it? You haven't been exactly fading away yourself."

His sigh ruffled the petals of the carnation in a silver vase on the crisp white linen. "Dr. Bodine says I ought to get some of it off. You ever thought about a bicycle? That might be worth a try." I twitted him by humming a bar or so of "Daisy Bell."

"Say, how about that! You and me could ride together."

"Which one of us would pedal?"

He was not to be put off. After he had ordered what he termed "a real first-class blowout," he said he would look into bicycling as soon as he had concluded his jaunt to Europe. Over the oysters, he remarked on the problem of losing weight when a body had worries to contend with. Over the bouillabaisse, he confided to me the source of those concerns.

"It's my ma and my brother Dan. I want to move out the house and get a place of my own, and she don't want me going. He's put it into her mind that I'm after setting up with some cutie, and she believes him, though he don't contribute one red cent to keeping her, and him with a wife that's loaded with the ready."

Once the hors d'oeuvres were served, he continued between bites of timbales, mousselines, palmettes, and croustades. "Dan's also got Ma believing I pimp for the big boys of every railroad in the country, and you know that's a pack of lies. I don't pretend to having the sweetest temper in the world, but, holy Christ, she flies off the handle as soon as I open my mouth."

We did justice to some dainty fillets of sole while he pursued his tale of woe. "You got to make allowances for her, mind. She ain't had it easy all her life, what with that bugger Lucas, then me and Dan leaving home so young. But I always done my best for her and put up with her nagging. 'Don't do this, Jim. Don't do that. Where've you been? Who was you with?'"

Lobsters smothered in a shrimp sauce were our choice for the entrée. "More than likely she ain't quite right in the head. Or perhaps it's them brown bottles with the stars on the labels that she's taken a fancy to lately. Anyway, Donnybrook Fair was officially opened last night with all the flags flying. I says to her, 'I'll be forty years old pretty soon, and I'm old enough to lead my own life.' She turns to me and says, 'I'll live to see you sleeping in the gutters of New York. You'll die with my curse on you.'"

The capon with savory mushroom stuffing and four vegetables was as good as I had ever tasted. "She even comes pussyfooting around the office, creating all kinds of scenes, poking her nose in, asking people about everything I'm up to. I dunno what's to be done with her, but one thing's damn sure—I'm getting out of the house."

"What do the girls in your office think of her?"

"Girls? I don't have no girls work for me, Nell. I got the best secretary within ten blocks of Cortlandt Street in Herb Haberle. You can't trust women in business."

I was sure my voice was as icy as the sorbet à la Bruxelles that had just been placed before us. "There's one thing a woman can't do as well as a man if not better, and that's cast a vote, because she isn't given the right."

His laughter rumbled like approaching thunder. "And there's another." I trusted him not to be coarse, and he was not. "A woman can't eat as hearty as a man."

"I wouldn't wager on it, if I were you."

"I will, though. I bet I can tuck away more'n you. If you

can go on matching me dish for dish, you'll have a new diamond ring in the morning. What do you say?"

"I say we're on, but you must excuse me for a minute." I came back from the cloakroom to resume the feast with a brace of duck à *l'orange*. "How are you going to vote next Tuesday, Jim?"

"Same as ever, for the Dems, like my pa woulda done. I don't see no sense in rocking the boat."

"But everybody's talking about Tammany graft. Why don't you prefer Strong?"

"Let me tell you. There's two kinds of graft, honest and dishonest, with a world of difference between 'em. Waiter!"

Next, we each tackled a plate of prawns in aspic, followed in turn by an airy cheese soufflé, butterscotch blanc mange, and Philadelphia ice cream. Between courses, as pauses separating the mouthfuls lengthened, Jim expanded on his philosophy and in his physical person.

"Take honest graft. You could truthfully say I'm an example of that. I work all the time for my own pocket. I see my opportunities, and I latches onto 'em. Dishonest graft I don't want no part of. No blackmail, no hush money, no boodle excepting straight commission, no payoffs."

"But that's hypocritical. You know very well your customers can get whatever they ask of you. Presents, parties, even girls maybe."

"Like I said, there's a difference. What I do is make an investment to get an order for the goods or else hold onto business already on the books. By the way, how you feel, Nell? Can you go another round?"

I was more than full but remarkably free of any oppression around the middle. "I should like a châteaubriand, underdone, juicy, and thick, and whatever you like to go with it." While the chefs prepared our order, we proceeded with this private investigation into Jim's articles of faith. "How do you reconcile what you're saying with dirty police graft? What about the bribes they extort from saloons and so forth?" Sometimes I sounded suspiciously like Mama.

"A feller running one of them has got a special kind of business to think about. If he don't pay up, he's out of luck, so he forks out like part of the overheads. You can't blame him for that. No point trying to shut them places down. If a customer's looking for that sort of thing, he'll always find it. I hope you ain't turning into one of them reformers. They got no place in politics. Reformers look lovely in the morning, but come evening they wither on the vine."

He talked so much that I finished my two or three pounds of delicately marbled prime beef ahead of him, leaving a plate clean of mushroom sauce, chantilly potatoes, sautéed sweet peppers, and petits pois—everything but the scraps. "Do you consider a woman like Georgiana Hastings or the French Madam or Fivepenny Fan as being in business, too?"

I knew I had him impaled. He swallowed his last morsel before he answered, weak in argument and manner alike. "There's got to be exceptions to every rule, and that's one of 'em. Well, Nellie, I reckon we can call it a draw. I always says when I sit down to eat as how I make a point of leaving just four inches between my stomach and the edge of the table. Now I can feel 'em rubbing together pretty hard, so I know I had enough."

I felt like an inflated balloon, but he was not to be let off so easily. "Aren't you going to have your usual box of chocolates?"

"Couldn't handle another thing."

"I think I'll try a box of Page and Shaw's assorted, if you please."

Under his incredulous stare, I unwrapped one of the nauseating little cubes, forced it down, then went on to polish off half a dozen more in order to clinch the conquest. The following morning, Jim delivered the promised prize, and I went back to Bustanoby's to retrieve from the proprietor, who had been its overnight custodian, the corset I had removed during my few minutes in the ladies' room.

On November 6, 1894, William L. Strong became the new mayor and straightway began implementing his campaign promises to improve the morals of New York. It was not the mayor, however, who commanded the attention of the newspapers and especially their cartoonists. One might have imagined from all the space devoted to him that his scrappy young chairman of the police board, Theodore Roosevelt, was St. George the Dragon

Slayer as he trumpeted, "I am fighting vile crime and hideous vice."

He did not need to be told that the root of much of the evil surrounding decent citizens lay in the police department, riddled with corruption like a rotten apple infested with worms. As I had seen for myself, blackmail and politics ruled the force. Officers, high and low, used their power to extort bribes for "protection" from saloonkeepers, gamblers, and prostitutes. A policeman's job and future promotion depended on his handing over cash to "the man higher up."

Teddy set out to put a stop to corruption and raise the morale of his troops by rewarding devotion and punishing venality, and my heart went out to him for his courage. We saw patrolmen on bicycles for the first time. We could read accounts of police misconduct trials when, as another novelty, they were opened to the press and the public. Mama shared my enthusiasm for the new commissioner, though politicians of both parties opposed him; most newspapers, respectable and sensational alike, jeered at him; and the criminal element threatened his life. She was thrilled to find that his pretty little daughter Alice and her young brother Ted came over the bridge with a detective guarding them to take music lessons in a house on Columbia Heights.

With a pistol in his pocket, Teddy prowled the streets by day and night, keeping patrolmen on their toes. In the course of an evening stroll, I turned a corner and almost bumped into him, a familiar figure after all the pictures that were printed, with his eyes squinting behind his pince-nez spectacles and the row of gleaming teeth that the cartoonists adored.

I gasped out his name and went on to say that like a majority of New Yorkers I gave him full credit for sweeping the city clean of the dirt that had besmirched it. "You are reminding all good Americans, sir, of the principles on which our country is based."

He surprised me by shaking his head under its black sombrero. "I am sure, my good young lady, that I have offended so many powerful interests and so many powerful politicians that no political preferment in future will be possible for me. If you will excuse me, I have duties to attend to, so I will bid you good night."

On November 24 I opened in *The Queen of Brilliants*. Jim was missing from his accustomed seats in the front row, but I had a letter relating the stir he aroused among British working-men on a visit to the Leeds Forge Company; his rapture over the sophistications of native French cuisine; and his exasperation with "damn foreign gabble." I missed even more the condolence he would assuredly have provided when the critics found this queen to be less than brilliant and proceeded to dethrone her in short order.

Had I not earned my chance on the stage of the Metropolitan nevertheless? Abbey, Schoeffel & Grau thought otherwise. To recoup the losses they had endured at the box office, they pinned their hopes on presenting me once again as the ancient war horse, *The Grand Duchess*, who should have long since been put out to grass, as the public was quick to realize.

Surely it was time now to portray Elsa or Marguerite or Abbey's choice of any heroine of grand opera? Not at all. Tickets to the theaters went begging when for a great many citizens prosperity was a thing of the past. I was one of the number who believed that in this most terrible year since Reconstruction our country would have gone bankrupt without the generosity of Mr. J. P. Morgan in raising $62,000,000 in gold for the Cleveland government at 3.75 percent. I had no sympathy for the hundreds of thousands of misguided laborers who laid down their tools to protest rising prices. Most of the unrest would be attributed to radical elements such as my own mother consorted with, European socialists, anarchists, and nihilists who should have long since been sent back where they belonged.

In Henry Abbey's timorous view, the times were too un-certain for experiment. As his next vehicle for me, he wheeled out another old stand-by, *La Perichole*. Timidity being con-tagious, I consented to ride in it. Unhappily the role was so vapid that I developed a tendency to hurry the pace to the point where listeners complained they had difficulty in following the plot and found themselves at the exit doors rather earlier than they felt was justified by the price of admission. Within two weeks of setting off, *La Perichole* was trundled back into the stable.

Abey's succeeding offering was equally vacuous. *The Tzigane* was something of a labor of love on the part of the librettist,

Harry Smith, whom I remembered as a classmate of my older sisters in the Chicago school system. Since few people could pronounce the title and still fewer knew that it meant "gypsy," recommendation by word of mouth was nonexistent. I did not care at all for my role.

These were depressing months made tolerable only by the excitement I caught from Jim over his new toy. The contraption known as an "electric" was in fact a two-seater buggy propelled by means of storage batteries rather than drawn by horses. He had foreseen inherent possibilities in these improbable inventions at the time of the Chicago Fair, when three of them rolled through the streets. They were so arresting a novelty that crowds gathered wherever they slowed to a halt. Even Jim's diamond displays could not rival an electric's power to win attention, and these machines were, of course, infinitely less dangerous than those dependent on steam hissing in a boiler or, even more perilous, on explosions of gasoline.

He sailed home to New York to find the order he had placed with the A. H. Woods factory ready for him. He had it warped to an open flat car under a tarpaulin for delivery to the New York Central's freight yards, together with a black engineer who formed part of the same order and rode from Chicago in the train's caboose.

Jim kept his purchase a secret until the mechanic, in a new bottle-green livery and nautical cap, had made early-morning practice runs along deserted streets adjacent to the West 57th Street stables where the contrivance was housed. Then Jim could contain himself no longer.

He sounded as jubilant as a Fourth of July picnic when he telephoned one Friday afternoon. "Nell, I bought myself a horseless carriage, the first in New York. There can't be no more than a couple of hundred in the whole country, most of them foreign-made, but this one's American-made, and she runs smooth as silk. I'm going to take a spin tomorrow, then you can have a go in her. I got a good steady driver, so you don't have need to be scared. I'm going to tip off the newspapers so's we don't get overlooked."

He generated glory for himself on Fifth Avenue between 57th Street and Madison Square. The crush of Saturday-morning

pedestrians gaped, and a pair of bays took fright and bolted, hauling a startled dowager in a victoria behind them. From 42nd
Street to 36th, five more teams of horses shied and whinnied
while coachmen wrestled with reins and whips. The vehicle
caused chaos in the heavy traffic of Madison Square where
broughams and phaetons, runabouts and tally-hos became hope-
lessly entangled until mounted policemen arrived to sort out
the mess with a squad from the Street Cleaning Department
in their wake. Sunday's newspaper headlines were pure gold to
Jim:

STARTLING HAPPENINGS IN MADISON SQUARE

JAMES B. BRADY DRIVES FIRST HORSELESS CARRIAGE SEEN IN NEW YORK

APPEARANCE TIES UP TRAFFIC FOR TWO HOURS

Sunday afternoon brought my turn. I tied a veil over my hat
to secure it against the wind, climbed up beside Johnson, the
driver, and we were off, leaving Jim to wave us bon voyage from
the curb. At my request, we made for Riverside Drive, where
Johnson, with one firm hand on the tiller, slid a lever along until
our speed quickened to what he judged was a full eleven miles
an hour. Our progress had the same effect on horses as yesterday's
outing, and even the swiftest carriages could keep up with us
only briefly. I would have been happy to ride as far as Harlem,
but Johnson informed me he doubted the batteries' supply of
current would be sufficient to bring us back over such a distance.
As a nation, I exulted to myself, we were on the threshold of an
age of mechanical miracles. If only I could afford it, I would have
ordered an electric next morning.

Bent on a further sampling of what the new century might
have in store, I took myself down soon afterward to Koster &
Bial's Music Hall on Herald Square, home of Professor Edison's
Vitascope, which up to now had failed to interest me. This palace
of pleasure had earned a reputation in the past for staging somewhat risqué entertainment designed for men about town, artists,
and writers; today its patrons covered the whole gamut of middle-
class citizens, women included.

On sight of me, the doorman summoned the manager, who

ushered me in for a complimentary showing. "Gentleman Jim" Corbett, three times his natural size, demonstrated in the darkness of the hall the telling blows he had delivered to wrest the heavyweight boxing title from John L. Sullivan. I found the flickering pictures dizzying but fascinating, though other spectators applauded. The frolics and simpering of the Gaiety Girls who followed him struck me as quite absurd, and the camera seemed to add substantial weight to their limbs.

I saw no more, for the manager came to whisk me away from my seat to his office, where the Wizard himself had stopped by and, being told of my presence, expressed a desire to make my acquaintance. With dandruff from uncombed hair flecking the shoulders of a rumpled suit, he appeared to have slept for a week in his clothing. It was necessary to risk straining my voice to hold any kind of conversation, since he was deaf as a haddock in his left ear and seriously impaired of hearing in the right.

He eyed my tight-waisted costume suit disapprovingly. "Is it not pure vanity, conceit, and folly to suffer bodily pain that one's person may have graces that are the outcome of secret agony?"

"Fashion enslaves us all, Professor Edison."

"Engraves what?"

"*Enslaves*. Holds us in bondage; robs us of our freedom."

A smile added more creases to his cheeks. "That is the function of corsets, lawsuits, and the nice, genial, generous lot of people they have over in Wall Street, who would have all of us their helots if they could. You have not met me before, but I have seen you perform in the company of the usual number of servant girls in tights. Beautiful voice, as I recall; I wanted to capture it for posterity."

"I was very busy at that time. If you might still be interested in an aria or two—"

"No. That was in the past, and now it's the future that beckons me. I am confident of the day when we shall make machines to transport us through the sky, make food from chemicals—diamonds, too—and breed the anthropoid ape to carry out menial labor."

"And when may we expect to live with such wonders?"

"My estimate would be by 1940, when I shall still be a year or two short of the century mark."

"Is all this to be brought about by electricity?"

His look was suddenly as craggy as the New Jersey Palisades. "Now that my name has been violated by Morgan's trust, I have no interest in electricity. People will forget that Edison was ever connected with anything electrical. I shall be remembered because I can do something that even God, on the unlikely assumption of his existence, has failed to achieve. I shall make man immortal."

Skepticism must have showed in my face. "You have seen the capabilities of the motion-picture camera, crude though it is as yet. I will link it to my phonograph, and there will be no limit to the possibilities. Grand opera, for example, given by artists and musicians long since dead, great plays, speeches, the sights and sounds of history recorded as it is made."

I half expected an invitation to his laboratories to be a pawn in his fantasies. Having seen how the Vitascope magnified one's proportions, I was wondering how to refuse, but the challenge did not arise. "You look nervous, Miss Russell. You might try doing what I do to steady my nerves: Read the Encyclopedia Britannica."

I excused myself. Much as I should have liked to stay longer, shouting was making me hoarse, and I had to sing that evening.

~ XIII ~

I REACHED my thirty-fifth birthday, one of the last of them to be acknowledged in my life, and in spite of all entreaties, the stage doors of the Metropolitan Opera House remained closed to me. Though my $1,500 a week was paid without fail, Abbey, Schoeffel & Grau complained that they lost money on the Lillian Russell Opera Company and were constantly casting around for a means of recouping. It was not a situation to inspire self-confidence, no matter how many portraits the *Police Gazette* sold or how many cigar bands carried my likeness.

I rejected the suggestion made by Abbey and others that one reason for my troupe's lackluster appeal was the homeliness of its other females and the mediocrity of the males. Audiences came only to see and hear *me*, and in my latest role at the Abbey Theater—as *The Goddess of Truth*, which was a tattered embroidery of *Pygmalion and Galatea*—the reviewers to a man agreed that in operetta I had no peer.

But there were thorns concealed in the verbal bouquets. "When you go to Abbey's," one mischief-maker wrote, "you'll see not only her diamonds, but some ultragorgeous gowns and as much of her pectoral flesh as she can reasonably be expected to exhibit." I was "as filling as a plum pudding stuffed with plums."

I could no more believe that a shapely figure would go out of style than give credence to Edison's farfetched dreams of flying machines, yet possibly it was time to shed a little super-

215]

fluous weight without going to extremes and reducing myself
to skin and bones like some goddesses of the younger generation. I came of sturdier American stock than Anna Held, the
bony French brunette imported by Ziegfeld; she weighed a
feathery ninety-five pounds, but he proceeded to make her his
common-law wife. Nor would I bring myself to ape the type
of lean-hipped womanhood exemplified by Charles Dana Gibson,
whose pen-and-ink drawings were gaining in popularity with the
weekly magazines.

Jim assisted by presenting me with a Columbia bicycle whose
frame he'd had plated with gold, the spokes of its wheels with
silver. Tiny diamonds and emeralds embedded in the handlebars
spelled out "L.L." I had a plush-lined leather container made
for the machine, with my name in white on either side so that
it could be transported without danger of scratches on my travels.
Jim already had his own velocipede, a specially reinforced tandem
with an inflatable seat in front large enough to accommodate his
derriere and a saddle for a former trick cyclist, Dick Barton, whom
he engaged at thirty-five dollars a week plus room and board
to pedal while Jim steered. Then, bitten hard by the bicycling
bug, Jim made a further contribution toward hardening Barton's
thighs by commissioning a three-seater on which he occupied
the bow and Barton the stern with a guest—often myself—
sitting amidships.

Mama applauded cycling as a forward step in the emancipation of our sex in the same way as she extolled the Remington
typewriter as a key for opening up commercial opportunities for
women. She and I were going through one of our intermittent
periods of amity now that I was experimenting with Christian
Science along with slenderizing in the hope that physical appearance and the spiritual content of the mind might simultaneously be improved.

She would, nevertheless, have been better pleased had I been
content to straddle something less gaudy than Jim's gift to me.
Mama could not utter the word "gold" without a curl of her
lips after absorbing the text of the speech that had won for
William Jennings Bryan the nomination for the Presidency of
the United States at the Democrats' July convention in Chicago.

I had long hoped that Cynthia Leonard, erstwhile Republican, would end her ties with Socialism and return to better ways. I was sorry to discover her a convert to the opposition. When *The Goddess of Truth* ran out of customers after two months of disappointments, she burst in on me, declaring the former Congressman turned newspaper editor to be "the greatest, most glorious orator in our history." She recited word for word the peroration he had delivered, and it was impossible to interrupt until she had completed "You shall not crucify mankind upon a cross of gold" with hands raised to the ceiling.

She realized only then that Jim had entered the drawing room. "Well, what do you say to that, Mr. Brady?"

"Speaking personally, I'm going to swap horses and vote for McKinley."

She was dumfounded. "But I have always gathered from Nellie that you were tied hand and foot to the Dems."

"Have been up till now. But if Bryan gets in, I might as well put up the shutters. The dollar will be shot to hell, and there won't be a wheel turning on any railroad from New York to San Francisco."

"So you favor the man who—and I quote Mr. Bryan—'was once pleased to think that he looked like Napoleon' and now seeks to fasten the gold standard upon us. If he succeeds, grass will grow in the streets."

"Then it'll make feed for horses, because McKinley's bound to come out on top. He'll have big money backing him, and cash hollers even louder than Bryan the Brave."

"Your cynicism offends me, Mr. Brady."

"That wasn't my intention, but there's no disputing a fact. Mark Hanna's made McKinley his man, and Hanna's going to fry the fat out of the banks and every other business for him if he can. I've chipped in myself. I like to stay on the right side of a winner."

As one of many grateful Republicans who foresaw Marcus Alonzo Hanna himself being elected President at a future date, I said a silent "hear, hear!" I appreciated the power he held in Cleveland, Ohio, from my appearances on tour in his opera house there. He also controlled the city's street railways and its newspaper, another *Herald*. At a reception held for me, I found this bald-headed onetime grocer overbearing, but his shrewdness could not be doubted when he had made millions in mining, banks, and railroads. Something he said then stuck in my mind: "Politics are the means to promote sound business, and sound business is the life's blood of this nation." He explained why he had been supplying McKinley with cash and a political machine for years: The governor of Ohio was "the advance guard of prosperity."

I knew for a fact that Hanna had bailed out his candidate after McKinley had been gulled into endorsing notes totaling $130,000 for an old friend of his, one Robert Walker, who finally declared bankruptcy. Hanna passed the hat around among other businessmen, reminding them how good the governor had been to them. Nobody could even guess how many millions he had raised in the eighteen months he set himself to win his man our party's nomination, but it was the most expensive, best organized campaign any of us had ever lived through.

There was a deluge of pamphlets, buttons, and posters. He gave many a delegation the train fare to go and visit with Mc-Kinley in Canton. He ordered swarms of handsome lapel pins in the shape of goldbugs as a symbol of his candidate's stand for firm finance. I was as happy to wear one as I was to sing one of the songs that Hanna sponsored, "The Honest Little Dollar's Come to Stay."

Mama was still crossing swords with Jim. "Where does humanity fit into your picture, pray? Does your new hero spare any thought for that? Remember, 'the humblest citizen in all the land, when clad in armor of a righteous cause, is stronger than all the hosts of error.'" She could not resist quoting the Boy Orator of the Platte.

"Humanity's got to look after itself. Always did, always will. You can hand out all the Christmas baskets in the world, but somebody's got to have made the wampum to pay for 'em first."

"What of those who labor in that factory of yours? Do they concur in your opinions?"

"I'd never fire a man for voting the way he figured was right, but I'll let 'em know if any of 'em votes for Bryan, I'm going to be mighty sore."

Mama could stomach no more. She picked up her shawl and

flounced out the door as fast as her old legs would carry her. I heaved a sigh. "What am I to do with her?"

"She ain't no patch on my ma. Now *she's* been parading up and down outside my office dressed to the nines, claiming I wronged her and swearing I'll burn for it. I'm going to have to get a doctor to take a look at her and see if she didn't ought to be put away, though to tell you the truth it'd break my heart to do it."

"She might be better off in an institution if her mind's wandering."

"She's had to put up with a lot of trouble in her life. I ain't always been the best of sons."

"You've done all you could for her, haven't you? She's never wanted for anything from the day you earned your first dollar."

"She ain't seen much of me lately, and that's a fact. She wants to hold onto everybody—do everything the old Irish way. But you can't always keep looking back over your shoulder at where you come from. You got to keep moving on if you want to make something of yourself. I'm gonna increase her allowance to make sure she don't want for nothing."

On the strength of the report from Dr. Paul Otterbridge, Jim tried to have her committed by a judge for treatment in a sanatarium. His brother Dan stepped in to tell her that Jim was living in sin and to file an objection with the court. Jim and the physician, he claimed, were scheming together to steal Mrs. Brady's money.

Jim carried his troubles to me. "That son of a bitch! She never sees a dime from him, and now he's after poisoning her mind against me."

"Big brother's jealous of little brother. You succeeded; he didn't."

"He's full of horse manure, goddamn holy roller down on his knees every Sunday and no more a Christian than a painted Indian. What a family I've got! But I'll get back at him somehow. I'm going to blacken his name all over this town so he'll never get another job any place."

How far he went in that direction I did not know, but whatever was done achieved no purpose. The court hearings dragged on, providing grist for the press, William Randolph Hearst's New York *Journal* in particular. Nothing Jim could say or do persuaded the judge that only spite spurred on Dan. In the end, a trio of jurists was appointed to handle Mrs. Brady's affairs, by which time public sentiment branded my friend not another Gentleman Jim but a blackguard who persecuted his aged mother.

He pretended not to need consolation. "I don't give a good goddamn, Nell. What do I care if a bunch of horses' asses think I'm a wrong 'un? It don't harm my business one bit. I'll go on making money and enjoying myself spending it."

"But it's all so unfair, Jim, when they mock you like this."

His huge head hung low. "Christ, Nell, ain't that the truth?"

Bicycling assuaged his anguish more effectively than it reduced his weight. I found singing to myself at the piano to be the best antidote for disenchantment, but every morning, rain or shine, I would mount my shining wheels for a turn into Central Park as far as the Reservoir, often with Marie as a companion, both of us jaunty in tweed knickerbockers. On occasion we would pump along as far as Jim's apartments in the Rutland at Broadway and 57th, where he lived not in sin, as his mother imagined, but in solitary splendor with two suites, each of half a dozen rooms stuffed to the gills with new furniture and his growing collection of old paintings.

On Sundays, if I were in the city and not visiting Daughtie at the convent, I rode with Jim. After taking a spill from the guest saddle of his triple seater, I was loyal to my own machine. These outings called for a white serge costume and matching hat of Tyrolean flair. Over the rear wheel of Jim's tandem was strapped a canister of ice into which fitted a gallon or so of orange juice, which was also essential to our Sabbath ritual.

Our entry side by side into the park caused as much stir as Barnum's elephants plodding into Madison Square Garden. Of the three riders, only Barton was too busy to spare a hand for acknowledging the shouts that hailed us. Not even the electric aroused more notice when similar quadricycles were no longer uncommon on the streets. Barton was invariably panting for breath by the time we reached a green knoll at 86th Street. There, as a gallery of strollers watched, we would dismount to take our ease by a "keep off the grass" sign, sipping the juice served by Barton before he stretched out to rest and massage his thighs. It was all peculiarly gratifying. With our show completed, Jim would provide a five-dollar bill for every police officer within range in consideration of their forbearance, and we would be off again with a rear guard of the curious on their own bicycles, eager to form part of the procession.

I had my machine packed in its pouch to join Jim at Saratoga Springs in the early fall. He was locked in battle with a rival manufacturer of undertrucks for railroad cars, the Schoen Pressed Steel Company, founded by a former letter carrier of Philadelphia.

At Jim's headquarters, open house was kept twenty-four hours a day. All I could see missing was a serving of geisha girls. I assumed that, had a prospective customer requested one, Jim would have been glad to arrange for any oriental delicacy to be supplied.

One of the cottages was reserved for Jim and me with no thought on the part of either for employing it as was customary when its tenant was one of the summer crowd from Wall Street who gave Saratoga its lively reputation. Now that the hills were splashed with brown and gold, the transients were fast disappearing. I should miss the August horse racing, but I had my bicycle, and I anticipated a few days of quiet, at ease in a community where I felt at home.

Newport, conversely, had never been for me. The snobs there were haughtier than Mrs. Potter Palmer in their attitude toward "that woman" who in their purblind eyes symbolized sinfulness. For all Jim's efforts to win friends in polite society, he was dismissed as a pariah by every hostess mindful of her place in the social register. By the standards of the *nouveaux riches* as well as of the more securely established families, we were both vulgarians.

He paraded the daily meetings, handing out cigars like the father of twins, hauling conventioneers into the cottages for a bite to eat or a bottle, leading the way down the street if they could afford a flutter at Canfield's elegant Club House. With Jim, I had previously met its courtly proprietor, who also operated the Nautilus Club in Newport as well as the most scintillating casino in New York, justifiably known as "the Monte Carlo of America." Despite his closeness to Frank Farrell, Jim had helped stake Richard Canfield when he was released from prison after serving six months for running a small-time gambling den in Providence, Rhode Island. The reading he did behind bars implanted a passion for collecting rare books and fine paintings. And today? "By God, Nell, he's got to be worth ten million dollars, made by skinning millionaires, and he's pally with Morgan, Vanderbilts, Johnny Gates, the Whitneys—you name 'em. And what does he do with his coin? Spends it on pictures I wouldn't give a thank-you for! Says if had his time to live over again, he'd be a college professor."

Canfield's rule could not be bent even for Jim, who had to be extremely selective about whom he brought in. No tinhorns gained admission through the electrically controlled doors of the Club House. If an acolyte could not withstand the heavy losses which, Canfield warned, were unavoidable in the long run, he was excluded. I was curious to see this Saratoga place, being already acquainted with the Manhattan casino which the ex-felon was reputed to have spent a cool million furnishing.

Once our little party had passed inspection, we progressed through a beautiful reception room into a thinly populated "public" salon, where the play was within the means of a prosperous master car builder, though one of our companions winced on learning that they were expected to begin by buying not less than five hundred dollars' worth of chips. If they wished to make the sky the limit, there were more secluded accommodations on an upper floor where such enthusiasts as Bet-a-Million might spend forty-eight hours in continual play. Personally, I decided that even the downstairs room was too rarefied for me.

Canfield, stately, clean-shaven, gray-eyed, came over to have a word with "Mr. B." and "Miss L." as we were addressed under a house regulation that lent anonymity to every patron. After congratulating him on the magnificence of all we had seen so far, I wondered aloud if I might be given a glimpse of some of his works of art.

The gray eyes penetrated mine. "I extend hospitality to two kinds of patron, Miss L.—those who search for a game of chance and those who appreciate a collector's mania. The two do not mix. Which is your category?"

"When I gamble, I like to collect, if that answers your question. I believe you are a friend of Mr. Whistler's?"

"I am proud to say I am. I have sat for him, in fact. The result happens to be hanging upstairs."

"I met him once in London in '83 and inspected some of the work he exhibited at the Grosvenor gallery."

This was enough for Canfield. While Jim watched over his charges below, I was taken up two flights of pile-carpeted stairs into the owner's personal quarters. For all the opulence of the furniture, it was the walls that took one's breath away. Whistlers by the dozen adorned them, oils, watercolors, etchings, drypoints, lithographs. Canfield, whose portrait depicted him as grave as a medieval prelate, treated me to a lecture on the influences that had affected the artist.

"I must say that I envy you this room, Mr. Canfield. If I had the money, I, too, would buy pictures."

"If I were Mr. B., I'd hand over one as a souvenir. But, alas, I am not. I will, however, interject myself and put you in touch with someone with a bigger heart than mine, a gentleman who may be even more charitable than Mr. B."

I smiled for him. "Would that be entirely ethical?"

"I do not know that I have any code of ethics. I don't care a rap about what other people think of me. I never did."

"Would it be moral, then?"

"As morals are considered by most people, I have no more than a cat."

And so Jesse Lewisohn entered the scene, stringy, mournful, sickly, and possessed of a fortune from his family's United Metals Selling Company, which had ambitions to put together a monopoly of every lead and silver smelter in the Union. The Lewisohns were not up in the Rockefellers' class, but they liked corporations that would grow like beanstalks once plenty of stock had been spread around as fertilizer. Jesse, one of Canfield's most dependable sources of income, was playing faro in a private room that night. I left an open invitation for him to call when we were both in New York again.

I returned home to quarrel with Abbey and company over their failure to raise me to prima donna status. They pretended to have lost $200,000 on my contract and posed no obstacles when I left them to be reunited with George Lederer in a new operetta whose strongest appeal for me lay in its title, *An American Beauty*. My qualifications had been increased by the recent loss of some ten pounds through bicycling.

An arduous two-month touring schedule called for travel from one city to the next to be done on Sundays to permit opening on Monday nights. This often meant going hungry, since dining cars might be omitted from Sunday trains, and I would have to survive the journey on snacks bought during station stops. Much as I had been looking forward to a hotel supper, appetite vanished when I read the telegram from Mama that was awaiting me in a pigeonhole behind the reception desk. Papa, visiting a brother in Detroit, had been seized with a heart attack. On Saturday night, he had passed away.

The decision confronting me was as taxing as any that ever had to be made. To attend the funeral would involve canceling all performances for the coming week. I alone in the company would receive salary in that event. I communed with myself in my suite, trying to determine what Papa would have desired. Then I seemed to hear his voice: "Don't worry about me, Nellie. Think about the rest of the people who work for you. Hide your grief. I'll understand."

I telegraphed Mama, my uncle, and sisters: Regretfully, I should not be in Detroit to see him buried. From the abuse to which the newspapers of New York and Chicago subjected me, one might have imagined that I had caused his end. I managed to atone in part for my omission, if that was what it was. After George Lederer consented to squeeze two extra days into our timetable, I made a sentimental journey to Clinton, Iowa, to sing *An American Beauty* there in remembrance of Papa. I was not in good voice; it was not easy to sing with a lump in one's throat.

At last, we got back to New York. On our first night, Jesse Lewisohn sat several seats away from Jim in the front row. Jesse's bouquet was the bigger of the two and the diamond concealed within it of equal size to Jim's.

Jesse more than made up as a stock speculator what he lost as a votary of Canfield's; he was already a second-generation millionaire. Jim fattened his own fortune on Tuesday, November 3, when what tomorrow's *World* would describe as "a sound-money cyclone" swept the country to elect McKinley, piling up unprecedented majorities against Bryan. Pulitzer's newspaper had reason for glee after its warning the Democrats in midsummer that "adoption of the free silver heresy would be suicide."

After the Tuesday-night curtain fell, I received a telephone call from Jim. Could I be tempted into going over to the Hoffman House for "a bit of fun"? Not in the bar, of course, since its celebrated Bouguereau canvas of carefree nymphs made it an exclusively masculine preserve, but in the Ladies' Parlor, which was doing nocturnal duty as a betting ring.

His eagerness for my companionship had been encouraged lately by the new alliance with Jesse, but tonight Jim's attention was divided between myself and his cronies who had congregated in another corner of the room. Gates was there, along with Gould's slippery henchman, Jimmy Keene, and some others bearing the brand of out-of-town riches. From time to time, Jim abandoned me altogether to grudging gallantry from his preoccupied comrades, whose minds were on the election, not on me. He was off to the bar, he would say, in search of easy money. I gathered that while individual stakes in the Ladies' Parlor ran higher, the sheer volume of wagers laid under the gaze of the Bouguereau maidens exceeded $400,000.

Whenever he reentered, he would make another bet among his fellows. Missouri, he declared unequivocally, would go to Bryan, Kentucky to McKinley. The Democrats would lose the Midwest, the Republicans take New York City for the first time in history. The returns posted on the bulletin board ten or fifteen minutes later as they flowed in by telephone and telegraph wire almost always showed Jim the winner.

Dawn was breaking when he took me home. I had not questioned his ability to make many a dollar before, but I was piqued by this newfound skill in politics. How had he done it? His laughter shook him like a blanc mange as he tugged back a coat sleeve to reveal a starched shirt cuff covered with penciled figures.

"I don't want you thinking I'm some kind of a magician. Look here, Nell. I never did go to the bar like I made out. I was popping off to McKinley's headquarters across the street in the Fifth Avenue Hotel. A pal of mine there give me the news before they got a smell of it over in the Hoffman House. I must have cleaned up damn near two hundred thousand dollars."

If he was driven by a sense of rivalry with Jesse, he would never admit it, but Jim forthwith took a plunge on the stock market, territory he had not ventured to tread before. His shares in the once bankrupt Philadelphia & Reading Railroad, bought dirt cheap on a tip from another champion of the Hoffman House bar, leaped to sixty-eight points following on Bryan's defeat. Jim sold out with a profit of fifty dollars a share. Now he, too, had made his first million and $250,000 more.

I wondered about the effect it would have on him, hoping not only for my sake that wealth would not sow the seeds of miserliness as it had in others who would shrink from doling out a plugged nickel to a blind beggar. There was no cause for alarm. "I'm going to do things in a big way from now on. There's a lot of people ain't been getting much from me, and this is a good time to do different."

That Christmas he inaugurated what Jesse promptly labeled the Brady Beneficent Society. At the Washington Market, Jim picked out one hundred and seventeen turkeys, each a twenty-pounder, and had them crated together with all the ingredients for Yuletide dinner. They went to those he thought of as friends —patrolmen, street cleaners, veterans of hook-and-ladder companies, railroad clerks, section bosses, even crews of trains on which he had traveled. Jim, one had to conclude, would always be a plebeian at heart.

With Papa gone, I counted myself fortunate in having two men eager to care for me, asking very little more than a share of the attention I attracted in public. I had speculated over what Jim's reaction would be to Jesse. It was comforting to find no jealousy apparent in either of them. Their tolerance of each other was readily explicable. Neither enjoyed any physical favor from me other than sisterly kisses, and I did not award those promiscuously. So far as I was able to judge, neither wanted anything more. Here were two males who had never married or shown any inclination to seek a wife. To myself, I posed the unutterable question: Would they be capable of satisfying the needs of a less fastidious woman? The only possible answer was no.

It may have been due to the absence of scandal associated with my name for the last three years, or perhaps theater managements were alert to the fact that my appeal as the epitome of wickedness was founded on legend, but my career was in the doldrums. Little bits of girls were suddenly basking in the limelight—Anna Held batting her big eyes and murmuring, "Won't you come and play wiz me?" and pale blonde Edna May, a chorus girl once scarcely worth her fifteen dollars a week, now the overnight toast of the town in *The Belle of New York*, a make-believe Salvation Army lass warbling, "They never proceed to follow the light, but they always follow me."

The day was coming when Jesse's brother Oscar would take shrimpish Miss May as his bride and she could retire to queen it in London. Jesse once or twice urged the same course on me, but I was leery of loveless marriages and too accustomed to singing for my supper to think of accepting him. He would have to be content with speaking of me as his fiancée and paying some of the bills, but never, I insisted, the costs of maintaining Daughtie.

One published barb came close to demoralizing me: "She has ceased to be a drawing card of pronounced magnetism." To disprove the accusation, I was prompted to lower my sights and accept equal billing with two others, Della Fox and Jefferson de Angelis, to ensure my return to a theater on whose stage I had triumphed in the past, the Casino. *The Wedding Day*, as the show was called, evoked cacophonous applause—and an echo of former days: Chatterton sued for divorce on the grounds that I had deserted him.

Over Abe's objections, I filed an answer to the petition, glossing over the more intimate details of his inadequacies lest they damage the aura of a goddess of supposed voluptuousness. I should have been better advised to be less discreet. In October of '98, a New Jersey court unjustly awarded the puppet Chatterton a decree against me. In theory, I was in a position to pursue a fourth husband, but the two men I admired above all others were not available. Rear Admiral George Dewey, hero of Manila

Bay and more recently liberator of Manila, whose name would
be immortalized in song, neckties, and a gum called "Dewey
chewies," was a widower about to remarry. Lieutenant Colonel
Teddy Roosevelt of the Rough Riders, who had put the in-
glorious Spaniards to rout on San Juan Hill, already had a wife.
Any contentment I was to find must derive from working and
earning money.

If New York's ideas of what constituted a handsome woman
were degenerating, German preferences remained steadfast.
When I was approached with an invitation to tour over there,
my initial reaction was to refuse. I foresaw no joy singing in the
Reichsland. But my most extravagant terms were willingly met.
I could select my own songs, deliver them whenever I pleased,
and be paid $2,500 a week plus expenses in the bargain. I took
Suzanne along for a vacation when I sailed on the *Teutonic*.

As I had expected, I disliked Germany and the Germans on
sight, but none more than Prince Henry, younger son of Kaiser
Wilhelm I, who appraised me through his monocle the day I
opened at the Winter Garden in Berlin. The arrangement of
flowers he sent the next morning, seven feet long from cut stems
to top blossoms, would have graced a winning racehorse. I responded with silence, as I did to the gigantic bouquet of violets
delivered on the second morning and the basket of red roses that
arrived on the third. Later in the day, Prince Henry raised the
stakes and sent a ruby-and-diamond brooch shaped like a dragonfly. It was such an inferior piece of craftsmanship that I asked
the Berlin advocate who represented me to return it, but he was
too chickenhearted to risk an affront to royalty.

On the fifth day, my sister and I were picking at an unappetiz-
ing breakfast in our suite, clad only in peignoirs, when a courtier
in black tails and pin-striped trousers strode in with an escort
of two uniformed Prussians. Suzanne paled at the prospect of
our being borne off to whatever was the Hohenzollern version
of a Turkish seraglio, but I gestured for her to be calm.

The emissary's heels and his ivory teeth clicked simultaneously. "His Royal Highness presents his compliments and
informs Fraulein Russell that he desires the pleasure of her
company for supper tonight at twelve o'clock sharp. She will
please not keep him waiting."

I lit a Melachrino. "Be so good as to inform his High and Mightiness that I am unacquainted with him, and I am not in the habit of supping with strangers." The factotum snapped his fingers to signal withdrawal, tendered an arthritic bow, and left without further word.

He reappeared the following morning, this time to present me with a note, signed by the irrepressible princeling himself. "Fraulein Russell should please take her bicycle and ride out to the Grunewald at eight A.M. tomorrow. On the North Drive she will notice on a white horse an officer in green uniform who, if she descends from her bicycle, will dismount and direct her."

Like Queen Victoria, I felt I had the right to be unamused. "You may tell your master that I would not arise at eight o'clock on any morning to see the Kaiser kiss the Pope. You can also let him know that I am an American who is not afraid to think for herself. You may as well give him this while you're at it." I deposited the gimcrack dragonfly into his tremulous hands.

Suzanne was equally trembly after he had clicked his way out. "Suppose they come to arrest us."

"They wouldn't damn well dare."

We returned to New York by way of England, where Jesse was awaiting us. "So what did you think of Germany, Lillian?" he asked when we were ensconced in our hotel.

"The audiences were kind, but they all looked so stolid and strange."

"And the big, blond Bismarck herring?"

"They amazed me. German men think they're the lords of creation. A woman is apparently created only for their comfort and pleasure."

The same peace-loving Suzanne who used to pacify Mama when we were girls suggested that we change the subject and sit down for a few hands of whist. The sores rubbed on my soul by Teutonic arrogance were quick to heal. After all, I had probably made more money in a few fretful weeks than if I had gone digging for Klondike gold.

After I had reestablished myself on West 77th Street, I was surprised when days went by without a call from Jim. I felt it was for him to contact me rather than the reverse, so I confined my bicycling to Central Park, staying clear of the Rutland. I was in Rector's one evening with Jesse, who was engrossed with the menu, hunting for something bland to soothe an upset digestion, when to my astonishment Jim entered with a young girl on his arm. Charles Rector sighted my raised finger and carried my invitation for Jim and his filly to dine with us.

His manner was a mixture of bravado, sheepishness, and concupiscence. "This here's Miss Edna McCauley, otherwise known as a niece of mine. Comes from Brooklyn. Used to work behind a perfume counter until I come across her in Peacock Alley. She dropped her handkerchief, and I picked it up."

She was a pretty little baggage with a mass of auburn curls and a winning smile, but she was certainly no relative of his. If picking up had been the start, I could guess which one of them did the picking. "What work engages you now, Edna?"

A nod from him was her green light to be frank. "I look after Jim. He's the most wonderful man. I have my own French maid and more clothes than I can ever wear."

His slits of eyes twinkled. "She come for tea and stayed for breakfast, didn't you, darlin'? We just got back from Atlantic City."

She was oh! so young. For a moment, I puzzled over what in heaven had impelled him to take up with her. Then all became clear. Jim modeled himself on others. The diamonds he flashed were a showoff's hobby copied from the like of Abe's partner, William Howe. As a promoter, Jim was a facsimile of Johnny Gates's species, though as a freshly minted millionaire he was a pale imitation, lacking the intestinal instinct to hold onto his money. Keeping a mere child as a plaything was a habit of his friend Stanford White's.

Stanny's latest chippy was a cow-eyed blonde named Evelyn Nesbit, who had arrived in New York from Pittsburgh at the age of perhaps fourteen to earn a living as a model and presumed bedmate for some of our local Bohemians. After Stanny came across her, he kept her to himself for a while, though Jim knew about her and even showed me a photograph of her, wearing nothing but a shawl draped none too respectably over her skinny shoulders, posing, if you please, as Mary Magdalene.

Apparently she fancied herself as an actress, so Stanny arranged to put her on view as a flower girl in *Florodora*, a show

I had stayed away from because I was sick and tired of reading press agents' puffs for the six so-called sizzlers who made up the sextette, all of whom—Agnes Wayburn, Vaughn Texsmith, Margaret Walker, Marjorie Relyea, Marie Wilson, and Daisy Green —landed a millionaire as a husband.

I wanted to see the Nesbit girl for myself, so with Jim and his Edna, Jesse and I took ourselves off to the Casino and the front row of the orchestra, timing our arrival nicely for a minute or two before the start of the overture in order to make a suitable entrance down the center aisle with an honor guard of ushers. It was necessary to squeeze past a dough-faced young man who occupied an end seat as if in a trance, staring vacuously at the curtain. Jim had to tap his shoulder twice to get him to move.

"I seen you here before, ain't I? You're Harry Thaw. I used to do business with your father, Bill, when he was with the Pennsy."

Young Thaw could have been stone deaf for all the response he made. "He's a weird duck," Edna whispered in my left ear as we settled down. "I wouldn't want to meet him on a dark night."

Florodora struck me as a fair example of the new sort of musical show that audiences were taking to nowadays with pretty tunes and attractive costumes, though the six daughters of Venus who warbled about being "pretty maids" would scarcely have drawn a second glance in the old days when men went for something sturdier. Nesbit turned out to be not much more than bones and a simpering smile, but from the moment she was on stage, Thaw jiggled in his seat as if ants had invaded his underwear.

"He's nuts about that flower girl," Edna murmured. I could not disagree.

If Jim had been my lover, I should probably have resented her, but he never had been. From the adoration in his face when he was with her, it was evident that he was hers, or was the relationship no more than a hope of his, impossible of fulfillment? I decided before our evening was over that I pitied him and silently wished him better from Edna than he'd had from me. She was no rival. I would not withhold my friendship.

Jim's infatuation with Edna was no blow to my ego; the

pounding came from a totally different quarter. The German expedition had not magnified my value in American producers' eyes. I had to settle for $1,000 a week when George Lederer and I let bygones be bygones and I was cast in the prima's role in *La Belle Hélène*, a work of some antiquity whose composer, Jacques Offenbach, had been dead for almost twenty years. The new American form called "musical comedy" was not suited for me, or so the managers believed.

A fellow performer was pert Edna Wallace Hopper, youthful bride of DeWolf Hopper. I used to wonder whether she was as tired as I was of hearing him reciting "Casey at the Bat" wherever he went. The wind begin to rise the morning after our debut when the *Journal* critic jeered: "Lillian has no beauty below the chin. She could not possibly wear three-quarters of a yard of silk and a corset lace with the confident effrontery of Edna Wallace Hopper, and she moves her grand-opera amplitude with the soft heaviness of a nice white elephant."

I bore with the exhibition she made of herself throughout our New York run, but when we moved on to Philadelphia she went too far. Her first entrance was made in a costume whose briefness had been further abridged by a dressmaker's scissors. A claque of students in the balcony hooted for more, or was it for less? Their desires were granted by an even scantier gown in her second scene, while their heckling of me approached the limits of tolerance.

For her third scene, the vixen came onstage in the remnants of a dress that in Anthony Comstock's heyday would have brought in the police to arrest her for indecency. This evening it caused an outbreak of unashamed lip-smacking from the gallery and cat-calls for my every song. At the earliest opportunity, I stormed in on Lederer. "I have performed for the last time. I will not share the stage with a half-naked slut."

He remained self-composed. "Walk out on me again, my dear, and I shall sue you again for breach of contract."

"I suggest you read that contract. I am under no obligation to perform for you outside of New York City. I came here to Philadelphia out of goodness of heart after you borrowed six hundred dollars from me to meet your first week's payroll. You never would have been granted a lease on the Casino without first signing me. You are a cheapskate, George. If you sue me, I'll sure as fate sue you."

That is precisely what happened; he claimed $15,000 from me, I a like sum from him. But it was a bout between Tweedledum and Tweedledee when Abe represented both of us. Not a penny changed hands in either direction.

The quartet of Russell, Lewisohn, Brady, and McCauley spent a great deal of time together in rare harmony. Jesse and I stayed with Beauty and the Beast in a summer cottage he took at Belmar on the Jersey shore. We went as a foursome to Saratoga Springs for the August racing. I had her to my parties as a useful extra girl whenever Jim was out of town. I spent many an evening with Jesse in the house Jim bought for Edna and himself on East 86th at a cost in cash of $87,000 with another $320,000 spent to furnish it.

In the basement, we played pool on a mahogany table whose legs were inlaid with red carnelians and azure-blue lapis lazuli, and roulette with onyx chips. When we were sated with these sports, there were dice boards and chuck-a-luck cages to amuse us, and tables for faro, poker, and even chess. Jim introduced us to the white-and-green marble kitchen, hung with spotless copperware; the new medicine men, the alienists, would have been fascinated by his dictate requiring all servants to immerse themselves at least once a day in the porcelain tub in an adjoining bathroom, while the kitchen itself must be hosed down every afternoon. I guessed that Stanny had taught Jim something about dining in Roman style. If Jim was going to serve a dryad scrambling out of a cake for dessert, he would make sure she was well-scrubbed both before and after her debouchment.

I giggled to myself at the sight of the bric-a-brac that swamped the Louis Quatorze living room, where the chairs were reinforced after one of them subsided when he sat on it.

In similar interests of hygiene, every bedroom had its private bath. His own sanctum contained more polished mahogany, a bed big enough for four, and a barbershop chair bolted to the floor. "It ain't beautiful, but it's damn comfortable when I get my morning shave." The top floor held equipment of a strictly utilitarian nature—a complete gymnasium with parallel bars, pulleyed weights, Indian clubs, and a rowing machine. I put them all to use during some of my visits, but he boycotted the place after he exercised just once in front of a floor-length looking glass that was set in one wall. "I never seen anything more repulsive."

But it was the Turkish Room on the second floor that revealed how Jim's tastes had flowered under White's influence. This harem was decorated with bronze and marble statues of coy nudes and amorous couples engaged in the practice of what euphemists would call love. Each corner was occupied by a divan whose velvet-covered swan's-down lay so thick that one was half submerged in it, Jim's, of course, being at least the size of two double beds. Brocaded draperies were suspended on rods from the ceiling in such a manner that they could be drawn to enclose any or all these nests. I began to feel compassion for poor Edna.

She confided to me that he allowed her a thousand dollars a month as pin money, hung her like a Christmas tree with diamonds, and accorded her permission to borrow anything or everything from his own collection. "But I'd rather not wear so much jewelry, and I'd like to choose some dresses myself."

"Then that is what you must do. You are a woman, not a toy."

After this, I went shopping with her whenever time allowed. The effect of my coaching dumfounded him. "God damn it, the girl's a lady. I'm going to get her into society if I bust a gut trying."

I had but one more thing to teach her. Undetected by Jim, I introduced her to the satisfaction to be obtained from puffing my latest fad, jasmine-scented cigarettes rolled to order in Havana.

XIV

I FOUND the opening of the twentieth century to have a lot
in common with a gathering of old friends on a New Year's
Eve magnified to the nth degree. We were all smitten by an urge
to weigh the unalterable past against the bright yet imponderable
future. Debate raged on interminably as to whether the new era
would dawn on Monday, January 1, 1900, or one year later.
Never one to dawdle, I opted for the earlier date.

As one of nearly 76,000,000 Americans, I felt we had reason
to celebrate the dawn of an age that would surely set us on top
of the world. We had remembered the *Maine*, blown up in
Havana harbor, and given the Spanish slavemasters in Cuba the
hammering they deserved; my soul still thrilled to recall Teddy
Roosevelt and his Rough Riders' charge.

With Mr. McKinley in the White House and looking forward
to four more years there, we had progress and prosperity at home
and prices that all but the most idle of the poor could well afford:
gingham for five cents a yard, a well-made corset for fifty cents, a
pair of shoes for $1.79, hotel rooms available at a dollar a day.
Of course, far too much whiskey was consumed at two dollars
a gallon, but I shared Mama's hopes for the Anti-Saloon League,
as well as for the spread of woman suffrage. To date, our sex had
the vote in only four sparsely settled Western states.

We had witnessed the miracles of American invention in
electric light, Edison's talking machines and Kinetoscope, the
building of skyscrapers and horseless carriages, and now something known as wireless communication, discovered by a Mr.

Marconi, was being advertised as the next marvel in our world of wonders.

In my profession, Americans were beginning to make their mark as authors, composers and internationally acclaimed performers, though in that respect the festivities were bittersweet for me; this phenomenon had arisen rather late in the day. I was an idol of the older generation. I might wear the fashionable new shirtwaists, but I was associated with the day of the bustle, and foreigners continued to win the kudos in grand opera that had been denied me. But I could give thanks that my health remained robust, delivering me from the hands of doctors who spoke so much about such developments in their profession as Roentgen's X-rays, radium, and the indecent prying into personal matters practiced by the followers of a Viennese Jew named Sigmund Freud.

The graybeards rushed into print with assessments of the events and personages that had left the deepest imprint on the previous decades: the most startling inventions, the greatest disasters, the best books, the superlative beauties, and so forth. It was pleasant to discover oneself placed first among the beauties.

Though acknowledgment on lists of handsome women was all well and good, it was no substitute for profitable employment. Caught up in the business of appraising my physical assets and liabilities, I realized that I must leap new hurdles or be put out to grass. I could not exist chewing the cud of former glory.

As it happened, it was Jesse who acted as intermediary in the opening up of a new vista. On an afternoon together at the Sheepshead Bay track, he had momentarily left our box to inspect a horse in the paddock. He returned with Lew Fields in tow, the elongated "Dutch" comedian who, with his partner, stubby Joe Weber, was in process of moving into new premises on 29th Street, a block above Miner's Fifth Avenue Theater.

Hearsay was all I knew of the team of Weber & Fields. The Pat-and-Mike jokes of my youth had given way to jests about Abe and Izzy. Weber & Fields had floated in on the tide, graduates of the old Dime Museum on 14th Street, where at the age of nine they acquired the art of slapstick, knocking each other around for six dollars a week, divided between them.

I was too busy picking runners by my own method—eyes

shut, a hatpin stuck into race card—to pay much heed at first. Then Lew posed a question: "Why don't you use a fork so one jab would give you win, place, and show?"

This was funny enough to gain him closer attention. Apparently he had come to bell the cat. He and his partner wanted me to be the leading lady of their burlesques, trusting that my reputation would sell tickets. What would it take to entice me? Their proposal was so preposterous that I tried the trick of quoting outrageous terms to quash it. "Twelve hundred and fifty dollars a week, guaranteed for thirty-five weeks, all gowns and costumes paid for."

Their new Music Hall held only six hundred and sixty-five seats, costing from fifty cents to two dollars. They had been forced to borrow from relatives and friends to acquire the little unkempt building which they were renovating themselves, sweeping, scrubbing, doing all the carpentry, while their fellow comic, Sam Bernard, plied his former trade as a house painter with pots of salmon pink and beige and touched up the cherubs with gold leaf.

Lew did not flinch. "Write your own contract. We'll expect you in August."

Thus it was that I commenced a reign in vaudeville, sometimes to be revealed as the curtains parted reclining in bed, clad in a negligée, or at other times in natty male attire, with plug hat on head and cigarette in hand—this when increasing hostility to smokers led three railroads to bar them from their cars and a woman risked arrest if she dared light up on the New York streets.

The sketches never failed to convulse our loyal followers. For months on end the roof was raised with laughter at the skit in which spry David Warfield played Sigmund Cohenski, a millionaire whose daughter Uneeda loved a Navy captain.

Uneeda: The captain is my ideal of a hero.

Sigmund: A hero? Is dot a business? A tailor is a business, a shoemaker is a business, but a hero? Better you should marry a bookkeeper.

Uneeda: A bookkeeper? I suppose you think the pen is mightier than the sword.

Sigmund: You bet your life. Could you sign checks with a sword?

It was like being landed on the moon in a Jules Verne fantasy, but it afforded maximum pay for a minimum of effort, and my girlish aspirations to sing the arias of Gluck and Mozart were easily forgotten. Backstage, the very air smelled differently with its scent of pickled herring, lox, and bagels. Pugnacious Joe Weber and deadpan Lew had followed the route of Oscar Hammerstein in escaping from the ghetto south of 14th Street, but they had not lost their taste for tasty Jewish delicatessen, and they had not put on airs or grown a beard like the maestro of the Victoria Theater. Jews were few and far between in our audiences, but they were proud of Lew and Joe.

Somehow, I had always associated vaudeville with its comparatively recent birth in Boston, Massachusetts, where a former circus employee, Benjamin Franklin Keith, opened a small museum and show in a vacant candy store next to the old Adams House on Washington Street. The chief attractions of the Gaiety were Baby Alice, a 1½-pound midget, and a stuffed "mermaid." Among his later lures to draw in the yokels was a chicken with the head of a semihuman—and a pair of apprentice comedians billed as Weber & Fields.

What brought most men in to see our shows was undoubtedly the opportunity to goggle at the legs of the longest chorus line visible on the Rialto. Frankie Bailey's were registered for copyright at the Library of Congress in her press agent's name, making her the envy of her peers—Bonnie Magin, Goldie Mohr, and Aimee Angeles, to mention a few—who were equally well endowed.

Yet young Keith set traditions of refinement which I found were carefully observed by his disciples. Vulgarity was frowned on behind the scenes, though one could catch the odor of whiskey and beer on the breaths of male and female performers alike. When everyone had only the few lines of a sketch to learn and improvisation was encouraged, the whole atmosphere was more easygoing than in more ambitious productions. But though my dressing room was more modest than I had been used to, I had no need to keep the door locked during my costume changes, as I had in such palaces of entertainment as the Casino. Thank God, we were spared the dog and pony acts which could turn corridors into a barnyard and keep porters on the trot.

On stage and off, there was no shortage of laughter, though some of the jokes were older than the costumes of the chorus. A soldier has been shot. "Where?" asks Joe. "In the excitement," Lew answers. "I got a pearl out of an oyster at Shanley's," says Bonnie Magin. "That's nothing," retorts Goldie Mohr. "I got a whole diamond necklace out of a lobster."

I was satisfied that I was abreast of the time, though I would have hesitated about expressing the thought aloud in those words backstage for fear of ribald chuckles. John J. Murdock had opened his Masonic Temple Roof as a vaudeville theater, Alex Pantages had found a new circuit, Hammerstein's Victoria Theater was a vaudeville house, and Gus Sun was doing fine in the same business in Ohio.

Neither could I feel I was desecrating a God-given talent when Maurice Barrymore played in vaudeville, like Mr. and Mrs. Sidney Drew, Sarah Bernhardt, and Nazimova. As I grew more reconciled to my new circumstances, parts were found for me in some of the playlets. DeWolf Hopper enlisted with us when "Casey" had palled on him, and he had also had enough of one-night stands and sleeping cars. Over the footlights, he explained, "When I finally climbed into a stationary bed, I had to hire two men to shake it all night and pour cinders down my neck."

I suppose the nethermost point was plumbed when the curtain rose to reveal Hopper and myself perched in the branches of a tree. William Randolph Hearst's chortle rang out above the others as Hopper and I prepared to climb down. "Have you got a safety pin?" my line ran. "My bloomers are coming down." He had not, needless to say, so it was up to me to decide how much anatomy I was prepared to disclose at each descent.

That was in the show entitled *Fiddle-dee-dee*, for which John Stromberg, whom we called "Honey," wrote the music. He suffered so gravely from rheumatism that he resorted to loading his pockets with rabbit's feet, four-leaf clovers, and any other kind of lucky charm in a futile effort to relieve the pain. He sent word one day for me to journey to Freeport, Long Island, where he lay in agony. He said he had "a very pretty song" in mind for me.

Not long afterward, he put an end to himself with a dose of the arsenical compound, Paris green. When his pockets were emptied, a manuscript sheet was found in one of them, the notes spotted with the poisonous green powder. The melody had the quality of the Negro spirituals which had not before appealed to me. But "Come Down, My Evenin' Star" could bring tears to every listener thereafter.

If its birth was counted as 1900, the new century produced fresh notoriety and guaranteed income, but it was not until November that I felt the surge of something more substantial. One erstwhile hero, Admiral Dewey, with his mustache that looked like painted cast iron, had made himself a laughingstock by marrying a young widow and aspiring to capture the White House from McKinley. But my other idol, Governor Roosevelt of New York, had no discernible blemish, apart from having a wife and half a dozen children.

Jim's trips to the West convinced him that without Roosevelt at his side McKinley would lose the Presidency to Bryan, and the country would be dosed to death with the quack remedies prescribed by that sham statesman. Hence I was elated when at the Philadelphia convention Roosevelt agreed, albeit reluctantly, to be our party's candidate for Vice President. My joy knew no bounds at the receipt of an invitation to take a seat on the reviewing stand in Madison Square on November 3, forty-eight hours before Election Day, when New York was to march for Teddy.

Politics set Mama and me against each other as usual. She was looking forward to the day when the jailbird Debs would run for the highest office in the land. Meantime, she was doing as much as failing health would allow in behalf of Daniel De Leon, her Socialist Labor Party's forlorn hope for the Assembly in the 16th District.

On the eve of the parade for Teddy, she came to my house with the light of battle rekindled in her rheumy eyes. "We are holding our rally tonight, Nellie, and I am to be among the speakers. It would do you good to hear more enlightened views than those of the cowboy Roosevelt. We are expecting an enthusiastic turnout."

I ignored her gibe about the governor. "And who is to look after you if there's trouble with the police?"

"There will be no trouble. Daniel is notifying Chief Devery of our meeting to obtain the necessary permit in advance."

(With Croker again the boss of Tammany, Big Bill Devery, sad to say, was back in charge of the police department.) "I am as capable as ever of taking care of myself."

I felt constant concern for this impossible seventy-two-year-old mother of mine, who was too stubborn to accept any financial help from me no matter how hard I pressed the matter. A shawl for Christmas or a new pair of shoes for her birthday was the limit of her tolerance, and if she thought any gift had cost too much, it would be sent back to me with a note of reproval.

She lived by the rules laid down in a sampler she had embroidered as a schoolgirl which hung over the chest of drawers in the tiny back bedroom she occupied at Mrs. Walker's: *Use it up; wear it out; make it do; or do without.* The landlady, fast approaching seventy herself, let her have the room rent-free and paid her a dollar or so a week, too, for her assistance in running the house, kept as spotless as it had ever been, though boarders now were limited to a maximum of four, including Mama.

The rest of her meager income came in the form of interest earned on the $874.72 left her by Papa, his total estate, deposited with a Brooklyn branch of one of the new national banks which were a legacy of the war. She questioned the ethics of drawing money she had not earned, and she distrusted the entire banking system, but Suzanne's husband succeeded in persuading her that it was a better solution than spending the capital and making herself a charity case.

She kept herself on a strict budget that allowed her to contribute small sums to the legion of causes she supported, though it excluded the purchase of newspapers; she shared Mrs. Walker's daily *Sun.* Doing the shopping was Mama's responsibility, since she could drive a harder bargain than the mistress of the house when she went the rounds of the butcher, the baker, the fishmonger and greengrocer. Her room she took as part of her wages, but board was a different question. She insisted on paying for a share of the groceries, always too great a share in Mrs. Walker's opinion, which led to an inordinate amount of haggling between them when Mama returned from an expedition to the shops with the price of every purchase carefully written down in a little black book maintained for the purpose.

Going down the stairs in my house that evening, she slipped

and twisted her ankle. I hastily applied a cold compress to reduce the swelling, but she shrugged off my plea that she rest in a spare bedroom. "I have given my word that I will speak. A bandaged limb will be no handicap."

I was due at the theater within the hour, but I was also concerned for her safety. First, I telephoned Suzanne to see if she or her husband might be willing to mount guard over Mama wherever her hare-brained meeting was to be held. Their maid answered: They were at a vestry meeting. I had no further recourse but to make a call to the stage manager, Felix Isman, and tell him with a piteous improvised croak that I suspected the onset of laryngitis. Old clothes, a hair net, and cheeks creamed clean of makeup substituted Helen Leonard for Lillian Russell. A hansom carried us to party headquarters at the corner of 7th Street and Avenue C.

There, amid the repugnantly evocative odor of stale smoke, printers' ink on cheap pamphlets, and unlaundered linen, we gathered that De Leon's efforts to book an outdoor site on 49th Street had been futile. As Chief Devery informed him, "Every one of 'em is engaged for this evening."

So the soapbox platform was set up right outside, and the citizenry of the dismal neighborhood thickened around it like ants drawn by a sugar cube. A weedy clerk and a burly drayman preceded Mama on the speaker's stand with familiar complaints of the "injustices" inflicted by "the system" on their "comrades." I stayed in the darkness at the rear, scarf pulled up about my ears, saying nothing to anyone. Mama's shrill voice had just declaimed, "There is no freedom for a people when the few own the instruments by which necessities for all are produced," when a police officer clambered up beside her, objecting that without an official permit the gathering was illegal.

To a crescendo of booing, three pairs of hands reached out of the mob to drag him down and frog-march him away. After some minutes of uproar, Mama resumed. She warmed to her theme. "What, you may well ask, must be done to bring about the regeneration of this land of ours? Is internal strife the answer? Are arms and blood to be employed to correct the sickness of our society?"

A captain of police trotted around the corner with reinforcements of two or three dozen men. As they thrust into the unruly swarm, they were resisted with blows and curses. At the sight of police clubs swinging, I climbed onto the stand to collect Mama. To her cry of "Cossacks! Cossacks!" I hustled her into the SLP offices to wait out the tempest.

It was an upsetting evening, much of it devoted to clasping her shaky hands as we huddled in a corner behind a bookcase, listening to the ebb and flow of the turmoil below. The police would charge and the rabble would scatter, only to reassemble, hooting in derision.

She continued to tremble as if with the ague after I took her home to a guestroom bed. She had undoubtedly suffered a chill, but she would not hear of staying with me the next morning. She left with a kiss more tender than I could remember having received from her in a lifetime. "I'm beginning to feel my years, Nellie. I doubt I shall be with you to see a Madam President in office, but to the Infinite Person I pray that you shall. Sinful men have tried to lead us into error for too long."

I paid for one cab to take her through the pelting rain to Mrs. Walker's, then engaged another to the Roosevelt rally at Madison Square. By some curious oversight, no canopy of any kind had been raised to shield the reviewing party on the platform opposite the Worth Monument. Since the board seats and wooden chairs were already waterlogged, it was evident that all hands would have to stand during the entire march past. Providentially, I had brought a mackintosh and umbrella, which gave me the advantage over most of the group, including a pretty little fair-haired thing of fifteen or thereabouts, the governor's daughter Alice, the only member of his family among the luminaries awaiting her father.

The less foresighted were drenched to the skin before a distant blare of trumpets, roll of drums, and rattle of hoofs on asphalt told us that a cavalcade of riders was about to loom into view. The clocks struck eleven.

Behind the fifty horsemen came an open carriage drawn by a pair of steaming grays. He was on his feet, ramrod straight, in the back with water streaming over his steel-rimmed spectacles and white teeth flashing in a nonstop grin as he brandished his Rough Riders' sombrero. Men's hats flew toward the dark sky, women's handkerchiefs fluttered, cheers exploded like a can-

nonade, and shouts magnified by megaphones of "Teddee! Teddee! Always ready!" dinned into our ears.

The clatter of wooden rattles twirled through the air and the
thunder of the brass bands' endless repetitions of "There'll Be
a Hot Time in the Old Town Tonight" made ceremonious introductions impossible. He strode to the forefront of the platform,
as upright as a general on dress parade, to accept the plaudits of
the hundreds of thousands who would pass beneath us in the
cold and penetrating downpour.

Old and young, millionaires and clerks, powers from the
spheres of finance and potentates of commerce all contributed
to the ovation. All carried a small but proud flag, giving the lie
to the Democrats' canard which claimed that workingmen were in
attendance only under duress from their employers. Edging in
close in order to overhear, I wholly approved of his comment,
"The poor, coerced people look remarkably happy, don't they?"

I recognized some of the city's most prominent retail merchants stepping out in the first contingent, comprising the dry-
goods men, some twenty thousand of them, led like every other
division in the procession by its own white-sashed marshal and
clangorous corps of fife and drum.

One hour later we had yet to see the last of their bedraggled
battalions, and the march was barely under way. "We've had so
many dry goods that I think I'll try a little wet goods," said Lieutenant Governor Tim Woodruff, who was in front of me, pouring some of the dark contents of a suspicious-looking bottle into
a gold cup.

Teddy turned to him. "Cold tea, Tim?"

"Not much. That's old rye. Will you take a swig?"

"Never on an empty stomach."

The clothiers appeared next, doffing their hats as they passed
and chorusing to the squelch of soaking wet feet, "Four, four—
four years more!" The black sombrero was circled high in greeting. Then came a cavalcade of men wearing the same Rough
Rider headgear, galvanizing Teddy into a fury of excitement.
"Bully for you!" he yelled, and he and his followers shouted back
and forth to each other like college boys at a football game.

A huge dinner pail mounted on a stand carried by four bearers led the succeeding regiment of marchers. "We want four years more of McKinley and Prosperity" said the legend inscribed on its circumference. "I'd like a full dinner pail myself right now," Mr. Woodruff groaned. Someone took the hint, and boxes of sandwiches were soon circulating among us.

Teddy waved them aside. "No, no. This crowd is all the nourishment I need at present. But surely Miss Russell—"

"I am perfectly content and not at all hungry, sir." This was a lie. I was famished.

"Perhaps later on, then, you will join me for a snack before I go back to Oyster Bay?" I said I could conceive of no greater honor. The afternoon wore on without let-up in the rain or break in the river of humanity. The florists made the square a veritable flower garden with yellow chrysanthemums wired to staves entwined with smilax; the railway and shipping men transformed it into a forest of yellow plumes affixed to similar poles. With tiny lamps aglow on their helmets, four companies of soot-encrusted miners swung their pickaxes into a "port arms" salute as they reached the stand.

Conspicuous in the ranks of the import and export trades was a man of Jim's dimensions. "Tammany says you're starving," Teddy called to him. "Are you?"

"What do you think?" Gargantua replied to another storm of applause.

The bankers and brokers pelted us with pink carnations plucked from their buttonholes. The lawyers satisfied themselves by skying their hats and echoing the chant that had bombarded us for the past five hours, "Teddee! Teddee!" Somehow, a group of interlopers infiltrated the columns to provide one unfortunate disruption. The streamer they flourished—"We came to see the wild one, but we will vote for W. J. Bryan"—was ripped from their hands. Teddy's grin vanished. "I'm sorry they did that. We don't want to fight them that way."

I was in pressing need of an intermission when the governor beckoned Chief Devery. I watched for signs of hostility between them. Police Commissioner Roosevelt in his day had come down hard on this former exile whom Tammany had restored to the force. There was not a flicker of animosity in their faces today. Big Bill swiftly arranged for a cordon of his men to part the sea of spectators and enable a small party of us to cross over to the Hoffman House.

"Fifteen minutes, no more; we shall be back," Teddy promised as I fell into step at his elbow.

"Have you no fear, sir, of catching cold after such a drenching?"

"Cold? Why, I never felt better in my life. It's not this sort of thing that gives a man a cold. Your flesh keeps you warm when you get a welcome like this." From experience, I knew exactly what he meant.

After necessities had been taken care of, our little group regathered briefly for light refreshments, though not of an alcoholic nature, save in the case of Mr. Woodruff, who prompted the governor into conversation while we sat as close as possible to the radiators to steam out a little of the moisture. "What do you suppose brought a turnout of this size in such foul weather?"

"Money, Tim, is the crux of it, not party loyalty or anything else. Not fear for their next pay packet if they declined to march, as our opponents would have us believe, but common-sense concern for a sound dollar. I was only a child, but I still remember the days when we had no currency except postage stamps and tokens of various sorts issued by shopkeepers. If we had not supplied ourselves with a currency, the war could not have been carried on. The issue of greenbacks was one of the great measures which saved the Union. We fought and won our revolution, too, on paper money of the most debased kind. If the paper had been subsequently repudiated after Appomattox, that would have been in the highest degree dishonest, but we have redeemed the greenbacks in gold, just as we have paid all other debts in gold. I am certain that most of Abraham Lincoln's 'plain people' desire the practice to continue, believing as I do that 'free silver' is the cry of a charlatan."

Asking whether he might now order something stronger for Teddy "to ward off the rheumatics," Woodruff received the answer, "I do not particularly like the taste of strong spirits. I use them on rare occasions when I am obliged to exert myself, but no exertion is involved in brandishing my hat to a crowd."

I had a question ready. "What are your plans after you and Mr. McKinley are elected, sir?"

The smile flashed on like a lighthouse lantern. "To read, write, study the law, and trust in the support of the plain people if my day should ever come."

"And the rich people, sir?" I recalled to myself that Mark Hanna had only recently described him as "this mad man."

The lantern was snapped off. "They had much better accept me. I am on their side. I believe in wealth. I belong to their class. They had much better accept me instead of some Bryan who'll come along and ride over them roughshod. It would be my intention for rich and plain to be treated on equal terms without favors for either. I have only a second-rate brain, but I think I have a capacity for action." He sprang to his feet. "Our time is up. A few more raindrops will cool our heads."

I said a hasty good night then and there. Torches lit the line of march as I departed. Another hour would elapse before the cheering died and the last of this army of close to a hundred thousand strong had dispersed into the darkness and the still falling rain.

I had never met a more vital human being or a man who overawed me to the same extent, and he was but two years my senior. My one concern, that in the shadow of the Presidency he might be lost to public view, vanished of course within a matter of months when the bullets of the anarchist Czolgosz took Mr. McKinley's life.

I mourned not for him but for Mama, who had predeceased him by a single week. She died early one September morning after a peaceful sleep, murmuring, so Suzanne said, "Ye shall know the truth, and the truth shall make you free." The end came so suddenly that I was not able to be present. At the funeral, I found myself wishing she might have been spared if only to see Theodore Roosevelt installed in the White House. If anyone might have inspired her to recognize the unreality of her political thinking, it was he.

A door was shut with the loss of Mama, but a window opened with Daughtie's springtime graduation. I excused myself from the Music Hall for a day to witness the convent ceremony. She had grown rather taller than I, and her jaw had a more resolute set, but in my view, anyway, her beauty equaled mine. Of necessity, I had been an absentee mother but not, I hoped, a neglectful one. The immediate question was what to do with her next. The city was no place for a sheltered girl just turned eighteen whom I wished to spare the challenges that had confronted me.

Irregular as my circumstances were, I was a model of middle-aged domesticity by comparison with most of my friends and acquaintances, notably Jim and Edna. Personally, after three marriages—or should they be counted as only two?—I would not have tried another for a million dollars. For Jim and his girl, bachelor and nominal spinster, things were different. It was incongruous for him to plead with her to become his wife and for her constantly to refuse him. Even Evelyn Nesbit was married now, as the world discovered when Harry Thaw was arrested during an automobile tour of the Alps and newspaper accounts mentioned that he was accompanied "by his young wife." When they returned to New York together, they were compelled to leave one hotel because they would not admit they were bride and groom. His mother showed some glimmering of common sense in her efforts to separate them, but finally she bowed to the inevitable, and they went through another ceremony. Jim was so partial to Stanny White that I did not know whether to believe his stories of the strumpet continually running back to her lover bearing welts from the whips her unnatural husband laid across her back.

I had a private talk with Edna one day in their atrocious living room. "Why are you so adamant? Jim's making all the money in the world, and he'd spend every cent to keep you happy." His fortune had indeed been swollen in recent months in a killing that he, Gates, young Bernie Baruch, and three or four others made by churning the stock of the Louisville & Nashville Railroad, then selling out to Morgan.

She fluttered her auburn lashes. "Do you think I'm worthy of him?"

Pretense infuriated me. "You talk like a milksop. What about that Turkish panel house on your second floor? What goes on there? What about the parties Stanny White throws for him with mirrors and swings and I can only guess what else? The real question is whether Jim is worthy of you."

"Perhaps he'll grow tired of me. I wouldn't want to be bound by marriage if he didn't want me."

"Fiddle faddle. A young thing like you is far better off married. Why don't you tell him yes?" She was older than Daughtie by no more than three or four years. I knew what I wanted for my only child.

"I don't know that I'd like a husband who had to be away so many nights as Jim."

"Edna, you may fool other people, but not me. You think you've a stronger hold on him by not being his wife, don't you? You like to keep him begging like a dog for a bone."

She could not be provoked. She crossed over to where I sat and slipped an arm around my shoulders. "Maybe you're right. I'm not sure myself."

Despite all the excuses that could be made for Jim, Daughtie must not be drawn into these circles. If Richard Canfield boasted of having no more morals than a cat, Jim's had been completely dispensed with. Kindness to friends and generosity to almost everyone, yes. But he was overcome by an obsession to make and spend money. Now that he was flying high among the "big fellers," as he called them, he had excessively broad-minded ideas of what constituted "honest graft."

His parties, either at home or, for the more outrageous affairs, in the Gilsey House below Greeley Square, were devised to ply railroad tycoons, stock-market manipulators, and legislators with unlimited liquor and obliging bedmates, blonde or brunette according to preference, coaxed from the choruses of the Broadway theaters he frequented with the promise of a hundred-dollar bill for each of them. His address book, handed to me for inspection once or twice, was replete with the names of girls willing to "go as far as you like," and Edna was his accomplice in recruiting them.

He had shown me suitcases packed with overnight attire for both sexes, with a bottle or two of wine included to ensure cooperation; he stored them in readiness in an upstairs closet. There were even occasions when they were put to use by a man and wife. If an intended victim came in from out of town with his legal spouse, Jim would invite them to dinner. Decked out to the teeth with diamonds, he would arouse spasms of envy in some female bosoms, then blithely insist on presenting the lady with an item from his collection. "It don't cost nothing in the end, Nellie. It's more than paid for in the commission I'm bound to make when him and me get together to do our little bit of business in the morning." And still he could not understand why society locked its doors against him.

I did not choose for Miss Dorothy Solomon to have contact with life at Jim's level. That summer I saw her off on a ship for Europe, where the finishing touches were to be applied to school her as an educated young gentlewoman.

I had not foreseen how greatly I would miss her. Visits to the convent, after all, had sometimes been erratic. Yet a sense of loneliness often overcame me when she was three thousand miles away. I endeavored to dispel it by hewing to long-established habit. The burlesques with Weber & Fields. The effort to reconcile a healthy appetite with the desire to control the numbers registering on the bathroom scale. Reading rather more than previously. I reveled in Marie Corelli and *The Sorrows of Satan*. Dining with Jesse at Rector's, Bustanoby's, and the other places on our circuit. Worshiping from afar our President and his determination to build a canal across the isthmus of Panama. Accepting with Jesse the hospitalities of Edna and Jim, who assured me he was worth about $12,000,000 after he had talked Andrew Mellon into backing a venture known as the Standard Steel Car Company, of which Jim was vice-president in charge of sales.

Daughtie sailed back in the steamer *La Savoie* the following May, in revolt against any furtherment of her education. I blamed myself for not devoting more time to her, not Daughtie for failing to share her secrets with me when she eloped three months later to Jersey City. Albert Louis Einstein, an attorney's son completing courses at New York University law school, was a Jew, like the first—and second?—of my husbands, but I disliked the furtiveness he and Daughtie displayed in leaving.

I wondered if she realized just how much she meant to me and concluded that she did not, otherwise I would not have been rejected in such brutal fashion. I had shielded her from the cruelties of the world from the day she was born at a cost in money I sometimes could not afford and in loneliness, which I had forced myself to accept. I could not credit how she had grown so much like me at the same age when our time together had been so limited. This, of course, was a blessing; a strong resemblance to her disgraceful father would have been too painful to bear.

She seemed to have erased him from her memory as I had from mine. I was glad for her sake that he had been no better as a father than as a husband, and she had believed me when I pretended that the reason she saw nothing more of him was that he had met with a fatal accident on a London street. I suppose in a sense he had. A certain amount of tinkering with the copy of her birth certificate I obtained from the British records office in Somerset House along with a copy of the certification of my so-called marriage to Solomon legitimized her so far as I was concerned.

Why, then, had she failed to confide in me? I had always imagined we were close, though it was not in my nature to gush over her and shower her with kisses, like some Italian mama, every time we met. It had been my intention to introduce her into social life by easy stages. She would return from Europe with enough polish to satisfy even Mrs. Astor, to make her debut at some upper-crust ball. Members of my profession were rapidly being accorded the entrée into what was called Society now that the walls were coming down, and Mrs. William Kissam Vanderbilt had her divorce and Mrs. Stuyvesant Fish threw parties for circus people.

Daughtie with my pushing might have had her pick of millionaires' sons for a bridegroom. She could have had a mansion on Fifth Avenue and a marble cottage at Newport, a staff of servants in livery, diamonds to wear, carriages to ride in, and not a care in the universe. Instead, she had run away from me without so much as a parting kiss. It is less harrowing to carry on the record of her foolishness in a single paragraph. The marriage failed. One year later, she appeared on the stage in a small role in *Olympe*. She was married to and divorced from other husbands. I recall one whose name was Dunsmuir. We were never as close as I recalled having been with Mama.

The bruises inflicted by Daughtie's flight were still painful when I was thrown out of employment and Jesse flirted with being clapped into prison. The first calamity resulted from a falling-out between the former inseparables, Lew Fields and Joe Weber. Why they quarreled after a virtual lifetime of harmony we never knew. Though they continued for a while to share the same dressing room, they spoke not a word to each other off-stage. I warned them repeatedly that they were committing theatrical suicide, but in May of 1904 the curtain was rung down on the partnership, not in their Music Hall, which the city had condemned as a firetrap, but in the New Amsterdam.

The turnout of society, clubdom, the judiciary, and the demimonde made that last night as sparkling as any opening. Players and audience alike indulged in an orgy of sentimentality. Tears streaked our makeup, and sobs sounded across the footlights as neighbor clasped hands with neighbor to sing the finale, "Auld Lang Syne." First thing in the morning, I must be off to see whether the Shubert brothers had a show suitable for me in the offing.

Jesse's brush with disaster was of the new District Attorney's making. William Travers Jerome, a graduate of the Lexow Committee, was an acknowledged candidate for the governorship of New York. Cleaning up vice in Manhattan was the strongest plank in the platform he was hammering together in advance. He led a raid on Canfield's at Number 5 East 44th, but the proprietor took to his heels and escaped. Jerome subpoenaed Jesse, one of the most faithful patrons of the "common gambling den," as the document stated, to testify against the missing Richard.

Jesse had the courage to refuse to answer questions on the grounds that to do so might incriminate him. Travers, determined to make him talk, went after him with two warrants for arrest, two judgments of contempt, two writs of certiorari, two writs of habeas corpus, and two appeals to the State Supreme Court. As the ultimate persuader, the lawman ushered the Dowling Act through the Albany legislature, spelling imprisonment for Jesse and all others who persisted in their silence. Small wonder that my friend's digestion faltered under the strain and he developed an ulcerated stomach.

He had no choice but to talk. Did he know Canfield? He did. Had he been in the club? He had. Had he witnessed games of chance being played and had he in fact participated in them? Yes to both questions. Richard was hunted down, tried, and convicted. The shutters went up on any number of places like his, and for the present a mainstay of the halcyon age was snapped like a thread of cotton.

The Shuberts lived up to their name for driving hard bargains. I was engaged only after undertaking to pay half the production costs of *Lady Teazle,* a musical rendering of Richard Sheridan's *The School for Scandal,* in which I was to have the title role. Instead of the comfortable $1,250 a week from Lew and Joe, I was down for a slim $700, but I was also to receive one half of the net profits. There was additional satisfaction to be had in once again portraying a lady rather than frolicking for five years in such Weber & Fields contrivances as *Whirligig,* *Twirly Whirly,* and *Whoop-dee-doo.* If this new gamble were to fail, I vowed to myself that I would sooner take in washing than set foot on a stage again.

Meanwhile, I threw my cap over the windmill that summer. For company in hours of solitude I bought a Japanese spaniel, "Mooksie," tiny enough to be kept warm within a winter muff, and Jesse supplied a bejeweled dog collar worth $1,800. With Jesse, I made an appearance in Saratoga Springs, where we had at our disposal not one but three gasoline-driven automobiles, each with seat covers of a different flowered chintz. I longed for the day the Albany lawgivers would raise the speed limit above a dawdling ten miles per hour.

He also helped me financially in acquiring a new house at Number 161 West 57th Street: Louis Seize music room, Marie Antoinette drawing room, Olde English supper room, early Dutch dining room, all-American bathrooms, pink-and-gold bedroom with a double bedstead of polished brass, and a Turkish room more elegant and decidedly less carnal than that of Jim, whose passion for questionable renown was impelling him to change every stick of furniture in his house at each spring cleaning.

I found an author hitherto unknown to me for bedtime reading. Marcus Aurelius Antoninus, Roman emperor and philosopher, had gone to his grave almost two thousand years ago, yet his *Meditations* touched sensitive chords in my soul. In twelve small leather-bound volumes, I found him saying all that Mrs. Eddy had written and saying it a hundred times better. *By a tranquil mind I mean nothing else than a mind well ordered....The universe is change; our life is what our thoughts make it....Death, like birth, is a secret of nature.* In these times of corruption and unreality the words seemed pure and unaffected, but not one person in ten thousand had the wisdom to reflect upon them.

Lady Teazle made her bow at the Casino on December 24. The enthusiasm of the press notices made as nice a gift as any actress could wish to find on a Christmas morn. Experience in burlesque, I realized, had given me a sense of ease and timing which had been missing in the past. The lyrics and libretto, both happily the product of native American hands, pleased me more than anything I had tackled in years, and naturally enough I had insisted that no expense be spared on my wigs and costumes, in particular a ball gown, all silver and shimmer. But one critic could not resist planting a poisonous barb: "Miss Russell as a spectacle certainly outshone the remainder of the show weighted against her en *masse*, and that is saying a great deal."

For all that, we scored a victory. Playgoers flocked to see us in their carriages and automobiles and even by the new subway that everyone was talking about, though I personally had no desire to try it. A slur printed just one year ago in the December issue of *Munsey's Magazine*, asserting that I was "a quenched star" was given a fitting answer.

I found I was on the verge of being acceptable at elevations on the social ladder previously barred to me. In earlier years I should have been flattered by the approach of Mrs. Stuyvesant Fish, who showed such determination to seize society's orb and scepter from the enfeebled clutch of old Mrs. Astor. Curiosity if nothing else would have taken me through the doors of the Venetian palace Stanny White designed for Mrs. Fish on a corner of Madison Avenue and 78th Street, where on one occasion she had a hundred yapping dogs to dine and on another a beribboned baby elephant passing out peanuts.

Mrs. Fish came upon me like a galleon under sail. "My dear

Miss Russell, you know I never shake hands with actresses, but I am going to shake hands with you."

Insolence deserved to be repaid in kind. "I can't possibly let you break your rule."

Would I, for a fee, sing some of Lady Teazle's songs for her and her guests? "That, my dear Mrs. Fish, would be incompatible with the dignity of my art."

I refused to disclose a more practical reason for haughtiness. Strenuous nightly vocalizing was telling on my throat. I was growing as raucous as a Saturday-night singer in a downtown concert hall.

A fortuitous fire, hurting nobody, partly destroyed the Casino two weeks before we were due to commence five months of touring. Telling only Jesse, Suzanne, and my household staff what I was about, I was admitted as a patient in the home of Dr. Peter Gibbons. His examination allayed anxiety. There was no malignancy, only growths on the membranes of the larynx. Under a local anesthetic, I watched their excision reflected in a hand-held mirror.

I took Bridget, whom I always trusted, with me when I rejoined *Lady Teazle* in Boston and experienced no further disability on our travels. Then came the day of reckoning. For months the Shuberts had paid me no more than $750 a week, claiming that, contrary to the evidence of sold-out houses, there were no profits to divide. My own little gold pencil said we had grossed $200,000 for profits of $40,000, of which half was mine. I needed a lawyer to gain access to the Shuberts' ledgers, but this time I could not turn to Abe.

With Howe dead these past three years and the Centre Street offices commandeered for a public building, Abe was installed in a cellar in the New York Life Building at Number 346 Broadway. He had also gone to ground in another way, hoping to elude his nemesis in the person of William Travers Jerome, who was after my little friend's shiny bald head.

~ XV ~

*T*WO DAYS after Jerome finally brought him to trial, my dear Abe was convicted of conspiracy to suborn perjury from a key witness in a shabby matrimonial affair.

Charles Dodge, a ne'er-do-well if ever there was one, had been a desk clerk at the Everett House, a residential hotel on Union Square, when his wife Clemence divorced him in order to take a far wealthier husband, Charles Morse, the malefactor whose monopoly, the American Ice Company, held everyone for ransom with the prices charged for deliveries to our kitchens.

Mrs. Morse's turn for the scrap heap came when Morse wanted a new wife, a Catholic who could not marry him if he were a divorcé. Abe applied a technique that had borne fruit many a time before: He would free his client of the bonds of wedlock by annulment of Clemence's divorce, back-dating her into Mrs. Dodge again. This was to be achieved by paying Dodge an initial $5,000 to swear ignorance of her original intent to be rid of him.

After Jerome sniffed a plot to subvert justice, Abe spent well over a million dollars of Morse's money to keep Dodge out of the District Attorney's grasp. Abe first hid Dodge in New Orleans, then paid for half a year of debauchery in the fanciest bordello in Houston until every tooth in the man's head fell out, then schemed to have him disguised as a tattooed lady before packing him off with a carnival troupe bound for Europe.

None of these stratagems worked. Abe, of course, knew the trial judge, but for once that did him no good. Nor did his attempt to buy off members of the jury during a recess on his second day in court. With Dodge mumbling on the witness stand through his new false teeth, Jerome had Abe trapped, and he knew it. He declined to testify in his own defense. He would search for some technicality to keep him from serving his sentence behind bars on Blackwell's Island.

I could do no more than send him my sympathy, for the course of my life was due to be recharted as a result of the fracas with the Shuberts. F. F. Proctor, the vaudeville promoter, pleaded with me to dignify his productions in the Fifth Avenue Theater by appearing for two shows a day, Sundays included. I sounded him out with a series of questions, seeking assurance that I would be presented in a fashion befitting my renown, still undiminished, though it was nearly twenty-five years since I had taken my bow at Tony Pastor's.

Proctor was all alacrity. I would have my own conductor and pianist. Only three songs would be called for at each performance. He would pay for a wardrobe of the latest Paris styles, but I must bedeck myself with the finest jewels in my collection. A property room at stage level would be cleared and refurbished with silk, satin, and pier mirrors for my use. The path to the stage and the stage itself would be pile-carpeted to protect my shoes and the hems of my gowns from snags and splinters. Only one point remained to be settled. "My terms are three thousand dollars a week, cash on the barrelhead." The deal was struck.

Eventually, I was glad that I tired of vaudeville before it tired of me. After my first ten weeks, I signed on for a further six but, though Proctor would have retained me indefinitely, not for a third engagement. "She's the same old Lillian," the *Sun's* reviewer wrote of my debut, "and her voice is the same old voice." He evidently lacked my keen ears. Cold water, massage, and application of cosmetics could preserve a complexion, but nothing could stave off the deterioration of a hard-used throat. The only way in which to extend my term as a public entertainer was to lay hold of the right play, a competent manager, and an able dramatic coach. In future, I would act rather than sing for my supper.

I was fortunate to find the second requirement in Joseph

Brooks and the third in Mrs. Scott Siddons, but the first eluded me. *Barbara's Millions*, an alleged comedy transcribed from a French original, contained only one dependable laugh. "Have you ever thought of marrying?" was a line spoken by my leading man. "Oh, once or twice" came my reply. We folded our tents after two pitiful weeks in New York.

Say and do everything according to soundest reason, says Marcus Aurelius. Reason urged me on to try again within two months with a gambol called *The Butterfly*, having to do with the frivolous young widow of a speculator who had gathered his millions by stealing railroads and earned salvation by investing a few thousands to support a church. But instead of throwing down the gauntlet before big-city critics, we would take to the train tracks and follow a brutal timetable carrying us to fifty-two smaller towns in a span of sixteen weeks. To make living halfway bearable, I chartered a private Pullman car to be staffed with my own servants. When I had completed its outfitting, the *Iolanthe* excelled Jim Hill's in luxury and compared favorably with Mrs. Langtry's *Lalee*.

Business proved so good wherever we played, with almost $2,000 a week going straight into my pocket, that the sixteen weeks extended into thirty-three, taking us as far afield as the coast of the Pacific. We omitted San Francisco, whose people were still nobly struggling with the task of rehabilitation after the previous spring's earthquake and fire. It was on a June day in California that I read of the death of Stanny White on the roof garden of his own Madison Square Garden.

I had never condoned the evil influence he exercised over Jim, luring him into lewdness if only as a spectator, coaxing him to savor degradation with Evelyn Nesbit. Nevertheless, his end shocked me. He deserved a fate less gruesome than having three bullets pumped into his body and brain by Harry Thaw's revolver. So far as I could piece the story together, the fatal trouble between the two of them began when they met by chance at Burns's restaurant on West 46th Street and sat arguing until the early morning. That evening, Thaw, his wife and another couple were dining at the Café Martin, unaware of White's presence until the unsaintly Mrs. Thaw spotted him and, pale and nervous, scribbled a note to her husband: "That dirty blackguard is here." Jim dismissed that detail afterward as a Park Row invention, but I was not so sure.

White returned to his eyrie in the tower of the Garden, then descended to the roof and took a seat at a table for the eleven-o'clock performance of *Mamselle Champagne*. Thaw threaded a path through the crowd, drew a pistol from an overcoat pocket and fired at point-blank range. As Stanny toppled to the floor, his murderer emptied out the remaining cartridges to demonstrate to those around him that the shooting was over. One of the theater's firemen grabbed him until a policeman was summoned, to be asked by Thaw, "Is he dead?" Yes was the reply. "Well, I'm glad I made a good job of it."

His trollop of a wife threw her arms around his neck and kissed him. "Oh, Harry, I did not think you would do it that way."

His friends begged the police captain to use the cab they provided to take Thaw to the Tenderloin station. I liked the officer's reply: "Millionaires will go to headquarters the same as any other prisoner" as he hustled him into the paddy wagon, handcuffed to a detective. Now he was in the Tombs, and the headline was reassuring: ALIENISTS DECLARE THAW SANE.

Like so much else in the universe, Thaw's deed had unforeseeable consequences: It would reduce the time Abe spent in prison. As he mentioned to me subsequently, his client White once took the Nesbit girl into Hummel's office to swear out an affidavit against her spouse, declaring under oath that Thaw had told her one day he would kill Stanny. When Jerome unearthed the document, Abe vouched for its genuineness, establishing premeditation on Thaw's part. Thus, after his every attempt to avoid jail had come to nought, Abe got off with a bargain sentence of one year, and Jerome, with another medal on his chest, looked to the day he might follow Mr. Roosevelt in the White House.

Abe was on one side of our continent and I, unfortunately, on the other on the night of the greatest party of his life, thrown on the eve of his donning penitentiary stripes. Jesse, who forwarded all the gossip, wrote saying that Abe was assigned to the prison bakery, but a digestive ailment soon had him excused from all forms of labor.

When *The Butterfly's* peregrinations were over and I was home again, I hastened to visit Abe. De Lancey Nicoll, who had represented him at his trial, kindly obtained passes for us. We stood on the East River shore across from the island, waving handkerchiefs as a signal for a boat to collect us. A keeper with a rifle across his knees sat in the stern while a surly convict crew rowed us over to the opposite pier. Abe awaited us there, strangely shrunken in a suit of coarse, banded flannel from which he constantly picked invisible specks of grime. He led us to his quarters, a commodious room in the workhouse.

"This must have cost you a lot, Abie." Nicoll's eyes took in the braided rug, the brass bed, lace curtains drawn back from spotless windows, a rolltop desk, an upholstered rocking chair.

"It did. It's the warden's." No *tee! hee!* punctuated his words today.

His manner was so wistful that I would have tried to comfort him had I the gift for doing so. "How do you pass the time, Abe?"

"Counting the days and asking God to grant me the strength to live through them, to resist the temptation to make an end of myself, because my sisters should be spared such shame."

"It never should have happened. What is it Charles Dickens says? 'The law is an ass, an idiot'? If only everything could have been delayed until after the next election. District attorneys don't last forever."

"Jerome deserves to be reelected; he knows what he's doing. About Dickens I don't know. Since I was a child my mother told me, 'Study hard. Be a lawyer. You'll be rich.' Every day now I am thinking about Oliver Wendell Holmes. 'The life of the law,' he said, 'has not been logic; it has been experience.'" The reflection of the daylight outside moved to and fro over his skull as he nodded. "Who can question his wisdom?"

Nicoll endeavored to dispel the gloom. "Now you're disbarred, I've got a plan for you. I'm going to get a good architect to design a nice place on Broadway, where you can have a good time, lots of drinks, nice girls, and everybody will have a wonderful time."

Abe was not smitten with the idea. Should he survive, he

said, he would sail to Europe to live with a sister—whether it was the widow or the spinster, I was not certain—but Nicoll could talk of little else on our way back except the "nice place" he dreamed of for Abe, while I could only grieve for him.

I missed Abe's counseling during the long months of his incarceration. I wondered afterward whether I should have acted as I did had he been available to advise me. Nearer now to my fiftieth than my fortieth birthday, I was anxious to simplify my mode of living. Manhattan had lost much of its charm in this era of ragtime and the ungainly cakewalk, whose steps were too frantic for me. This was mongrel music not worth singing even to myself, but "Come Down, My Evenin' Star" had tempted me into the field of Negro spirituals, surely as moving a form of art as any race had devised to picture mankind's ultimate destiny. I especially cherished

> O Lord, remember the rich and remember the poor
> Remember the bond and the free.
> And when you done remembering all 'round
> Then, O Lord, remember me.

I desired most of all to be free of the city so as to establish closer contact with the open sky. It was one thing, however, to enroll in the Farmers' Union and invest my earnings in land in West Palm Beach and New Jersey, where a tenant set about raising crops of celery, eggplant, and other vegetables. It was perhaps a less rational move to burn my bridges and put my house up for sale and all its furnishings for auction. This I did in the belief that Cedar Hill, the mansion with fourteen guest rooms and thirty acres which I had been renting for some time past in Far Rockaway, would serve most of my needs. With its outdoor gymnasium—barbells, punching bag, medicine ball, ping-pong table, and rapiers for fencing—it was part and parcel of my goal.

Suzanne, a frequent visitor, accepted the establishment rule that guests should exercise with me for a minimum of sixty minutes every day, rounded off with a hot shower, a cold plunge, and a rubdown to leave us all hungry and happy. Dressed alike from my stock of bloomer suits, sweaters, and track shoes, my girl friends and I vied with each other in the interests of health. Jesse and Jim were the only males on the calling list, one too emaciated to compete, the other too bloated. Edna was always a wallflower, too, scornful, if I guessed correctly, of something a reporter wrote after interviewing me there: I was "lithe, dapper, and beautiful." It brought a glow to my ageless heart.

The proceeds of the auction were a grave disappointment. These were not the best of times for household treasures to go under the hammer when consternation beset Wall Street on the heels of a court's finding John D. Rockefeller's Standard Oil guilty of strangling its competitors by granting secret rebates to railroads for transporting its fuel. My Limoges cigarette box fetched a paltry $16.50, the inlaid ivory chair in which I habitually posed for photographers a ridiculous $22.00. Hand-carved breakfast-room chairs, which had cost $700 apiece, were disposed of as a job lot for $200, a whole suite of Louis Seize furniture for $2,950, a fraction of the original price. All in all, the three-day sale at the Fifth Avenue Art Galleries gave me not quite $70,000, which on my instruction was deposited in the Knickerbocker Trust Company at the corner of Fifth Avenue and 34th Street.

That was on Monday, October 14. One week later to the day, the Knickerbocker collapsed. Between the nine-o'clock opening of its wrought-iron doors and their shutting six hours later, $8,000,000 was paid out to a jostling mob of depositors demanding the return of their savings after the Standard Oil crowd had dumped untold thousands of shares to deflate the market. There was nothing left at the bank for the rest of us to whom it owed another $52,000,000. My auction money had gone up in smoke.

The news induced a curious sense of calm. I was poorer, of course, and my ever-present battalions of creditors would have to keep cooling their heels. The loss represented perhaps more money than Papa had earned in half a lifetime, and I might just as well have given away my prized possessions to the Salvation Army or set them afire with Rockefeller kerosene for what I had gained in cash. But I was not certain that it mattered too much. The desire for recognition had always been the spur that drove me on. Fame brought money in its trail. I would far rather choose to be renowned than merely a rich nobody, and I had no patience with self-pity, which was excusable only in the immature. Besides, my latest dramatic role was evoking such nightly applause that it served as a salve to cure the pain of bidding farewell to all those desirable dollars.

Cincinnati, Ohio, "Queen City of the West," as its natives called it, adored *Wildfire*: its heroine, another engaging young widow, and her costumes, every one of them just off the boat from Cherbourg. It should not be difficult to recoup my losses. Similar acclaim awaited us in Chicago, Rochester, Scranton, Philadelphia, and Boston, though in that last city a whipper-snapper on the *Transcript* had to dilute his praise—"As a comedienne, Miss Russell is a revelation"—with acid: "obesity has not bested Miss Russell yet." Then we rested before testing ourselves in New York.

A week after his release from prison, Abe sailed for Southampton aboard the *Lusitania*, prison-pale but spruce in a new black suit and crippling pointed shoes. He was going into retirement, he said, in London, at a sister's house on Grosvenor Square. A delegation from the world of footlights went down to the pier to bid him farewell. Charles Frohman was there, princely John Barrymore, Marcella Sembrich, the Metropolitan's latest Polish coloratura, and others besides myself. I lingered in the stateroom long enough to see a steward deliver my flowers. Abe read the card I had attached to them: "For the man who never squealed." I walked down the gangway with the sound of his shrill "Tee! hee! hee!" making music inside my head.

I had hoped Jesse would be well enough to meet me at Grand Central when the train bearing our *Wildfire* company steamed in from Boston. The condition I had left him in had worried me while I was away. Perhaps it was the aftereffect of his ordeal with Jerome or possibly Jesse's addiction to late hours, gaming, and drink, but in the spring the flesh had melted from his already scantily covered bones. His doctor had been sharp with him. Jesse's only chance of restoring his health lay in giving up dissipation and retreating to the countryside for a rest cure. He, Jim, and I had discussed this unwelcome prescription.

Jesse was loath to surrender his pleasures. "What about Nellie here? She'll never manage without me. I refuse to leave New York unless it's to go on the road with her."

He was being ridiculous. "I am more than capable of taking care of myself, thank you. I was doing that well enough for thirty years before you came along. Just do as you're told to repair the damage you've done to yourself."

Jim, to whom the very idea of illness was repellent, exploded. "God damn it, you *will* listen to your doctor. Pack your bags and go out to the farm. Edna'll stay down there to look after you. Nell won't mind if you forget about her for a while to get back into shape again, will you, Nell? She'll be here when you get back."

Jim's Ellesdale Manor Farm in South Branch, New Jersey, was a comparatively recent acquisition, bought for $68,000, primped and prettified for $100,000 more. He could well afford it. The inside tips he garnered from his friends of the Hoffman House bar enabled him to move in and out of the stock market ahead of the vast army of innocents—barbers, waiters, widows, doormen and the rest—who bought any old thing and got their fingers burned in the process. When he wanted to impress the "big boys" he invited to the farm, he would have his cowmen milk his herd of Guernseys into gold-plated buckets, or entertain his guests over carefree weekends with their current lights of love.

Jim, not Jesse, was standing on the platform when our train pulled in. The severity of his expression alarmed me. "Jesse's all right, isn't he? After all these weeks, I imagined he'd be much better by now."

"He's better, right enough."

"What's wrong then?"

"I been away a lot meself. I bust in on the two of 'em at the farm the other night, and I could smell something fishy right away. We was having a game of cards after dinner when I asked 'em, 'What's going on around here?' Jesse turns red as a beet root and says, 'Edna and me are in love, and we're going to get hitched.' Now the bastard's run off with her, a girl who's never looked at another feller for God knows how long."

"Poor Jim." What else to say? That she, too, was old enough

to take care of herself? It would sound callous. That she and Jesse could never hit it off? They might find in each other what neither had found from Jim or me. That I was heartbroken at losing him? Jesse had not meant that much to me. I gave an absent-minded tug at one of Mooksie's feathery ears.

Jim growled, not Mooksie. "I don't give a hoot in hell for her. What are you going to do?"

"My driver should be outside to take me to Cedar Hill. Would you care to come?" Another time, he said, as forlorn as a beaten puppy. I found what I was looking for on my bedside table that night, in the fourth of the dozen slim volumes: *Whatever happens at all happens as it should; thou wilt find this true, if thou shouldest watch narrowly.*

The runaways wasted no time in living up to Jesse's promise, and Edna became Mrs. Lewisohn. On February 8, 1909, they sailed on the *Deutschland* for a European honeymoon. My cablegram to the ship said only DON'T BE IN SUCH A HURRY.

These days, though he had $1,000,000 a year coming in, Jim usually looked like a half-stripped Christmas tree, the former displays of diamonds being reserved for those gala nights when we resumed parading together to first nights and the familiar eating houses, where the names of Jesse and Edna were only whispered within our hearing. Jim replaced every stick of furniture in his house and gave away most of his clothes to erase the memory of her.

My figure, unfortunately, was still out of fashion, but Jim's was back in favor, with the new incumbent of the White House setting the style. I regretted that Teddy Roosevelt had abided by his pledge to withdraw from further consideration after serving almost eight years in office, but Mr. Taft, after all, was his personal choice as successor. He was so fat that four men of average size could fit in his bathtub.

Though my appetite never faltered, exercise served to keep one's tissues in tone. Jim, on the other hand, set no bounds to his gourmandizing. It was useless to chide him while, after starting with the inevitable gallon of chilled orange juice, he plowed through a dozen courses, with three or four helpings of the tastier dishes, until he finished with a five-pound box of chocolates. Without Edna to deluge with his shekels, he began accumulating his glittering lifeless "pets" again as greedily as he tackled a saddle of mutton or a twelve-egg soufflé, avid to possess a different set of jewelry for every day of the month. He tried harder than ever to justify his extravagances. "What the hell! Why wouldn't I spend every dollar I make? There ain't nobody to leave it to."

Now he talked openly and continually about the state of his health, which as anyone could detect was deteriorating. He was so dropsical that unless we watched an exceptional musical comedy or bedroom farce he was likely to fall asleep before the first act was over, needing a series of prods in his spongy ribs to interrupt his snoring, which vastly amused our fellow first-nighters.

He complained to me about pains in his joints, palpitations of his heart, and his problems in the bathroom, yet rather than put himself into a physician's charge, he laid his trust in syrupy Swamp-Root, which he consumed by the caseful on the strength of its advertisements ("thousands have kidney trouble and don't know it"), disregarding my warnings that the secret of this evil-smelling elixir was its staggering content of raw alcohol.

Happily, time for brooding over Jesse's jilting was limited during the unsettling early months. *Wildfire* lasted for a phenomenal five hundred and sixty-six performances, and long before it was over I was making plans for my next attraction, *The Widow's Might*—plans that involved a shopping trip with Anna Held to the couturiers of Paris and, upon returning, a daily regimen of two hundred and fifty body rolls on the parquet floors of my newly rented apartment to reduce adiposity.

All was in vain. The curtain at the Lyric seemed scarcely to have rung up for the first time before it was rung down for the last. Without Jesse's largess to fall back onto and with no wish to go cap in hand to Jim, I had one recourse: to look for still another play. Had there been a race card for Broadway, I might just as well have relied on blind luck with a hatpin. *The First Night*, which was not as improper as its title implied, was unveiled at the South Broad Street Theater in Philadelphia on the day after Christmas. We barely held on into the New Year, and the same icy response was met with throughout our curtailed tour.

I was at liberty once more when my old friend, Blanche Bates, unforgettable in *Under Two Flags*, invited me to appear at a benefit concert for the local hospital in Ossining, New York, a town best known for its Sing Sing Prison and its ever-busy electric chair, plus its proximity to Rockefeller's immense property at Pocantico Hills, through which the old gentleman had built his own private railroad line.

As soon as the announcement was made that I was to lend myself to this charity affair, a check for $500 arrived from Mr. Rockefeller with a request that I present myself to him, since he had a personal favor to ask. After a tedious drive along the Hudson up the Albany Post Road through Tarrytown, a platoon of uniformed sentinels halted my automobile outside the wrought-iron gates in the massive fieldstone walls that encircled the Pocantico retreat, to walk me through into a waiting Franklin limousine which would take me the rest of the way. What appeared to be almost a half hour's journey along curving gravel drives laid out between velvet-green lawns and towering stands of shapely trees brought us to the master himself, engaged in overseeing a team of sweating gardeners who, with the aid of a derrick, were uprooting a seventy-foot elm.

All the strength remaining in his frail body seemed to be concentrated in the steely eyes set in a face as wrinkled as a pharaoh's mummy, its outstanding features being the beaked nose and curious bumps behind ears that hung out from under a quite obvious wig.

His first words were to the driver as he hopped out to open the vehicle's door for me. "How many miles are you getting to the gallon?" Eighteen, sir. "Why, you will ruin me!"

He extended a hand as limp as a rag "I have seen you once before, Miss Russell, with DeWolf Hopper in *Hoity-Toity*, 1901. I have no abiding taste for the theater, but I was amused beyond words."

"How sweet of you to remember."

"My eyes, my hearing, and my memory are in excellent condition, and I have a passion for detail even in such matters as this task that occupies us today. We keep a set of account books for each place we own and plant trees by the thousand. If we transfer one from Pocantico to our home in Lakewood, New Jersey, we charge one place and credit the other. We make a small fortune out of ourselves by selling to Lakewood at two dollars each trees which originally cost us only five or ten cents here. Moving a very large horse chestnut actually in flower costs us no more than twenty dollars."

"It must take a considerable staff to accomplish everything."

"We employ very nearly one thousand, including the guards. We ourselves wish merely to lead a prudent, orderly life free of pomp and elegance, but we have enemies who would use guns and bombs if they could. They are resentful of what we have accomplished in bringing tidiness into big business."

"I have met men like that. Were you always tidy, sir?"

"I began business life as a bookkeeper in Cleveland, which taught me respect for facts and figures, no matter how small. From early boyhood I kept a little book I called Ledger A, containing my receipts and expenditures as well as an account of the small sums my mother instructed me to give away regularly. When I was seven or eight years old I owned some turkeys and sold them all in businesslike fashion. My receipts were all profits."

The sun emerged from behind a bank of fleecy cloud. At a snap of his fingers, one of his attendants produced a pith helmet, which he carefully placed over his wig. "Do you attribute your wealth to that early training, Mr. Rockefeller?"

The restless eyes fixed on mine. "God gave me money. I endeavored to fulfill His divine purpose by applying good old-fashioned common sense, always a rare commodity, and patience, which is a virtue in business affairs as in other things. I have never wronged any man. My enemies, of whom we know there are a few, are inspired by envy. I don't mind what they say about me and other rich men, but I resent their attacks on my son."

A hint from this disciple of the Lord's on how to improve the handling of my microscopic fortune would have been welcome, but I doubted whether even Jim would have had the gall to introduce the subject when the old gentleman was celebrated for screening his operations from the public's gaze. In any event, I was curious to learn his views on another subject. "Are the wealthy happier than the poor?"

"The very rich are just like all the rest of us. If they get pleasure from the possession of money, it comes from their ability to do things which give satisfaction to someone besides themselves. I am told by those who profess to know that the purchase of material things soon palls upon one. These rich men we read about in the newspapers cannot get personal returns beyond a well-defined limit for their expenditure."

I could detect a certain similarity in the thinking of my host, worth an incredible billion dollars, and Jim, who was a pauper by comparison, but Jim still had a lot to learn from this model of piety.

"The rich cannot gratify the pleasures of the palate beyond very moderate bounds. They cannot lavish very much money on fine raiment without suffering from public ridicule. In their homes, they cannot go much beyond the comforts of the less wealthy without involving themselves in more pain than pleasure. As I study wealthy men, I can see but one way in which they can secure a real equivalent for money spent, and that is to cultivate a taste for giving where the money may produce an effect which will be a lasting gratification."

For a moment, I wanted to argue with him. Money to me meant enjoying myself first and foremost. What else was the purpose of having it? Then I wondered. How much true pleasure had it brought me? I should have to give more thought to that. I reverted to chitchat. "You have a beautiful place here, Mr. Rockefeller."

"It is kind of you to say so. My friends address me as 'J.D.' as you may if you wish." Borrowing a pair of clippers from a courtier, he bent creakily over a nearby flower bed, snipped a single bloom, and handed it to me. "The American Beauty rose. It can be produced in all its splendor only by sacrificing the early buds that grow up around it. It can no more achieve its best in competition than this country can. Cooperation, conservation, benevolent assimilation—these are the keys to the great economic era we are entering. It will give splendid opportunity to the young men of the future, whereas in my young manhood we had everything to do and nothing to do it with."

A thorn pricked a finger through my doeskin glove. "Would your rivals of the past agree with that view?"

The threadlike lips flickered. "We left them to the mercy of the times, and they could not compete with us. But today, no matter how noisy the pessimists may be, we know that the world is getting better. All I wish is that some day we shall have a real businessman as President."

"Unlike Mr. Roosevelt? To my way of thinking, he was a great—"

"Like some others among the rich men we read about, I supported him in 1904 to see if I could do something to keep the wolf from the door. He had value as a safety valve of change. Mr. Taft falls within the same category."

I inhaled the scent of my rose while I framed the next question. "If you were asked, 'What is the most important piece of advice to be given anyone in business today?' how might you answer?"

There was no hesitation. "Never lend money to your friends —it will spoil your friendships. But I must not waste your day. You will have other matters to attend to. I shall be at the concert in Ossining. Will you sing 'Come Down, My Evenin' Star'? I have heard it on the Victrola. I should like to hear it from you."

"I shall be charmed. It's a favorite of mine, too. The man who wrote it, John Stromberg, was a dear friend who lived on borrowed time, not on borrowed money." I waved the rose to him as I was borne away to the gates in the Franklin at an expenditure of something approaching half a gallon of gasoline. Inquisitive as I was about the internal affairs of a Rockefeller, I had not been invited inside any of the score or more dwellings on the estate for any refreshment. J.D. knew his place in the world and mine, too.

> My evenin' star,
> I wonder who you are,
> Set up so high

Like a diamond in the sky.
No matter what I do,
I can't go up to you.
So come down from there, my evenin' star . . .

He sat in the audience, grimly impassive among a group of his own people. I could only assume that he enjoyed the song. He had such force of character that I fancied no star would hesitate to descend at his beckoning. Yet for all his might and his billion dollars, he could not ward off the Supreme Court's order for Standard Oil to be broken up the following year, which struck me as an act of ingratitude to the richest man alive.

Daughtie always sought me out between her marriages. She had either just become or ceased to be Mrs. O'Reilly—my memory was cloudy on the point—as we sat together in the apartment one evening when Jim showed up, twisting the rings on his fingers in nervousness. "Can I have a word with you, Nell?"

"Alone?"

"No, no. Don't run away, Mrs.—ah, I'd better call you Dorothy same as I used to. I could use your help to pluck up my courage."

Gasps as if from a stranded porpoise made me inquire if he was feeling quite well. "I'm okay. What I come to say, Nellie, is . . . I mean, I want to ask you . . . How shall I put it? . . . How would you like to be Mrs. Brady?" His smile was pitiable. "I recall as you once said you'd only marry for a million dollars. I'm going to give you this for a wedding present." From his commodious wallet he peeled out ten unsullied $100,000 bills and, before my incredulous eyes, spread them like a fan across my lap.

Daughtie gulped. I picked up the uncrinkled oblongs of paper, feeling tears about to flow. I had never had such wealth as they represented, every one of them backed by Treasury gold, nor actually handled such a sum before. He was trying to make up for every loss I had suffered in cash, esteem, and kindness, some very real, others magnified in his imagination like the disappearance of Jesse. But I was too discriminating to want a husband so plain and unsatisfying as Jim.

"You must have misunderstood me, Jim. I remember saying I would *not* marry again for a million dollars, nor would I for ten or a hundred times more. Let us be what we always have been—dear friends." I folded the money back into one of his huge hands and added a pat for consolation.

He stuffed the bills into a side pocket, then drew out an embroidered linen handkerchief the size of a pillow case to blow a blast on his bulbous nose. "I can't blame you. Who'd want to be wed to such an ugly devil as me?"

That wasn't it at all, I said, and rambled on in an attempt to apply balm to his feeling by recounting the virtues of his generous heart.

He brightened up somewhat after five or ten minutes of this. "Then I'm going to take this jack and build you a theater all your own. I'll come and watch you, every performance. What do you say to that? The Lillian Russell Theater. I'll put your name up in the brightest lights on Broadway."

"There'll be time enough for that when I'm dead, Jim."

The draining of blood from his cheeks left them the color of papyrus. "I can't stand hearing that word. It's like somebody was already walking over your grave. If I ain't allowed to give you a theater, what about a party? The best damn party you ever been to?" I agreed that he could do that, and he ambled out, forlorn but not desolated.

"Mother, weren't you tempted a little bit? I certainly would have been."

"Your grandmother sometimes called me a foolish, headstrong girl. She would lecture me by the hour, urging me to mend my ways, use my brains, make something of myself. Perhaps Mama was right, and I was impetuous in those days. But not any more, my darling." That was more a hope than a certainty, but surely there had been some improvement lately.

A detachment of New York's finest deterred common folk from walking across the Turkish carpet laid between the curb and Jim's front door on the night of the party, but a score or so of bystanders watched the guests arrive in the blaze of electric light that shone from the house's every window.

In the entrance hall, Jim shone brighter than the crystal chandelier suspended over his head. He was wearing his "transportation set," 2,548 diamonds and nineteen rubies by his careful count, worked into representations of every conceivable animal or item of equipment having some fanciful connection with the trade he had pursued for forty years. His ring, shaped like a locomotive's wheel, had a hub weighing ten carats, he said. One shirt stud was a miniature bicycle of one hundred and nineteen stones, the other a diamond-and-ruby automobile. A lion and a tiger rampant (five hundred and forty-six gems in all) made up the buckle of his belt. A jeweled donkey adorned his fob watch, a camel his tie clip, a locomotive his eyeglass case. Cuff links, vest buttons, collar buttons—everything was diamonds. "I paid $105,000 for this lot, which was cheap," he was pleased to tell anyone who asked.

The sliding doors between the living and dining rooms had been opened to accommodate the thickening crowd. In the first, the Katzatz rug had been rolled up to clear space for dancing. Before the night was over Jim had given it away as a memento to a visiting Pennsylvanian. At an upright piano of intricately carved rosewood inlaid with mother-of-pearl scenes from Italian opera, a black musician, skull shaved bare, was rattling out a new jingle called, if I heard correctly, "Alexander's Ragtime Band." The sturdy dining-room table and equally stalwart sideboard bore up bravely under solid arrays of covered dishes: kidneys, meat pies, lamb, veal, and pork chops, sweetbreads, fish rissoles, flapjacks. "I ain't aiming to let nobody go hungry before we clear all this away and get down to some real eating."

He stole a few more minutes from his duties as host to conduct me upstairs for a glimpse of his latest notion, which he termed his "Tiger Room" for understandable reason. The frames of the mirrors that hung on every orange-and-black wall and the headboards and footboards of the double-sized divans— all were decorated with tigers ablaze with fire opals, emeralds, and bright red rubies. Pelts of the beasts with jaws agape covered the floor. The woodwork was satinwood, planed to its natural grain to give the effect of the feline's stripes. The plaster of the ceiling had been molded like a canopy of tropical trees painted in shades of green. At its center, ropes were looped like jungle vines.

We went down to mingle with the guests. Flo Ziegfeld had

arrived with his Anna, who gained never an ounce of superfluous flesh. "When are you going to continue the grind, darling?" She was always so insouciant. I told her I was contemplating a drama entitled *In Search of a Sinner*, which I might take on the road in the fall.

"Haven't you found any sinners yet?" She was such a merry child.

I spotted Marie Dressler in the crush of theatrical friends and went over to her, glad that by comparison with her I was a sylph. Nat Goodwin spoke of his plans to open a café. DeWolf Hopper was inching away from a stranger—from Pittsburgh undoubtedly—who was pressing him to recite "Casey at the Bat." Young Lionel Barrymore was making excuses for the absence of his brother John.

Richard Canfield surprised me with his presence. I ascertained that all was well again with him, with business booming at a new address. I was reluctant to leave this old friend to make the acquaintance of an immense being with a face like carmined concrete, but Jim would have been upset had I not shaken hands with the great "Jawn" L. Sullivan, whom I knew was paid $100 a night and all he could drink to impress Jim's customers at these soirées now that the ex-champion was a bankrupt.

Hired lackeys were in constant circulation, holding silver traysful of beverages aloft above the bobbing heads. At the piano, argument had broken out between one group of music lovers wanting more of "the Swanee river played in ragtime" and another who clamored for the more sedate strains of "East Side, West Side, all around the town."

Jim extracted me from an admiring circle of outlanders, all dressed like three-card monte men, to take me over to another prize showoff, imported to impress his clients. I had previously seen Buffalo Bill Cody only on horseback, circling the tanbark in Madison Square Garden. Tonight, his costume was little changed, but he was too tipsy to have stayed aboard a horse. I was glad to see no trace of his sidekick, Miss Annie Oakley, who, when in her cups, was known to have a penchant for shooting out electric light bulbs.

Most of the younger generation turned up late. First on the scene was Marie Wilson of *Florodora*, who on a stock-market

tip earned from Jim Keane, Morgan's trusty henchman, made
$750,000 before Freddie Gebhard made an honest woman of
her. Fatuous Freddie, who came with her, I remembered from
his days as Lillie Langtry's $250,000-a-year fancy man. Charlie
Gates, Bet-a-Million's son, who had inherited his father's estate
last year, arrived soon after with his bride, boasting of the
fortune he was spending on a new home for them in the Lake
of Isles district of Minneapolis and their private railroad car,
Bright Eyes. I thought, "Shirt sleeves to shirt sleeves in one
generation," wondering how long could his life last when Bill
Cody was his constant drinking companion.

And so the night wore on, with fresh arrivals, louder chatter,
mountains of food, oceans of liquor, nonstop jangling of the
piano keys, and gambling in the basement for those who sought
it. The one person I should really have enjoyed more time with
was Marie Dressler, but we were interrupted whenever we closed
in on each other.

At dinner, a porcine Pittsburgher inquired if I was "going
to entertain."

"Jim has asked me to sing, but no more than a single song."

"I heard he was forking out five hundred dollars a head to
some girls he's bringing in."

In my ingenuousness, I didn't know what he was talking
about. "I assure you, not to me."

It was a surprise to find that the exhausted pianist could
play everything I suggested from my repertoire. Since I was not
prepared to compromise my standards for an audience of this
sort, I sang Tosti's "Good-bye" as I had for the late king of
England, Edward VII, when he was next in line for the throne
over there. The accompaniment was flawless and the applause
so rousing that I responded with an encore, Sullivan's "Let
Me Dream Again." Before beginning, I noticed disdainfully
that the Pittsburghers were slipping out on me.

One song inspired another, and I had supplied a full half
dozen until my voice tired. I thought it time to end the concert,
bid Jim good night, and take my self home.

Since he was not to be found in the ground-floor rooms, I
ascended the stairs. Sounds of carousing from the Tiger Room
tempted me to open the door. There stood Jim with his back

to me, the jovial master of ceremonies, topping up the glasses held in the uncertain hands of his outlandish guests, who with coats off and ties loosened sprawled either among the trophies of the hunt on the floor or on the seductive divans. The ropes from the tropical ceiling had been lowered and the level of lighting dimmed. I closed the door unnoticed, to proceed along the hall past the intervening bathroom to the entrance of the next chamber.

Fainter sounds—girls' giggling this time—came from inside. With utmost caution, I peeped in. Five or six of them, one apiece for the Pittsburghers, were in process of removing their clothes, one of them a recruit from Ziegfeld's chorus line, all of them with war paint on their faces and goose bumps on their pallid flesh.

I shut that door gently, too, and went downstairs. I had grown rather too mature to wish to know any more about this sort of frolic.

XVI

*T*HE MALES of the towns in which we appeared were
perhaps reluctant to stir their wives' speculation by entering any auditorium bedizened with posters advertising "Lillian
Russell: *In Search of a Sinner*." Whatever the cause, we found
neither sin nor ready customers of either sex. We subsisted by
the skin of our teeth, and for this I blamed my manager, Brooks.
In Pittsburgh, business at the Nixon Theater fell to such an ebb
that I had to bestir myself or the performers behind the footlights would have outnumbered the occupants of the seats.

A stopgap remedy was to canvass the publishers of the local
newspapers, seeking cooperation in my scheme by which they
would purchase blocs of tickets at advantageous prices to give
away to their readers. The *Gazette-Times* was not interested,
and neither were the *Sun-Telegraph* and the *Dispatch*. The
Leader, however, rose to the bait, though it was by no means
the most affluent of the journals.

I outlined the plan to its proprietor, Alexander Pollack
Moore, an aging, affable gentleman: Why not offer evenings
at our play as prizes for solving a simple puzzle to be printed
in his pages? The novelty of the idea and my physical attraction
seemed to impress him equally. We sealed our bargain over
dinner, a welcome diversion in the aptly christened "Smoky
City," whose atmosphere, reeking with the effluvia of factory
chimneys, was as noxious as its *noveaux riches*.

Mr. Moore was eager for details of my personal life, which
were traded for confidences of his own. He was untainted by

steel money, being a comparative newcomer from Baltimore, where he had lived with Lucille, his wife of fifteen years, before she divorced him in 1910 for "incompatibility of temperament." Like Papa, he had started out as a cub reporter. Like me, he idolized Theodore Roosevelt. The gleam in his eyes testified that he would have liked us to clasp hands under the table, but he was too well behaved to make any such overture.

On a subsequent evening, he showed more backbone. Would I consent to being the new Mrs. Moore? Before I began weighing the pros and cons of a fourth run in the matrimonial sweepstakes, I wanted to determine the conditions of the track. "I have discovered, all too slowly, Alec, that marriage must be an equal partnership. There must be tolerance, and there must be understanding. I would insist on having my own undisturbed privacy, as I have now."

"That would never be contested, my dear."

"I set great store by spiritual and mental beauty as well as the purely physical. I believe that earnest, intelligent women of all ages will come to subscribe to this same creed, for as education and culture grow every woman will desire the good, the true, the beautiful."

"A spiritual union—I quite understand."

"What is more, I intend to devote much of my time to a cause my mother held dear—women's suffrage. Does that strike fear in your heart, Alec?"

"Not so long as they vote Republican."

"And finally, I could not bear to spend twelve months of the year here in Pittsburgh, where the sky is dark by day and lit like Dante's Inferno by the furnaces at night. Exercise in clean, fresh air is essential to my well-being. You shall have my answer in a month or two. I am closing the play next week to go back to New York. Did you know that Weber and Fields are together again? They patched up their squabble at Lew's father's funeral. They want me with them at two thousand dollars a week."

"I'll be there for the first night, my love, praying that you will tell me yes."

Alec sat in the second row since I cautioned him against spending the $250 a front-row seat fetched at the Broadway Theater at the auction for *Hokey-Pokey*. He was awarded my most blissful smiles after I made my first entrance, sprinkled with $150,000 worth of gems, wearing a black velvet chapeau, gold shoes with diamond buckles, and flesh-colored net embroidered with genuine jewels, treading in state over a carpet of American Beauty roses that was spread over the stage. *In Search of a Sinner,* I had decided, had brought me an honest, accommodating man I could safely marry in my advancing years. I gave him my answer at the Friars Club supper held for the company and guests when the show was over.

Jim was there, but shortly thereafter he lay cursing his fate, as we were told, in his enormous mahogany bed, drinking orangeade, a quart at a gulp, laced with two pounds of sugar a day. After eight weeks in New York, I was on the road again with Weber & Fields when the rumor swept Broadway: Jim was dead.

If only he had listened to me was the first thought. More exercise and less gourmandizing could have postponed this wretched ending. *I am glad I had better sense* was another thought. It would have been less than frank to pretend I was immune from that surge of feeling which can often blunt the cutting edge of grief: *I have survived.*

As Alec remarked afterward, if Jim had been partial to Mark Twain, he might have repeated the words cabled from London by that master of the ironic a generation ago: "The reports of my death are greatly exaggerated." I was provoked by having to piece together from the newspapers what had actually befallen him because there was no mutual friend who cared enough or knew enough to write to me.

He was within an ace of dying when his doctor prevailed upon him to be rushed by ambulance to Pennsylvania Station, where a special train was waiting to hasten him to Baltimore. The staff at Johns Hopkins Hospital there was compelled to labor around the clock, reinforcing a surgical table to hold his elephantine weight. In the meantime, through the use of Professor Röntgen's X-rays which we had heard so much about for the last decade, it was discovered that a lifetime of abuse had stretched Jim's stomach to six times normal capacity and a kidney stone of excruciating size had lodged itself in a ureter.

The odds against successful surgery were astronomical. Jim,

a diabetic, had an enlarged heart as well as a cavernous digestive system, and his entire frame was swathed in obesity. The one chance in a million to save him from succumbing to uremia depended on the surgical skill of a Dr. Hugh Young, who had perfected the technique and necessary catheters for reaching up within the body to locate and crush a kidney stone without opening up the abdomen. The operation was performed early next morning. Within a week, Jim was holding court in his room, dispensing two-carat rings to his nurses, wolfing down the food he ordered sent in from the Hotel Belvedere because he could not take to the fare prepared in the hospital kitchens.

A letter of condolence from me brought a note signed by him but obviously written by a nurse to his dictation: "I have been doing a lot of thinking lately," it said in part, "and have come to the conclusion that I would kind of like to help the doctors who are getting me back on my feet again. I am going to give a couple of hundred thousand"—an excited ink blot marred the page at this point—"to build a new clinic for the likes of me and an extra fifteen thousand every year to help keep it going. Dr. Young says there's only two places like it anywhere else in the world, one in London and the other in Paris. He wants to see this new one called the James Buchanan Brady Urological Institute! I read in the paper here that you figure on getting spliced. Even in my present state of health, you could of done a lot worse than take me on, but that's only a joke, Nell, and I send my regards and wish you the very best of everything."

I had been beset by reporters the moment a whisper got around concerning my engagement to Alec. "We shall be married," I stated, "when Mr. Roosevelt is once again nominated for the Presidency at the forthcoming convention in Chicago. Should he fail to obtain his party's backing, the wedding will be postponed."

I spoke for myself, not with Alec's concurrence. My statement, in fact, was calculated to place him squarely in Teddy's camp and stop his hemming and hawing about leaving the choice of candidate to the national committee. In my view, the committee was more than likely to go for Taft, despite Teddy's announcement as far back as February that his Rough Riders' hat was "in the ring."

Chicago, Cleveland, Kansas City—we played to sold-out houses all the way. Then to conclude the tour, *Hokey-Pokey* pulled into Pittsburgh, where I sensed immediately that my fiancé and I would have to come to terms. I would bow to his desire to be married without delay if he gave me his word that, irrespective of what deviltry occurred at the convention, Alec as a delegate would stand firm for Teddy. Otherwise, I implied, I might be content to remain Miss Russell to the end of my days.

We were married in the Hotel Schenley on June 12 with Lew Fields and Joe Weber as our witnesses. It was as simple a ceremony as each of the others had been—no Mendelssohn, no feasting. In lavender silk and a new diamond pendant from Alec, I had Suzanne as matron of honor, while the manager of the Nixon served as best man (a hollow term in his case). That evening my bridegroom took the train to the convention. On the train back to New York, I played solitaire to maintain a private tradition.

He proved to have retained his touch as a journalist in his letters to me, sent from the Congress Hotel, where Teddy established his headquarters upon arrival at the scene of carnage. "This has come down to be a fight of honesty against dishonesty," he declared, and I agreed with him. Alec wrote that his heart fluttered, as mine certainly did, at our champion's avowal, "We stand at Armageddon, and we battle for the Lord." But the traitors convening in the Coliseum nominated Taft, forcing Teddy to bolt the party, which was the only course open to a man of his honor.

My husband brought glad tidings when he came to our New York apartment. On June 22 he had been among the faithful who pledged support to Teddy at a rally in Orchestra Hall. Alec would return to Chicago in August, paying his own expenses to the first convention of the Progressives, known now as the Bull Moosers, and I would accompany him to this unique event in our nation's history, where women at last could serve as delegates and rank as man's equal when the ballots were cast.

From Michigan Avenue we entered the self-same Coliseum that had seen our inept President reacclaimed six weeks ago, to find it draped with what could have been the same red, white, and blue bunting and flag-draped portrait of Abraham Lincoln which had served before. I lifted my voice to its joyous limits to join in singing:

> *I want to be a Bull Moose*
> *And with the Bull Moose stand,*
> *With antlers on my forehead*
> *And a big stick in my hand.*

Oscar Straus, the Jewish aspirant for the governorship in Albany, marshaled the New York State delegation down the aisle, and we all sang again. "Onward, Christian Soldiers" would be our anthem for the campaign ahead. Teddy's address—he labeled it "Confession of Faith"—revived the same passion within me that I remembered feeling on the inspiring day when, borne over freshly laid railroad track in Montana, I had a vision of the might of our young nation. Of course the old parties were, as Teddy said, "husks with no real soul," and of course his platform called for votes for women.

I examined the others who packed the hall around me. These were no potbellied politicians but fellow citizens—farmers, professors, small businessmen, high-thinkers, and, above all, women like Jane Addams, who most fittingly would second our idol's nomination. We also learned that Mark Hanna's son and heir, Dan, was already raising fighting funds for Teddy through his Ohio newspaper.

I took to a different kind of stage to speak before female audiences, pulling out all the stops to tell them, "The election of Theodore Roosevelt will mean an advancement of one hundred years for women in this country and the world. Woman will be accorded the rights she has been unjustly denied since the founding of our land. We shall stand up in glory to be counted. Ours will be the power and ours the glory."

The receptions I received were so stimulating that on one occasion I caught myself declaring, "If women ever get the vote, I would willingly run for mayor of New York City." But that was unduly impetuous. I calculated that even if ten thousand times more votes came to me than had gone to Mama in '84, victory would still be elusive, and I had an antipathy toward being defeated by Tammany Hall.

The news of Jim was worrisome. Discharged after eight weeks in the hospital, he had reverted to his old patterns of living. I also had to write him off politically as a recidivist Democrat whose vote in November would inevitably go to Woodrow Wilson, the muddleheaded prophet of "reform" who, like Taft in this first real three-way contest since I was born, was concentrating his fire on Teddy.

Jim was captivated by the new craze that infected New York like an epidemic of the Saint Vitus dance. The graceful waltz, schottische, and lancers of my youth had been supplanted by animalistic capers identified by such grotesque names as the turkey trot, the camel walk, the bunny hug, the kangaroo dip, with the mixed drinks called "cocktails" served between times for refreshment. Rector's was catering to the mania by restyling itself "the Balmoral Club" at 1:00 A.M. every morning with saxophones blaring jazz until dawn. Bustanoby's was pursuing the same downhill course in the guise of "the Domino Circle Club."

Jim did the rounds every night like an ocean liner under tow, the tugboats hauling him into harbor being half a dozen young girls who fussed around him, all attired with the new high heels and hobble skirts that made them look like drainpipes. For $25 a head, free food and drink, and a fur coat on loan from a collection of them he had accumulated for the purpose, they would take turns dancing with him, clutched against his belly by one hand while he fondled their backs with the other. Two of his favorites were young married women, the Dolly Sisters, professional dancers who invariably brought their husbands along to form a bizarre quintet and were rewarded in Jim's unfailing fashion with gifts of diamonds plus an automobile apiece.

I should have been inclined to dismiss these accounts of his behavior as figments of journalistic invention if I had not seen him myself one night after I had gone to New York to take part in a demonstration of the strength of our suffrage movement.

Serene on a snowy steed, the beauteous Inez Mulholland led the parade organized by Mrs. O. H. P. Belmont (once the wife of Willie Vanderbilt) that commandeered Fifth Avenue from 59th Street to Washington Square. All 50,000 of us—scions of society, factory workers, shopgirls, schoolteachers, housewives, and typists—wore virginal white as we marched for hours on end in a defiant sisterhood between ranks of jeering males who resented our soon-to-be-won equality.

For old time's sake, I asked Alec if we might drop in at Rector's after dining at the new Ritz-Carlton. There I saw the restaurant's postprandial transformation into an arena of terpsichorean madness with Jim in the center, jigging around like a bear with the itch to the beat of Tin Pan Alley.

I caught him during a rare interval of comparative quiet. How could he bring himself to this? I asked. There was wretchedness in his eyes. "Hell, I got to have some fun. I ain't got much longer."

The inanity of the Republican Party junto was revealed on Election Day. If they had not lost their minds and had chosen Teddy instead of Taft, we should have had Roosevelt as our President once more, making our country strong enough to keep the world's respect for us as a mighty force for law and order, that would tolerate nonsense from nobody.

To diminish my chagrin over Teddy's defeat, I took to the road again, this time with an illustrated lecture, "Health & Beauty," rather than in a play. I retrod a similar route repeatedly thereafter as an accepted voice of authority on any number of themes—suffrage, jewels, philosophy, love, marriage, divorce, and the hypnotic merits of scopolamine, which I had not experienced myself, in childbirth during "twilight sleep." On that subject I must have been especially convincing. The newspapers buzzed with the lie that I was expecting another baby myself at the official age of forty-eight, which was five years short of the actuality.

At the behest of the Chicago *Tribune* and for $12,000 a year, I wrote with the aid of a more experienced newspaperwoman a series of daily articles on beauty care. Sold throughout the country, they attracted such an avalanche of mail that six assistants had to be engaged to answer it. One day the editor wired me: WRITE LESS ABOUT SOUL AND MORE ABOUT PIMPLES. From then on, the rival *Record-Herald* had the benefit of my services at the typewriter.

In addition to my name, I gave precious time as a part-time saleswoman in department stores, demonstrating the products of Lillian Russell's Own Preparations, Incorporated, which I dreamed would make me $1,000,000 on an investment of $25,000 while I was young enough to enjoy it. Some twenty-four months after the line of face powder, rouge, and skin creme went into the shops, I had to sue the company's management for arrears in royalties amounting to $10,000.

Europeans were fighting with each other in the trenches of France when I was tempted into exploring an area of entertainment I had previously neglected. Moving pictures had come a long way since the day of my talk with Thomas Edison. If one could believe the drum beaters of the press, Gladys Smith, the little curly-haired Canadian who acted under the name of Mary Pickford, was earning $1,000,000 a year from Adolph Zukor's Famous Players Company.

My invitation was forthcoming from a Jewish immigrant from czarist Russia whose jewelry store I had now and then patronized in Pittsburgh before he upped stakes and moved to New York. Lewis Selznick, born Zeleznick in Kiev, had recently spent his savings to buy a modest holding in World Film Corporation when he got into touch with me. His scheme for making a fortune in a hurry was to arrange with the Shubert Brothers and their like to photograph successful plays of yesteryear with as many of the original leading players as he could corral.

I knew when I responded to a barrage of telephone calls and telegrams that his prize catch to date was a buxom brunette with eyes like saucers. Clara Kimball Young, the principal asset of World Film, was also his bedmate, though I understood him to be married and the father of three sons. But where I had the advantage of maturity, she had youth on her side, so I reluctantly accepted the fact that I should never be given equal treatment in the matter of advertising and promotion of the version of *Wildfire* that he proposed to record on celluloid.

The hustler with the pince-nez eyeglasses who introduced himself to me in his sumptuous Broadway office gave the appearance of having been chasing a fast dollar from the moment he was out of the cradle. Mr. Selznick was disarming in his frankness when I asked who my leading man was to be.

"Lionel Barrymore. What a beautiful actor. Such a voice, such dignity! Do you know him?"

"I question whether he has the brains of his sister Ethel or the looks of his brother John."

"Less brains are necessary in the motion-picture business than in any other you could think of. Tell me whether you know another business where you put in a thousand dollars like I did and take out a hundred and five thousand in ten weeks. With Lionel you will have it easy. He'll make you look like a diamond on velvet."

"What shall we decide about the terms of my engagement?"

"Money. Everybody wants to talk about money. I tell my sons, 'Spend it all. Give it away, but get rid of it. Live beyond your means, because then you'll have to work hard to catch up.' I will say to you, Miss Russell, 'Never try to save money.' If you do, then you'll have two things to worry about: making it and keeping it."

He was evading my question, but eventually he wheedled me down to a fee so far below what Weber & Fields had paid that I had to tell myself it would have to be tripled for the next photoplay I made.

I continued to have reservations about what I had let myself in for during the journey to Los Angeles, the latter-day Mecca of an industry that had discovered one way of reducing overhead was to film as much as possible outdoors, using the dependable California sunshine in lieu of more expensive interior electric lighting. The better class of legitimate artistes had so far withheld themselves from the temptations of this tawdry new medium that suppressed civilized intercourse in speech and song, relying instead on crude gesture and melodramatic pantomime. Moving pictures were a magnet for second-raters like Maurice Costello, Francis X. Bushman, the acrobatic "Bronco Billy" Anderson, and, let it be said, dear Marie Dressler with her golden heart and face like an amiable chimpanzee. I doubted whether a performance in front of the cameras could be given the restraint and subtlety I aimed for when the whole business was largely controlled by Jewish immigrants without formal education, hungering for easy money.

Los Angeles itself was not unattractive with its streets of little Spanish-style houses and tiled roofs the color of the fruit on the citrus trees, groves of which covered miles of the dusty hillsides under the relentless sun. The atmosphere was as relaxed as what I imagined life on a hacienda to be. Water carts driven by indolent Mexicans sprinkled the quiet thoroughfares in the early mornings, gaily shawled women peddled exotic flowers on the street corners, and somewhere there was usually the sound of a chorded guitar.

The contrast was startling on the erstwhile empty lots hurriedly transformed into what were grandiosely termed "studios." There, turmoil reigned, such as I had never witnessed. Since the cowboy reigned as king in this land of make-believe, these lots bore a marked resemblance to Madison Square Garden when a Wild West show was playing. Bronzed young men in outlandish costumes featuring revolver belts and white sombreros were forever mounting livery-stable horses to go whooping down streets of false fronts to volleys of blank cartridges. The costumes of the production staff were equally droll with their emphasis on khaki shirts, riding breeches, puttees, and megaphones. The bizarreness of the limited number of females engaged in these fantasies lay in what they wore on their faces as well as in the wardrobes, seemingly ordered in haste from the Sears, Roebuck & Company catalogue, worn on their backs. The mascara, the carmine and talc were applied so heavy-handedly as to make them look like clowns, yet they were so taken by the effect that most of these unknown ingenues, whose talents consisted of little more than the ability to simper to order, daubed themselves with similar makeup to go off to a party when sunset ended the working day.

On the one visit Jim made here soon after he came out of the hospital, he had entertained Marie, who had migrated to this quarter of the globe they called Hollywood to make comedies known in the local patois as "two-reelers" with an English graduate of the music halls, Charlie Chaplin. I saw *Tilly's Punctured Romance* for her sake but was not enthused. Now Marie must respond by playing hostess for me.

I made a point of wearing my very finest gown and leaving my hotel a little late. The Ford in service as a taxicab turned out to be driven by a youngster who, after recognizing me, claimed that he was an actor awaiting further employment, though his experience to date had been confined to falling off horses, pretending to be shot by rifle or bow and arrow.

He proved to be a garrulous chauffeur, deluging me with gossip in the course of a journey whose duration would have surprised anyone accustomed to the briefer distances involved on evenings out in Manhattan. Did I know Mary Pickford? I allowed that I had heard of her. "Wistful face and a mind like a bear trap, I hear. I'd like a chance to work with her." Mae Marsh, the Gish sisters? No, I hadn't had the pleasure. "Those three are going to make it big. What I wouldn't give to be in pictures with them!" "Fatty" Arbuckle, perhaps? I did not recognize the name. "Very funny when you see him on the screen, but he's got different kinds of tricks when he's out for a good time. Girls are his weakness, and there's plenty of quail out here for anybody's hunting if you can afford it like he can. I reckon I'll take a stab at being a comedian."

I was tired of his prattle by the time we reached the house Marie had rented up in the hills, identifiable this evening by the sound of a Mexican band playing what she said was "marimba" music. After a hug and a kiss, she ambled out with me onto the patio, where things were well under way, enveloped in the light of Chinese lanterns and the scent of steak sizzling on a barbecue fire of some fragrant wood. I swallowed hard at the appearance of the crowd, attired for the most part not in tails and dinner jackets or gowns approaching mine but in the very same kind of dishabille sported during working hours.

The first person I must meet, Marie said, was the celebrated Mr. Charles Chaplin. He was a wisp of a man, half her size— or mine, I feared—with a mop of black curls, white teeth showing in a fleeting smile, but bereft of the mustache I expected. For the London Cockney I knew him to be, he had remarkably good manners, and he accorded me the greatest respect. "You're the lady Jim Brady's always talking about. He thinks there's nobody quite like you."

"He's a dear. When did you run into him?"

"Soon after I arrived in New York with Fred Karno, before Joe Schenck took me up and introduced me to Mack Sennett." (Who were these people?) "I slept one night in Jim's bathtub at his place on 86th Street."

A throng of admirers, sycophants, and starry-eyed "quail" gathering around the little fellow soon made further conversation impossible. I turned away to a gaunt, solitary stranger who was regarding the scene like a director at rehearsal. In no time at all I was listening to an idealist's dreams for the infantile business I had fallen into.

"Moving pictures are the most revolutionary invention since the printing press. I grant you the Wright brothers' flying machines are more spectacular, and telephones and sewing machines have more commercial value, but none of these rank in importance with the moving-picture camera. It can present a vision of all the wonders of the universe in a language everyone can understand, the simplest language known to man—pictures."

I murmured insincere agreement, which unfortunately encouraged him. "We can read the history of the cavemen of France from the drawings they left behind. Egyptian hieroglyphics speak to us over the centuries. Now we have the means of expressing anything we choose in moving pictures—drama, history, art, literature." And so he rambled on until I excused myself with a parting "I didn't catch your name."

"Griffith, D. W. Griffith." I forgot all about him until I watched and marveled at *The Birth of a Nation* at a later date.

The evening would have been less taxing if I had known others besides Marie. As it was, everything was too strange, too alien for my taste, from the faces to the clothes to the rum cocktails, to the food, with appetizers too mushy and steak with a flavor of firewood. I pleaded that fatigue persisted after the days spent on the train and took myself off as soon as I decently could.

For all this, I became quite fond of the way in which we worked in front of the unwieldy cameras under the open sky with property men crouched around us, holding metal reflectors to shine sunlight under our chins, which made it difficult to pretend that the flimsy backgrounds were genuine theater sets. Although the continual repetition of fragments of scenes could be tiresome, Lionel and I had many a chuckle over his ad-libbing. One piece of action, for instance, called for him to pore over my right hand, to which had been added one of my better emerald rings. The subtitle would have him utter something to the effect of "What delicate fingers! When may I press them to my lips?" Only a lip reader could descry that his actual words were "What beautiful green glass! Was it made from a beer bottle?"

I made no more photoplays; *Wildfire* fizzled when it was released. The kindest thing any reviewer could find to write about my performance was "She carries expensive gowns with a distinguished air." I committed myself to the road only once more, in "Lillian Russell and the Big Feature Festival," ten weeks of travel, toil, and trouble, and the critical abuse became unbearable. How could I construe it except as a sentence of professional death when I read, "Some real good, honest friend ought to take Lillian by the hand and gently lead her home that we might be left with a happy memory of the days when she was in her prime"?

If Teddy had been attending the 1916 convention of either the Republicans, held again in the Coliseum, or the Progressives in the Auditorium, I, too, would have gone to Chicago proud to pin on my Bull Moose badge, sing the songs of 1912, and rip out yells for him. But he stayed in Oyster Bay and I in Pittsburgh, the Progressives crept back into the fold, and the bearded iceberg, Charles Evans Hughes, was the reunited party's selection for the Presidency. Jim was there, wandering through the hotel lobbies, disillusioned with Wilson, I was pleased to hear, and with the trumpeting of the Democrats that "he kept us out of war." The battles that raged on the far side of the Atlantic were a boon to Jim, whose company had an order on its books from the French government to build $100,000,000 worth of freight cars to replace those lost to the invaders.

That November of Hughes's defeat saw the beginning of Jim's irreversible decline. His doctors diagnosed gastric ulcers as the root cause of the attack, but that was not all. His heart was diseased and his kidneys, too, and his diabetes was uncontrollable. Surgery would accomplish nothing. He was given only a few more months to live.

He chose to end his days in Atlantic City, where he'd once had Edna McCauley as his plaything. Alec did not question my desire to see my old friend for what could only be the last time. I found him in a $1,000-a-week apartment at the Shelburne, whose entrance opened off the boardwalk. A matronly nurse led me out onto a verandah enclosed with glass, where he sat wrapped in steamer rugs, swollen legs resting on an ottoman.

His voice was down to a phlegmy whisper, and loose folds of flesh hung over the collar of his striped flannel nightshirt. "God, it's good to see you, Nell. I ain't had a visitor all week."

"Nor last week, either." The nurse sniffed as she left us together.

I endeavored to be Miss Sunshine. "What are you doing with yourself these days, Jim boy?"

"Sitting here watching the sea mostly. It gets you thinking, you know, seeing the waves come rolling in, then rolling out again."

"They're happy thoughts, I hope."

"Sometimes they are; not always. I ain't much for being left alone. I don't know what's happened to all my pals. Must be sick, too, I reckon."

"Perhaps you need a pretty face to cheer you up."

"I got yours today. There never was anybody prettier than you. I wish I could have made you happy."

"Of course you did. We had wonderful times, and you're not to make yourself upset by doubting it."

"You never loved me like I loved you, did you? If you had've done, I'd have turned out different. I been a sinner, Nell, and the tide's going to go out soon and take me with it."

I controlled myself and reached under the covers to hold his hand. "And you'll swim right back again. You've nothing to worry about; nobody's done more than you to make all kinds of people happy."

"You're wrong, and I don't like to contradict you. I could have done a lot more 'cause everybody can if he tries and if somebody loves 'em. I don't want to be buried in some hole in the ground, Nell. I've left word I want to be cremated. My ma would have said that was a sin, too."

"Jim, you mustn't talk yourself into dying. Think of everything you've done with your life. You've made millions of dollars and hundreds of friends and done no harm to anybody if you could help it."

"There ain't too many friends in sight just now, is there? Sure, I made some money, and I ain't sorry about that, but I should have done something better with it than make a public spectacle of myself like I was some two-headed calf. I got a lot of attention, but that wasn't what I wanted, not deep down under all this mess of flesh I been carrying around."

I could check the tears no longer. "So much of it was my fault. I wish I could have loved you, but I couldn't, and I can't stand to see you so unhappy now. Jim, I'm sorry, but I couldn't."

There was no strength in the fingers that squeezed mine. "Don't go blaming yourself. Not even the angels could take to an ugly devil like me."

It would do him no good to stay on, crying. "I'll come again, Jim, as soon as I can."

His tallowy face attempted a smile. "Don't leave it so late that the tide's gone out." No friend was present when he was borne away in the early morning of Friday, April 13, a week to the day after we declared war on Germany.

Throughout Saturday afternoon and all day Sunday, his body lay in the living room of the house on 86th Street, whose first floor was massed with flowers, from wreaths more splendid than mine to ten-cent nosegays placed by ragged newsboys close to the blanket of orchids drawn back from the open coffin. His number-one set of diamonds glittered on the dress suit he was clad in. His executors ruled against cremation. They would have him buried in a mausoleum in Greenwood Cemetery after the jewels had been stripped off in accordance with state law.

On Monday, at the Catholic church of St. Agnes on East 43rd Street, police reinforcements had to be called in to handle the overflow. Railroad presidents past and present filled the pews along with other titans of industry, merchants he had enriched, recipients of his charity, policemen he had bribed, and a swarm from my own profession who had enjoyed his bounty. Had any one of us been a true friend to him? I doubted it.

His will ordered most of his millions to be shared between Johns Hopkins and the New York Hospital. The bulk of the diamonds went to his legion of acquaintances, with a chain of sixty-five pearls for Rose Dolly and twenty-four carats of his "little doodads" for her sister Jennie. Nothing was left to me, and I was glad.

I put aside thinking about the nature of Jim Brady to busy myself in the spirit of 1917 by drumming up recruits for General "Black Jack" Pershing's American Expeditionary Forces, selling Liberty Bonds like Mary Pickford, starting my very first diary, and taking up knitting khaki socks. I would stand on a jerry-built platform in the middle of a town square in some corner of Pennsylvania, thrilled by some of the most emotional moments ever experienced in my varied career. "Men and women," I would cry, "our boys are knee-deep in mud in the trenches of France, fighting the Hun for you and me." It was a joy to know that Theodore Roosevelt was stumping the land for similar purposes.

My best night came in McKeesport, where two hundred and fifty-nine lads stepped up to offer their lives for their country. In Pittsburgh, a "Lillian Russell Recruiting Day" was proclaimed, and onto the breast of every young man who volunteered I pinned a Stars and Stripes emblem bought from a jeweler by Alec. A little later I was awarded a badge of my own, designating me a sergeant in the United States Marines, which was only a prelude to speedy promotion as honorary colonel in the corps.

Brave men like Sergeant Alvin York were responsible for winning the war, and Wilson was guilty of losing the peace. When he came back from Paris patently broken in health and spirit in the summer of 1919, I felt compelled to tell audiences at my lectures, "God was not at the Peace Conference, and He's not in the Covenant of the League of Nations." I agreed with the Senator from Ohio, Warren G. Harding, who explained to his colleagues that he was opposed to establishing "a new internationalism paralyzed by socialism."

On the political scene, the solitary saving grace that year was the Nineteenth Amendment, bestowing nationwide suffrage upon us women. "Liberty! Equality! *Sorority!*" as I wrote on a diary page.

The following June I went with Alec to the extremely odd

convention that met in a sweltering Chicago—always Chicago! I was rooting for Teddy's old comrade, Hiram Johnson of California, and doing my best to avoid an encounter with that ancient bore, New York State's Senator Chauncey Depew. The sale of intoxicating liquor had been constitutionally prohibited for the past five months, but the law of the land obviously meant nothing to many of the bleary-eyed delegates I beheld swaying through the public rooms of the Blackstone, where we had a suite on the thirteenth floor, not far from another occupied by George Harvey, editor of the *North American Review*, an owlish-looking individual but a notable kingmaker, as the constant stream of visitors to his door indicated.

The Coliseum was already as hot as a glasshouse when we arrived there for the first session on Tuesday, and ragtime rattled over the amplifiers from the band perched up under the girders. By nightfall, one candidate appeared to have been eliminated. Warren Harding of Ohio, whose portraits showed him handsome enough to have attracted me as a leading man in earlier days, was the subject of a scurrilous pamphlet—some fanatic distributed copies in the Blackstone's lobby—which made the outrageous claim that Negro blood ran in the Senator's veins. I could not believe his name had been dropped from the party's councils on that account.

The following day's sitting was even briefer, over in ten minutes before we had left our hotel, where the mysterious comings and goings on the thirteenth floor continued unabated. Alec, who was present at some of George Harvey's confabulations, told me that evening that Harding might accept second place on the ticket.

"Will he be asked?"

"That manager of his, Daugherty, hasn't given up trying, but Harding would like to chuck the whole thing, too, and go back home to his newspaper. Warren's wife, Florence, and Harry Daugherty nagged him into trying in the first place."

On Friday, the nominating speeches lasted until five o'clock, by which time a noticeable odor of perspiration permeated the hall. The roll of the states was called thrice more before the deadlocked convention broke up in a thunder of protest from those who would have chosen not to have their labors interrupted. More than anything else at that moment, I wanted to be back in the Blackstone to do my exercises, bathe, and go to bed, leaving Alec to go about his political affairs.

I was still awake when Alec tiptoed in, the pungency of his clothing telling that he had called at the smoke-filled suite along the hall. "They've been shuffling names like a pack of cards, Nell. Colonel Harvey's just sent for Harding. They're going to try to put him over in the morning."

It was accomplished on the tenth ballot that next evening in an auditorium where the temperature had not dropped below ninety degrees all week and not a clean shirt was to be seen on any man's damp back. "Will you take to the stump for him?" Alec inquired when all was over.

"I will speak for our party, but first I should like to meet the man in person."

We were invited to lunch with the Hardings at their home in Marion on a day in August. From Union Depot, the route up Center Street was hung with bunting. A fife-and-drum corps had just finished a serenade outside the house on Mount Vernon Avenue. The Stars and Stripes fluttered nobly from McKinley's old flagpole, brought from Canton and set up in the yard. In the orchard at the rear, temporary quarters had been erected for gentlemen of the press. We watched the Senator pose to be photographed on the porch, arms around two little neighborhood girls who had come to show him their dolls.

I sensed the warmth of the man as he declared, "I would rather have a houseful of kiddies than anything else in the world."

The Harding and Coolidge Theatrical League had come by special train from New York. The master of ceremonies was the currently popular coon singer Al Jolson, who had made his name by debasing Negro spirituals into "jazz." He was president of the league and composer of the song he proceeded to deliver:

> We think the country's ready
> For another man like Teddy.
> We need another Lincoln
> To do the country's thinkin'

Jolson's arms flapped to bring everyone in for the chorus: *Mister Harding, you're the man for us!*

After the choristers had departed and comparative peace had been restored, our future President conducted Alec and me into his modest library, where a foot-high stone elephant occupied the mantel above the tiled fireplace and an armless, truncated Venus de Milo the top of an adjacent bookcase. Florence was waiting there, the inevitable velvet choker encircling her throat to conceal what I suspected were wrinkles.

He flashed an instant smile. "I think you've met the Duchess? She's a good scout who knows all my faults and yet has stuck to me all the way. We have to call her Snow Bird these days—she's just been made an honorary Indian."

At the simple luncheon she served, I was seated at his right as guest of honor. He spoke of his early boyhood on the farm and of a father who went off to medical school and came back a qualified physician. He told of his mother's dreams of making him a preacher and, most movingly, of his work as a printer's six-year-old errand boy. He brought Papa to mind with his reminiscences about buying his newspaper, the Marion *Star*, for $300 cash and acceptance of its mortgage, but he was more like Mama in his unashamed confession that he relied upon God's guidance every day.

I had seldom been more charmed than by this model of a man who carried his years—five less than mine—almost as well as I. He was, in my opinion, every inch a President. I was flattered to be called upon to campaign in fifteen states for him, making three and four speeches a day. He, of course, had my vote and probably those of the vast majority of women, with whom his sheer good looks may have counted as much as his advocacy of restoring America to what he termed "normalcy."

Alec and I were advised in advance not to be disappointed when the first prizes of victory were handed out, naming Harry Daugherty the Attorney General, millionaire Mellon the Secretary of the Treasury, and the President's old friend, goateed Albert Fall, Senator from New Mexico, the Secretary of the Interior. We were assured that our services in the election would not be overlooked. There was even talk of an ambassadorship for Alec.

My reward was given earlier than his. We answered a summons to visit the White House over our President's first Christmas there and arrived in a snowstorm to find confusion within the Executive Mansion. Florence was in a state of alarm over the deluge of poison-pen letters threatening death to her husband, which had been climaxed by an anonymous warning that his life would be taken on Christmas Day. Happily, she and "Wurrn," as she called him, had been invited to spend that day with Eva-lyn Walsh Maclean, Florence's dear friend, at her house on Eye Street.

Christmas morning found the Hardings in church. Alec and I made our separate way to a united luncheon, entering the Macleans' house under the gaze of Secret Service agents stationed on the street outside and encountering others in the hall. During a lull in the afternoon's pleasantries around the immense tree in the three-story living room, I heard from the President what my assignment was to be.

He had chosen me as his emissary to Europe! I was to con-duct an investigation on the spot there into the problems our country was suffering as a result of the ceaseless influx of immi-grants seeking to take advantage of our vastly superior standards of life. A report from my hands was to be presented to the Secre-tary of Labor, James J. Davis. The President's dark-brown eyes twinkled. "You know, Mrs. Moore, a woman's ear can get more information than all the intelligence and diplomacy any govern-ment can lay hold of."

"I am sure the country is safe in your hands."

A frown crossed his patrician brow. "Truth is, I have decided that it is more fun to be a candidate than it is to be President, with all the annoyances, irritations, and burdens. I listen to one side, and they seem right, and then—God!—I talk to the other side, and they seem just as right, and here I am where I started. I hope you can give us some simple, one-sided proposals."

I imagined he would have had more to say but for the familiar cry of "Wurrn!" with which Florence broke in on us, nervously fidgeting with the diamond sewn into the band around her throat. After a turkey dinner with an abundance of trimmings— and drinking by most of the group—she approached me again. "Wurrn's going with some of the boys for a poker game, and we ladies are going to enjoy a picture show—Mary Pickford in *Little Lord Fauntleroy*. That book's a real favorite of mine."

It would have been a breach of good manners to tell her

that I would much prefer to join in the game upstairs with the President, Harry Daugherty, Ned Maclean, Senator Charlie "Indian" Curtis, and John Weeks, the Secretary of War. From Alec's accounts of such evenings, I had a shrewd idea of what this one would consist of: waistcoats unbuttoned, feet up, cigars lit, a spittoon for the President, who preferred plugs of chewing tobacco. The one thing of which I could not approve would be the trays of bottles containing every variety of illicit whiskey.

The next day Mr. Harding welcomed Eugene Debs, whom he had pardoned from Atlanta penitentiary as a prisoner unjustly incarcerated as a result of Wilson's hatred of conscientious objectors. Mama would have applauded the President's act. I could not.

I devoted most of the spring to ferreting out the truth from our embassies and consulates in England, France, Italy, and elsewhere. What I learned only confirmed what I had known from girlhood. "Give me your tired, your poor, your huddled masses yearning to breathe free" was a policy that spelled disaster for our country. The hordes of foreigners, 350,000 of them every year, that we allowed through our golden portals threatened us with the fate that befell ancient Rome.

Europe teemed with "relief" organizations which, for the sole purpose of making money, hoodwinked my fellow citizens into believing that "humanity" demanded the unchecked influx of immigrants. The result was a swarm of parasites who, incapable of speaking a word of our language, infected our nation's bloodstream with alien philosophies of internecine strife like Sacco and Vanzetti or with horrible physical diseases.

I observed that every able-bodied Frenchman or Italian was hard at work restoring the damage wrought by shot and shell. The class of people seeking to flee that responsibility were for the most part wastrels and riffraff who as immigrants were only obstacles in the path to developing our country's wealth and resources. On the other hand, they deprived Americans of jobs in an hour when unemployment at home was rising to dangerous levels.

My ire knew no bounds when, on the return voyage, I suffered a bruising fall down a companionway after being nudged by an overdressed, pock-marked idler of Mediterranean origin, undoubtedly en route to leech on us, who pretended it was all accidental. The sickly look on his swarthy face indicated lack of either physical or mental health.

The program I recommended, well received in Washington, boiled down to this: Slam the doors to all immigrants for a period of five years. Make every alien who had already infiltrated our land wait twenty-five years, not five as now, before qualifying for the privilege of naturalization and the attendant right to vote. Screen every man, woman, and child on their own shores to weed out the unhealthy in mind or body before granting visas to enter our gates. Our slogan, as I said in my report and repeated from the lecture platform, must be "America for Americans!"

~ XVII ~

*E*XTRACT FROM THE DIARY of Dorothy Solomon Calbit, May 28, 1922:
Thank God I came to Pittsburgh today to see Mother. I would
have been here days ago had I known how sick she really is, but
there was only a vague hint in her letter. When Alec met me at the
station, he said she had not been well for a week and more. She
takes no more notice of him than of me and refuses to go to a
doctor. For all her talk about Marcus Aurelius, there's a Christian
Scientist lurking somewhere inside her.

She won't even be put to bed, though she has lost so much
weight she looks like a shadow. That might be better for her, of
course, in the long run. She blames her trouble on the fall she
had on the ship, raving on about the man who pushed her. I saw
the bruises, still black and blue, and I don't like the look of all
the swelling.

I think that for once she was pleased to see me. It's always
hard to tell with her. She isn't exactly an emotional woman, but
the kiss I got was warm for a change. If she hasn't improved by
tomorrow, I am going to telephone a doctor because Alec's too
scared to. I do wish he wouldn't keep urging me to call him
Father.

May 29. Well, Dr. Shieldecker answered my call right off and
was at the house in his Packard within thirty minutes. I wondered
whether she would let him examine her, but she did. I think the
pain is beginning to get her down. She even accepted his advice
to stay in bed, though I'm sure she won't take her medicine. She

talks about something called "homeopathy," a word I remember
my grandmother using. I'm no wiser about what it is than I was
then.

There's certainly nothing wrong with Mother's spirit; she's
as strong-willed as always. Today she told me, "I intend to get
well very shortly in order to resume my work for the President
of the United States." I'm happy she has something to occupy
her in her old age. She still pretends to herself that she will do
another show before she gives up the stage completely, and she
says she has to finish a book she is writing. When I tucked her in
for the night, she insisted on lending me one of her little bedside
companions—Marcus Aurelius, no less—marked with a passage
she wanted me to read: "This Being of mine, whatever it really
is, consists of a little flesh, a little breath, and the part which
governs." In her case, the part which governs is the most important. Dr. Shieldecker doesn't seem to know what's wrong with
her.

May 30. The first tests didn't prove anything, so they are going to take some more. At last she's agreed to swallow her
medicine, which makes her drowsy, and I find her dozing when
I go in to her. She dreams a lot, she says. This afternoon it was
about her baby, the one she lost. "Strange to think," she said,
"that had he lived, he would have been forty-two this year, and I
might have been a nobody."

She is determined for me to admire her philosopher. Another passage marked up for me tonight: "All is ephemeral—
fame and the famous as well." If she believes that, and she says
she does, it's a miracle.

June 2. Alec stayed home from the office today and won't go
back until she's turned the corner. He's more of a hindrance than
a help, puttering in and out of the bedroom all day. I can take
good care of Mother, but he is getting a nurse in the morning.
Dr. Shieldecker came again, talking about X-rays. She finds it
hard to explain where the pain is, and I suspect it's everywhere
by the look on her face. Her eyes glaze over sometimes, and her
mind wanders.

She seems to appreciate it when she finds me lying on top of
the covers next to her. She comes out with some odd remarks.
This evening she said, "I was certain that Mama and Papa were

here a moment ago. They were holding hands and looking so happy at being together that it brought me to my senses, knowing this could not be real."

I wish I could persuade her to eat, but her appetite has disappeared. Now she asks me to read to her from the bedside books. She nodded off to sleep tonight after she'd had me repeat, "Whatever may befall thee, it was preordained for thee from everlasting."

June 4. She is back from the hospital and feels better, she says. We dare not tell her what the X-rays showed. She had ether for some of the tests, but her brain went on working. "I was as certain as you are sitting there," she told me, "that I was on the stage of the Metropolitan and yet also sitting in the audience, applauding myself as I sang *Lucia* better than anything I have done in my life."

There are so many answers I need while time is left to ask the questions. Why was I packed off to places like a Railway Express delivery when I was a child, aching to be with her? Why did she send me away to the convent after my father left us and she was all I had? Why didn't she let me share in her life when I was so proud of her and could not tell her so because she kept herself so aloof from me?

I don't want to upset her now, so I don't know what to do. Even if I asked her, she probably could not understand, her thoughts go so far away. I was tiptoeing off to my own bed when she suddenly opened her eyes, which were bright blue at that moment, and said, "Money is, too."

"Money is too what, Mama?"

"Like fame. Ephemeral. Sweet dreams, Daughtie dear."

June 5. She has no more strength than a kitten, but her mind is clear now that she takes her pills only at bedtime. I would not have brought up the subject of myself, but she did. "I have been lying here, wondering about you, my darling, wondering why it took you so long to come close to me."

"I've always wanted to be if you did but know it."

"Then why did you do the things that hurt me so? Run off to be married without a word? Go on the stage instead of marrying someone to look after you all your life? Marry I can't remember how many husbands? You can't imagine the grief it brought me."

"Mama, didn't you know? Can't you guess? I did all those things to be like you. There was nothing I did that you didn't do, except you were a thousand times better and richer and more famous. I wanted to show everybody I was your daughter, not somebody you didn't much care about, which was what I felt was true."

"Didn't you ever realize that I loved you?"

"I was sure you didn't."

"Do you realize now?"

I knew I must not lie to her. I answered by kissing her forehead, wrinkled like a peach that is past its bloom, as I burst into tears.

June 5. She took her pills and went to sleep after she had found the sentence she wanted to have me read to her: "I am privileged to make necessity my choice."

Extract from the New York Times, June 6, 1922, headlined: "LILLIAN RUSSELL DIES OF INJURIES. Noted Stage Beauty of Years Ago Succumbs after 10 Days of Illness."

Pittsburgh, Tuesday, June 6—Mrs. Lillian Russell Moore, wife of Alexander P. Moore, publisher of the Pittsburgh *Leader* and a noted stage beauty of a score of years ago, died in her home at 2:20 this morning, after an illness of several days. At the bedside at the end were her daughter, Mrs. Dorothy Calbit, Mr. Moore, and Dr. C. B. Shieldecker.... While it was recognized that the situation was grave, members of the household, nevertheless, made it known late in the evening that no alarm was felt....

Author's Note

*T*HE FOLLOWING listings of principal research sources is included for the reader who wishes to determine the fine line that divides what is factual from what is fabulous in the preceding pages.

Chapter I. Appleton's Railway and Steam Navigation Guide, 1875; the Association of American Railroads; Ann Bowbeer of the Clinton, Ohio, Historical Society; *This Was New York!* by Maxwell F. Marcuse (hereinafter "Marcuse"), New York, LIM Press, 1969; *Incredible New York* by Lloyd Morris (hereinafter "Morris"), New York, Bonanza Books, 1951; *Our Times* by Mark Sullivan (hereinafter "Sullivan"), New York, Charles Scribner's Sons, 1926; "Lillian Russell's Reminiscence," *Cosmopolitan*, February–September, 1922; *The Promised City* by Moses Rischin (hereinafter "Rischin"), Boston, Harvard University Press, 1962; the Robinson Locke Scrapbooks in the Theater Collection of the New York Public Library (hereinafter "Locke").

Chapter II. "Reminiscences"; Ann Bowbeer; Iowa State Guide; Sullivan; *The Transportation Frontier* by Oscar O. Winther (hereinafter "Winther"), New York, Holt, Rinehart & Winston, 1964.

Chapter III. "Reminiscences"; Marcuse; Morris; *Gilbert and Sullivan* by Christopher Hibbert (hereinafter "Hibbert"), New York, American Heritage Publishing Co. Inc., 1976; *Children of*

305]

the Slums by Jacob A. Riis, New York, The Macmillan Company, 1903.

Chapter IV. Lillian Russell: The Era of Plush by Parker Morell (hereinafter "Morell"), New York, Random House, Inc., 1940; "Reminiscences"; Hibbert; *Duet in Diamonds* by John Burke (hereinafter "Burke"), New York, G. P. Putnam's Sons, 1972.

Chapter V. Morell; Sullivan; Locke; Marcuse; Morris; "Reminiscences"; Hibbert; *Gilbert* by Hesketh Pearson, New York, Harper & Brothers, 1957; *The Prince and the Lily* by James Brough, New York, Coward, McCann & Geoghegan, Inc., 1975.

Chapter VI. "Reminiscences"; Locke; Herbert; Morell.

Chapter VII. Howe and Hummel by Richard H. Rovere (hereinafter "Rovere"), New York, Farrar, Straus, 1947; *Diamond Jim* by Parker Morell (hereinafter "Morell II"), Garden City, Garden City Publishing Company, Inc., 1934; Morris.

Chapter VIII. Morell II; *Fortune*, October 1954; *The Age of the Moguls* by Stewart H. Holbrook, Garden City, Doubleday & Co., Inc., 1954; Winther; Morell.

Chapter IX. Morell II; "Reminiscence"; Locke; Sullivan; *Edison* by Matthew Josephson (hereinafter "Josephson"), New York, McGraw-Hill Book Co., Inc., 1959; Morell.

Chapter X. Morris; Locke; "Reminiscences"; Sullivan; Marcuse; *My Memories of Eighty Years* by Chauncey M. Depew, New York, 1922.

Chapter XI. Morell; Rovere; Josephson; Morell II; *King Edward the Seventh* by Philip Magnus, London, John Murray, 1964.

Chapter XII. Morell II; Josephson.

Chapter XIII. Locke; "Reminiscences."

Chapter XIV. Sullivan; Burke; Locke; Rovere; *Roosevelt* by Henry F. Pringle, New York, Harcourt, Brace, 1956; *The Roosevelt Family of Sagamore Hill* by Herman Hagedorn, New York, The Macmillan Company, 1954; *Crowded Hours* by Alice Roosevelt Longworth, New York, Charles Scribner's Sons, 1933.

Chapter XV. Rovere; "Reminiscences"; Locke; Morell; *Random Reminiscences of Men and Events* by John Davison Rockefeller, New York, Doubleday, Page & Company, 1904.

Chapter XVI. "Reminiscences"; Morell; Locke; *The Shadow of Blooming Grove* by Francis Russell, New York, McGraw-Hill Book Co., Inc., 1968; *The Incredible Era* by Samuel Hopkins Adams, New York, Capricorn Books, 1964; *Selznick* by Bob Thomas, New York, Doubleday & Company, Inc., 1970.